FATHER OF LIES

"Outstanding character ⸴ development that reveals personality develops in the ⸴ ﹍﹍﹍ in excellent fiction." LIONEL F⸴

"Serena Cairns has done an excell⸴ ⸴ob on her first novel. I felt like I was in the inner chambers of the Vatican. Father of Lies holds the reader's interest mainly through characterization, plot and atmosphere. This is a very clever story. Benvenuti is a terrific character who revels in his evil. I'd like to read the sequel." BRUCE G. HALLENBECK author / filmmaker

MerrieOak Publishing

Also by Serena Cairns

SHORT STORY COLLECTIONS

Wyrd Stories

Between Stops

'Feeding the Fish' short story broadcast twice on BBC Radio.

Serena Cairns

FATHER OF LIES

Father of Lies

Published in Great Britain by MerrieOak Publishing 2015

A CIP catalogue record for this book
is available from the British Library

ISBN 978 0 9931600 8 0

MerrieOak Publishing
Great Britain

This book is also available in e-book format
ISBN 978 0 9931982 3 6

I would like to thank the following people for their help, without which this book would be full of glaring errors: Viv Laine and Eleanor Piper for endless proofing, Ernest Harris for ecclesiastical advice in the early stages, Terry Mugridge for being 'my man at the morgue', Peter Holbrook and Shane Briant for their encouragement, and Simon Cornish and Jenifer Braund for final readings.

FATHER OF LIES

PART ONE

GENESIS

Lightning snaked across the heavens with the hiss of serpents startled from eons of slumber. Something stirred in the dark; something moved across the wastes of time and the surface of deep waters.

Another flash of light turned night into day, as molten rock cooled in the turbulent water, crusting in layers, fiery blood pumping from the earth's torn arteries. Again the serpents hissed, as the earth thrust itself above the surface and rain sheeted across the smouldering rocks.

That night, the earth turned beneath the light of myriad stars, their reflections mirrored in the restless oceans.

Even then, the birth of good was balanced by the birth of evil. Later, as life teemed in the ocean, something undulated in its depths and, like all newborn, it was hungry.

FOUNDATION

"...for he is a liar and the father of lies."
JOHN 8:44

ONE

As the stone lid cracked open, putrid air escaped the sarcophagus with a hiss and lay over the debris for an instant before dissipating in the empty building. A shape trembled beneath its ancient, rotted shroud and, instead of settling, the dust stirred anew and rose towards the light.

The loud crash brought Father Graham Phillips running to the entrance of St. Jude's. It had sounded from deep within the dark interior of the church, making the ground tremble beneath him. He instinctively glanced up at the tower, long overdue its current renovation, thinking it had been struck by lightning. It stood firm, defiant against the slate-grey backdrop.

Even with daylight on its side, the porch light fought a losing battle under the leaden sky. Despite his haste, Graham made a mental note to get the timer fixed. After a brief struggle with his umbrella in the close confines of the porch and coming near to using a profane word or two, he stepped, dripping, into the nave in a temper almost as black as the weather.

Graham had seen images of bomb-blasted buildings after the war, rubble wounds gaping to expose charred ribs of houses and, for a few timeless moments, he was back amidst the dust and carnage.

But this time it was in his sanctuary, within the safe walls of this ancient Norfolk church.

He stumbled over workmen's buckets, scaffolding and tools, all of which added to the bombsite appearance. That wasn't what bothered him. After all, renovation couldn't be accomplished merely by a wave of the bishop's hand, even if the bishop liked to think so. Graham's fears for the medieval carvings on the pews and the ornate lectern paled into insignificance at the sight before him. It was almost as if a vengeful deity had smitten the church and turned the elements against it when it was at its most defenceless.

As he squinted through the centuries of dust shaken loose and spiralling in its new-found freedom, Graham was unprepared for the devastation that met his gaze. Like a wooden thunderbolt, an immense beam had fallen from the high, arched roof, shattering the flagstones, where cracks now grinned obscenely about a yawning hole.

Shaking, he grasped the edge of a pew to steady himself. It felt clammy under its shroud of white plastic sheeting. Dust now seemed the least of his problems. Bright flashes revealed a steady trickle of rain from somewhere in the darkness above, as drops were caught in the dull light reflected through a stained glass window.

"Holy…" Graham stopped himself.

He shivered. It was mid September and St. Jude's was never warm, but the chill in the air reminded him of an empty tomb. Words from the Gospel of St. Matthew sprang to mind: "…upon this rock I will build my church, and the gates of Hell shall not prevail against it." Right at this moment, he felt his church had been slain, wrapped in a plastic winding-sheet and now a mighty stake had been thrust between its polished ribs, impaling it so it might rise no more.

"How?" he muttered, scrambling back to the light switches by the door. No illumination came, either to his question or at the switch of a button. Of course, the workmen had cut the electricity inside the building. He hurried forward again, tripping on cables and bags of cement. He remembered the warden kept a torch in the utility room to the right of the chancel. Unable to see the full extent of the damage, he slipped between the pews to the south aisle, then made his way forward.

The room was windowless, crammed with chairs stacked dangerously high in tilting columns, lime-encrusted vases and cleaning materials. Graham felt his way cautiously, brushing against dried flower arrangements and plastic palm leaves, to where he last remembered seeing the torch resting on an old velvet curtain. He blessed the warden for being a tidy man and, turning, stubbed his toe on the manger from the children's nativity play.

Clasping the torch tightly in an effort to hold it steady, he shone the beam up into the roof. It picked out the cold, stone features of Green Men staring sightlessly across the aisles and chancel, silent pagan watchers over centuries of Christian congregations.

It seemed the temperature had fallen even further now and Graham's breath clouded in the air. Hooking one arm about the end of a pew, he leaned perilously over the gaping hole, disturbing the dust that swirled in the torch's yellow light. He waited for it to settle, eyes straining in the gloom.

The beam had split the top of what appeared to be a

sarcophagus, wedges of stone now angled like an arrowhead upon an ancient oak shaft. As he hung at arm's length, Graham was unable to tell if it was a family vault or part of a vast catacomb. The hole was only a few feet wide – just large enough for a man to squeeze past the beam and climb through – but it was impossible to see beyond a few feet on either side of the smashed coffin.

As he hauled himself upright, he knew he should phone the diocese and possibly get someone in to look at the damage. The whole roof could be poised to fall. He also knew that, once the discovery was made known, let alone when workmen began to swarm over the building, his chance of taking a close look inside the hole would be gone for good. His curiosity demanded satisfaction, and he hurried outside to where he'd spotted a ladder lying alongside scaffolding poles and clamps. The church would have already been webbed in metal if the bad weather hadn't set in.

It felt warmer out in the open, the rain no longer heavy, although the sky held little promise of leniency. Dark clouds threatened an early dusk as Graham struggled back inside with the ladder. Manoeuvring it into the hole, he felt as if he were ten years old again, living an Enid Blyton adventure, on the brink of discovery with blood racing in his veins.

As he descended into the blackness, the torch beam arced across the vaulted roof like a spotlight. Then the dark wrapped itself about his shoulders, drawing him into its depths, velvet silence cushioning all sound from above. He stepped onto a stone floor covered with rubble and broken chunks of flagstone. His teeth began to chatter. The cold down here felt more intense, but he couldn't smell any trace of damp in the dry air.

The room was smaller than he'd expected, with what appeared to be stone walls on all sides. The light from the torch barely penetrated the darkness that was made even more intense by black walls. The batteries must be going, thought Graham, straining to see in the weak light. The room was empty, but for a coffin almost central to what would have been the original church. Whatever else there might have been had long since turned to dust.

An empty niche gaped blackly in what he estimated was the north wall and, as he moved forward to peer into its depths, broken pottery crunched at his feet. He stepped back guiltily but the contents, whatever they were, had long ago been lost.

Turning his attention to the sarcophagus, he noted its patched, dark colouring, like black lichen, as though the stone itself had bled, or had – he shuddered at the thought – been fed with blood, appeasement from the living to the dead. He shook his head, wondering where such dark thoughts came from, and shone the torch into the murky interior. A shape, unrecognisable beneath a rotted cloth and distorted by the centuries and shadows, lay in pitiful decay, grey like the dust it had almost become.

He raised the torch. Colour assailed his eyes, vivid red, gold and green. He gasped, turning his head away, the swirls of brilliance jolting his senses as he recoiled from their onslaught. Unsteady, he slowly faced again the painted sides of the coffin, warily this time, as if a coiled serpent might strike out from the confusion of colour. Circles dissolved into circles, brilliant maelstroms reaching out from the chaos, merging together. They devoured his breath whilst spewing out images into the edge of his consciousness, images he couldn't grasp but which he felt were seeding in his mind.

He fought back nausea, disorientated now and struggling to breathe. Flinging himself towards the ladder, the torch falling to the ground, he pulled himself up into the nave. He staggered out into the darkening night, retching against the buttress, his forehead pressed against its wet stone flank. Only when he could feel the rain on his face, the wind cooling it against his burning cheeks, did he lean back into the porch and steady his breathing.

How stupid he'd been, he thought. The stale air in the crypt, the dirt, the rotted corpse; breathing in the dust and decay of centuries, he was lucky not to have felt worse. Less dizzy now and heedless of the rain, he hurried back to the vicarage. He must do what he should have done when he'd first seen the fallen beam: ring the warden to notify the diocese and arrange for someone to look at the damage. He'd wasted valuable daylight playing at being the great explorer. Whatever had he been thinking of?

One phone call and two mugs of steaming tea later, Graham relaxed and waited for the warden to ring back. A headache threatened, a black cloud heralding the storm. He neatly divided one paracetamol and took half with the last of his tea. It was hardly any wonder he was feeling the effect of the day's exertions.

He was dozing when the call came to say there'd be workmen at St. Jude's first thing, along with someone from the diocese to assess the damage. The following day was already promising to be stressful enough in its own right and the headache hadn't lifted.

It was almost midnight when the switchboard at the Vatican lit up. Within minutes, robed figures hurried along the labyrinthine corridors. Excited voices shattered the quiet and a chartered plane was put on standby. Urgent plans were still being drawn up as Monsignor Benvenuti hurriedly packed. Like a monstrous spider's web, a trembling thread had alerted the Ordo Autem Serpens to long-awaited movement. Now it sent its blackest spider scurrying towards St. Jude's.

Graham woke with a throbbing pain in his temple. He'd overslept and should have been at the church an hour ago. The sky was overcast, the air chill. At least the rain had stopped, but the damp permeated clothes, and moisture dripped from leaves, gutters and railings. To hell with restraint, this was a two-paracetamol morning.

St. Jude's seemed busier than on a Sunday. Hard-hatted workmen crawled like insects over more newly-erected scaffolding, their large haulage truck blocking the tarmac path up to the church. Graham picked his way around graves, his feet sinking on the spongy wet grass. Just who were all these people? He was greeted in the church porch by the archdeacon.

"Ah, at last, Father Graham."

Graham resented the implied criticism that he should have been waiting at dawn for the world to inspect St. Jude's.

"Archdeacon," he acknowledged, wondering what had drawn him here quite so early.

"We seem to have a slight problem," said the elder cleric. "Shall we go inside?"

FATHER OF LIES

Graham considered the collapse of half his church far from slight. He held his tongue and motioned the other man through the door, whilst casting a guilty look at the spot where he'd been sick the previous evening.

The workmen had wasted no time in fixing heavy chains about the fallen beam and lifting mechanisms had been hauled into place high in the arched ceiling.

Looking up, the archdeacon said, "It would appear the rain has been seeping in at one corner for some time and rotted the wood. It's been up there since at least the thirteenth century. We must be thankful the church was already closed and there were no injuries. It could have fallen during a service and, if anyone had been hurt, I doubt we could claim it was divine retribution for their sins."

"I've been trying to get financial help for years," replied Graham. "Had the diocese been prepared to help earlier, this disaster might have been averted. The church funds just haven't been enough." He was aware he was treading on eggshells, but he refused to be made the scapegoat for ecclesiastical negligence.

The archdeacon chose to ignore Graham's comments. "We must also be thankful that work was already underway when this happened. I hate to think how long we'd have had to wait otherwise, or what further damage might have resulted from a delay."

A group of men, strangers to Graham, stood about the edge of the hole. Wearing long, black raincoats, they had the appearance of sentries guarding the opening. The archdeacon followed his gaze.

"The bishop from the Catholic diocese and some priests," he said, in answer to Graham's unspoken question. "You see, whatever lies beneath here would be pre-Reformation, in other words, left here by the Roman Catholic Church. I informed the bishop as a matter of courtesy, but I'm surprised by their arrival so soon. Still, if they decide to take responsibility for it, that's fine by us. It would certainly make a change!"

"Does that include responsibility for costs incurred?" replied Graham, thinking of time and money spent in excavation. The archdeacon ignored him.

"I have to admit, it's most unusual and I'm puzzled by their interest. However, if there's anything down there, and tentative examination suggests a tomb, then it's of Catholic origin. We have no records of any cellar or crypt, though they could have been lost of course. It looks as if you'll have to hold services in the Church Hall for longer than we'd hoped, Father."

Graham thought of the draughty hall, tepid radiators and poor acoustics, and inwardly groaned. He knew the parishioners would understand but, with his own church, however temporarily, back in the hands of the Roman Catholic Church and his congregation relegated to the hall, he suddenly felt denuded, stripped of the security his church represented.

"It's a lot of red tape, I know, but it would seem it's out of our jurisdiction, so to speak," continued the archdeacon.

Graham was introduced to the four men, who paid lip service to protocol but showed no signs of friendship.

"I'm afraid we're going to prove somewhat of a nuisance," began the senior of the group, a dour-faced individual with a thin fixed smile. "Of course, no-one can be allowed down there until our special emissary from the Vatican is present." He guided the archdeacon and Graham away from the hole as chains snapped taut, taking the weight of the ancient beam. It swayed slowly, as if reluctant to be freed, then jerked up, swinging out above their heads.

Graham swallowed. The Vatican! What would they say if he told them he'd already explored the chamber? He noticed the ladder had been removed, probably by the workmen earlier. Deciding it politic to remain silent, he asked when that visit might be.

"Monsignor Benvenuti is expected later today," rejoined the archdeacon.

Well, they weren't wasting any time, thought Graham. Just how important did they think this tomb was? His musings were cut short by a loud crack and sudden urgent shouts from behind and above.

"Watch out!"

"Christ, it's going."

"Move!"

A hand grabbed Graham's arm, pulling him off balance so he fell between the pews. As though in slow motion, he watched the great oak beam swing loose from broken chains, then plummet down. He heard the crash of shattered pews and cracked stone. Staggering to his feet, he choked back a sob. An arm protruded from beneath the fallen beam, black raincoat visible amid the shards of broken wood. A steady stream of blood pooled from the crushed body, trickled to the opening in the floor and dripped into its dark interior.

Hours later, when the police had asked their questions and the beam had been hauled clear, after the ambulance crew removed the body of the priest and dust was already caking the dried blood on the floor, Graham sat hunched over his fire, his tea cold beside him, his body tense and strained. Again and again, he replayed the accident behind closed lids until, exhausted, he let his mind retrace his exploration of the underground tomb. At the memory of the coffin's decorated interior, he felt as though green, red and gold snakes spawned in his head, trying to map out circular designs as if they were the key to memories long forgotten, buried like a corpse beneath the foundations of his church.

TWO

As Pope Gregory XVII raised his frail hand in blessing, millions of heads bowed to receive the Holy Spirit, one man the instrument of God's will.

When did a blessing ever alter anyone's character? The pontiff could be calling down the spirit of Lucifer himself into the crowds and no-one would know any different. Dermot O'Shea stabbed at the remote in disgust and the picture changed to a game show compère, bearing a false smile and a handful of question and answer cards.

"Your next question for ten," mimicked O'Shea, before switching channels again and finally settling for none. He glanced at the whiskey bottle on the sideboard, offering its own illusions. Alternatively, a large folder of students' papers needed correction and comment. He was still wondering if getting drunk was the best course of action when the phone rang.

"O'Shea," he growled, his voice like sandpaper on rough plaster. He seldom received calls and it showed.

"Dermot, is that you?" The man's voice on the other end of the line sounded shaky and strained.

"Who's that?" said O'Shea, softening his voice somewhat.

"Graham, Graham Phillips. I know it's been a time but can we meet for a coffee? I need to talk."

Sitting opposite Graham in an all-night café just outside of Newmarket, O'Shea felt as if twenty-four years had slipped away. He remembered sharing long, animated discussions into the early hours of countless mornings when Graham attended theological college

13

in Dublin and he, the seminary. They had been young and fired with enthusiasm then. He wondered how they had both become so jaded.

"You look well," said Graham, obviously reluctant to take the step from banalities to the reason for the meeting.

"I thought priests weren't supposed to lie," O'Shea said, keeping the tone light and with only a hint now of his original Irish brogue. He slept badly, ate badly and had aged twice as fast as the agitated man opposite. Yet somehow, seeing Graham again filled him with that spark of energy so lacking in his life nowadays. When Graham remained silent, he said, "Something's shaken you up, old friend, so what is it?"

"You always did come straight to the point, Dermot. Does it show that much?"

"That much."

Graham took another sip of his tea, wished he'd ordered coffee, and began.

O'Shea listened intently, wondering where Graham's story was heading.

"…and if I believed in such things," Graham said finally, "I'd say St. Jude's has been cursed – or I have. The next thing I know, I'm told I can't go back into my own church, there're two new locks on the door and I'm being moved from Adderidge to a parish south of Bedford somewhere. It's unheard of. I wasn't even allowed back in to collect my personal belongings without an escort, as if they thought I'd leave with the damned missal under my arm."

Graham's agitation grew as he related the happenings of the past week.

"It hurt, O'Shea, I don't mind admitting it," he said, "but now…"

14

"Now it doesn't?"

"Oh, it still hurts but now I'm scared. Something strange is going on, Dermot, and I mean more than parish manoeuvrings. Crazy as it sounds, I'm convinced I'm being watched."

"Oh, come now, Graham, why would anyone…?"

"Maybe because I've been down that crypt. I've seen the inside of that thing. I realised after, they must have found my torch."

"That proves nothing. You could have dropped it when you were leaning over the edge."

"And disturbed the dust down there as well? I think not. I no doubt left footprints in the rubble and muck that came down with the beam, or did I accomplish that by leaning over as well?"

"You're saying you saw, or disturbed, something you shouldn't, is that right?"

"It can only be that coffin."

"So it seems, but why? An empty coffin…?"

"You didn't see those paintings in its interior. They seemed alive, like something dreamed up in Hell. Even now, when I think of those colours, those designs, I feel…" Graham swayed, a hand to his head, eyes tightly shut, trying to block the images from his mind.

O'Shea reached out a steadying arm. When Graham seemed in control again, he asked, "And what is it you want me to do?"

Hope shone in the eyes of the frightened priest. "You have access to museum and university libraries. You know how to research these things. You must have contacts. Find out who was buried under St. Jude's or, perhaps more importantly, why."

"It's a tall order you're asking," O'Shea replied. "If

the church has no records, I doubt I'll turn anything up." He wasn't sure he wanted this job, though he saw no way out, not without turning away an old friend – perhaps, he considered, his only one. Graham needed help, that was certain, but whether it was practical help, spiritual or straightforward psychiatric, he wasn't sure. If Graham wasn't paranoid and all he said was accurate, then O'Shea had a distinctly uneasy feeling about the whole business.

"Why me?" he asked, in a last ditch attempt to avoid involvement. "You're surely in the best position to ask questions yourself?"

"Like I said, this is no game. They're watching me. You have no love for the church, I know, but you trained as a priest. You know almost as much as I do. You were certainly cleverer than me when you were at the seminary."

"That was all a long time ago."

"But you haven't lost touch. You may teach philosophy, but philosophy is akin to belief. With your academic background, you'll know where to dig and any investigations you make will be unbiased."

"I doubt that," returned O'Shea. However, he promised to do what he could.

There was still activity around St. Jude's when Graham reached Adderidge. Cables led from an outside generator in through the porch, and the interior of the building had never been so well lit, throwing huge, grotesque shadows against the stained glass. A tall figure was silhouetted in the doorway but, whether he was looking in or out, Graham couldn't tell. He fervently hoped Dermot would find out what was going on, as he hurried past to the vicarage and the last of the packing.

Unbiased! O'Shea smiled grimly as he drove back to Cambridge. The meeting with Graham had unsettled him. Back in his study, he felt justified in pouring the large whiskey he'd denied himself earlier. How could he feel any love for the church or any religion for that matter? Slumping in his worn armchair, he pulled the wallet from his breast pocket and carefully withdrew a dog-eared photo. He gazed at the child, her hair a mass of unruly curls, her eyes full of laughter and promise. It was the only one he had of her and he carried it next to his heart, a reminder of both love and hatred. He'd no other photo of any of his family, just this one of his niece. The love he'd felt for this golden-haired child was equal to that of a father, but his capacity for love had been destroyed, first by other men's hatred, then by his hatred of other men. A man of the cloth should have been able to forgive, so he'd turned his back on his god and left the forgiving to others.

Through tears, he saw again the pleading in his niece's eyes as she'd begged him to let her run ahead. His sister needed time alone to shop for presents and he was only too glad to take her daughter off her hands for a couple of hours. The store was full of Christmas shoppers. She'd wanted to look at the toys; he wanted to buy gifts for the family. The explosion had racked the building. He heard again the screams, the sirens, the hastily-whispered prayers, and felt his stomach constrict with dread as he remembered running through the smoke, the staggering figures and shattered glass. He'd found her lying amidst fallen decorations, as lifeless as the broken doll she clasped, whilst somewhere the strains of 'Silent Night' reached out into the frosty evening air. He'd had no time after that for a religion that inspired men to plant bombs and kill innocent children.

"Damn them all to hell," snarled O'Shea, gulping down the remains of the whiskey, angry that he'd allowed the demons in again. Sleep would be a long time coming but the bottle was still half full and somewhere, he was sure, he had a history of the early church gathering dust amongst his vast collection of books. Maybe Graham's troubles were just what he needed, after all.

"Woman! You are the gateway of the devil... Because of you, the Son of God had to die." Laura Coatman snarled as she jotted down Tertullian's words. The further into the sermon she got, the more her blood boiled. What had begun with a few pert comments on female priests had turned into a diatribe against men's hostility to women in general. She wondered if she was wasting her time trying to convey her feelings to the congregation. Many of them resented her for being female, and even her friends had been against her ordination, but she was convinced that, in time, women would be accepted more within the church and not just the Anglican faith. It may not happen in her lifetime but, one day, Laura sincerely believed, there'd even be a female pope.

It wouldn't be the first time, she reasoned, and wondered if she should include a few words about Pope Joan. The more she thought about it, the more she warmed to the idea. It only went to prove that a woman was just as capable of running the church as a man, not to mention how easily men were deceived.

FATHER OF LIES

She reached for a blue folder bulging with scraps of paper, articles torn from newspapers and magazines and endless photocopied pages from diverse books and the internet. At last she found the article on the ninth century pope.

Laura respected courage and the story of Joan had enough elements of romance and adventure to fill a best-selling novel. There seemed too much detail for it all to be a myth. Joan had been elected pontiff on the death of Pope Leo IV, calling herself John VIII. Two years, five months and four days later, disaster struck when she gave birth to a baby during a procession between the Colosseum and the Lateran Church. Neither she nor the baby had survived. The church maintained the story was mere legend and without any foundation, but Laura preferred to believe all legends have their roots in fact. From her point of view, Pope Joan knocked spots off Joan of Arc.

A mug of hot chocolate might calm her down and help her to collect her thoughts. She was used to late nights and, as she waited for the milk to boil, she considered her own position within the church. She was ambitious and the Church of England was now accepting women not only as priests but also as bishops. The parishes had the right to reject women priests, and bishops couldn't be forced to ordain them. One step at a time, she told herself. She'd heard somewhere that the Vatican, although still against women being ordained, had approved altar girls, and were allowing women to be servers, administering the chalice. Today, altar girl, tomorrow, the head of the Holy Roman Catholic Church. Now there was a thought.

Hands clutching the steaming mug, she returned to

her sermon notes. She knew what the problem was: fear of the inherent power within women, who are more in touch with the earth and not so easily led into wars and needless cruelty. Pretty pagan thoughts for a Christian, she thought, with a grim smile.

With pen in hand, Laura poured out all her resentment of a system that kept women in a lowly position, that had a history of repression and persecution of her sex, a system that she ached to be a part of but which shut her out but for a token title, and that a male one. Priest! How she hated the hypocrisy of the title. Why not 'Priestess'? It was just another way of saying she wasn't good enough. But Laura knew they were wrong. Like Pope Joan, she'd use whatever means were at her disposal for advancement.

When she finally finished, she read the sermon and then calmly tore it into shreds. Too much, too soon, she thought, and began to write about desire, prayer and the power of faith.

Later, when the only sound was the occasional slamming of a car door or the howling of a territorial cat, she stood before her bathroom mirror, leaning on the basin, and stared at the stranger's face that her tired eyes tried to convince her brain was hers. The longer she stared, the less familiar the features became. Her long face, short-fringed crop and sloping eyebrows had earned her the nickname 'Spock' at school, a likeness enhanced by the shape of her reading glasses, but her ready smile and easy laugh quickly banished that image when people met her. Now, strain etching shadows beneath her eyes, she wondered if she'd chosen the right path after all. An ardent feminist by nature, she'd stepped into a male domain in which she fought the dogma not only of her peers, her congregation and the church itself, but also at times the very teachings she was expected to relate. Once, in a moment of weakness, she'd wondered if she would have even considered the priesthood if she'd been born beautiful. One never thought of great beauties teaching the gospel. She wondered what Pope Joan had looked like.

The following morning, after delivering her sermon to a sea of blank faces, she felt as if she'd let them down, betrayed them through lack of courage. She'd fed them watery platitudes instead of the fire of inspiration. Depressed, she wandered back to her tiny flat, hoping the gusting winds would blow away her doubts and the cobwebs of two thousand years of repression. All they blew away was the rain. Patches of blue sky were visible between the high moving clouds but it stayed cold. Autumn had come early and the few leaves that remained on the trees had begun to wither. When the sun finally appeared, its pale light added no warmth to the bleak day. It was at times like this Laura felt isolated, and her faith seemed a poor substitute for the comfort of a fellow human's touch.

Even when she received the phone call, telling her she'd been offered the appointment as a locum to a parish church, she'd found it hard to raise her spirits. She wasn't sure why protocol had been broken. Locums were usually retired priests but the archdeacon had asked it as a favour, so who was she to refuse? Give her a parish, tucked conveniently away in some remote district, and she'll be happy whilst the position is advertised. The system moves slowly, so it will keep her quiet where she can't do any mischief. If we must tolerate women priests, let's put them where they can do the least harm. That was the impression Laura got and, unreasonable as it may be, it dulled the edge of her pleasure. It's just the beginning, her inner voice comforted.

She reached for her AA road map and looked up Norfolk. Now, just where was this St. Jude's anyway?

THREE

It had been cold in the crypt, with nothing to mark the passing of the years, save the saintly drone of endless sermons and discordant voices reaching for unsaintly notes. Awoken now, it hungered. The centuries had seemed eternal. The trickle of fresh blood had revived memories of times when it had flowed freely over the stones. The movement of the chill air disturbed the shape beneath the cracked stone slab, dissolving it into dust with the faint whisper of dissolution. A draught stirred the motes, spiralling them up till they caught the feeble light, where they shimmered green, red and gold.

I should have guessed, Laura thought, as she stood looking up at the scaffolding and planks encasing St. Jude's. She wasn't going to conduct services there at all, but in a hall. In fact, she hadn't even been allowed inside the church. It was too dangerous, she'd been told, the whole roof liable to give way. The stained glass windows stared back, dull, with no light from within to illuminate their coloured icons. Gargoyles gazed out with sightless eyes, prisoners in chiselled granite until the centuries would finally grant them their freedom and reduce them to sand. The whole building had the appearance of something that had died.

I shouldn't be surprised, thought Laura. After all, St. Jude *is* the patron saint of lost and desperate causes.

The creak of the gate hinge made her turn. A figure was watching her from the cover of a dying yew. He dodged back behind the foliage but not before she'd made out a dirty tweed coat and striped woollen hat. She relaxed. The tramp had been hanging around since she'd arrived at Adderidge, but seemed more concerned with concealment than in posing a threat. He disappeared as, hunched now against the feeling of being watched, she made her way back towards the road. But this time it was the church itself that seemed to be watching her, and she shivered despite the sunlight.

Her lodgings were comfortable and homely. Mrs Lyle, the widow with whom she had been housed, seemed quite in awe of Laura, as if she was of a different species entirely. She gave the impression of being about to curtsey whenever Laura crossed her path, giving a little bob of acknowledgement. Laura wondered if she should mention it but decided it might make her landlady even more self-conscious.

Laura had hoped she'd be housed in the vicarage, but then nothing seemed straightforward with this assignment. Some of Father Phillips' larger personal belongings were still in the house, though no mention had been made of his possible return.

One of the churchwardens had met her at the hall.

"Taken poorly quite sudden-like," he explained. "Good of the diocese to get someone to step in so quickly and take services."

It seemed that was the limit of her responsibilities: the midweek Eucharist on Wednesday and two services on Sundays.

"'Course, I don't hold with women priests," the warden gruffly informed her. "Voted against one in this parish meself but seems most folk didn't object, least not strong enough. They didn't know Father Phillips was going to be taken badly, mind. P'raps then they'd have voted different."

Laura got the impression he would have been against women getting the vote as well, had he been around a century earlier.

"And what of the other warden? Does he share your views?"

"He don't have views, he don't, not any more." When Laura looked shocked, he added, "Been ill, he has. Job got too much for him. No-one has the heart to replace him. Went a bit funny, he did, but I manage." With that the warden began banging one of the radiators with a spanner and Laura took it as a sign she had been dismissed.

Her room overlooked an allotment, then open fields, their soil freshly turned after the late harvest. The land was flat and bare, making her aware of the onset of autumn. Maybe that accounted for the chill she'd been unable to shake off since leaving St. Jude's. She might have put it down to suddenly being thrust into a strange new environment, but she'd always been a loner. It wasn't that she wanted it that way; she'd just never known any different.

The phone call took her by surprise.

"A Mr O'Shea for you," gasped Mrs Lyle with a bob, puffing after the exertion of the stairs. "Says he got this number from the diocese."

Laura was glad of an excuse to visit 'The Peal of Bells' pub and warm herself with a brandy by the open fire, though she failed to see how she could help Dermot O'Shea with his enquiries. He'd said little on the phone and she anticipated a wasted journey on his part. However, he'd not found her hard to persuade. The alternative of watching 'Coronation Street' and 'Inspector Morse' with Mrs Lyle had quickly decided her. She arrived before him and sat gazing into the fire's heart, letting the heat soothe her as the brandy reflected its glow within.

"Laura Coatman?" the burly man asked. "I'm Dermot O'Shea." The soft Irish brogue was barely discernable. "Can I get you another?"

Laura watched him as he ordered another brandy for her and an Irish whiskey for himself. When he had settled opposite and taken an unhealthily large gulp of his drink, she spoke.

"I did try to explain earlier, Mr O'Shea. I only arrived in the parish this morning. You, no doubt, know more about St. Jude's than I do."

"Well, Fath… er, what do I call you?"

Her face relaxed into a smile. "The jury's still out on that one. Laura will do just fine."

"Right, Laura, I'll get straight to the point. I'm aware that a priest is not moved to another parish until his appointed period is up, but that's exactly what's happened to my friend. I was wondering if you'd tell me what reason you've been given as to why this vacancy has arisen?"

"I presume this friend you're speaking of is Father Phillips?" When O'Shea nodded, she continued, "I was led to believe he had suffered a shock of some kind, a sort of breakdown, and needed rest. I have to admit it wasn't a stated fact, merely implied. I gather there was a death within the church, an accident?"

O'Shea related what he knew of the grim details concerning the death, but avoided mentioning

26

Graham's fears surrounding his hasty removal from St. Jude's.

"No wonder it gave me the shudders when I was there," said Laura. "I pick these things up," she added, noticing O'Shea raise a quizzical eyebrow.

"And what's the chance of you picking up some information, about the corpse in the cellar, so to speak?" he asked.

"May I ask just what your interest is in all this?"

"You could say I'm a bit of an amateur historian, I suppose," lied O'Shea, "and Graham, Father Phillips, well, I'd just like to know what's going on."

"Well, there are records of course, but there won't be anything going back that far. The upkeep of graves is paid for, whenever possible, by the deceased's families, and that includes renovation of crypts and such. The church has even been known to locate the families of very old graves and bill them, but there's a limit even to their endeavours. The fact no-one seems to have known of the tomb's existence means any identification will rely on evidence within the tomb itself. It certainly sounds intriguing. I need something to occupy my time whilst I'm here. Not much else seems required of me."

O'Shea looked surprised. "I would have thought this first week, at least, would be busy for you, meetings with parish officials, church council, churchwardens…?"

"Oh, I've already met one of the wardens and been put in my place. Not the most tactful of men. As for the PCC, if the warden's correct, there'll be little enough for us to discuss. I'm not exactly being deluged with responsibility. My work load seems to have been kept to a minimum, though I can't understand why they agreed to me being appointed if they don't think I'm up to all the job entails."

"It certainly doesn't seem normal."

"What's normal? Anyway, I'll have time to help you, if I'm able."

"Good, and if you don't mind, I think I'll stay on for a couple of days. I've no classes till next week. I gather the food here is acceptable and I'd like to be on hand."

That settled, they exchanged mobile numbers and Laura left O'Shea to book a room and order a nightcap. She'd enjoyed their talk, but it wouldn't do for her to make a bad impression on Mrs Lyle the first night under her roof. There was no need for her to have worried. Soft snores competed with a political discussion on TV as Laura tiptoed past the living room and up the stairs to her room.

With the nights getting colder, Blakey needed somewhere to shelter. Hedgerows were protection against the wind but did little to keep out the cold and wet. The few farms he'd come across kept over-zealous dogs. They'd sniff him out in no time if he hid in any of the barns.

His sights were set on the church. It didn't seem right, it standing there empty and him out here, huddled under the protective wings of a white marble angel. There were heavy locks on the main door and he'd tried the south porch without success.

The north door looked more promising. He fumbled in the pockets of his old tweed coat until he found what he was searching for – a small well-used screwdriver. There were few locks he'd come across that he couldn't master, apart from the new-fangled ones, that is. His luck seemed to be holding. A few minutes more and he'd be fixed up with a pew for a bed, a hassock for a pillow and, if he was really lucky, a cup of communion wine to send him to sleep. Now that's what he called sheer Heaven!

Maybe it was the unfamiliar bed or perhaps the cold wedge of moonlight that sliced through the room where the curtains didn't quite meet. No matter how Laura lay, she found sleep elusive. She heard Mrs Lyle struggle up the stairs and coughed to let her know she was in her room. She imagined her landlady bobbing in response on the far side of the door. From somewhere across the allotments came the excited 'yakking' of foxes, testing each other for land rights as grown cubs prepared to venture into the autumnal world.

When sleep finally came, it brought with it strange dreams in which Laura found herself within an unfamiliar church, dwarfed by its vastness, disturbed by its alien structure. She knelt as shadowy figures performed a dark and savage Mass. Offered the host, she saw in it her salvation but, at the moment of opening her mouth to receive it, she realized that it was not the body of Christ but the putrid remains of something long-dead and unspeakable that was being presented to her. She struggled to be released, but unseen hands held her firm and the unclean host, rotting and maggot-ridden, was forced between her lips and she was made to swallow.

She woke gagging, struggling against the confines of tight, twisted bed linen. Lost in unfamiliar surroundings, the residue of horror raced her blood and stifled her thoughts. Her throat felt like sandpaper.

The bathroom light was harsh and unforgiving. Laura carried a glass of water back to her room where, feeling calmer, she finally drove away the last of her unease with her favourite whispered prayer.

O'Shea was the first on the scene. He reasoned there'd be few people about if he visited the church before breakfast. He wanted to gauge how much damage had been done to the building and how soon work might begin again on repairs and possible archaeological work. He circled St. Jude's anti-clockwise, unable to see inside, frustrated by the sight of gleaming new locks. He was almost back where he'd started when he spotted the north door with its lock hanging by one screw, an inch of dim light inviting him to trespass.

The door swung open easily and he stepped quickly into the half-light of the north aisle. Dust motes slowly danced in the beams from the high windows, the only movement in the still air. The sound of his own laboured breathing seemed loud enough to wake the dead, for the church was certainly as silent as the grave. He thought of leaving, perhaps returning later with Laura and a flashlight, but the possibility of finding it freshly secured against unwanted visitors prompted his feet in the direction of the Lady Chapel. It was a long time since he'd set foot in a church. It seemed odd and unfamiliar, like a photo of a childhood haunt, remembered but distant, something from another time and place.

The pulpit and lectern, hung with white sheeting, resembled giant, cowled monks. He turned between the two into the chancel. Draped across the altar rail was what had once been a human being.

O'Shea always considered he had a strong

constitution but the sight made his stomach lurch and he fought for breath. It was too late in the year for flies, but even their charnel drone would have been welcome in the cloying silence.

Somewhere, in that part of the human brain that goes on reasoning even during the most traumatic events, O'Shea wondered what held the shredded body together. The chancel and sanctuary walls, choir stalls and altar looked as though they had been airbrushed with crimson paint. He reached out and touched the sticky substance before the bile rose in his throat.

He was still sat on the grass, huddled beneath a blanket, his unsteady hands about an already cold mug of tea, when Laura arrived. The area was cordoned off, police trying to look important, bystanders shaking their heads and muttering together.

"I really think you ought to let us take you in for a few hours. You're suffering from severe shock." The ambulance technician hovered anxiously over O'Shea.

"I'll be fine. What I need is a whiskey."

A policeman approached. "Excuse me, Miss. I'm sorry, but you'll have to stay the other side of the tape."

"It's all right, officer, I'm the priest for this church," replied Laura. "What happened?" Before he could reply, she turned to O'Shea. "Are you all right? Are you hurt? What on earth's been going on?"

O'Shea's eyes crinkled as he tried to place her against the bright sky. "Yes, I'm all right, no, I'm not hurt and, as to your third question, I'd rather tell you over a stiff drink, if you think you can prize this limpet paramedic from my side."

Laura smiled. He sounded fine. "Be back in a

minute," she said, making a move towards the church and a group of senior police officers talking amongst themselves.

"Laura!" She turned at O'Shea's call. "Don't go into the church. Even if they'll let you, don't. I mean it."

She paused before nodding. O'Shea looked in a bad way. She was in no hurry to share whatever he'd seen but they both knew she'd go inside. She approached the officers, a couple of whom stood back, somewhat surprised to see a woman, especially one wanting answers.

"We seem to have only slightly more chance of discovering the body's identity than its cause of death," admitted the detective inspector. "I mean, he – and we're assuming it's a 'he' until an autopsy confirms it one way or the other – died because no-one could survive whatever happened to him. However, what caused it is beyond my imagination."

"Perhaps I can help."

"You know what happened?"

An overalled figure had just left the church, carrying a clear, plastic bag through which bright stripes added an incongruous dash of colour to the washed-out day.

"No," replied Laura, "but I recognise that hat."

Although the remains of the body were covered, the metallic smell of blood, stale incense and fear hung in the sickly air of the chancel. Laura had intended taking a look at St. Jude's despite the 'Keep Out' and 'Danger' signs but, as she glanced around at the damage, the police tape and forensic team, she felt an alienation from the building she would previously have found hard to imagine. This was the first church

she could call hers – and it sickened her to her
stomach.

Taking large gulps of clean air after the claustrophobic
atmosphere inside, she rescued O'Shea and made for
the gate, where the constable was arguing with two
irate men in long, black raincoats. Press, she thought.
They could sniff out death better than any
bloodhound.

Once more ensconced in 'The Peal of Bells', she was
relieved to see a touch of colour returning to O'Shea's
cheeks. Despite his protests, she'd insisted he eat a
sandwich as he'd missed out on breakfast.

"There was evil in that church," said O'Shea, his
voice low, not wishing to attract unwelcome listeners.
"I can only think it was the scene of some diabolical
Satanic rite."

"Real evil has nothing to do with Satanism, or any
other form of religious activity for that matter. It was
around long before man thought up his own brand of
horrors." Laura clutched her drink. Her hands were
still shaking but she wouldn't let O'Shea see she was
unnerved.

"But it needs the hand of man to do the work,"
replied O'Shea.

"Perhaps."

"Perhaps?"

"There are places that feel wrong, make you uneasy
just by being there. It uses mankind, that's true, but
something that strong doesn't need any help from us."

"Laura, I saw the body and I'm telling you that,
whatever it was that did that, I'm pretty damned sure it
wasn't the power of suggestion."

"But you automatically assume Satanists or devil-worshippers are to blame and that's how evil works. It often uses the guise of organised belief to mislead and point a finger at the innocent."

"Innocent? What are you trying to say?"

"Well, take the church for instance."

"St. Jude's?" O'Shea felt the stirring of unease, the same gut reaction he'd had to fight back when entering the church.

"No, the establishment. It wages war on all other religions. The Muslims and Sikhs are too numerous to mess with, but witches, Odinists, Druids, what have you, all make perfect ready-made scapegoats, not to mention Jews. It's simple to persecute those groups already suffering from media misrepresentation. They're easy victims."

O'Shea shook his head. "But you're talking about the witch trials, the Inquisition and the like. That's all in the past."

"It still goes on. Look at the myth of Satanic Abuse. Fortunately, reason won over the fundamentalists in that case, but not before a lot of innocent people suffered. Anything other than mainstream Christianity is still looked upon with suspicion."

O'Shea couldn't believe what he was hearing. "But you're part of that very body you're accusing," he gasped. "I have to say you're certainly unusual for a priest."

"I'm no ordinary priest."

"You mean because you're a woman?"

"Let's say, I'm an unblinkered one. There *are* a few about, you know."

"Unblinkered enough to believe Satanists are

innocent?" he asked sarcastically.

"Of this atrocity? Yes."

"Why?" Something was niggling at him and he didn't know why.

"Simple. There was nothing to show they were involved. Those people don't hide what they've done. There were no symbols smeared in blood, no black candles, you know the scenario. It defeats their object somewhat if no-one is shocked."

"Not shocked?"

Laura fell silent, aware suddenly of O'Shea's vulnerability.

He sagged in his chair like a man vanquished. "The church used to be inviolate," he said. "It used to be a refuge, a sanctuary."

"It still is for most people," replied Laura, "but I suspect it has enough trouble protecting itself." O'Shea looked lost. "Opposites attract. It's like…"

"You're telling me," O'Shea interrupted, "that evil is drawn to a church?"

"Something like that, yes. It's possible."

"Surely, if that was the case, it would be happening all the time?"

"Maybe it is," said Laura. She looked deep into the bottom of her glass. "Maybe it always has."

FOUR

Forensics had been all over St. Jude's. Both the protective sheeting and the pews, and just about everything else within the church, had been dusted with a fine film of powder and enough prints lifted to fill a large filing cabinet.

What was left of the body was somehow removed, the doors sealed once more with police tape and a constable positioned on duty, wishing uneasily that he'd watched 'Peter Pan' with his kids the night before rather than 'The Woman in Black'.

Two men arrived, dressed in white overalls, contract cleaners who were allowed under the ribbon now flapping noisily in a cold wind. They were keen to finish before nightfall. Used to dealing with spilled blood, they set to washing the walls, their chatter echoing in the still chancel. Gradually, silence enveloped them, every sound a disturbance that vibrated through the frozen air. The men peeled off their rubber gloves and blew on chapped hands, eager now for clean and open spaces.

"What's that?"

The shadows seemed to grow and slide towards them.

"Sod this. I'm finished. How 'bout you?"

"Yeah, as good as. Let's get out of here."

When all was quiet, the shadows reached further, slithering softly, silently over the stone flags and around carved railings. They paused where a few splashes of spilled water shimmered in the fading light, their faint red tinge obscured by the growing darkness.

FATHER OF LIES

O'Shea was troubled. He'd gone over his conversation with Laura a dozen times. Could centres of good draw evil to them? If that was the case, surely the church would always have been under attack. What was it Laura had said, 'Maybe it always has'?

At first, he focused his thoughts on derelict buildings and remains. They'd had their share of vandals, Satanic misuse and desecrations, but the same thing happened to any empty or ruined building. Still, certain activities lent themselves to old religious sites in particular, even when they were just hollow shells.

That was not what Laura meant and he knew it. He was avoiding the issue, refusing to consider the living body of the church. He'd always thought of the church as a defence, a bastion against all forms of evil. Even if it attracted the Devil himself, it could withstand him. Other thoughts insinuated their way into his smug self-delusion. How many times had he read or heard of corruption? What about promiscuity and homosexuality within the very priesthood? Temptation had not always been withstood and the stain of sin had remained.

'Maybe it always has.' O'Shea shook his head. History had painted priests as notorious lechers and debauchers, cardinals sneaking mistresses into their homes, monks abusing novices, young girls leaving the confessional with more to confess than when they entered. It had even become a source of humour over the years. Then there were the misguided ventures such as the Crusades to consider, the torturous Inquisition, the Massacre of the Cathars and exploits of over-zealous missionaries. Whoever first thought up the expression 'Soldiers of Christ' must surely have had a helping nudge from the Devil, and how any war could be called holy defied all logic.

It occurred to him that even Christ himself had been tempted by the Devil, and he doubted there'd been a man since who could withstand all temptation.

Graham smiled weakly at the young waitress as she pushed the tray onto the table. Lifting one of the two stainless steel pots, he eyed it suspiciously before starting to pour. He usually managed to choose the one with hot water by mistake and felt irrationally pleased with himself at the sight of brown liquid filling his cup. He felt he needed a cup of tea more than anything else in the world.

A moment later, he revised his priority listing. A new identity, fake passport and swift removal to a secret location shot to first place. He was convinced he'd seen the tubby man in the trilby before. He met the man's gaze and quickly turned his attention to an unsavoury-looking chip on the cup's rim that had escaped his notice before. When he glanced up again, the man in the trilby seemed to be playing the same game.

He wondered if he'd read one too many thrillers and paranoia was setting in but, however rational he tried to be, he was still convinced he was being followed. Without even sipping his tea, he sidled from his seat and out into the street.

The rain stung his face, whipped into ferocity by the bitter wind. He could see the tubby man still seated at the Formica table, his back to Graham, intent upon his coffee and Danish. Definitely paranoia, thought Graham with a stab of regret at the memory of his abandoned tea.

Leaving the newsagent's a few minutes later, clutching a bag of liquorice toffees and a paper, he failed to notice a figure step back and blend into the shadowed doorway of a nearby building. A headline rooted Graham to the pavement. It wasn't the main story and Graham was forced to juggle toffees and subdue the wind-whipped paper before locating the full story on page four. Paler than the page in his hand, he hurried towards his new vicarage.

Why hadn't O'Shea rung him and who was the murdered man? A fearful thought crossed Graham's mind. His hand trembled as he rang the number O'Shea had left him. It seemed to ring endlessly before a female voice answered.

"I'm sorry, but Mr O'Shea left about half an hour since." He recognised the voice of Judy, the landlord's wife at 'The Peal of Bells'.

"Thank you. I'll try again later."

She sniffed discouragingly and hung up. At least O'Shea was alive. Glancing back at the phone, he noticed the answerphone flashing.

"Where the devil are you?" O'Shea's gruff voice was music to Graham's ears. "All hell's broken loose. I don't know what you've stirred up, but I certainly intend to find out. Damnation, I wish you'd switch on your mobile. Ring me."

"Tried that," muttered Graham.

Hollow echoes tap-danced their way along the corridor in the wake of Cardinal Scappucci. It had just turned seven a.m. and Pope Gregory was at Mass. The cardinal paused outside two large, polished, wooden doors, aware of the silence that descended at the sound of his footsteps.

The cardinals gathered within each had a folder before them containing photographs of St. Jude's and of Father Graham Phillips.

"We mustn't delay, but we must still act with caution." Scappucci's glance fell on each man present. "It would, of course, be simpler if we were to remove Father Phillips entirely, but we mustn't be seen to be involved."

The tall, gaunt figure of Cardinal Vanni rose to his feet. "Everything will be swiftly resolved, providing he has talked to no-one."

"Can we be certain of that?"

"Things are in hand. He is being watched. The seeds of his destruction have already been planted and tonight they will begin to grow. As long as St. Jude's is secured, but – er – there has been an incident…"

"Incident?" Scappucci's head turned sharply towards the Prefect.

"…a traveller, I understand, no-one of importance. It has caused some difficulties. The church was not protected as it should have been, but we have Monsignor Benvenuti's assurance that those responsible have been dealt with." The gathering stirred uncomfortably. "This has posed a delay, I'm afraid, nothing more. The arrangements will go ahead as planned, as soon as the church is free of police surveillance."

Scappucci nodded. "I need to be kept posted on all developments. You will be held personally responsible if anything else goes wrong. Do I make myself clear?" He looked directly into Cardinal Vanni's eyes.

"Nothing else will be allowed to get in our way."

Without answering, Scappucci left the room but his warning hung about the members like a living being, reluctant to let go. The Prefect broke the silence.

"Brothers, we have work to do."

For the second time in forty-eight hours, Laura stood within St. Jude's and, for the second time, fought back nausea. She'd explained to the police officer on duty that she needed things for the midweek service. She hated having to set foot within these walls again. The warden, it seemed, had forgotten to collect everything together, or had been prevented from doing so in the wake of the murder. Even though the services were being conducted elsewhere, Father Phillips had insisted on keeping church items within St. Jude's when not in use.

Piling hymnbooks into a dustbin bag, Laura looked about her. Only an effort of will stopped her running from the building. Where was her faith now, she wondered? She needed items from the altar. The chancel smelled damp, its walls stained despite the efforts of the cleaners. She told herself she was alone here, that God was her sole companion, yet caught herself looking over her shoulder, listening for sounds within the shadows that seemed to deepen and stretch further at each glance.

She hurried through into the vestry, gathering up anything and everything she might need. She didn't want to have to make a return visit.

Staggering with the bulky bags, Laura retraced her steps. Their weight slowed her down and she felt her shoulder muscles pulling painfully. She had to rest for a moment, even though she wanted to get out of the stale air of St. Jude's as quickly as possible.

She lowered the bags and sat unsteadily on the pulpit steps. She felt far from well and pressed her forehead against the cool woodwork rising round her. She tried to steady her breathing, noticing her hands had begun to shake, and closed her eyes. Instantly her lids flew open.

Something had touched her leg, she was sure of it, but there was nothing there. Perhaps the plastic bag had brushed against her. But there was no breeze, no draught, and the closest bag was at least a foot away.

Pulsing blood beat against her eardrums as she strained her senses, probing the shadows and silence. Again, a touch on the leg made her gasp aloud and she sat upright, rigid, as something unseen slithered slowly under the hemline of her dress. She couldn't move, though she willed all her strength into that one simple act. She was caught in a vice of fear, held tight by her own imaginings. Nor could she cry out. The scream that had begun to form seemed frozen in her throat.

Whatever was exploring her body was not human, nor had it human form, yet it was producing a heat between her legs that she was incapable of extinguishing. It seemed to be in contact with every part of her, penetrating and shifting, until she no longer cared that she was an ordained priest writhing on the steps of her own pulpit, that whatever was doing this to her was older than time and baser than instinct. When her scream finally escaped, it was the howl of the she-wolf upon ancient mountains, the screech of an eagle on the dark winds of time.

It was dark when Laura finally regained consciousness. She stumbled to the door, pain jabbing its fiery fingers into her bruised body. She had no trouble slipping past the police car at the gate. The constable who had been on duty when she arrived had been relieved long ago, oblivious to the fact Laura was still in the quiet church.

She hurried through the hall of her lodgings to the sounds of a 'Poirot' episode coming from Mrs Lyle's sitting room. Locking the door of her room, she threw herself onto the bed, where she curled into the foetal position and lay trembling, unable to shake off the chill that gripped her. Finally, stepping into the shower, she scoured her flesh in the steaming water but the memory remained. No amount of soap could cleanse her mind of the horror she'd experienced. No amount of holy water could wash away her body's betrayal in the pleasure she had felt.

Within the still walls of St. Jude's, the air stirred and something silent, invisible and restless brushed against one of the discarded black bags, spilling its contents across the stone flags. It lingered by the pulpit, caressing the wooden steps with tendrils of fetid air.

O'Shea was used to burning the midnight oil, only usually he was in no state to know the hour. He sat back, fired now, not with alcohol, but a slow-burning conviction that was fanning itself into flames.

"The flames of Hell," he mused, but there was no humour in his voice.

What had begun as an idle exercise had taken on an impetus of its own. The more he discovered in the pages of the high piles of library books he'd collected earlier in the day from Cambridge, the more he was led to further discoveries. Few made for pleasant reading. His view of the church as an institution had been poor before he started, but now he was ready to tear it down, stone by bloody stone.

He had begun with the obvious black marks against its pure white mantle. The tortures of the Spanish Inquisition headed the list, the direct outcome of a papal bull, the Summis Desiderantes, issued by Pope Innocent VIII who, three years later, appointed the infamous Torquemada as Grand Inquisitor.

"Innocent!" snorted O'Shea. It was designed to eliminate secularism, heresy and witchcraft, all of which threatened ecclesiastical authority. Words were fed into minds confused by barbaric torture, acceptance bringing the only release from their suffering.

The witch trials were no less horrendous or devastating, the result of the famous quote from Exodus, 'Thou shalt not suffer a witch to live'. Thanks to King James, those few, mistranslated words had probably caused more deaths than any others ever written. It laid the foundation for the later persecution of countless innocent people. Whole communities were hanged or put to death at the stake, nearby walls running thick with human fat, women being the chief victims. He discovered that even today the horror reared its ugly head.

O'Shea was sickened by accounts of the mania that swept Europe for 650 years. The accused were tortured, maimed and abused, all in the name of religion. They were condemned by testimony extracted under torture, but the diabolical disclosures came often from those obtaining the confessions, not from the dry throats of the innocents they tormented. Obscene and evil rites were the produce of religious minds, not the admissions of simple peasant folk. The ancient folk religions knew of no Hell, apart from that created by man, something O'Shea understood only too well. Imps, demons, incubi, succubi and the Devil were all created, it seemed, by the church to instil fear and control the people.

And to think I wanted to be part of this, thought O'Shea. The church had seemed a safe, benevolent body to him but, behind its public face, he was discovering a history more violent and diseased than he had ever imagined. He knew Graham had always thought of it as a substitute parent. Until now, that is, when it had seemingly turned against its child. It surprised O'Shea that Graham had never married. He'd always seemed destined for slippers, pipe and a doting wife.

Bigotry, prejudice and fear, they were still rife. His thoughts turned to Northern Ireland and then to his niece. Finally, he poured a large whiskey and downed it in one.

FIVE

Graham screamed. Stripped of his garments, he stood naked and trembling in front of the chancel of St. Jude's, facing an altar draped in flayed human skin. At his cry, a sigh arose from the pews behind him and he spun, trying to cover his nakedness, but there was no-one there, or at least no-one visible.

He straightened and let his hands fall to his sides. A new strength suddenly flowed through him, his surroundings as meaningless as his state of undress. He turned, purposefully mounted the pulpit steps and faced the rows of pews.

As he spoke, another sigh whispered around the empty church. Graham felt only contempt for the gullible congregations that had gathered here for hundreds of years. Venom-soaked words poured off his tongue, veiled obscenities within the sermon, temptations masked in holy prayer.

Reaching onto the shelf under the pulpit, he retrieved a knife, sticky with congealed blood. A striped woollen hat fell at his feet like a handful of gold, red and green serpents. As he ground their writhing bodies into the floor with his naked heel, his own screams woke him.

The faint glow of dawn lit the cracks that snaked across the whitewashed ceiling and the seeds of nightmare germinated in the half-light of his room.

Later, sunk deep in a soft brown leather chair, cocooned against the weather, he tried ignoring the niggling feelings of unease that had lingered from the dream and now kept intruding on his concentration. He wasn't given to premonitions or idle fancy, and besides, he was getting to the most exciting part of the crime thriller he was reading. Nevertheless, thoughts of St. Jude's kept finding their way into scenes of Mafia murder and blondes' bedrooms. Finally laying down the book, he sighed.

It was still raining heavily when he exchanged the warmth of the vicarage for the dubious shelter of his umbrella. A missing rib allowed water to gather in the fold like a caved-in tent until a sharp gust lifted it, spilling its contents to the wind. He muttered a few reproachful words in the general direction he perceived Heaven to be, pulled in his collar in a useless attempt to prevent water dripping down his neck and hurried towards St. Botolph's, his new church, his long black cassock smacking against his ankles.

"Confound it," he grumbled, as the waterlogged garment wrapped itself around both legs, endeavouring to trip him at each step. It was obviously designed for drier climes and not the British weather. Alternate overhanging horse-chestnut and sycamore trees, instead of providing shelter, seemed in competition to release their heaviest drops of gathered rain as he passed beneath. Swerving, he tried in vain to avoid the large puddles that threatened to completely flood the uneven tarmac path.

Once inside the church, he hurried forward to the front pew to pray but, try as he might, he found himself reliving the dream and wondering if he'd ever be able to face a congregation again.

A middle-aged woman, busying herself with the flower arrangements, cast a suspicious eye over him as he gathered his wet clothes about him and left the church. For the first time in his life, he wished he need never step inside one again.

"Well?" Cardinal Scappucci looked frail but his voice was strong, tinged now with urgency. "Is it done?"

"Yes, Your Eminence. The Reverend Graham Phillips shouldn't be a problem for much longer and our agent will be seeing to the transfer of the coffin within days. There was no trouble with officials once we contacted the right people." Cardinal Vanni was pleased with how things were going.

"Excellent, but I want to be kept in the picture. I shall not be happy until we have the coffin and its contents here, safe within our fold."

"Your Eminence." Vanni was eager to get away. He still had to prepare storage for the large stone sarcophagus and there was the appetite of their guest to consider. But then, as he had always maintained, the poor had their uses.

Laura examined her pallid features in the bathroom mirror. The harsh light illuminated her sunken eyes, the small lines forming around their edges and the furrow of her brow. Were it not for the bruises and occasional stabs of pain, she might have put her experience down to a vivid nightmare in a night of restless sleep, but there was no deluding herself. Each breath felt as if it was forced to claw its way free of the dread that threatened to crush her, body and soul, and each second added to the weight of her dark memories. Yet, even as she sank beneath the waters of her misery, she felt a warmth in her loins and an uneasy desire stir within her.

"No," she moaned, as her body remembered feelings her mind fought desperately to forget.

FATHER OF LIES

She splashed cold water onto her face, stinging her burning cheeks. Somewhere her reason screamed for her not to give in. Whoever – whatever – had abused her in St. Jude's wanted her to drown in shame and guilt. She knew it instinctively and she'd be damned if she'd allow it to defeat her. She refused to feel guilty for her body's responses, but fear, now that was another thing altogether. Damned either way, she thought ruefully, and winced as pain shot through her abdomen. As her eyes met their reflection, she was shocked at what she saw within them.

"Come on, girl," she whispered to herself. "You're stronger than this." As she spoke, the pain eased and she cautiously pulled herself erect and straightened her shoulders, breathing long and deep. She may look like a hollow shell but she had work to do, work that couldn't wait.

"Pre-Reformation bell... narrow lancet windows... south doorway of trefoil shape... herring-bone masonry... dedication crosses of sexfoil pattern on nave walls... There's plenty about the architecture of St. Jude's but little of its history, I'm afraid." O'Shea was frustrated, whereas Father Graham Phillips was agitated. "Painted rood-screen... nave of four arches with octagonal piers... embattled west tower... See for yourself, Graham."

"There must be something. Not all the records can have disappeared. I can only assume the room was built under the original church, dug out during the first centuries of Christianity. I've often wondered if the site was originally a place of pagan worship; that was frequently the case with early churches. It was believed that much of the present St. Jude's was built in the eleventh century." Graham scanned the photocopies before him. They covered every surface. He already knew most of it. He could picture every corner of St. Jude's, each archway and carving, but what he was searching for eluded him, just as it had eluded him through years of sermon-preaching within its walls.

O'Shea shrugged. "It's not for want of looking. Most churches were laid low during the Reformation. It's hardly surprising no written records remain."

"I know! I'm not a fool," snapped Graham. Then, more softly, "But this is something special, Dermot. St. Jude's isn't your average church. It…it's…" His voice trailed off.

O'Shea lifted his gaze. His friend's gaunt features shocked him. He'd driven over that morning and they were now sat in the rather austere vicarage that needed the clutter of Graham's still unpacked personal belongings to give it warmth. "Hey, I'm on your side," he said, offering what grain of comfort he could. He'd kept his description of the events at St. Jude's to a minimum, sticking to the bare facts of the media reports.

"And it was a passing visitor who found the body, you say?"

"A stranger to the village, yes." O'Shea hadn't admitted to being that stranger. He didn't want to answer the inevitable questions, didn't want to relive the horror he'd seen within the house of God. Whether he kept silent for Graham's sake or his own, he didn't know.

"But how did they get in?" Graham persisted.

"Look, I've a colleague in Hampstead who might be able to dig something up," said O'Shea, ignoring

FATHER OF LIES

Graham's question and gathering up the sheets of paper. "I've got to go down to London anyway, and I've cleared an extended leave of absence with the university. Still got to visit the British Museum. I'm glad I kept my reading pass up to date."

He was worried about his friend. There was a restlessness, an uneasy alertness, about Graham that was alien to the quiet, mild-mannered cleric whose eyes now shone with a strange light. It was as though he was listening, straining to hear sounds beyond the door of the vicarage, and it was making O'Shea edgy.

"I'll travel down tomorrow," he said, "See what I can come up with," but Graham didn't hear him. Nor did he hear O'Shea's farewell and the closing of the door. He was listening to something far more interesting, more direct, more seductive and, like a serpent in his brain, its whispered words were for Graham's ears alone.

William Dorcas had a passion for old books. He spent most of his spare time browsing through shops that dealt in antiquarian volumes. The rest he spent rummaging through dusty piles of forgotten gems in second-hand shops, jumble and car boot sales and house clearances. His collection was diverse to say the least, ranging from Victorian morality tearjerkers to cult sixties drug and sexploitation novels, ancient historical works in almost indecipherable English to first editions of the classics. Alchemical treatises lay next to the poems of Tennyson, Punch illustrations alongside illumined monastic theology.

It was never an easy task to find a particular novel or subject, but one which provided him with hours of pleasure as he let himself be diverted down many a curious literary byway. It had taken him most of the previous day to locate the information O'Shea had asked for and he'd photocopied the relevant pages of the thin book he'd at last uncovered, hidden at the back of a dark corner shelf. He had no recollection of putting it there or, for that matter, having ever set eyes on it before, but would be quite relieved to bury it away again as soon as O'Shea's visit was over. There was something distasteful about the softbound cover and an oily feel to its pages. To someone who loved the smell and touch of musty tomes, this was a rotten apple in a storeroom of fragrant orchard produce.

It crossed his mind that he should perhaps offer it to a museum. Each page was hand-written in a clear, ornate style, possibly making it unique and deserving of more care than his twice-yearly dusting.

He was spared the decision by the ringing of his doorbell.

"O'Shea! Come on up." He pressed the button to open the street door.

O'Shea shook himself free of his wet overcoat and scarf in the hall before mounting the stairs and stepping into his idea of Heaven.

"Dorcas! Good to see you."

"Come in, come in."

O'Shea handed over his coat and scarf. An inviting gas fire crackled deceitfully in the cluttered study, its warm light tingeing the laden bookshelves with red. He made for one of the armchairs and, on being offered coffee or something stronger, settled for both. He lent back into the soft womb of the chair, relishing his surroundings whilst he could. He'd be born again into the wet London streets soon enough.

"So, what have you found for me?" He was

comfortable, warm and relaxed and didn't really care if Dorcas had come up with anything or not.

"Would I let an old colleague down? They said it couldn't be done but here you are, 'Ye Suppression of Evyl in Ye Countee of Norefolk' by Wesley of Ely. It may not qualify as history exactly but you didn't specify fact." He handed O'Shea the book.

O'Shea passed it from one hand to the other, looking at his fingers as if to see traces of whatever made his skin crawl and feel slimy and sticky at the same time.

"Unpleasant, isn't it?" said Dorcas, seeing O'Shea's reaction. "I wondered if it could be skin but it's too white and supple. Suppose I could get it tested."

O'Shea grimaced. The pages looked and felt greasy, reminding him of rancid fat.

"Here, read the photocopies if you prefer." Dorcas exchanged crisp, clean pages for the book.

It took O'Shea a while to sift the story from the meanderings and inventive spelling typical of its period. By the time he'd finished, he was sat bolt upright, lethargy and disinterest washed away in a flood tide of excitement.

"My God, Dorcas, you're a genius. Have you read this?"

Dorcas shook his head, his mouth full of fruitcake. Spitting crumbs, he said, "Of course I've read it. How else would I have found it for you?"

O'Shea barely heard him. He was re-reading the papers, disbelief and understanding competing for supremacy in his mind.

"That's it!" he muttered. "That's bloody it." He should call Graham, tell him what he'd discovered, but knew his friend was close to cracking. No, he'd talk to

Laura first. Maybe then they could both pay Graham a visit. He didn't want the responsibility of being wrong to rest solely on his shoulders. If that made him a coward, so be it.

"Seems like your St. Jude's, according to this Wesley of Ely chappie, was built where it was to prevent the evil spreading." Dorcas broke in on his thoughts.

"Or, perhaps, to protect it," returned O'Shea. Could it be possible, he wondered, for the church to unwittingly house something evil.

"What? What do you mean?"

"Look, I'm sorry to dash off, Dorcas, but I need to get this to someone as quickly as possible. You do understand, don't you? Thank you so much for, well, for everything. Must do it again." He was collecting coat and scarf as he spoke and stumbling down the stairs, followed by a bemused Dorcas. "I'll ring, yes, I'll ring you soon, return the favour. Knew you'd understand. Genius!" And he was gone, his feet splashing in the dirty London puddles, a wave without turning, papers clutched firmly in his hand.

"Well, I can't say I understand at all," said Dorcas, as he watched O'Shea disappear around a corner. "Not at all," he added, closing the door and shutting out the cold and rain. He returned to his room, which felt strangely empty, and turned up the gas fire. O'Shea hadn't even touched his slice of cake. Waste not, want not, thought Dorcas as he reached for O'Shea's plate.

It was sometime later that he picked up the book, running his fingers over its pallid cover, puzzled again by the impression of touching skin. It was like caressing the dead, except it managed to seem still alive. He shivered.

Becoming aware suddenly of intense pain in his hands, he let the book fall, blisters forming on the tips of his fingers, the burning sensation making him cry out and wave his hands in a frantic cooling motion. The heat spread through his fingers, beneath the nails, as though he'd held them in an open flame.

When the worst of the pain eased, he looked at the book lying open on the tiles before the fire. Its cover was turning brown before his eyes, the pages curling as if unable to ignite, acrid, foul-smelling smoke twisting up from the warped paper. When it finally burst into flames, Dorcas cried out again, startled by the sudden combustion. He watched, shaken and terrified, still clutching his painful hands under his armpits, until all that remained of Wesley of Ely's carefully scribed book was a grey pile of ash and a stench that came straight from Hell.

O'Shea wasn't sure what to make of Laura. He'd never come across a priest or a woman like her and couldn't quite decide if she inspired or offended him. Right now, he just wished she'd give him her full attention.

"Apparently, there was a huge battle between this oh-so-godly Jude and a stranger accompanied by a swirling serpent or dragon who, we must presume, represented the Devil. The fighting went on week after week, neither giving way, each gaining or losing strength with the hours of darkness. Finally, Jude got the upper hand, killing the stranger and overcoming the serpent, although, being mortally wounded himself, he was unable to kill it. This is where it gets interesting." He looked at Laura, expecting some sign that she was listening. None came.

"Laura, are you all right?" She certainly didn't look

it.

"Yes, yes, I'm fine. Sorry, I'm just not feeling too good." She felt guilty for not showing interest. "Do go on, but just don't expect fireworks. O.K.?"

Unconvinced, O'Shea nodded. "Seems, with Jude dead or dying, the people of the hamlet didn't know what to do with this creature and were in fear for their lives. At this point, some travelling monk conveniently arrives and tells them to build a stone coffin for the beast. He, himself, takes control of its design, in fact. How the serpent was coaxed into its prison isn't stated but this monk, or whoever he was, then tells the people to build a church over it, commemorating the supremacy of good over evil. The body of Jude was interred with the beast. Once this was done, there seems to be no further records. There's no mention of the name of the hamlet or any clues to its whereabouts, but there seems enough there to tie it in with our St. Jude's and the recent find." O'Shea sat back.

"But this was all hearsay, just some morality tale handed down, if it's even that. This Wesley of Ely might just have been a hopeful Stephen King of his day."

"And what if he wasn't?" O'Shea was annoyed. He felt like a child who'd just had his balloon burst.

"All I'm saying is we have to be careful. This doesn't constitute proof of anything, merely a possibility. If your friend, Graham, is as unstable as you say, the last thing he needs is food for his paranoia."

O'Shea sighed. "Yes, you're right of course, but I did promise Graham I'd find out who that damned coffin belonged to if I could, and this seemed a possible explanation, even if it wouldn't stand up in court."

"A dragon?" said Laura. She raised an eyebrow and smiled.

O'Shea sighed. "So what's the next step?"

"I'm going to ask that Vatican official," said Laura, with sudden determination. "We seem to be jumping to conclusions but we've never bothered to ask. After all, they must have an inkling who it is, otherwise why insist on removing it?" She forced a strained smile. "Besides," she added, "they have no power in Britain beyond what we give them."

The answer seemed so simple; O'Shea wondered why they hadn't thought of it before. "Have you a way of contacting them?" he ventured.

"If I haven't, I'll want to know why."

As he stood before Cardinal Scappucci, his hands folded before him, Vanni radiated a calmness he didn't altogether feel.

"When we discovered a copy of the book, we immediately took appropriate measures. I can assure Your Eminence that it was totally destroyed."

"But can we be sure no-one read those passages that pose a threat?"

"No, Your Eminence, but we have the location. We will tidy up the loose ends, I promise you."

"See that you do," replied Scappucci, his appearance belying the power behind his words. "Nothing must be overlooked."

Vanni hoped fervently that nothing had been.

It was late. O'Shea wondered if he should give Graham a call; he was worried about him. He fished for the paper on which he'd scribbled down the numbers. Getting no answer from the mobile, he rang the landline Graham had given him. It took a while before there was a disgruntled answer.

"He's gone," came the abrupt reply when he asked for Graham.

"Gone? Gone where?"

"You tell me," snapped the voice. "Packed a bag and left. Right to-do, I can tell you. He's supposed to be taking services."

By the time O'Shea put down the phone, he was even more concerned. Just where had Graham gone and how could he contact him if he wasn't answering calls? There was nothing he could do but wait, and waiting was something O'Shea found very hard to do.

SIX

A crowd had gathered in the damp Hampstead street, whilst, thanks to the revolving blue and red lights of the emergency services, figures appeared to move in the jerky fashion of early films. The road was blocked by two bulky fire engines, coils of hose curling like a giant snake along the gutter and across the pavement.

"Move along there. There's nothing more to see." The police constables ushered the curious onlookers back to their homes and signalled a few waiting cars up onto the opposite pavement, around one of the red engines.

"Where do they all come from?" The constable was young and experience hadn't yet taught him about the elusive, yet unfailing, allure that draws people to disaster sites.

"Wherever it is, let's get them back there as quickly as possible," said the older constable, relieved that a senior officer had arrived on the scene to take charge. He could hear his superior questioning the leading firefighter.

"Any ideas?" the sergeant asked.

"Your guess is as good as mine at this stage. Could have been the gas fire. Anyone report an explosion?"

The two men stepped back to let the ambulance technicians through, carrying a stretcher.

"We'll have the Fire Investigation team in tomorrow. Between them and your forensics, we'll soon know. Funny, it was as hot as hell in there yet the fire seemed oddly contained."

"Could it be spontaneous human combustion?" chimed in a voice from behind them. Larry Markham had arrived on the scene simultaneously with the police, having picked up their messages on his radio.

"Print that and you'll be doing yourself no favours," said the constable.

"How about you doing me one then, like filling me in on the details?"

"I'll do you a favour by not running you in for scanning our airwaves, hindering the police and fire service in their work, loitering, harassment..."

"O.K., O.K., I'm going." Larry sighed. "I'm only trying to make an honest buck." He'd got some good photos and enough information to be going on with.

As he drove away, no-one noticed the second car pulling out in his wake, or its two occupants. No-one had noticed them amongst the crowd of onlookers either, two more strangers in a street full of strangers, standing apart in their long leather coats.

Graham slipped from his room into the night. He needed to breathe the cool air. His new lodgings in London were stuffy and the light poor. Economy bulbs reduced everything to a dull glow, straining his eyes when he tried to read. Without his books to distract him, his mind wandered down paths he'd rather leave untrodden and, for the first time in many years, he wished he had a television.

Left alone with only his thoughts for company, he'd begun to doubt his own sanity. He wondered if he'd sent O'Shea on a wild goose chase, that in fact there was nothing extraordinary going on and that his fears were only the product of his imagination. Then he'd remind himself there had been a murder committed in St. Jude's. There was no denying that fact. His head reasoned that perhaps there was no connection, but then that inner sense of knowing that plagues everyone from time to time stepped in and he was sure, deep down inside, that something was wrong, very wrong indeed.

There was frost in the air tonight and his breath formed clouds as he walked the empty streets, going nowhere, walking to clear his head. The crispness of the night seemed to clarify his thoughts. He'd had to get away, lose himself in the city, give himself time to think. Or maybe time not to. He felt safer having no-one knowing his whereabouts.

Heedless of where he was going, Graham's steps led him past rows of houses, all similar. Nothing distinguished them from each other in the camouflage of night. It was late and there were few lights signalling life behind the closed curtains and blinds. Graham envied the sleepers within. How he would love to shut out the world with all its threatened menace as they did. He sensed the thing he had most to fear was inside him and he had nowhere he could hide. Except the church, he thought. Not St. Jude's or St. Botolph's, but one that didn't know him, one where he could sit quietly in prayer and perhaps find relief from the thoughts eroding his mind.

Two streets further on, he spotted the tall, dark building set back from the pavement. Black iron railings separated the church from the community it served. He hurried up to the unwelcoming door. He half-expected it to be locked, but the handle turned easily in his grip and the door swung inwards.

It was surprisingly light inside and he was able to make his way forward without difficulty. Sliding into a pew halfway down the length of the nave, he knelt and prayed in the yellow glow from the street. He let out all the horror and pent up emotions of the past few weeks. He asked to be forgiven for his weakness and begged for guidance. As he prayed, he felt the shadows gathering around him. With an effort of will which would have been impossible earlier, he pushed them back into the recesses and, when his prayers were finally finished, he was filled with new resolve. Fired with the certainty that all would be well, he rose on numbed limbs, lifted his head high and ventured back into the night, confident now. No longer the hunted, no longer afraid.

Perhaps, had he raised his head a little further, his eyes would have picked out the detail on the church's stained-glass windows. In the sickly glow from the street lamps, the main window depicted St. George standing astride a coiled serpent. In the uncertain light, its writhing body engulfed the saint in coils of red and green and gold.

Larry Markham supported himself with one hand against the wall whilst he relieved himself with the other. The whole alley smelled like a toilet so he felt no qualms about using it as one. He'd only meant to have one quick drink but that barmaid certainly had a way with words and a bosom to die for. Now, his head only somewhat lighter than his wallet, he wished he'd gone straight home after the fire.

Swaying, he found he needed both hands to zip his fly and, for a foolish moment, wondered where he'd parked the car. Before the foolish thought could become a foolish act, a blow from behind sent him sprawling in the fouled garbage, where two well-aimed kicks to his ribs and head granted him welcome oblivion.

He had no idea how long he'd lain in the filth. His throbbing head, the acute pain in his ribcage and the dreadful stench surrounding him made him vomit into the gutter, before he hauled himself upright against a drainpipe and tried to collect his thoughts. He knew instinctively his cameras were gone. The case was such a part of his life that it was like an extra limb. He checked his pockets but his wallet and credit cards were still there. He almost wished they'd been stolen instead.

He let out a groan as he tried to walk and wondered if he could make it to the end of the alley.

O'Shea was glad he didn't have to shoulder Graham's paranoia and its attendant horrors alone. That's if it was paranoia and everything that had happened wasn't just a series of unrelated circumstances. There were folk who believed there was no such thing as coincidence and O'Shea had found himself wondering if they were right. However, reason told him that, of the two deaths in St. Jude's, one was certainly an accident and the other – whatever form it had taken – most definitely wasn't. Maybe they were only finding links because they were looking for them. They had nothing concrete whatsoever and Laura's course of action, simply asking the official from the Vatican who was buried in the sarcophagus, seemed so logical and straightforward. Still, O'Shea felt a twinge of unease.

Something was bothering him about Laura too. Guiltily aware he'd dumped all his suspicions onto her, not only expecting but getting her help, it seemed little wonder she appeared distracted and worn. Maybe they should listen to what the Vatican official had to say and then call it a day. In the meantime, he'd needed a break away from St. Jude's.

There were more people than he'd imagined strolling along the Cam embankment. A couple of hardy souls were even punting, despite the chill winds. Piles of leaves clustered in soggy heaps along the edge of the path, forming terracotta borders to the shaven grass. A laughing couple jostled past, lost in their own world, rolls of Christmas paper jutting from a carrier bag.

Thoughts of his niece came automatically, as though to a hypnotic command triggered by the yearly festival. He guessed she would have been about Laura's age had she lived. With a jolt, he realised that he'd have been proud of her if she'd turned out like Laura.

His thoughts led him down familiar darkened avenues and his footsteps slowed as if in respect. He turned from the path and sat on a bench, hunched, staring at the river with unseeing eyes, the dampness of the wooden seat working its way through his clothes and chilling him to the bone.

As the grey afternoon began to lose its light, he rose and headed for the nearest Catholic church, where he paused only long enough to light a small white candle for a long-dead child with golden curls.

It had taken Laura almost an hour and fourteen separate phone calls before she was able to make an appointment with Monsignor Benvenuti, and that indirectly.

"It is not our way to give interviews," said the Monsignor, ingratiatingly, as they sat in the otherwise empty lounge of an extremely expensive hotel. "You are a very fortunate woman."

"Neither is it normal for you to retrieve ancient remains from a Protestant church, Monsignor, and, having had two deaths in that same church, I don't consider myself fortunate at all."

"Quite so, but surely you are not suggesting there's a connection?"

"I'm suggesting nothing. I would merely like to know why you're removing the remains and whose they are."

Benvenuti crinkled his eyes, hinting at a smile without moving his lips. The way Laura looked him straight in the eye, almost challenging, reminded him of his sister. Not that he'd seen her for years but, as a child, she would look up at him with the same challenge, pushing her chin forward determinedly despite the trembling of her mouth. It had somehow increased the pleasure as he'd forced her down the cellar steps, locking her alone in the dark and damp whilst their mother was out at work. He'd stand on the opposite side of the cellar door, listening until the screams became whimpers and finally silence. He'd always been able to think up new reasons for her tear-stained face when their mother returned home.

He now beamed at Laura, wishing he could hear her screams, excited by thoughts of her confined in that very darkness that he had dreaded. When he was young, he'd been terrified by what it might hide. How much sweeter it was now that he knew.

"My dear young lady, I am not in a position to divulge such information, even if I was able. We presume it is an elder of the Holy Roman Catholic Church but, beyond that, I can be of no assistance."

"Then why," insisted Laura, "remove it? If it has lain peacefully for so many centuries, why disturb it now?"

"For just that reason, that it has already been disturbed. Now, if you will forgive me, I have much work to do." He was reluctant to bring the conversation to an end but he had observed protocol. He could continue his darker thoughts regarding the Reverend Laura Coatman at a more conducive time.

He rose from his chair in one elegant movement, whilst Laura, who had been fighting to stay dignified and upright in the soft cushions, chose to remain seated. She'd tumble out when Benvenuti had gone rather than give him the satisfaction of another patronising smile.

"Shit!" she said, when he was out of earshot. She was sure he knew but he hadn't told her a thing. She was also sure that she never wanted to see him again.

"Time to knock on a few doors," announced O'Shea, when he and Laura were ensconced before a log fire in 'The Peal of Bells'. A red light, hidden behind the inglenook beam, shone on the beaten copper fireguard, reflecting a warm glow back onto their serious features.

The afternoon stroll beside the Cam had cleared O'Shea's head. "We're assuming we're the only ones to feel unsettled within St. Jude's. It's time we asked the parishioners."

"How do you plan to approach them?"

"Me? OK, OK, so it was my idea, right? Leave it to me, young lady, if I'm allowed to call you that? I'm sure a touch of blarney will work its charm. I'll just tell them I'm doing some research on the history of the place. They don't have to talk to me if they don't have a mind to."

"You won't get much co-operation from the churchwarden that I've met. He tore me off a strip today for leaving the items I need for services in the church; said he wasn't my servant, as if I'd left it to him on purpose. You could start with the other one who, I'm told, has been unable to fulfil his duties for a number of months now, due to ill health. Go gently with him though. I understand he's quite elderly."

"Gentle as a lamb. How did you get on with the Monsignor?"

Laura grimaced. "He made my flesh crawl."

"Clergy has had that effect on me for years," grinned O'Shea. At Laura's startled expression, he hurriedly added, "Present company excepted, of course."

"Well, I think I've managed to put a spoke in *his* wheel, at least." She waited for O'Shea's reaction. "The Vatican isn't going to be shipping anything anywhere just yet. A team of archaeologists is arriving from Cambridge tomorrow to check out both tomb and occupant." She sat back smugly as O'Shea let out his breath in a long low whistle.

"Just how did you manage that?"

"I simply pointed out the age of the tomb and its possible links to that old legend written by Wesley of Ely, and they were falling over themselves to examine it. I can't prevent the remains from being removed, but I can certainly slow things up, if only to upset the contemptible monsignor. He'll find it hard to speed up the slow wheels of British academia."

O'Shea grimaced. "You really did take a dislike to the man, didn't you? Remind me never to cross you."

After a moment, he added, "What brought you to the church, Laura?"

"You can blame Saint Hilda," Laura smiled.

"She's one I've not heard of," said O'Shea.

"I'm just a Yorkshire lass at heart," replied Laura. "Both my parents were killed in a car crash when I was young and I lived with an aunt and uncle at Robin Hood's Bay. I never felt close to them. Saint Hilda of Whitby was my heroine. She founded the monastery there."

"The one on the cliff?"

"That's right! Three hundred feet above sea level. It was a double monastery, men and women, with women taking precedence. Maybe because of the proximity of men, Hilda became a sort of mother figure and even kings and bishops sought her advice. She proved that female leadership was possible within the church, that the rules needn't be rigid."

"Quite a lady," O'Shea observed.

"Yes, she inspired men rather than dominated them. She and Joan were the biggest influences on my early years and I decided I'd follow their example." She refrained from naming which Joan. "I suppose the church offered the support, guidance and protection I'd been deprived of when I lost my parents."

Both fell silent for a while, the warmth and alcohol drawing each into their own unspoken thoughts, each needing to talk but not wanting to break the silence. Finally Laura asked, "Where were you this afternoon? I tried to contact you."

"Just walking. Christmas isn't my favourite time of the year."

"Do you want to talk about it?"

"No." O'Shea shook his head. "It wouldn't do any

good," he added.

"You could try. I'm a priest, you know?" said Laura, smiling.

That, one too many whiskeys and the fire highlighting her concerned expression was all it took for O'Shea to pour out the bottled feelings he'd held in check for too long. A tear rolled unattended down his cheek as he told Laura of his niece, the bombing and the guilt he'd been carrying for nearly twenty years. When he'd finished, he felt tired and hated himself for his weakness. Laura laid her hand over O'Shea's for an instant.

"I suppose you're going to tell me she's happy now," he said quietly.

"Have you never thought of returning to Ireland?" she asked.

"No, no! There'd be too many memory lanes to wander down." He straightened, locking his personal thoughts away in the Pandora's Box that was his mind.

"And what of family? Your sister?"

"We lost touch. She blamed me or, perhaps, resented me for still being alive. I've no family now, not to speak of."

She shook her head. "Give up the grief, Dermot." It was the first time she'd used his Christian name. "Only when you cease to grieve can the loved one be truly free."

"Free?"

"To move on, to be at peace."

"You're preaching again." Despite himself, a slight smile lifted the corners of his mouth.

"I know, it's what I do best," she replied, then added, "but I'm going to give you the chance to do the same."

"Me? I'm long past doing that." Something in her tone made him turn to look at her. "What is it? What's wrong?"

Laura took a deep breath before replying. "I want you to hear my confession."

"I'm not comfortable with this, I have to let you know," remonstrated O'Shea. "I'm not a priest and you're not a Catholic. If you feel the need to unburden yourself, surely you should be alone and pray?"

"You need to hear this, Dermot, and I don't think I can go through it more than once. You and God must share this, like it or not." She was not to be swayed. "Haven't I heard you say the church doctrines have been altered by men from day one? Well, I'm altering them again. Besides, you know confessions aren't unheard of in the Anglican Church; it's just usually to one of our own." She paused. "You might need another drink though, before we find somewhere private."

SEVEN

The proxy confessional turned out to be a path alongside a dyke skirting the village and separating it from the flat surrounding land. There was no-one about at this hour and a bracing wind caught their words and flung them out across the bleak fens.

O'Shea was glad of the dark as he knew he couldn't prevent the dismay showing on his face as he listened to Laura's account of the events that had taken place in St. Jude's. No wonder she had seemed troubled of late. He just wished she'd told him sooner. She, in turn, held nothing back, including the guilt she felt at what she could only see as her body's betrayal of her long-held values.

When she had finished, they walked on in silence, only turning back when they heard the last revellers leaving 'The Peal of Bells'.

"No prayers in penance, no comforting words of absolution?" She glanced at O'Shea.

"You don't need forgiveness, Laura, not from me or from God. You could no more control your body's reaction than will yourself to stop breathing."

"But…" Laura felt she needed something from O'Shea.

"But nothing! What kind of God would condemn us for feelings and responses beyond our control?" He paused. "Why didn't you tell me all this sooner, Laura?" When she remained silent, he continued, "I was beginning to believe we were giving in to our imaginings, but now I'm sure we've encountered something truly evil. I don't know what form it takes, its purpose or how to fight it, but if you want a penance, Laura, you'll help me to find out."

O'Shea couldn't sleep. It wasn't the first time he'd broken with convention and he had no remorse at easing Laura's burden of guilt. He guessed that, even had Laura been a Catholic, she wouldn't have wanted to confess in church, especially after her previous ordeal. They desperately needed to know more. Dorcas had come up trumps before; maybe he could again. He'd call him first thing. He rose from his bed and closed the chink of window he'd left open for air, but his room remained chill and a whiskey nightcap held the only promise of sleep.

"It's no good," O'Shea told Laura, in what passed as a breakfast bar in the pub. "I've been trying to get hold of Dorcas since seven. I know he's an early riser. I think I'll just take a chance and go on down to see him. If he's away at a book fair or the like, I'll just have to wait."

"If you don't mind company, I'll tag along on the journey. I'd like to do a little research myself." When O'Shea looked at her questioningly, she added, "There's a shop I thought of that might just know where I can get information. It's worth a try at least, and I'd rather enquire in person than over the phone."

"Delighted to have you along," chuckled O'Shea, "if only to wake me if I snore on the train."

When Benvenuti got off the phone with Cardinal Vanni, his face was burning and the conversation's repeated replays in his head were fuelling the fire.

His brothers in the Vatican obviously had no idea of the problems he was facing on the 'front line'. He'd had the devil's own job preventing the Cambridge team from wrapping up the contents of the coffin and shipping it back to their labs at the university. He'd stressed that whatever remains were there, whether bones, mummified tissue or just plain dust, the Holy Roman Catholic Church considered them as holy relics and the sole responsibility of the Vatican. It had been a hard-fought battle but he'd finally won. He'd agreed to let the sarcophagus remain in situ whilst they dug and scraped about it, but insisted two representatives of the church remain with it at all times. It was imperative the contents were not disturbed.

The professor in charge of the dig had been irritating and exuberant and was gushingly grateful at having received a call from the vicar to notify them of the find.

Laura Coatman was becoming a thorn in Benvenuti's side, one, if he was given the opportunity, he would take great pleasure in removing.

Laura and O'Shea parted company at King's Cross, O'Shea catching the Northern Line to Hampstead, Laura taking it in the opposite direction to Tottenham Court Road. From there she made her way to Great Russell Street and the Lemuria Bookshop, wedged neatly between a film nostalgia shop and one selling ancient coins.

She had never been to the shop before but had known of its existence since her teens. Although its books were not required – or recommended – reading for an ordinand, she had purchased one or two from their website over the years, under the pretext to herself of checking out the opposition.

Laura was both surprised and delighted to find that, although in the heart of Bloomsbury and opposite The British Museum, it was an old-fashioned style bookshop. Its cramped interior begged the customer to spend time browsing the new and second-hand books that jostled for space on the overflowing shelves, and the evocative smell of incense made Laura feel immediately at home.

She was overwhelmed with the sheer number of books on all aspects of the occult and felt as if she'd stepped straight into Harry Potter's Diagon Alley. Where to start?

A woman with a cushion of blonde, upswept hair and half-rimmed spectacles smiled from behind a glass counter containing packs of divination cards and a variety of crystals. Maybe she senses my confusion, thought Laura. She took a deep breath and approached her.

"Excuse me, but do you have any books that deal with the subject of evil. That is, evil within the church?" It sounded so silly now she'd put it into words, but the woman didn't turn one gravity-defying hair.

"Are we talking desecrations, clerical corruption, demonic forces, exorcism, their treatment of women, the Devil, what exactly?"

"It seems I'm spoilt for choice," gasped Laura. "I'm not sure where to start. I suppose reputed dark associations or maybe with manifestations. Oh dear, I really don't know." She had been surprised by the choices offered and realised this may take a great deal longer than she'd bargained for.

The woman looked anxiously across at two customers waiting to be served, their arms sagging under piles of books.

"Would you mind if I just attend to these people?"

As Laura waited for the woman to return, she scanned the titles on the immediate shelves. There were books on witchcraft, magic, astrology, tarot, the Kabala and much more besides, covering not only their history but 'how to' and 'what if'. She seemed to have entered an Aladdin's cave of esoteric knowledge and arcane practice, and had begun to feel uncomfortably out of place when the woman reappeared at her side.

"Sorry about that. Right, evil? In the church, you said?"

"Yes. I suppose, if I'm honest, I don't know in what form. Possibly legends connecting the buildings themselves to evil, but I'm open to anything you have really. That is, if you have anything at all."

"I'm sure we have plenty on it in one form or another but you're actually in luck. One of our regular customers studies evil in all its guises, and that's him standing over there. Maybe I should introduce you, that's if you're willing?"

Laura gulped. She almost imagined him to have cloven hooves, horns and a forked tail. In fact, he looked very ordinary, blending so well into his surroundings that she had failed to notice him till now. When they were introduced, his ready smile and twinkling eyes put her immediately at ease.

Marcus Cook turned out to be charming and intelligent, with light, limpid eyes and an ever-present smile playing on his lips. Laura wondered if he found her amusing or maybe that was how he viewed everything. Seated in a nearby café, with a coffee and

Danish, she discovered Marcus's appearance belied his deep fascination with all things evil.

"Is your interest a general one or are you looking for something specific?" he asked, in a slightly rasping voice and eyeing Laura with shameless curiosity.

"I'm looking for reports, myths, legends – I'm not sure what you'd call it – of evil associated with a certain church in Norfolk. Would you know of anything or where I can look up such information?"

Marcus bestowed another smile on Laura and lifted his mug to his lips. As he took a sip, Laura noticed for the first time his long fingernails, each filed to a point. It was all she could do to drag her attention from them as he began to speak.

"I take it you've tried the internet?"

Laura nodded.

"What about the church itself?"

"There's nothing."

"And its name?"

Laura took a deep breath. "St. Jude's. In Adderidge. I've read an account by a Wesley of Ely that might have a bearing on it, if that helps?"

"Ah, that rings a bell. Have you tried the Dean of Ely Cathedral? Also the Ely museum archives? That's where I'd start."

"You're right!" Laura brightened visibly. "I'll see what I can find there."

"Look, I feel pretty sure I can come up with something. Leave me a contact number and I'll do some digging. How does that sound?" He smiled at the thought of what might prove to be an interesting diversion.

Laura returned his smile, feeling that maybe the trip had proved fruitful after all. She took his proffered hand but averted her gaze, still finding his nails repugnant. What did they matter though, if their owner uncovered information that would help her and O'Shea face whatever lurked in the cold shelter of St. Jude's?

O'Shea stood in total bewilderment, staring across the busy street at black-stained brickwork around the window of William Dorcas's flat. He sidled through the two-way traffic and gazed blankly at the doorbell. He knew it was useless but pressed it anyway. "You're wasting your time," came a voice from the doorway to the left, that led into a delicatessen directly under the flat. The generously-proportioned lady who was watching O'Shea retreated, crablike, into her gastronomic refuge as he headed after her into the shop.

"Miracle it didn't come down through the floor. Not even the smell of smoke, much to our insurer's relief. A real miracle, that's what I call it."

"What happened?"

"A fire, that's what happened. Silly old git probably fell asleep reading too close to the fire, that's what I think."

"He's …?"

"Dead? Better be. They carried him off in a body bag, or what was left of him." The thought that O'Shea might be a relative about to go into mourning never seemed to occur to her. "Friend, was he?"

"Yes, yes, I suppose he was." O'Shea felt a sudden sense of loss.

"'Course, he'd have done us a favour if the fire had come through. Might have been able to get new cabinets and freezers, maybe get some designer units. Most of this stuff came out the ark." She seemed all set to begin itemising all she could have done with a sizable insurance payout, so O'Shea bought some garlic sausage and olives and made his getaway. His head was swimming with unanswered questions and the smell of the sausage was making him feel nauseous.

The fresh air helped and he stood still in the middle of the pavement, wondering what his next step should be. A moment later, jostled by annoyed passers-by, he set out for Hampstead Police Station on Roslyn Hill.

"Something smells good," said the desk sergeant, nodding toward the deli bag in O'Shea's hand. "What can I do for you?"

As O'Shea explained, the desk sergeant shook his head. "Nothing suspicious, as far as I recall." He checked anyway. "No, as I thought, a tragic accident. Place was full of old books, it seems. Went up like tinder. Our presence was needed more to keep back onlookers and press and make sure they didn't get in the way of the fire services than to investigate."

"Press, you say? So there would have been photos?"

"Just a minute, Sir, I'll see if anyone knows who was there." He left O'Shea staring at the posters warning of the danger of fireworks and where to ring for drugs advice. He'd just started reading a third on help for AIDS when the sergeant returned.

"Seems I mislead you. There was just a freelancer there. He may or may not have taken some shots."

"Do you know where I can contact him, by any chance? It really is important." O'Shea didn't expect co-operation, so was surprised when the desk sergeant handed him an address.

"Larry Markham is his name. Yank! Always

looking for a story."

O'Shea expressed his thanks and hurried out.

"Sir?" called the desk sergeant but was too late. He picked up the deli bag and put it under the counter, secretly hoping it wouldn't be claimed.

The address was for a house in Chalk Farm, typical of so many now divided up into bed-sits with rents larger than their floor space. A quick check of the door buzzers showed O'Shea that Larry Markham had a room on the ground floor but there was no answer when he rang. He glanced at his watch. Where had the day gone? He wanted to stay and wait for Markham to return but had promised Laura he'd meet her at King's Cross. It was getting near rush hour. He reached for his wallet and a pen. After scribbling a brief message and his mobile number on the back of a Tesco receipt, he pushed it through the letterbox and hoped it would reach its intended reader.

Laura was sitting in the British Rail café over a cold cup of coffee.

"I wondered where you'd got to," she smiled. "I thought maybe the two of you had got buried in piles of antiquarian books." On seeing O'Shea's expression, she added, "What's wrong?"

"What time's our train?"

"We've got almost half an hour. Do you want a coffee?"

"I'll get it. Do you want another? That looks dead."

"No thanks. I've had three."

O'Shea came back with a coffee and greasy-looking muffin. He sat down opposite Laura, took a sip of coffee, grimaced and added three sachets of sugar.

"I'm not coming back with you tonight," he began. He went on to tell a shocked Laura of the day's events.

"And this Markham, you think he may… what? Help? You've no reason to believe the fire was deliberate. What do you expect to find in his photos?"

"Probably nothing, but it's just all too much of a coincidence," said O'Shea. "How did you get on?"

"It can wait till you get back. A lead, nothing more. Where will you stay?"

"Don't worry about me. There are hotels all around here. I'll see you tomorrow. Now, you'd better rush. You don't want to miss your train."

After Laura had gone, O'Shea sat watching the frantic commuters, many laden with pre-Christmas shopping. He gulped down the last of the coffee, wished he hadn't, and headed out into the dark in search of the nearest bar. From an adjacent table, a dirty, gloved hand reached out and grasped the neglected muffin.

The carriage was crowded and, though clammy from tightly-packed humanity, still managed to keep its chill, like frosting round a warm cake. Laura was forced to stand till Welwyn Garden City, where she clambered over stretched legs to reach a vacated seat by the window. She rubbed the steamed glass and watched the moisture run down the pane in trembling lines.

Gazing out into the darkness, she couldn't shake off a growing feeling of dread. As the train passed the various towns en route, she found herself gazing into uncurtained windows, wishing she were a part of the comfortable, ordinary worlds within. She didn't want to go back alone to the Parish of St. Jude's – her parish – and found herself praying fervently for the strength to get her through the night.

EIGHT

Once again, Graham's bedding was soaked with sweat. He couldn't recall his dream but felt as if he'd cut himself on the sharp edge of a scream and couldn't stop the bleeding. He hauled himself from the bed, wondering how long he could go on like this. Standing barefoot on the cold bathroom lino, he stared into the mirror but the pale, gaunt face reflected there offered no consolation or trace of his earlier resolve.

He couldn't stay cooped up with just his thoughts for company. He felt the need to walk, no matter the hour. He looked at his watch. Two thirty-four a.m.. Not the best time to walk the streets of London, especially alone. He decided to head towards the centre, where lights and laughter defied even the darkest night.

He was surprised to find so many people out on the streets, but then the old cliché was true, cities never sleep. No-one bothered him or even seemed to glance his way. He might as well not exist. That might be preferable to the existence he was experiencing, he thought.

On reaching Waterloo, he headed east along the South Bank and gazed across to the illuminations on the opposite side of the river. The theatre audiences had long since dispersed, and there was a peace of sorts as he descended the steps to the Embankment.

He was so immersed in his thoughts that he failed to notice the bundle of sleeping bag and homeless humanity until he nearly tripped over it.

"Spare any change?" came the muffled voice from within its folds.

"Oh, er…" Graham fumbled in his pocket, finally

spilling its contents onto the concrete. He looked down at keys, purse and the rest of accumulated detritus that had made his pockets sag, and made no move to retrieve them.

"Are you all right, mate?"

"Yes, yes, I'm fine," Graham answered automatically, still making no attempt to salvage the items. They were like rats leaving a sinking ship and he had no need of them.

The young man crawled from the warmth of his sleeping bag, gathered up the pocket's contents and reached up, offering them to Graham, who he thought had obviously had one too many. Graham took them all except his purse.

"Keep it," he said. "Your need is greater." It occurred to him that was a truly Christian act and the thought warmed him. Suddenly, he felt giddy with relief and gloriously happy. He had only to cast off this cloak of desolation he'd been wearing and cleanse his soul of the clinging thoughts that had been gnawing away at his beliefs. He could be baptised anew and relieved of the dread that had coiled about him ever since he'd climbed into the crypt beneath St. Jude's. He'd never believed in original sin but it had seemed as though that tomb had housed it, an original sin waiting for a host, and now it must be removed.

Leaving the bemused, though uncomplaining, recipient sliding back into his bag, Graham crossed to the wall and looked down at the black water. The Thames reflected back the Christmas lights, red, green and gold, but they trembled as it moved, watered down and powerless.

He edged forward onto the steps that led down to the water. There was no rail and he reached out a steadying hand to the wall as he slowly descended out of sight of the vagrant.

The lapping against the lower steps whispered to him of centuries of ebb and flow, of continuity, of purpose: enough water to wash away a million sins, or maybe one big one.

The steps were slimy now, covered in algae, and Graham leaned against the embankment wall so as not to slip. Could one baptise oneself, he wondered? Could he offer his soul to God, immerse himself and finally be cleansed? Surely it would be possible, if he had the right intent. He smiled and stepped forward.

For a moment the cold caught at his breath but it was fleeting. He was still smiling as he went beneath the dark water. As he felt the pain and fear being washed away, he looked up. The ripples above him danced in fragmented light, green, then red, then gold, but Graham no longer cared. The current caught at his clothes. It felt like the gentle embrace of his saviour, offering him the gift of absolution, and he gave way to its pull.

O'Shea was tired. He'd slept badly. The toilet on his floor was blocked and the bathroom mirror cracked. He studied his reflection. It was hard to believe he'd once been a young man, full of enthusiasm and hope. He could only remember being old. He splashed water onto his face, peed in the sink and headed for the near-empty dining room.

He'd found a hotel that was both cheap and reasonably central, situated above an Indian restaurant. What had seemed like a good idea after an evening in the bar, lost its appeal in the early light of day. The smell of last night's cooking permeated the building and ensured the patrons wouldn't linger over a breakfast that was barely worthy of a corner café. The clientele seemed to be mostly made up of salesmen trying to keep their costs down. When O'Shea finally caught someone's attention to ask for a second cup of coffee, the waiter seemed shocked he should have the audacity to do so. He was thankful when he had a call from Larry Markham, who agreed to see him in just over an hour. He left his table and the hotel, the bill having been paid in advance. It had been insisted upon at reception, no doubt to avoid disgruntled patrons fleeing the crime scene.

Markham's bed-sit would have been quite roomy if it hadn't been piled high with boxes, files and heaped books, newspapers and magazines, all of which somehow fitted with his image, casual dress and shoulder-length fair hair. There was just room enough for a single bed, one chair and a cluttered table. Larry ushered O'Shea to the chair. He was unaccustomed to entertaining and used his washbasin to rinse a couple of mugs and fill the kettle. As the water boiled on a single electric ring, he sat on the edge of the unmade bed, unashamedly scrutinizing O'Shea, who made no comment but, in turn, studied the cracks in Markham's walls and ceiling. However, the steaming coffee eased the discomfort as O'Shea made clear the reason for his visit. He'd deliberately been vague with Markham earlier, not wanting a refusal over the phone.

When he heard which photos O'Shea was after, Markham shook his head. "You're out of luck there, I'm afraid," he said, with just the hint of a soft southern drawl. "That night, right after the fire, I was mugged. Bastards took my camera bag and left me out cold. Didn't touch my money and cards, just took the bloody bag. My Nikon was in that. My life, that is. Bastards! Fucking bastards!"

O'Shea flinched. He didn't swear but thought he might take it up. A mugging would explain the nasty gash on Markham's temple and a couple of fading bruises.

"I'm freelance, you know. No paper to foot the cost of new ones. The only one I've got left is broken. Meant to get the Nikon insured. Fuck!"

"Can you tell me all you remember, then? Did anything seem unusual? Anyone look suspicious?"

"What is it you're looking for? Can't say I recall anything out of sync."

"The flat that was burned belonged to a friend of mine." He faltered over the word 'friend' but realised it was probably true. "He was killed in the fire."

"I'm sorry! You think it might have been started deliberately?"

"Maybe! It just seems fishy – too much of a coincidence – with everything else that's been going on."

"Care to elaborate?"

"Not really." O'Shea wished he had a flask of something to add to the coffee.

"Sorry you've had a wasted journey. There might have been something on the photos but there's no way of knowing now."

"Another coincidence," said O'Shea, bitterly.

"You're thinking my cameras being snatched was connected to the fire somehow?"

"It's possible. Maybe you photographed something, or even someone in the crowd, but we'll never know."

Markham narrowed his eyes. He was good at

sniffing out a story and O'Shea was emitting a strong smell of fish.

"Look, I'm pretty stuck without my cameras. How about you telling me what this is all about and maybe I'll climb aboard and help."

O'Shea considered for a moment. It might be useful to have an outsider's view on things. Maybe Markham's input would help. Either that or highlight how ridiculous their suspicions were.

"All right, but on one condition," said O'Shea. At Markham's quizzical glance, he added, "We find something stronger than coffee."

Laura wasn't sure when O'Shea would return. She felt at a loose end, just waiting around. There was no need for both her and O'Shea to go to Ely. After all, it may well be a waste of time. Though cold, the sun was shining and a drive would take her mind off St. Jude's, at least for a little while.

Despite the need to keep occupied, she didn't want a wasted journey. The museum was accommodating enough when she rang and agreed to let Laura view their archive material, most of which had been transferred to microfiche. Anything else that she may wish to view would be under supervision. The attendant Laura spoke to had never heard of Wesley of Ely or his book but pointed out, rather brusquely, that she wasn't familiar with everything held within the archives.

Laura then rang the Chapter House at Ely Cathedral. She assumed she would have to make an appointment to see the Dean but, to her amazement, was put straight through to him.

She deliberately refrained from mentioning her

position within the church to avoid awkward questions. The Dean was charming and as helpful as he could be, but had not long held the post and wasn't as familiar with Ely or its history as he hoped he might become. However, he didn't hesitate in passing on the number of his predecessor, who had only recently retired. Laura thanked the Dean and rang the number.

Almost an hour had elapsed when she finally got off the phone. The previous Dean was obviously already missing the human contact of the cathedral and was delighted to have someone to talk to. He had never heard of Wesley of Ely but took the mention of his work as an excuse for a rambling account of Ely ghosts, which, it seemed, were of particular interest to him. Laura tried to be patient, and might even have found it as fascinating as he did, had not her mind been on the recent events at St. Jude's.

"Jude, of course, was also one of the twelve Apostles," said the somewhat droning voice on the other end of the line, when Laura asked if he knew of St. Jude's. "I've never heard of any legends linked to that name. The closest we have is the story of the Jude Tree but I expect that was connected to that other one." By that, Laura presumed he was referring to Judas Iscariot but sought clarification, just in case.

"No, no, my dear! It was an ancient tree somewhere in these parts. I think, according to old legends, it was somehow connected to the slaying of a serpent. People shunned it. That's all I know. Why it was named the Jude Tree, I have no notion. Maybe it was near your St. Jude's."

Laura thanked the elderly clergyman and considered the long conversation may not have been entirely fruitless. She had another lead, however tenuous, to follow up in Ely Museum. She looked at her watch. Still time to drive to Ely. She'd had no word from O'Shea and resisted the urge to call him. Hurrying now and with purpose, she picked up her car keys and headed for the door.

Parking in the cathedral car park in Barton Road, Laura walked up Church Lane past the impressive cathedral. She had no need to call in there now, but made a note to herself to visit again when she had time to view it properly and could admire it at leisure. From Palace Green, it rose skyward, reminding Laura a little of a fairytale castle with turrets and flag flying in a brisk northeast breeze. A large canon on the green added to the illusion.

Continuing up Lynn Road to the museum, Laura felt quite carefree. The place spoke of tearooms, souvenir shops and day excursions, with coaches depositing hoards of tourists into the ancient city.

Unlike the previous Dean of the cathedral, the museum attendant didn't seem inclined to chat. She swiftly showed Laura to a cubicle and instructed her on how to view the records. An hour later and Laura had still found no mention of Wesley of Ely, though she had found mention of his book. It seemed there had only been a few copies of 'Ye Suppression of Evyl in Ye Countee of Norefolk', all hand-written and all burned in a medieval church cleansing. 'All except one,' thought Laura. She turned her attention to the Jude Tree.

Here she was a little more successful. A newspaper, dated August the 19th, 1886, told of a terrible storm that caused havoc all across the fens. 'Trees were uprooted as it traversed the region, leaving destruction in its wake. One such tree was an oak, known locally as the Jude Tree, growing as it did within the ancient churchyard of St. Jude's. Its demise caused little concern, as it had long been held to have an evil reputation.' The piece failed to state where St. Jude's was located, but it didn't take Laura long to check that there was only one in the vicinity.

She obtained photocopies of the article and also the reference to Wesley of Ely's doomed book. Not a total waste of the day, she thought, as she headed back to her car.

O'Shea was waiting for her when Laura called in at 'The Peal Of Bells'. Both had barely eaten all day, so it was only after steak and kidney pie with all the trimmings that they finally compared notes.

"Markham is coming up here tomorrow," said O'Shea, "just to get the feel of the place and, of course, to meet you." At Laura's questioning glance, he added, "Well, it can't hurt. We're not making much headway ourselves."

That annoyed Laura. She felt she hadn't done too badly playing Miss Marple, but she kept quiet. She'd listened in dismay to O'Shea's description of the fire in Dorcas's flat and the coincidence of Markham being mugged.

"Where on earth do we go from here?" she said, putting down her empty glass and shaking her head at O'Shea's offer of a refill.

"Didn't you say there was another warden, an older chap who had been unwell? I know I was given the task of speaking to him but maybe you could ask him what he knows? And meanwhile, I'll keep trying to get through to Father Phillips. I have to admit, I'm very worried about him in his present state of mind." After a moment, he added, "You know, Laura, we'll need to go back into St. Jude's."

Laura visibly blanched. "What do you think we're going to find?"

"It's anybody's guess. I don't even know what to look for but, whatever it is, we'll be more likely to spot it now than before." O'Shea took another drink. "Have you considered doing an exorcism?"

"I'd have to apply to the bishop and that would mean giving him a reason. I can't tell him what happened, Dermot, I can't."

"The church will have to be re-consecrated before services resume there, violent death and all, but I doubt that will destroy whatever's there. It hasn't up till now." He downed the last of his drink. "I believe you were wrong, Laura. I don't believe St. Jude's attracted evil to it; I think it was there all along."

It was agreed Laura would call on the warden the following morning. Both of them were weary and in need of a good sleep. They bade each other goodnight and, as she left, Laura turned back to wave at O'Shea. She frowned, knowing he hadn't seen her as he made his way over to the bar and ordered a large nightcap.

If there had been a more direct route back to her digs, Laura would have taken it. She didn't want to go anywhere near St. Jude's, but she was tired and wanted to get into the warmth before the heat of the meal and drink wore off. The sound of her hurried footfalls echoed in the chill air. The church stood stark against the night sky and the thought of setting foot under its roof again filled her with dread. She found herself wondering where the ancient oak had stood, and shivered. Keeping her eyes averted, she almost ran past the old church, and it wasn't until she was safely back under Mrs Lyle's roof that her breathing steadied. Even the sound of CSI reruns couldn't keep her awake tonight, though she feared what dreams might visit her in the darkness, and left the bedside light on like a frightened child.

There was a distinctly festive feel to the London streets, as commuters bustled with extra shopping and store windows dazzled with scenes of snow, gifts and Santa.

Pathologist, Russell Dryer, didn't even see them as he made his way to the Westminster City Mortuary. The lead up to Christmas was always busy. This year was no exception. It meant long hours. A body could hardly be left unattended until after the holiday. In a way he was glad he had to work. His Decree Nisi had come through in today's post, along with a smattering of Christmas cards sending wishes to the two of them. One of them should notify distant friends and relatives, but he was finding the break-up hard enough to handle without being the recipient of pity and well-meant sympathy. No, work was what he needed and work was definitely what he was getting.

"Evening, Doctor! Just one so far but the night's still young." Gary was a bright lad, always smiling no matter what state a body was in on admittance. "I've tagged him and sent the bloods to Toxicology," he added.

"What have we got?" said Dryer, changing into his scrubs and donning rubber gloves.

"Caucasian male. Possible suicide – drowning. There was no money on him, so it could have been a mugging. Can't see any obvious signs of violence but I haven't got very far. He's not been long over from St. Thomas's. Haven't got far with photographs yet either."

"Has he been identified?"

"Yeah, get this. Seems he was a man of God."

Dryer was getting irritated. The body before him was still fully-clothed and needed more photos taken, both with and without clothes, before he could get started. "What are you talking about? Come on, try talking at the same time as you take your pictures."

Gary began carefully removing the body's clothes.

"He had a New Testament in one of his pockets, inscribed to a Father Graham Phillips. We're checking dental records just to be sure though, presuming he had a dentist. 'Ere, you don't usually get priests, vicars or whatever topping themselves. It's supposed to be a sin. 'Course, we won't know till we get the blood results. Maybe he was at the Communion wine!"

Gary had finished removing the clothes, folding each item separately before placing them in individual plastic bags. He then weighed, measured and X-rayed the body. Only when he had finished did the older pathologist step forward.

Dryer looked down at the cadaver, the pale flesh seeming even whiter under the harsh fluorescent lights. He felt reluctant to begin. Maybe it was the fact the deceased was a priest, though such considerations had never bothered him before. Or, perhaps, it was because this man lying on the steel autopsy table should be celebrating the birth of his saviour instead of joining him. He began the external examination, commencing with the neck.

Finally, taking up his scalpel, Dryer began incising the large Y in the torso for his internal examination.

He always felt it was a body's way of asking final questions of the living: Why must I be defiled? Why must I be exposed? What has brought me to this? But it was those very questions that Dryer always sought to answer.

After reflecting the fat and muscle to expose the rib cage, he reached for the shears. Why was he sweating? He looked down at his hands. They were trembling, only slightly, but enough for Dryer to wonder if he'd caught a chill. Had the patient been alive and he performing surgery, he would be forced to stop. 'Well, that's not the case,' he thought, 'so I had better get on with it.'

Cutting through the costal rib cartilage, he then removed the sternum, followed by the organs from the top half of the torso, placing them on the smaller dissecting table. Considering the body had been fished from the Thames, he began by examining the lungs, measuring, weighing and finally slicing into the spongy surface tissue.

As Dryer made the incision, Thames river water spilled out onto the dissection table and down the drain. He was used to finding sand, weed and small marine life, swallowed when water replaced air and death replaced life. It was to be expected, but what spewed out before him made Dryer gag. Never before had he seen anything like the writhing mass that twisted and turned in the unforgiving light. He'd heard of young elvers being found in bodies, though he'd always believed it was a folk tale. These weren't elvers. The squirming creatures on the table were worms of some kind, extending and contracting, interlaced, red, brown and green. He tentatively peeled back a flap of the lung. Inside, more worms continued feeding. Dryer just made it to the men's room before throwing up.

Later, hands cupping a strong coffee, he awaited identification of the worm samples he'd sent for analysis. The biodiversity department at the Port of London Authority had promised him they would get right on to it. Fortunately, it seemed they had staff working unsociable hours too. Even so, it was a couple of hours before the phone rang.

"Dr. Dryer, where did you say the body was found?" The woman on the other end of the line sounded as if she thought he was drunk in charge of a cadaver.

"Blackfriars Bridge. At a rough guess I'd say he'd been in the water twelve to fifteen hours. The clothing had snagged onto something, stopping it from being swept further down river."

"It doesn't make any sense."

"What do you mean?" He asked the question, even though none of this made sense to him.

"I've consulted with the Environment Agency. Firstly, although these worms are found in estuaries, one wouldn't expect to come across them at this time of the year. They all appear to be young ones, as the adults grow to some considerable length, especially the Lineus longissimus."

"Sorry, the what?"

"The Bootlace-worm. They're the blackish-brown ones. Some of the red and green ones are smaller species, although some of those reds, the Ribbon-worm for example, can get to a sizeable length. They're all found in crevices, under rocks and sediment. Even if they were to somehow find their way into a body, there wouldn't be so many types and in such propensity. I'm at a loss to explain it."

"That makes two of us," said Dryer. "I suppose we'll just have to put it down to some freak occurrence, unless it's repeated elsewhere."

"And they were in his lungs, you say, eating him away from the inside? Is that usual?"

"About as common as snow in the Sudan," replied Dryer.

"You'll let me know, I hope, if any more turn up?"

"You'll be the first person I'll contact," said Dryer and hung up. Turning back to Father Graham's body, he prayed fervently that no more would.

NINE

O'Shea had agreed to meet Larry off the train in Cambridge, giving Laura a welcome few hours to catch up with church paperwork. For one thing, she had sermons to write, albeit short ones. She was forced to acknowledge that the parishioners expected her to take services and not put them all on hold while she pursued her own enquiries.

She was far from happy with O'Shea dragging this Larry Markham into things. 'What things?' she found herself wondering. Maybe they were both becoming delusional. Well, if there was anything to ferret out, a photographic journalist was maybe the one to do it.

She hadn't heard anything from Marcus Cook and wondered if she would. Another dead end!

Finally closing up her laptop, Laura decided to make herself useful and have a word with the elderly warden, who had been conspicuous only by his absence. Finding his address in the folder of church papers she'd been given, she headed outside. Fresh air filled her lungs and lifted her spirits.

Leonard Pargeter looked very frail as he opened his front door and peered cautiously at Laura.

"You from Social Services?" he wheezed.

"No, Mr Pargeter," Laura replied. "I'm the Reverend Laura Coatman. Maybe I could have a few words with you?"

She thought at first he was going to refuse, but he shuffled back and opened the door further to let her squeeze through. He waved a thin blue-veined hand, ushering her into a small sitting room. The curtains were almost closed and the room was in semi-darkness.

"I must apologise. I should have come to see you sooner. I understand you've been unwell."

"You come to say I can't come back? Can't be a warden no more?"

"Heavens, no, Mr Pargeter, nothing of the sort. I merely came to introduce myself, pay my respects and," she paused, "to ask you a few questions, if I might?"

"Questions? What sort of questions? About my illness, is that what you mean?"

"No, not at all." He was so defensive, Laura wasn't sure how to proceed. "As you are aware, I'm new here. I wondered if you could tell me a little about the history of St. Jude's."

Mr Pargeter looked doubtful.

"Please! It would be greatly appreciated."

"Well, Reverend… Coatman, was it? I suppose I knows as much or more than most about St. Jude's. What did you want to know?" He'd relaxed a little and sat back now in his chair.

"Are there any legends connected with the church? Stories? How have you found working there? Have you noticed anything unusual?"

"Who's been talking to you?" Mr Pargeter sat forward again, agitated.

"No-one, I assure you." Laura back-peddled. "What I mean is, I'm interested in folklore and history. Being such an old church, I felt sure it must have some fascinating stories attached to it."

"You mean, is it haunted? That what you mean?" Pargeter sat back a little but was obviously still uneasy about the questions.

"Yes, well, anything really. Suppose you just tell me anything you've heard or experienced?"

"Ain't seen no ghosts, not exactly anyhows. Seen shadows. Do they count?"

"What sort of shadows? A person?"

"No, more like coiled smoke. Maybe that's all it is, smoke from the candles caught in a sudden draft."

"Is that what you believe, Mr Pargeter?"

Pargeter's eyes shifted from Laura to the darkened corners of his room.

"What else could it be?" From the frightened look in his eyes, Laura had the distinct feeling Pargeter knew, or at least suspected, there was more to this 'smoke' than he was saying. She didn't want to press him and have him close up altogether, and her own memories threatened to rise up and choke her.

"You must have heard about the crypt that's been uncovered. It was a surprise to everyone."

Pargeter narrowed his eyes but remained silent.

"Have you any idea who might have been interred there? There are no records that we can find."

"If there are no records, then maybe you shouldn't be asking." He was beginning to get defensive again, so Laura tried a different approach.

"I wondered if you'd heard of the Jude Tree? I believe it was associated with St. Jude's."

He nodded. "Aye, I know of it. My grandfather saw it too, when he was a boy."

"Where did it stand? Do you know?"

"Easier to show you."

He rose and moved towards the window. Laura followed and stood to one side as he pulled back the curtain. In the revealing light, she saw how threadbare and old his clothes were. No wonder he didn't want to lose the pittance he earned as a warden. She hadn't realised before that his cottage looked out across the dyke, with an uninterrupted view of the church. The path she'd taken to get here had led her in a semi-circle.

"See that raised up bit of land between the church and the cemetery wall?" He inclined his head in its direction.

Laura nodded. "Yes, I hadn't taken any notice of it before."

"That's where it was wrenched from the earth, writhing and flailing like it was fighting for life, my grandfather said. The roots stretched right to the church walls, though you wouldn't know it now. They've flattened that bit of land since then. The villagers all huddled together to watch."

"It was said to have an evil reputation?"

"Wouldn't know about that. Believe a couple of witches were hanged from it but that was God's work being done."

Laura flinched. "But surely they wouldn't hang someone on consecrated ground?"

"Wouldn't have been consecrated back then. The tree was outside the graveyard till they extended it in the mid eighteen hundreds. Folk used to make offerings to it and tie clouties to the lower branches, believers and non-believers alike."

"Offerings? You mean like with holy wells and such?"

"It don't sound holy to me; does it to you?" It was a rhetorical question.

Pargeter stepped back from the window, being careful to draw the curtain across again, plunging the room into half-light. Laura couldn't help but notice that the folds neatly hid St. Jude's from sight.

"Well, I'm sure it will have provided some of the

villagers with firewood," she said, trying to lighten the mood.

"No-one hereabouts would burn wood from that tree. Local man carved the present rood screen for the church from it. He was the only one who'd touch it. The rest was left to rot."

"Really? I shall have to take a look at the carvings."

"If you must," replied Pargeter, gruffly.

"You've been a great help, Mr Pargeter. Thank you." She was sure he could say more, but equally sure he wouldn't.

Pargeter sniffed in response and showed Laura out. She felt his eyes follow her as she started along the path. She turned to see him hastily step back from the small front window but waved anyway.

Lunch was accompanied by a pooling of ideas and information. Larry Markham felt as if he'd just stepped through a rather dark looking glass.

Both O'Shea and Larry were intrigued by the Jude Tree connection. In fact, Larry wanted to visit the church as soon as possible, but they'd all lingered too long over lunch and the day was already losing its winter light. Dark clouds were rolling in from the east and neither Laura nor O'Shea wished to explore St. Jude's once the sun went down, no matter how medieval that may seem to the sceptical London photographer.

"I'm positive Pargeter knows more than he's telling, but I didn't know how to draw it out of him. Maybe I can come up with another reason to call on him and try again."

"It's probably because you're a stranger. We all are.

He may have opened up to Graham," said O'Shea. He frowned at the thought of his friend. "Wish he'd get in touch. I'm getting really worried. I haven't heard from him and I don't even know where to look." More   by luck than careful planning, they managed to get Larry a room at 'The Peal of Bells', and Laura left the two men, heads together in a corner, clutching their respective drinks. She suspected they would spend the evening in the bar and she didn't want to stay and watch them trying to drink each other under the table. Besides, she was sure O'Shea would win. Back in her room, she checked her mobile. One missed call.

"Reverend Coatman? This is Marcus Cook. Maybe you can call me back when you get this. Thanks."

Laura dialled his number but reached the messaging service. Maybe he'd come up with something after all.

Things were taking far too long. The Cambridge archaeologists exasperated Benvenuti. They were quite aware that the Vatican had no authority in England and almost seemed to be taunting him with their methodical investigation.

"Surely there is only so much to be learned from a crypt. After all, there are dead buried beneath the floors of many churches and cathedrals."

"What you say is true," said Rudi Clements, patiently. He was the senior of the group and was tired of Benvenuti's constant harassment. "This one dates way back to Anglo-Saxon times but it wasn't until much later that corpses were buried beneath churches. It's quite unique. Besides," he added, "there are unusual aspects that we need to record."

"Unusual?" Benvenuti turned casually away to hide

his concern, afraid his eyes would convey his unease.

"Yes, for one thing, the stone walls were painted black, possibly with pitch. Now why would anyone do that? I've not come across it before. There was an unusual grave uncovered in Lichfield Cathedral, I believe, much more recent than this though, and its walls had been whitewashed. That particular grave had originally been outside the building in Norman times, but then had been included when the later cathedral was built. That can't be said for this one though, as it's central to the church."

"I see nothing odd in that," said Benvenuti, dismissively. "Is that all?"

"No, there are other things but I'm not ready to discuss them yet. Bottom line, I'm afraid, is we'll be hanging on to your sarcophagus a wee while longer. Now, the more time I stand here talking…"

Benvenuti reluctantly let him go.

Clements was more than glad of an excuse to get away from the Vatican official. There was something about the man's presence that made him feel unclean and, even now, as he hurried through the churchyard, he found himself trying to shake off its cloying residue. Something unsettled him about this excavation too and, despite his comments to Benvenuti, he would be glad to pack up and leave. The two black-clad Vatican officials who seemed to be always watching didn't help any. They never smiled and reminded him of vultures.

"Ready to call it a day?" he called out.

Karen Martin looked up from the now well-lit interior of the crypt and grinned. She looked excited.

"I think you'll want to see this first." Her voice

sounded hollow in the closed surroundings.

She stood back as he clambered down the ladder. There was barely room for two people in the confined area that was now filled with boxes and camera equipment. Once everything had been recorded, there really was very little left for the archaeologists to do. However, it seemed Clements wasn't the only one to find Benvenuti's high-handed attitude abrasive. The university had told him to take as much time as he wanted, and that's exactly what he intended to do.

"As you suggested, I was examining the walls for unusual marks and found a fine channel between two of the stones. Take a look. The groove seems to have been gouged out before the walls were painted. It looks as if it probably had a few layers put on. It's quite shiny and smooth but, at the same time, it feels tacky."

Clements reached up and ran his finger down the gully, then fished in his pocket for his glasses and a small but powerful torch.

"Hand me a precision tool, Karen." Gently, he began scraping the surrounds of the channel where it disappeared into the stonework, then slowly he inserted the instrument. "There's definitely a channel going back through the stones. You know what I think we've got here, don't you?"

"A libation tube?"

"It would confirm this crypt was here under the earliest church."

"Wouldn't that mean the offerings would have to be made from inside the church?"

"You're right, unless, of course, the tube stretched outside the walls of the building but that's unlikely. We haven't a hope in hell of finding the opening if they did. The ground would have been dug up for the foundations of the Norman church." Clements retrieved the tool and began scraping the smooth lining of the gully. A black residue flaked up under the sharp metal and Karen put a plastic bag into his outstretched hand. Carefully, he transferred the scrapings into the bag and sealed it.

"How soon can you get this to the lab?"

"I might catch someone if I give them a call and set off now. Do you need me for anything else?"

"No, I'm just curious to know what they were feeding whoever was down here. I know, I know, no patience," he added, when she raised an eyebrow.

She laughed. "OK. I'm on my way. See you tomorrow."

Clements didn't answer. He was already deep in thought. Who had been buried here? Why were they fed libations? Was it a holy man, a healer, someone of great importance or much loved? And the biggest question of all, would they ever know?

TEN

Laura met O'Shea and Larry at the gates of St. Jude's. The sun was putting on a brave face, almost as if trying to reassure the trio as they made their way across the gravel.

"Looks a bit of a mess," observed Larry, eyeing the scaffolding and the earth churned up by workmen's vehicles.

"Wait till you see inside," returned O'Shea. He cast a concerned look in Laura's direction. "You OK?"

She nodded but O'Shea noted the firm set of her jaw and the taut skin about her eyes. This was going to be a far greater strain for her than either Larry or himself. As they entered the porch, he let Larry take the lead and briefly took Laura's hand. He gave it a quick squeeze, then, feeling foolish, marched through the door.

Laura couldn't suppress a shudder as they entered the church. If anything, it felt even colder than she remembered and the two men from the Vatican, sat together on the back pew, looked none too happy with their allotted task. The air seemed to vibrate as a generator supplied by the university throbbed near the opening in the floor, lighting cables snaking down into the interior.

Larry whistled. "Wow, I'd like to have had my camera poised when that baby fell," he said, nodding in the direction of the roof beam that had been hauled to one side and now lay across the pews. He glanced up at the rest of the wooden structure resting on the solid stone walls like the skeleton of an upturned boat.

Laura moved closer to O'Shea. It was only will

power that kept her there and it was getting pretty thin.

Larry, oblivious to the effect the place was having on the other two, stood looking up in awe.

"Just look at all those Green Men. Where do they fit in?" He glanced back at the other two.

"Looking about me, I'd say everywhere," said O'Shea, softly.

"Was that an attempt at humour?"

"Sort of. Mind you, I can't recall seeing so many in one place before. Have you noticed they seem to leer out from every beam and corner?"

"And gargoyles," said Larry.

"Grotesques!" cut in Laura. "These are grotesques, not gargoyles. Gargoyles are waterspouts, put up to drain water away. These have no use other than to scare evil spirits a…" She stopped short. Looking at O'Shea, she added, "And the Green Man was for protection too."

The two of them looked up at the silent watchers and shivered.

"Maybe I was right, Laura." O'Shea's voice was low, for her ears only. He needn't have worried. Larry had moved away towards the altar and out of hearing. "If Wesley of Ely was right, and the church was built to imprison a serpent, then evil wasn't drawn to the church; it was here all along. Any means of containing it would be used," he gestured to the carvings overhead, "whether pagan or Christian. They would also use the same means to protect themselves. What we've been missing is the fact that, just as with any prison, it doesn't only protect those on the outside, but also whatever is within."

Before Laura could reply, Larry raised a hand. "What's that?"

107

In the stillness, they could hear a scraping sound, like something clawing its way through stone. All three felt the hair on the back of their necks rise. Laura reached for O'Shea's hand.

It's coming from over here," said Larry, moving to the gaping wound in the church's underbelly, the edges of which glowed with a sickly yellow light.

The scratching stopped and a face suddenly looked up at them.

"Sorry! Didn't mean to startle you," grinned Clements. "Not used to visitors."

Laura swayed, letting go of O'Shea. She didn't know what she'd expected to see but her relief made her feel unsteady.

"How's it going down there?" asked O'Shea.

"Very interesting. Want to come down and have a look?"

"Too right," said Larry, eagerly. "You two coming?"

O'Shea was about to agree when he saw Laura take a step back from the hole. She obviously had no intention of climbing down into its depths. If he went down at the same time as Larry, it would mean leaving her alone up here.

"There doesn't look to be much room. I'll come down after you," he said. He noted the intense relief on Laura's face.

Left alone, they both seemed uncomfortable. What they knew about each other, instead of drawing them closer, was like a wedge driven between them.

"Laura…" began O'Shea.

"It's this place," Laura interjected. "It's as though it's listening. It knows we're here and it's laughing at us." She hugged her arms about her.

"Now you're being fanciful."

"No. There's something here, watching. Everywhere you look. Eyes."

"You said yourself that all the Green Men and what was it, grotesques, are for protection."

"Can't you feel it, Dermot, or have you finally pickled your finer senses?" She regretted her words as soon as she'd spoken. "Dermot, I'm sorry…"

"I think maybe we ought to get you out of here. Why not leave me to look around and keep a watch over Larry?" He took Laura's arm and she let him lead her out of the church. "How about meeting us for dinner at about seven? My treat."

Laura nodded. "I guess it took more out of me than I expected," she said. "But Dermot, be careful."

"Hey, it takes more than a church to rattle me, otherwise I'd have given up years ago, you know that." He gave Laura a reassuring smile that faded as he watched her walk away.

Back in St. Jude's, he called down to Larry.

"You finished down there?"

Larry's head popped into view. "Sorry, be right up." He clambered out of the hole. "Wow!"

O'Shea smiled. There was something about this young man that lifted his spirits. "My turn," he said.

"Where's Laura?" said Larry, looking round.

"She wasn't feeling too good, so I sent her home." It wasn't far from the truth. He was still smarting from her jibe.

It was the first time O'Shea had seen inside the crypt and he recalled Graham's description of it. He tried to imagine it as his friend had seen it, without the lighting and cables, the bags, boxes and tools.

The coffin was a box tomb in design, the lid

overlapping its edges, or at least it had, until it had been smashed inwards by the weight of the beam. The colours and patterns that Graham had described so vividly were conspicuous by their absence. O'Shea frowned. He wondered if Graham had imagined them. The interior walls of the sarcophagus were rough granite, with no sign of ever being painted.

"I was just telling your friend," cut in Clements, "we've found something really exciting over here."

O'Shea edged his way round to stand by the archaeologist.

"See this?" Clements pointed to the channel he'd been working on. "It's a libation tube, used to make offerings to the dead. If you look at the coffin lid, you'll see there was a small hole in the corner to allow a feed to go straight into it. Whatever the tube was made of has long since turned to dust. It was sheer good fortune that led us to this."

O'Shea was speechless. He turned and looked at the smashed lid. Without scrutiny, the small hole would have been taken as part of the overall lid damage. "Is this common?" he asked.

"Not uncommon in tombs this old, no, but I've never seen one like this. It's unique in my experience. It was a widespread practice among the Romans."

"What did they pour down?"

"Wine mostly, or oil. Pass me that, would you?" Clements motioned to a coil of tension wire lying near O'Shea. The end was bound in tape and he inserted it into the passage between the stones.

"I don't know if this will work but thought it worth a try. Maybe we can get an idea where the opening was, if the passage isn't totally blocked. It seems amazingly free of debris this end." He began pushing the wire gently forward. "I expect it's blocked solid but it could give us an idea of direction."

"What would it have been made of?" asked O'Shea, as he lifted the coil of heavy wire to aid Clements. He noticed it was marked off in metres.

"The pipe, you mean? I've no idea. As I said, this is unusual. It was commonly a groove between slabs. Could be clay. A build up of oil residue might have given it some protection but I doubt it would have lasted long. I'm amazed we've found any trace at all."

Slowly, O'Shea fed more of the wire to Clements as it disappeared into the hole.

"Something is definitely odd here," said Clements. "I can't believe the channel could remain intact over all these centuries."

"I take it that it would have led outside the church?" said O'Shea.

"Outside the original one, definitely. Wherever the entrance was, it would have been destroyed during the building of the later church."

They were both startled by a shout from above. Larry arrived at the tomb's entrance.

"Hey, you two, what are you doing? I hope you're responsible for what I've just seen."

The three men stood looking down at the floor behind the pulpit. Poking out from a joint between the flagstones was the now-blackened end of Clement's measuring wire. The small hole would not have drawn any undue attention normally, tucked into a corner and shadowed by the pulpit.

"I'm stunned," admitted Clements. "This suggests libations were still being carried on for hundreds of years. Why the entrance should be positioned where it is, well, I can't account for it. Most odd."

"I'm learning there's a lot about St. Jude's that's odd," said Larry. He met O'Shea's gaze. "Very odd indeed."

Laura joined Larry and O'Shea at the pub as arranged. O'Shea was relieved to see she had a little more colour in her cheeks. He'd been seriously worried about her.

At his questioning look, Laura said, "Fine. Really. I had a sleep this afternoon. Think it was just the result of accumulated rough nights." She smiled, though O'Shea still thought it looked rather forced. "So, come on then, what did I miss?"

The two men told her about the discovery in the church. They'd stayed there most of the afternoon, watching Clements as he fussed, photographed and recorded the find. The light had been fading before O'Shea was able to drag Larry away.

"Dermot showed me where the murder took place," said Larry. "Pretty grisly, I gather," he added with all the subtlety of youth. O'Shea winced. "Wish I'd still got my Nikon. Still, I took a few shots on my cell."

"Has Clements any idea when the libations ceased?" asked Laura.

"None whatsoever. I think he's totally baffled, not that he'll admit it. Probably hoping to get a paper out about it all, if I know anything about university professors," said O'Shea.

They placed their order at the bar and bought drinks.

"Just realised, left my phone in my room. Back in a sec.," said Larry and hurried off.

"He's keen, I'll say that for him," laughed Laura.

"He's bloody exhausting, that's what he is," replied

O'Shea, gruffly but with good humour.

"So what does he think?" said Laura, as they took their drinks to the table. "Does he think we're certifiable or not?"

"Hmm, he hasn't said much," replied O'Shea. "I get the feeling he wants to find something, but whether he actually thinks there's anything to find…"

"Dermot, about earlier…"

"Hmm?"

"What I said in the church. I'm sorry. I had no right…"

O'Shea stopped her. "It's forgotten. Besides, you were only telling the truth. That's what priests do, don't they?" She nodded and he smiled.

They both jumped as Larry dropped a newspaper onto the table. Without realising the effect on their frayed nerves, he flopped into a vacant chair and started flicking through his photos.

"What's this?" said O'Shea, motioning towards the paper.

"Yesterday's Evening Standard if you want a look. Otherwise I'll bin it."

O'Shea reached for it and idly leafed through the pages whilst Larry showed Laura the shots of the libation tube. They looked up as his hands abruptly clenched the paper taut, his face ashen.

"Dermot, what's wrong?"

Without speaking, he pushed the paper over to Laura.

She skimmed the page, her eyes coming to rest on a few lines near the bottom. Under the heading, 'Priest's body found in Thames', she read:

'Information is being sought regarding events leading up to the death of a priest, whose body was found floating in the Thames on Tuesday. Witnesses and anyone with information are asked to contact either the police or Westminster City Mortuary. The name of the deceased has been withheld, pending his family being informed.'

"Oh, Dermot!" Laura could see how shaken O'Shea was. "It might not be him. There's no description here, nothing. It could be anyone."

"And just how many priests do you know who might go swimming in the Thames, who'd be in such a fragile state of mind to end up there?"

"Anyone could have an accident, Dermot."

"I'll go down tomorrow. See the body, if they'll let me."

"Then I'll go with you." Laura had no intention of letting O'Shea go through this alone.

"We'll all go," said Larry. "I need to pick up some things from my flat anyway."

The meal was eaten in silence, O'Shea leaving most of his.

Feeling uncomfortable, Laura rose to leave but, as she reached for her coat, Clements materialized by their table.

"Can't stop, but thought you'd be interested to know the lab just rang through with the results. The scrapings I took from the tube, it was blood, and human blood at that."

"What!" Larry exclaimed. "You're kidding?"

"I don't kid. I'll know more tomorrow. Sorry to rush off but just thought you'd like to know. What a day it's been. Bye!"

"Curiouser and curiouser," said Larry. "Looks like you two might have been onto something after all."

Before leaving, Laura took Larry to one side.

"Keep an eye on him. Try to see he doesn't drink too much."

"You want me to move the pyramids while I'm about it?"

"Yes, I know, but try. Please."

As Laura walked away, Larry wondered if moving pyramids wasn't the easier option.

Laura got hold of Marcus Cook on the third attempt.

"I haven't come up with anything on your St. Jude's specifically," he informed her, "but I have enough ammunition to condemn the Holy Roman Catholic Church for crimes against humanity."

Laura was taken aback and wished he wouldn't refer to it as *her* St. Jude's.

"What on earth do you mean? Oh, I suppose you mean witch trials and the like?"

"And the rest," snorted Cook. "You have to remember, they may not be aware of it, but most people aren't worshipping God, they're worshipping the church. It can get away with practically anything."

"You make it sound like it has evil intent," said Laura.

Cook ignored her comment. "Look, do you want me to send you what I've got, or do you want me to give it to you in person?"

"I'll meet you, if that's OK." She resented his aggressive attitude and would have been happy just to let him put his findings in the post, but O'Shea would need company when he visited the mortuary, and she could fit in picking up the papers at the same time. "Look, I'm coming down to London tomorrow anyway. Can I call you when I'm down there? I'm not sure yet how the day's going to go"

"Fine! Let me know." And he was gone.

Laura looked at the paperwork needing her attention, then at the bed. It was more welcoming by far but, when she finally stretched out, all her muscles aching from tension, it was like lying on a bed of writhing serpents and sleep was a long time coming.

FATHER OF LIES

ELEVEN

The following day, it was decided Larry should accompany O'Shea to the mortuary, leaving Laura free to meet up with Marcus Cook. Neither of them had any intention of letting O'Shea face the ordeal of identifying Graham alone, if indeed it was him. Using Marcus Cook as an excuse was Larry's way of shielding Laura from the task. He didn't get the chance to play the hero very often and was surprised to find he liked it.

The Coroner's Court turned out to be a typically Victorian, red-bricked building on Horseferry Road, at the back of which lay the Westminster City Mortuary, a single storey building that had obviously been refurbished over the years. O'Shea and Larry walked around and pressed the intercom to the right side of the glass door. The mixture of old and modern somehow emphasized the continuity of death.

Once inside, they were required to sign in. As O'Shea fumbled for reading glasses, Larry looked about. The building seemed to be divided into red and green sections, although they were led through a 'grey' transition area to the viewing room.

It reminded Larry of the type of room often shown in American TV crime dramas, where agents of various government bodies watched interrogations taking place. In this case, however, he doubted the glass between them and the body was 'one way'. Graham was laid out on a trolley, his body hidden by a red cover, his head resting on a white pillow. But for the cleric's grey features, the scene was almost regal.

"Would you care to be left alone for a few

minutes?" asked the attendant.

O'Shea could only nod, overwhelmed by a tidal wave of grief. As the attendant quietly left, Larry slipped out behind him.

"I was wondering," he said, as the man turned towards him questioningly, "if there was anything… unusual connected with the Reverend Phillips?"

"And you are?"

"We're friends of the deceased," said Larry, stretching the point and feeling justified in doing so. He doubted O'Shea would be in a fit state to ask questions.

"Well, as it happens, I do know that the pathologist who performed the autopsy was rather shaken up by it."

"In what way?"

"I'm afraid I don't know the details, and wouldn't be able to discuss them if I did. I do know the death is not being treated as suspicious though."

"Can you just tell me if any relatives viewed the body?" persisted Larry, despite the attendant obviously wanting to get back to his work.

"I really can't help you. A couple of rather official-looking gentlemen viewed the body and confirmed his identity, but I have no idea who they were, I'm afraid. I don't have that information."

"Thanks, anyway," said Larry. He returned to the viewing room and O'Shea. "Ready?"

Putting his hand on the older man's shoulder, he led him from the room and out into the street. The sun was trying to break through the hazy cloud but there was no warmth to it.

"If you don't mind, I'd like to be on my own," said O'Shea. When he saw the look on Larry's face, he gave a thin smile. "Don't worry! I just want to walk for a while, say goodbye in my own way. Couldn't do it in there, too formal."

Larry wasn't happy about it, but O'Shea had the right to some peace if that was his wish.

"I'll catch up with you both at King's Cross," continued O'Shea.

Larry watched him walk away, O'Shea's shoulders perhaps a little heavier than before, then turned and hurried to meet Laura.

The café in Great Russell Street was filling up with lunchtime customers when Laura got there, but she was lucky enough to find a corner table by the window. She got herself a sandwich and coffee and sat back to wait for Marcus Cook. He'd been vague about what time he'd arrive and she hoped she wouldn't have to take up a table for too long on her own. Fortunately, most customers seemed to want their food 'to go'. It had begun to rain and Laura found herself wondering how Larry and O'Shea were getting on. When Cook finally arrived, it was obvious from the books wedged under his arm that he'd probably been close by for the last half hour or so. He unceremoniously dumped them on the table, along with a folder, and bought himself tea and a large Chelsea bun.

"Right, Miss Coatman – er – Reverend, I think this might be what you're looking for." He wiped away some crumbs with his sleeve and pushed the folder towards Laura before attacking the bun. Laura averted her eyes.

"You'll see there's a great deal about the church in general being thought of as evil," he said, showering more crumbs as he spoke. "There's plenty of that. I couldn't find anything directly connected to St. Jude's, although I came up with mention of a Jude Tree which..."

"Yes, we've located that. It used to be in the graveyard at St. Jude's."

"Really?" He fell silent as he gave his attention to licking icing off his sticky fingers. Although he was being amiable enough, Laura sensed a reserve that hadn't been there when she first met him.

She was surprised by the amount of paperwork. Cook had certainly accumulated a lot of references. It would take her some time to sort through it all.

"According to our old friend, Wesley of Ely, St. Jude was supposed to have slain a serpent, so I devoted some time to following that line of enquiry." Cook reached across the table and placed his still-sticky hand over Laura's to emphasise his next words. "And that's when it really gets interesting."

Laura fought the desire to pull her hand away and was thankful Cook released it almost immediately. She surreptitiously slid it beneath the table and wiped it on a napkin.

Cook gulped down his tea. "I'll leave it with you. I hope you find what you're looking for." He rose abruptly from the table.

"But you'll want paying for this. How much do I owe you?"

"NO! No, I won't take any money."

"But..."

"I said I don't want paying. Oh, and please don't contact me again. I really won't be able to help you further."

"I don't understand..." began Laura.

"You will," he returned, and was gone before she

could ask what he meant. She ordered another coffee and began to read.

Waves of nostalgia washed over Laura as she stood at Larry's window, hugging a mug of coffee. The street was full of dissected houses, each converted into bedsits and small flats, mostly bedsits. Greedy landlords crammed as many into a house as possible. She reflected on how, when you're young, it's all part of the excitement of living alone. Next-door's front garden was full of bursting black bin bags, a sure sign of someone moving in or out.

Larry fussed about self-consciously. He couldn't remember when he'd last entertained a member of the opposite sex in his room and was disconcerted to find he was drawn to Laura. She was not the sort of woman that normally attracted him. He would be the first to admit he preferred curvaceous stereotypes, being more interested in their cleavage and availability than how well they could hold their own in conversation. Maybe it was the novelty of Laura that attracted him. He didn't know but, whatever it was, the attraction was there.

"Do you think O'Shea will be all right?" broke in Laura. "I wish you hadn't let him go off on his own like that. Didn't he give you any idea where he might go?"

"If I told you, I'd have to kill you," joked Larry, but Laura didn't laugh. "He'll be fine, I'm sure," he said, coming to sit next to her. "And what could I do? He's a grown man, after all."

"Yes, but…"

"But nothing! He'd just seen his friend laid out on a table, for Christ's sake. He wanted to be alone and take a walk along the Embankment. If you think he's going to do anything stupid, I think the nearest pub would be far more dangerous."

Laura turned to face him.

"You're right." Then, after a pause, "Sorry. Did they say when the funeral is likely to be? I expect he'll want to attend."

"Next week. We've to ring to confirm. It's Christmas the week after, so it needs to be soon. Hey," grinned Larry, "fancy something stronger? I think we deserve it."

"After your comment about a pub?"

"Yeah, well, that's different. Sorry, only got one glass," he said, handing it to her and rinsing out an almost empty jam jar for himself.

"What have you got?" Laura crossed over to look into the cupboard next to Larry. An unopened bottle of vodka nestled in amongst the baked beans and packet soups.

"Not exactly a well-stocked bar," she said, smiling. "Anything else?"

"Warm beer. The fridge broke."

A few vodkas later, they no longer cared that it was neat.

"To us," said Larry, lifting his jar to Laura's glass.

"Us?"

"Well, I think we've toasted just about everything else," laughed Larry. "And why not? Don't you think we deserve it?"

"Why not." This time they didn't move apart after the toast, but remained close enough to feel each other's breath. They both sensed something had changed.

"You're a priest," said Larry, softly, stating the

obvious.

"I was a woman before I became a priest." She wanted to forget for a short while that she was a minister of the church, a church that no longer offered her the solace and joy that she craved and expected from it. She wanted to feel someone's arms about her, to surrender to someone else's will besides God. She was tired of being strong and needed the warmth of human contact.

Larry put down the jam jar and took Laura's glass, placing it beside his makeshift one. Gently and rather nervously, he placed a hand on her cheek and drew her close.

Their kiss was long and sweet, like two teenagers on their first date. Larry pushed aside a pile of magazines and gently lowered Laura back onto the bed. At the back of his mind a little voice was shouting, 'No, you can't, she's a priest,' but he was past listening.

O'Shea couldn't know the route he took was the same one Graham had followed on his last night. He wasn't taking in his surroundings. Something had led Graham to the river, whether intentionally or by chance. No-one knew and probably no-one ever would. O'Shea felt he had let his friend down. Why hadn't Graham called him, talked things over, shared what was going on in his troubled mind?

A gloved hand reached from a tartan sleeping bag and O'Shea handed over a coin.

'Poor bastard,' he thought, momentarily distracted. Someone had shovelled grit onto the steps but O'Shea still kept a steadying hand out at his side. Cold concrete, cold river, cold thoughts.

Reaching the wall, he looked down into the fast-flowing water. The tide had turned and was eager to get back to the open sea, its ripples undulating like the shadows of birds long flown.

Even though he couldn't know if Graham heard him, he whispered softly, "I promise you, Graham, old fellow, we'll find out what all this is about, if it's the last thing we do." As he said the words, it occurred to him that might well be true.

"I'm sorry!" Larry handed Laura a mug of steaming coffee where she sat on the edge of his bed, a blanket wrapped about her.

"It's OK." Laura hugged the hot drink to her, but its heat wasn't the sort she longed for.

"It didn't seem right. I know you were fine with it, but I just couldn't."

"It's all right, Larry, really. It was a stupid idea."

"No, no, not stupid. I wanted to, but…"

"But the collar got in the way?"

"I'm not sure it was that exactly. It's hard to explain. I didn't feel it was wrong, but then, I'm not that religious. I just felt I couldn't, like you were already spoken for somehow." He paused, then added with a rueful smile, "Not that that's ever stopped me in the past."

"It's nuns who are married to Christ, Larry, not female priests."

"I know! Jeez, it's embarrassing. This doesn't usually happen to me."

"Drink your coffee and stop fretting," said Laura, realising that, for all her longing to offload responsibility, here she was taking control again. "If it makes you feel any better, it probably wasn't the cleverest of ideas. We didn't even think of safety measures, for one thing. I guess I just wanted to relive my past somehow, when life was so much simpler. Pass me my clothes, will you?"

As she sipped her coffee, Laura looked about the cluttered flat. She smiled. It fitted Larry to a T. Even had he been a successful photographer working for the New York Times, she still imagined part of his home would look like this, comfortable chaos.

She leaned down to straighten a pile of books and glossy magazines and noticed a small box protruding from the heap, causing their dangerous angle of incline. Carefully retrieving it, she found it was a pack of tarot cards.

"I didn't know you were into fortune telling," she called out.

"What? No, why?" Larry appeared around the partition. "Oh, those! Ex-girlfriend. She left them here when we split. Probably hoped I'd read them and take her back."

"Or read them and see why she left," Laura teased.

Larry grinned sheepishly, feelings of inadequacy still uppermost in his mind.

Laura opened the pack. She'd never had a proper look at 'The Devil's Prayer Book' before; it was frowned upon by the church.

The cards felt heavy and cumbersome as she admired the vivid illustrations. Sifting through, a card slid from her grasp and fluttered to the floor, face up. Before she could retrieve it, Larry reached down, glancing at it before handing it back.

"'La Papesse!' That's amazing." When Laura looked puzzled, he added, "The High Priestess."

Laura smiled. "Don't get me on to the subject of

titles."

"Still, 'priest', 'priestess', you have to admit that's kind of spooky."

"Unlike you, Larry, I'm not so easily impressed. I see no point in cards that tell a person what they already know." She put the cards back in their box and then, as Larry washed up, made herself respectable.

"Ready?" she asked, as Larry started rummaging in drawers and stuffing various things in his pocket.

"Right with you," he replied. "You never know what might be useful."

"Right, let's go and meet Dermot."

The teabag floated to the top of the cup, buoyant with air, where it remained like a bloated carcass bobbing in the water. Perhaps, if O'Shea hadn't been so weighted down with his own thoughts, he might have noticed a difference in the way Laura and Larry acted, like two animals circling each other for fear of their intentions being misread.

"That looks cold," said Larry, nodding at O'Shea's tea.

He didn't answer.

"The train's in," said Laura.

They made their way to the platform. It was going to be an uncomfortable journey and Laura was glad of the folder of notes she'd got from Marcus Cook. At least she could bury her head in that. Larry chose to sleep, or gave every appearance of doing so, but O'Shea stared out into the darkness. The well-lit interior of the carriage reflected in the window and the darkness stared back in.

A weak sun greeted Larry the following morning as he

left 'The Peal Of Bells'. It was Sunday. O'Shea hadn't surfaced yet and Laura had a service to attend to. The church should be quiet, and Larry decided it was an excellent opportunity to have a good look around on his own.

The inevitable two Vatican guards were standing in the graveyard, catching what little comfort the sun offered. One of them started over, saw who it was, and relaxed as Larry gave a cheery wave.

"Just having a quick look inside," he shouted. "Not going to steal your damned coffin," he added under his breath.

The chill struck him immediately. It wasn't surprising, he reasoned, considering the time of year and the fact the church was out of use. Still, he wished he'd muffled up more. The sight of a little sunlight had duped him and he should have known better. The church had the feel of a building left empty for too long, combined with the sharp smell of damp wood.

He gave the opening to the crypt only a cursory glance. He'd never found archaeology very interesting until now and had already seen all there was to see down there. Getting excited over a few old bones or stones seemed more than a little odd to him, although he had to admit he'd been excited by the tomb when he first saw it. That was it though; he'd seen it and was now more interested in looking at the rest of the church in greater detail.

Thinking about the death of the tramp, Larry made his way forward for a closer look at the scene of the murder. Where light shafted down through the stained glass window, it cast the area surrounding the libation tube into deeper shadow. Apparently, there had been no body as such but someone had sprayed the vagrant over the walls and altar. Someone or something.

St. Jude's original rood screen would have been destroyed during the Reformation. In its place, a low chancel screen had been set up to separate the clergy from the congregation. This was obviously what Pargeter had referred to when he told Laura of a villager carving the rood screen from the Jude Tree. Larry moved closer to look at the detail.

The ability of a local man to carve such intricate coils and figures astounded him. He guessed the pictures worked into the design were episodes from the Bible. He recognised Eve taking the apple from a malevolent-looking serpent whilst Adam stood helplessly by, and wondered how the carver of the piece had been allowed to emphasise Eve's voluptuous figure with quite so much accuracy.

He guessed one of the end carvings depicting graves torn open was a scene from The Book of Revelation. Here again, a serpent appeared, wrapping itself about some of the risen dead, presumably to drag them down to Hell. 'Cheerful pre-TV viewing for the sinners in the front rows,' he thought.

He slowly backed along the screen, trying to make out other recognisable scenes. His hand casually slid across Eve's breasts as he traced the intricacies in the wood and he felt a sudden excitement that took him by surprise.

The feeling grew stronger and, at the same time, his head began to swim so that he grasped the edge of the screen for support. He couldn't move. He was aware of the rising heat from his body despite the now icy cold church, as something applied pressure first to his ankle and then slowly moved up his inside leg towards his groin.

128

FATHER OF LIES

Larry moaned. He wanted to break free but his body seemed to have other desires, forcing him to lean over the rail as though offering himself to something he could neither see nor hear, but which was even now violating his willing flesh.

His brain was screaming for him to fight, to push himself free of whatever was entwined about him but, despite this, his body responded to its intruder. Aroused now beyond his control, Larry twisted and writhed until, with a deep guttural groan that he no longer recognised as his, he was finally spent.

He hung over the rail for endless minutes, trembling and too exhausted to move, then, turning as he did so, he slowly slid to the floor. Gasping, he tried to reconcile the empty church before him with what had just happened.

He was surprised to find he could walk, albeit rather unsteadily, using the end of the pews as an intermittent handrail.

He hurried from St. Jude's. He didn't notice the guards looking quizzically in his direction. Nor did he notice the aggrieved regulars whom he pushed past in 'The Peal Of Bells'.

When he got to his room, he fell face forward onto his unmade bed and sobbed like a child.

TWELVE

Laura arrived at the pub shortly after lunch. O'Shea was perched on a stool at the far end of the bar.

"How are you feeling?" asked Laura, shaking her head as he motioned to the barman.

"I'm perfectly all right, Laura. Don't fuss. Are you sure you won't have an orange juice or something?"

He certainly looked better than she'd feared, more like the O'Shea she'd come to know.

"No. Thanks though. I just wanted to check on you after yesterday. I'm up to my eyes preparing the Christmas services. Have you seen Larry?"

"Not today. Gather he went off early this morning. I thought he might be with you." He motioned to the barman. "Larry Markham? Have you seen him at all?"

"Not since he nearly knocked two of my customers off their feet earlier," grumbled the bartender. "Came storming in here as if all the hounds of Hell were after him. Don't know what got him so riled up, but I haven't seen hide nor hair of him since."

O'Shea snorted. "Doesn't sound like Larry."

"Look, I need to get back to work," said Laura. "I'm getting behind with parish duties and I think someone must have reported me. I had a reprimanding email from the bishop, sort of a verbal wrist slap, and it won't look good on my record – dereliction of duties on my first assignment."

"If anyone did report you, I have a good idea who it might have been."

"You mean Benvenuti?" Laura asked in astonishment, but, when she thought about it, it seemed highly probable. She was being a nuisance, and telling the bishop she was meddling with Catholic business, instead of attending to her duties, would be one way of warning her off.

"Look, you go ahead. I'll see if I can find Larry. I presume we'll see you this evening?"

"I'll probably need that drink by then," laughed Laura.

"Oh, and Laura," he called after her.

She stopped in the doorway and looked back.

"Graham's funeral. I've just heard. It's tomorrow."

Larry didn't put in an appearance until the evening meal.

"We were wondering where you'd got to," said O'Shea, brusquely. "I knocked on your door a couple of times but decided you were out."

"Sorry," said Larry. "I wasn't feeling too good. Went back to bed and hopefully I've slept whatever it was off. I didn't hear you."

"You're feeling OK now?" asked a concerned Laura. Larry certainly didn't seem his usual bright self.

"Fine! Probably just tired. It was quite a day yesterday." He glanced at O'Shea but saw no reaction.

"I managed to make inroads into Cook's notes this afternoon," said Laura, drawing attention away from the previous day. "It makes for interesting reading."

"Funny that Cook seemed not to want any further involvement," said Larry. "I would have thought it was right up his street, all this. Didn't you say he studied evil?"

"Maybe this was all *too* disquieting, even for him," broke in O'Shea. "It's OK being interested in something from afar, but not when it comes knocking at your front door."

"I'm not sure I follow," said Larry.

"I think he means that this was too much. It had suddenly become believable," said Laura.

O'Shea nodded. "That and, going by what's happened to some of the others involved with this particular line of research, maybe Cook was astute enough to pick up on something nasty hovering in the shadows. It's even possible he was warned off."

"That's sounds a bit melodramatic," said Larry. He took a sip of his drink. When no-one spoke, he added, "OK, I'll buy it."

Under his breath, O'Shea muttered, "Make mine a double."

As they ate, Laura told the two men a little of Cook's findings.

"There's quite a lot about how others see the church," she began, "and he's including all denominations as well as the Old Testament, which is, of course, Hebrew. There are lots of references, such as Ian Paisley denouncing the Pope as the anti-Christ, and the Egyptians describing the encounter between Moses and Pharaoh in a slightly different way to its Biblical rendering."

"How exactly?" asked Larry.

Laura grinned. "To them, Moses practised witchcraft and, along with his followers, worshipped a foreign and loathsome god. Of course, most of this is simply one religion distrusting another." She swallowed a mouthful of lasagne and continued. "He goes on a bit about dubious aspects of Christianity, such as mass exorcisms, trances, the Toronto Blessing, talking in tongues, etc."

"How do you mean?" This time it was O'Shea who interrupted.

"Well, he points out there's a fine line between visions say, and possession, and mentions shrines, for example, Fatima. He asks how a bright light can automatically be accepted as a holy vision. The church condemns healing, saying it's the work of the devil, yet what about the healings at Lourdes? It's all down to our perception of source. The same with trances. What makes one possession by voodoo gods and the other the touch of the Holy Spirit?"

"Interesting notion," said Larry.

"Indeed," agreed O'Shea. "We believe what we're told. We presume – in fact we're indoctrinated from the cradle – that good will conquer evil in the end and we're even led in what we perceive to *be* good or evil. What if we believe what we're told because we want to, or life would simply be too unbearable?" He fell silent.

"It's like political manoeuvrings," said Larry. "Biblical teachings tell us to turn the other cheek, not to retaliate, not to defend ourselves. That's tantamount to offering ourselves up for further abuse. Control by a few simple words is so much more effective than by force and, if force should be needed, reducing the opposition's strength by religious doctrine is a frighteningly ingenious ploy."

"The church has always been a political power or, at least, a power for politics," said Laura.

"What else did he say?" asked Larry.

"There's a great catalogue of horrors laid at the church's door. The usual ones, persecution, torture, ethnic cleansing, wholesale slaughter." Laura laughed. "It's bizarre, really. There are a few interesting ones thrown in though."

"For instance?"

"For instance, in drought-ridden countries where humanity is starving, birth control is frowned upon by the Catholic Church. Consequently, the suffering is increased ten or a hundred fold. Cook questions whether the church is doing the Devil's work. After all, the Christian religion was born out of bloodshed, torture and death. Without the slaughter of an innocent, there wouldn't even *be* a church." She paused and sipped her drink. "There's also the old criticism of the church, and we're not just talking about Catholics here, having untold wealth, yet not following Christ's example. Instead, they hoard the wealth rather than using it to help the poor. I must say he's really gone to town in his research. I've only looked at about a third, if that."

"Not really what we're looking for," said O'Shea.

"Not yet! He mentioned 'serpents' when we spoke, but I haven't got to that yet, apart from a brief mention of a supposed secret order within the Vatican, associated with snakes or serpents, which seems highly unlikely." Laura finished off her now cold lasagne and pushed her plate away. "By the way, what time is the funeral?"

"Two-thirty," said O'Shea, "but you two don't need to be there."

"Try and stop us," they said, almost in unison.

Graham's funeral was a sorry affair, not helped by the appearance of two men, obviously Vatican officials, who hovered some distance from the grave. What they were doing there was anybody's guess. They certainly weren't paying their respects to the dead priest.

The clergyman performing the brief service approached Laura, O'Shea and Larry beforehand and asked if they could tell him anything personal about Graham, that he could use in the eulogy. However, only O'Shea had known Graham and that was when they were so much younger. The request brought it home to O'Shea how little he really knew his friend.

As Laura and Larry steered O'Shea from the grave, a steady rain set in. It pooled in the mud around the edge of the opening, brimmed over and trickled down onto the coffin within.

O'Shea had remained stony-faced throughout the service, showing no trace of emotion. That worried Laura. He remained silent for most of the journey home, only speaking when it was absolutely necessary, and retired to his room as soon as they arrived. This worried Laura even more. She was also feeling unwell and was afraid she might have caught whatever it was that had upset Larry. Either that, or it was the result of last night's lasagne. She had felt queasy since breakfast and hadn't been able to shake the feeling till they'd reached London.

"Come on," said Larry. "I'll walk you back to your digs. I don't know about you but I could do with an early night too."

When they reached Laura's lodgings, she popped her head around Mrs Lyle's door.

"Oh, you're back," said Mrs Lyle, stating the obvious but unable to curtsy from her chair in front of the TV.

"Yes. Sorry to disturb your viewing. Is it all right if I make Mr Markham a coffee in the kitchen?"

As Laura boiled the water, Larry placed a couple of mugs on the flowered, plastic tablecloth.

"There, just like an old married couple." His attempt at jollity didn't fool either of them. Although it wasn't late, they were both exhausted. "He'll be OK, you know. O'Shea. He's a tough old cookie."

"I guess you're right but I've grown fond of him. I can't help but worry."

"I'll look in on him when I get back to the pub, just to be sure, if you like."

"Yes, I'd appreciate it." Then, after a moment's pause, "Thanks! Tell me, Larry, what made you leave America?"

Larry gave a wry laugh.

"I thought it would be safer," he said. When Laura looked surprised, he went on, "I took some photos at a crime scene that certain parties would rather I hadn't. Those certain parties have a long reach and I figured an ocean between us sounded a good idea. So here I am, though I'm not too sure about the 'safe' part."

They'd barely taken a sip of coffee before a loud banging at the front door jarred them both into full wakefulness and they shared the same thought, 'O'Shea!'

Raised voices came from the hallway and Mrs Lyle entered the kitchen in full sail.

"Reverend Coatman, there's something odd going on at the churchyard. They say you should come quick." Breathless and red-faced, she bustled out of the way to let Laura and Larry through, handing Laura a torch as she did so.

There were half a dozen figures gathered outside the low churchyard wall. Their attention was fixed on a wailing figure kneeling beside the church. The group parted as Laura and Larry hurried up but quickly closed ranks again as they ran through the gate. Scared though she was, Laura could tell the despairing cries were all too human, and humanity she could deal with.

FATHER OF LIES

Larry kept pace with her as she approached the figure huddled in the church's shadow. Bent double, a man was clawing at the damp earth with bare fingers, and from his slight build it was obvious it wasn't O'Shea.

As they drew closer, Laura avoided pointing the full beam of the torch in his face for fear of frightening him further, but it offered enough light for them to make out the ravaged features of Leonard Pargeter. Both his hands and clothes were covered in dirt and blood, and tears had washed gullies down his hollow cheeks.

He was crying out, "I'm sorry," and "Forgive me," over and over, as he dug his torn fingers into the mound of earth.

"Be careful," said Larry, as Laura moved towards the distraught man.

"Mr Pargeter? It's Laura – Reverend Coatman. It's OK, everything's all right. Mr Pargeter?"

Pargeter didn't stop clawing at the soil until Laura gently but firmly clasped his wrists and held them. She slowly helped him rise as Larry stepped forward, removing his jacket as he did so and wrapping it around the shoulders of the frail old man.

"I'm sorry," wailed Pargeter. "It's all my fault. Oh God, forgive me, it's all my fault." His arms now hung limp at his sides and fresh tears rolled down his cheeks. "All my fault."

"Larry, get rid of them," said Laura, nodding towards the onlookers, "and see if you can get hold of a doctor."

"I'll call for an ambulance."

"No, it may not be needed. If it is, the doctor will call for one."

"Will you be OK?"

Laura nodded. The elderly man let himself be led towards the porch where there was a seat. It was as if all life had been drained from him and the empty shell didn't care what happened now. He was still muttering softly, the words the same, but they were no longer filled with desperation, only resignation and defeat.

Laura could see he was in shock, though she couldn't imagine what had caused him to behave the way he had.

"Mr Pargeter?" she said, her voice soft with persuasion. "Mr Pargeter, can you tell me what happened?"

"It's my fault," he began. "The tree."

"Do you mean the Jude Tree?" Laura realised the spot where he'd been digging was its supposed location.

"Yes, yes. My fault."

"But the tree was destroyed in your grandfather's time. How can you be to blame?"

"No, no. My job… to feed it. The roots. I'd stopped doing it. I'd stopped believing." Before Laura could ask what he meant, he continued, becoming agitated again. "If I feed it everything will be all right, but I couldn't get in the church. It's all been my fault."

Larry had done a good job of clearing the onlookers, who seemed to have wandered off towards the pub. It wasn't long before he came trotting back, followed a few feet behind by a puffing, middle-aged gentleman, who turned out to be the local doctor.

"Now, what's all this? Good God, Pargeter, what the hell have you done to yourself?" Suddenly remembering where he was and in whose company, he coughed but didn't apologise.

"Doctor Reynalds!" said Larry, by way of

introduction.

As Reynalds began a cursory examination, Laura introduced herself and described how they had found the elderly warden. She omitted the actual words, preferring to lie, in the light of all that had happened. She wasn't sure how trustworthy the doctor was and didn't want it spread around the village.

"You say he was babbling incoherently?"

"Yes, it was more of a wail actually."

"I need to get him to my surgery to check him over properly. That porch light is next to useless, but I can't see any major damage. Still, I'd like to make sure. Can either of you help me with him? I'm sure he'll be happier if he can sleep in his own bed tonight. The old never like being admitted to hospital. They always think they won't get out again."

Larry volunteered, "I'll stay the night with him if it will make you any happier." He turned to Laura. "Try and get some sleep. We'll catch up tomorrow."

As Laura followed their slow progress out of the churchyard to the doctor's waiting car, she glanced over to where Pargeter had been digging. She breathed in the smell of moist, freshly dug earth. A light mist had formed. As she watched, it shifted and coiled, and she dragged her eyes away from it, afraid both of what it hid and what it might reveal.

Larry arrived whilst Laura was still eating breakfast. Mrs Lyle made him a coffee and then left them alone.

"How did it go?" asked Laura, as she downed bacon and eggs.

"Poor old man," said Larry. "The doctor checked him over, cleaned and patched up the cuts and grazes and gave me some sleeping tablets for him. Then he ran us back to Pargeter's and said he'd call by today. The old guy had shredded his fingers on stones and his nails have some nasty cracks in them. They'll be pretty damned sore for a while."

"Did you stay all night with him?"

"Yeah! Not the most comfy of nights, curled up in a chair. He slept like a baby once I'd gotten the tablets down him. Seems a bit out of it this morning, but I think he'll be OK."

"Has he said anything more about what happened?"

"No, and I thought it best not to ask. I'll tell you something though, not all the blood on him last night came from his fingers. There were a couple of deep gashes on his forearm and, before you suggest it, they weren't made by catching them on anything. It had all the appearance of him having ripped the flesh with his teeth."

"What do you mean?" said Laura, fork poised en route to her mouth.

"I mean, it wasn't the first time dear old Mr Pargeter has been blood-letting. There was blood on his lips too. He had numerous scars on both arms. The doctor said some of them probably dated back years. Wouldn't have put Pargeter down as the self-harming sort. Sorry, forgot you're eating," he added, noticing Laura's pale face.

"Oh, that doesn't worry me, not usually anyway. Maybe I should have just had toast this morning." She waited for her stomach to settle. "What does worry me is the picture you're painting of Pargeter making a regular habit of this. I need to have a talk with him."

"Is that wise?"

"Well, even if I don't, someone else will now the doctor's seen the scars. They'll probably want to send him for some psychological assessment." After a moment she added, "Have you seen O'Shea this morning?"

"No, I came straight from Pargeter's. I'll get along there now. What will you be doing?"

"I'll pay a call on Pargeter. After all, he is one of my parishioners, and it's only natural I should be concerned about him."

"Hm, one of your flock."

"One of the church's flock anyway," replied Laura.

When Larry had left, she thought about what she'd just said. Flock. Flock of sheep. Sheep follow each other unquestioningly. Sheep can be herded and led. Sheep can be slaughtered.

She gulped down the remainder of her coffee and hurried after Larry.

THIRTEEN

Laura couldn't get much sense out of Pargeter. Despite the medication, he was still very agitated.

"People are dying – will die – and it's all my fault."

Laura laid a hand on his bandaged arm and then, remembering his wounds, quickly withdrew it. "None of what has happened is your fault, Mr Pargeter." She wasn't even sure if he could hear her. He made no response at first. "Mr Pargeter?"

"It was my job. My father's before me and his before that. I didn't believe no more, you see, I didn't believe."

"I'm not sure I understand…" began Laura.

"Feeding the tree." When she still looked at a loss, he continued, "It had to have blood, and it was my job to keep it fed."

"*Your* blood?"

"No, no, any blood, but when I couldn't get it elsewheres, yes, I'd use my own." He paused. "But then I stopped believing. Thought that the roots under the church had died long ago. More fool me."

"You used the libation tube by the pulpit?" asked Laura.

"I was a churchwarden. No-one ever questioned me going into St. Jude's, nor my father before me. It was our duty, see? Now they won't let me in."

"And you thought you were feeding the remains of the Jude Tree?"

"Of course. What else would we be feeding?" He gave Laura a pitying look. "Me, and my father before me. Our family's job, see? Our duty."

"Who told you it was your… job?" asked Laura.

"No-one told us. No-one had to. It was our duty."

FATHER OF LIES

Laura realised she wasn't going to get much else from him. Leonard Pargeter's troubled mind was addled, like an egg rotting from within, and his sanity was already questionable. She saw to it that he was comfortable and then, deep in thought, returned to her digs. Her breakfast had left her feeling off-colour and the thought of writing the Christmas Day sermon was daunting. Joy and hope seemed a far cry from the brooding presence of St. Jude's.

By four thirty, Rudi Clements had finally finished his work documenting and photographing the crypt and its contents. He wasn't sad to be leaving. He couldn't quite put his finger on it, but there was something not quite right about the place. He reasoned that it might be the knowledge there'd been a recent unexplained murder within the church's walls, but he felt there was more to it than that. There had been times when he'd welcomed the proximity of the servile Vatican guards. Knowing someone else was within earshot had been a comfort. No, he'd be glad to say goodbye to this one.

Recently, he'd detected a smell, sickening and all-pervading. He concluded a small rodent had somehow got into the libation tube, died and was now rotting within the narrow passage. He'd searched everywhere else and it was the only answer he could come up with. If anything, the smell was growing worse, and it was an odour that he just wasn't able to ignore.

He looked round one last time. Everything was as it had been when he'd arrived. It was cleaner, that was the only difference. Permission had been adamantly refused for a sample of the dust within the coffin to be sent for analysis. He'd been tempted to take one anyway but decided it would add little to the investigation. Whoever had been in there would give up little more than trace elements now. Instead, the top of the sarcophagus had been covered with thick plastic sheeting and securely sealed.

As he turned to leave, a slight movement stopped him in his tracks. The strong lights had already been packed away in his car and he had to strain his eyes in the comparatively poor light from his torch.

He crossed over to where the libation tube opened into the crypt and leaned forward to see it better.

"Aagh!" He jumped back as a large maggot crawled out and fell from the hole. It was followed by another and then another. There were already huge, black flies clinging to the surface of the wall. Thank God the job was finished and he didn't have to contend with them in the confined area.

Finally, leaving the churchyard, he gave an involuntary shudder. He didn't like turning his back on the church. He threw his bag onto the rear seat of the car with his other gear, laid the folders on the vacant front seat and climbed in. Turning on the radio, he pulled away from St. Jude's with a feeling of relief.

In the darkness, he didn't see the black bodies crawling from his camera case and gathering on the rear side windows. Humming along with the carols that were playing, he didn't hear the increasing buzz of bloated flies.

It was the day before Christmas Eve and Laura was rushed off her feet. As neither Larry nor O'Shea had anyone to spend the festivities with, they'd voted to stay at 'The Peal Of Bells' and, at the very least, spend the holiday in a blissful state of inebriation. Fortunately for Laura's peace of mind, she was unaware of that part of their plan. Despite her full working schedule, she had picked up an email that morning that wrenched her mind back to St. Jude's, and she hurried to the pub to relay the contents to the two men.

"Hello," greeted O'Shea, the first to spot Laura. On seeing her face, he added, "What's wrong?"

"Rudi Clements is dead," she blurted out. Larry had joined them and the two men stared at her in disbelief.

"How?" It was Larry who spoke first.

"Driving home after finishing his work at St. Jude's. They think he hit some black ice, skidded off the road, rolled and hit a tree."

"They?" queried O'Shea.

"Well, the police, I suppose. I had an email from the university this morning. Thing is," she added, "when they opened the car door, they said the inside was swarming with flies."

"Flies?" said Larry. "It's December, for Heaven's sake. You don't get flies in December."

"'Behold, I will send swarms of flies upon thee, and upon thy servants, and upon thy people, and into thy houses: and the houses of the Egyptians shall be full of swarms of flies, and also the ground whereon they are'," quoted O'Shea.

"What?" Larry looked confused.

"Exodus!" said O'Shea. "Chapter eight."

"'And the land was corrupted by reason of the swarm of flies'," added Laura.

"Of course," said Larry, "Lord of the Flies! Isn't that another name for…?"

"The Devil," cut in Laura. "Now there's a surprise!"

"What about all Clements' notes, his photos?" said O'Shea.

145

"Ruined," said Laura. "When the car rolled, the roof caved in and crushed his head. The folders were on the seat beside him and he'd bled over them to such an extent they simply weren't salvageable."

"How very convenient," replied O'Shea, almost to himself, then emptied his glass.

Benvenuti was fuming. At last the sarcophagus had been signed over to him and the haulage company had arrived at St. Jude's at nine o'clock precisely. He'd overseen the removal of the coffin, ensuring it was well padded and crated, hoisted clear of the hole and put aboard a truck heading for Southampton. Now he'd learned it would stay in a container at the docks until the New Year.

"Why wasn't this explained to me in advance?" he growled down the phone. "No, I did not ask. I said quite clearly it was a matter of urgency. No-one mentioned the whole company would close down for the holiday."

He had deliberately engaged a company used to shipping antiques and antiquities, but this unforeseen delay infuriated him. The longer the sarcophagus remained outside of Vatican jurisdiction, the more risky it became. There had already been enough delay, thanks to the interference of Reverend Coatman.

The thought of Laura brought a warm feeling in his groin. What was it about her that made him desire her, he wondered? She certainly wasn't attractive in the usual sense, yet, at the very thought of her, he envisaged several delightful scenarios that both aroused and frustrated him. In some ways it was a shame he was required back in Rome.

Finally slamming down the receiver, he realised

there was nothing he could do but wait. He was sure Southampton would hold some avenues of interest, even for his unusual tastes.

"Will I see you two at a service over Christmas?" asked Laura that evening.

"Speaking for myself, I think not," said O'Shea. He seemed surprised she should even ask.

"It's not really my thing," said Larry. Then, on seeing Laura's crestfallen face, he gave way. "OK, as long as it's not too early."

"Can't I persuade you, Dermot? Not even the Midnight Mass?"

"Especially not the Midnight Mass," he replied. "I'll see you for Christmas lunch, that's if I've surfaced by then."

"I'll do the Mass," said Larry. "Then I'll see you safely home."

"Thank you. I'd like that." Laura was glad O'Shea had invited Larry to join their investigation. She wasn't sure she could have coped with St. Jude's and O'Shea on her own.

Christmas Eve was even more hectic for Laura, as she got everything ready for the services and went over the sermons once more. It was cold in the hall but not nearly as cold as St. Jude's would have been, she reasoned. She didn't think the parishioners would want to linger after the Mass, and she guessed most of them would wrap up as if preparing for an Arctic expedition.

She skipped lunch and grabbed a sandwich in the evening. She didn't feel like food and wasn't sure if she felt cold from lack of body fuel or the icy temperature.

Watching the congregation gather before her, seated on uncomfortable wooden chairs in the bitterly cold hall, Laura was reminded of the simple, honest folk who made up the church she loved. But did she love it, she wondered? Only a couple of months ago, she would have answered with a resounding 'Yes', but now... So much had happened in such a short time. She doubted her vocation, her beliefs and even herself. How could she stand up before these people and lead them in prayer?

Looking at her watch, she saw it was almost eleven-thirty, time to begin. She nodded to the two parishioners who were acting as servers. Everything had to be downsized since moving out of the church. Even the hymns were sung to organ music played on a cheap CD player. One of the servers moved to her position by the player, finger poised to switch it on with a noisy click.

Looking past them, Laura saw Larry arrive in the doorway, and her spirits rose. He was another question needing an answer. She wasn't sure what her feelings for him were; all she knew was she needed him around. Why, was another unanswered question.

He made his way forward and edged along the second row to sit near the wall and one of the malfunctioning radiators, giving her an encouraging smile once he was seated.

The questions would have to wait. Laura owed it to these people to perform the Mass to the best of her ability, to send them home with renewed faith and peace of mind. Whatever her own misgivings, that was what she was going to do.

Larry was impressed by the way Laura delivered

the sermon and led the congregation. She had such strength but, towards the end of the service, during the recital of the Lord's Prayer before the distribution of the Holy Communion, she stumbled over the words, "Lead us not into temptation, but deliver us from evil."

There was a pause as waves of panic washed over her, but then she caught Larry's eye. He nodded reassuringly and she finished both prayer and service without causing anyone a second thought.

Afterwards, as Larry helped her pile up the Bibles and hymnbooks and straighten the chairs, she said, "Well?"

"Well what?" he said.

"How was I?"

He smiled. "I thought it was the man who asked that."

"Larry!"

This time he laughed. "Come on. Let's get you back and into the warm."

"I'll see you both for lunch tomorrow," said Laura, as they hurried through the cold night air, their breath visible before them.

"I'll be there with crackers and streamers," he said.

"And Larry? Let's try to make it a Jude-free celebration."

Creeping up the stairs past Mrs Lyle's room, Laura wondered if that would indeed be possible. She had the awful feeling that nothing would ever be Jude-free again.

O'Shea's cheeks were already rosy from alcohol when Laura met him and Larry for lunch. He'd insisted on the full Christmas menu with all the trimmings.

"How are we supposed to eat all that?" gasped Laura, seeing the plate piled high before her. She really didn't feel hungry and the sight of so much rich food made her queasy again. She obviously still had Larry's bug.

"Eat up," urged O'Shea. "Got to build our strength up for the battle to come."

Laura and Larry exchanged glances but neither spoke, nor did O'Shea attempt to elaborate.

"I wonder how Leonard Pargeter is," said Laura. The thought of him alone at Christmas in his darkened room saddened her.

"He's doing all right. Still confused but enjoying his holiday lunch," said Larry.

"How do you know that?" asked Laura. "Have you been to see him?"

"Not only that," laughed O'Shea. "Larry got the pub to prepare a full Christmas dinner for the old guy and took it round to him earlier."

"Oh, Larry, that was wonderful of you. Thank you."

Larry concentrated on the food before him, embarrassed at being found out. He didn't tell Laura that he'd discovered the old man staring out of the window at St. Jude's and how he'd had trouble dragging Pargeter's mind back to the present and the meal he doubted he'd eat.

Afterwards, both Larry and O'Shea felt bloated from too much food and wine. Laura, who'd skipped desert and limited herself to only one glass, left the men to sleep it off in their rooms. She felt tired too.

Mrs Lyle greeted her in the hallway, proffering a plate of mince pies. Laura just made it to the bathroom in time. Lying on her bed, she felt shivery. She'd wondered earlier if she'd make it through the morning service without being ill. Fortunately, there wouldn't be an evening one. She looked at Cook's file lying on the bedside table, reached for it then changed her mind. St. Jude's could wait until tomorrow, and she crept beneath her quilt and slept.

Benvenuti's cell phone roused him from a most pleasurable dream.

"Yes," he almost shouted into it. "Yes, I am he." He wasn't altogether surprised by what he was told. "I trust there's no question of police rooting around in the container?" he said. "Good. Keep me posted."

So, a body had been found at the docks, not far from the Vatican's container, one of the security guards. It had all the appearance of the man having fallen and split his head open. Messy! Benvenuti gave a half-smile. He had felt the energy radiating from the coffin, fed on it for his own private pleasure. It was only natural that it, in turn, needed to be fed.

He pulled back the mesh and looked out of the hotel window. Christmas decorations hung from every lamppost and lights sparkled in the bare trees. He heard some revellers in the street below. He doubted they were celebrating the birth of their Saviour. The laughter turned to abusive threats and he heard glass shatter on the pavement. Smiling, he turned away. He had celebrating of his own to do.

Laura was growing concerned. She'd been sick again this morning and her period was well overdue. If she didn't know it was impossible, she'd think she was pregnant. She would have put being late down to the stress of the last few weeks, but the sickness was something else. It wasn't constant, but was enough for her to consider making an appointment with the doctor now that Christmas was over. She was relieved that nothing had happened in Larry's flat. That really would have given her something to worry about.

There was, of course, the possibility that she'd picked up a bug from the stale air from the crypt. Although she hadn't ventured down into it, the outpouring of air could have lingered in the closed church. She shivered at the mere thought of the place. The whole building had smelled of corruption and death. She knew archaeologists had to beware when entering sealed tombs, for fear of what the fetid air contained. This, she reasoned, was no different. She would tell the doctor of the stench. Yes, it was definitely something she'd picked up there.

When she left the surgery, her head was reeling and she was trembling violently. It wasn't possible, but the fact remained, she was pregnant. When she'd blurted out to Doctor Reynalds that she hadn't had sex, he'd given her a pitying look. Perhaps, if she hadn't been a member of the clergy, he'd have given his usual response to the claim of immaculate conception, 'You wouldn't be the first'. At least he hadn't looked shocked, just perhaps a little disappointed.

Laura needed to be by herself for a while, to think, maybe to pray. She walked through the village to where the dyke separated the houses from the expanse of fens. Looking out across the winter landscape, she could have been the last living creature left standing at the edge of the world.

It was here she let the fearful thought she'd been

suppressing filter through to her awareness. Willing though she may have been, Larry had not been able to make love to her, but something had. Something inhuman had violated her within St. Jude's and awoken feelings in her that she hadn't known she had. Whatever that thing was, it was the only possible father to what was growing inside her. She fought the urge to rip her body open and tear the child from her womb. This couldn't be happening, but she knew it was, knew from the moment Doctor Reynalds confirmed the pregnancy, that things could never go back to how they were. Dark clouds were massing towards the east and she shivered. Reeds bent their heads in an icy blast, carrying whispered words from the father of her child. Turning, she made her way back to her room, but now the panic had subsided and a gentle feeling of peace cloaked itself about her, shielding her from the cold easterly wind that drove in across the bleak flat marshland.

"So, when are you going to let us read the notes you got from Cook?" asked O'Shea later that day. "Laura?"

"Sorry, notes?"

"Yes, the ones from Cook. Are you all right?" Laura seemed distracted. O'Shea had been watching her with Larry and had the niggling feeling something was going on between the two of them. It was nothing he could pinpoint but it left him feeling unsettled. The last thing they needed was personal problems on top of everything else.

"I'll let you have the folder. I haven't had a chance to go through it all and you may find something important amongst the waffle."

"Waffle, is it?" snorted O'Shea. "Since when did it

become waffle?"

"Well, not every crime committed in the name of the Christian religion has a bearing on what we're looking at here."

O'Shea felt a sudden twinge of guilt. If anything, his desire to find out what happened to Graham and the events that followed had given him new purpose. It had made him feel more alive than he'd felt for a very long time. Death sometimes had that effect upon the living. But Laura was young and the strain was showing. She appeared pale and drawn and he hadn't realised until now how tired she was looking.

"I'll look through the stuff, separate the wheat from the chaff and share what I find. How's that?" he said, more gently.

Laura nodded. She hadn't meant to snap at O'Shea, but the recent development had played on her mind almost constantly, tearing her first one way, then the other. Logic told her this couldn't be happening but the reality was different. She resolved briefly to have the child aborted and, at first, that seemed the only answer if she was to save her career and her sanity. But she believed in the sanctity of life, all life, and could see no way to absolve herself from guilt should she take that course. It would be murder.

Somewhere, deep inside, she was already feeling a mother's love, the need to nurture, to protect. This was new to Laura and something she never believed she'd feel. She had never wanted a family, children, the things most women took for granted. And what *was* this child, this thing that was growing in her belly? What monstrous horror might she give birth to?

Despite the fear, however, Laura felt surprisingly calm. It seemed that all was unfolding as it should and that she had a part to play in something far greater than she could ever have imagined. If she caught herself trembling at the thought of what might be, she would sit quietly and let the euphoria wash over her, and all seemed well again.

She would leave O'Shea to read the notes and decide what was to be done. It seemed unimportant to her right now. There was only one thing truly worrying her above all else. Tomorrow, she would have to tell O'Shea that this less than holy priest was carrying a less than holy child.

FOURTEEN

"I was afraid of this!" O'Shea looked as if his world had just caved in about him.

"You thought this might happen?" Laura was incredulous. "You thought it but it never occurred to you to say a word?"

"Why would either of you listen to me?"

"Either of us? I don't understand."

O'Shea sighed deeply before replying. "I'm not a total fool. I see how you both behave when the other's around. I may be old but I'm not blind."

"Wait!" At last Laura realised what O'Shea meant. "You think Larry is the father?" She laughed but there was no humour in it.

O'Shea glanced at her for the first time since she had told him she was pregnant. She preferred the term, 'with child', but it sounded too biblical, although she could think of one New Testament woman who might know exactly what she was going through.

"You mean someone else fathered it? My God, Laura, you're certainly not the woman I thought you were." He looked as if he might dissolve into tears.

"Dermot? Dermot, look at me." He'd turned his head away to hide his moist eyes. Now he turned back to look directly at Laura, disappointment adding years to his weathered face. "Dermot, I haven't slept with *any* man. Do you hear me? Have you forgotten my confession to you so soon?"

He stared at her. "You're telling me," he faltered, "you're telling me the *thing* in St. Jude's is the father? You want me to believe…"

"Dermot, you're the only person who must believe

me. It could so easily have been Larry's but it isn't. Larry and I never … I'm not proud of myself but I'm telling you the truth. Besides…"

"Besides?" O'Shea was having difficulty taking in what Laura was saying.

"I *know* that thing, whatever it was, impregnated me. Don't ask me how I know, I just do. I can feel it – its presence – like a shield. It was deliberate, and I'm now carrying its offspring."

"So, you're saying…"

"Yes!" Laura almost shouted. "Yes, Dermot. If you could once believe that the Holy Spirit could impregnate a young girl in Judea over two thousand years ago…" She lowered her voice. "…then you have no choice but to believe that something evil is capable of doing the same today."

He remained silent, considering her words. Despite the absurdity of Laura's claim, he felt inclined to believe her. She could have lied, said it was Larry's child, and he would have accepted that, so why pretend the father was some invisible entity. Neither of them were gullible fools and Laura had nothing to gain from such a pretence but derision.

"All right, supposing, just supposing, I was to go along with what you've told me," said O'Shea, "the next question has to be, what do you want to do about it?"

"I have the feeling that what *I* want is not going to have much bearing on what happens from now on."

It was after New Year before Laura met up again with the two men. She'd played upon having to write inspiring sermons to herald in the New Year, but the truth was much more personal. She needed to come to terms with what was happening to her. She also needed a break from O'Shea. She tried not to notice the curious looks he unconsciously gave her. Maybe he was still weighing up whether she was telling him the truth.

Part of her rejoiced that she was carrying a life within her, but there were times when the realisation of who the father was broke in on her thoughts. The feeling of well-being that had calmed her at the outset of her pregnancy now frequently deserted her and she'd find herself trembling and unable to cope. It was then that she fell on her knees and prayed, begging for both a solution and absolution, an end to this nightmare she was being forced to live. But no deliverance came. She'd be left feeling let down, even betrayed, her weeping prayers producing nothing apart from puffy eyes and a headache. Where had God and his angels been when she'd cried out for them in St. Jude's? Once or twice, she even found herself directing her pleas not to them, but to an equally ancient entity, one that had a vested interest in keeping her alive and well. At least for the time being.

It was whilst she was sat in her room, going over everything yet again but resolving nothing, that she heard raised voices from Mrs Lyle's living room and the wail of a fire engine racing through the quiet village.

She called down from the landing. "Mrs Lyle?"

Getting no reply she raced down the stairs, nearly knocking her landlady off her feet.

"There you are. I was just about to call you. Your Mr Larry has just called. The church is on fire."

Leonard Pargeter couldn't rid himself of the thought.

However hard he tried, it just kept coming back. He blamed himself for the crippled church and the mysterious death of the vagrant. If he'd known of the other deaths, he would undoubtedly have taken on the blame for them as well. He'd neglected his duty and the tree needed to be appeased. Perhaps it was not too late to put things right.

With the coffin gone, the heavy padlocks had been removed and there was no-one to stop him. The electricity was still off in the church but Pargeter knew where the candles were, and felt his way carefully round the back of the church to where the spare Bibles and hymnbooks were stacked. There was no moon to outline his path with its cold light. He moved slowly, fearful of falling. As he shuffled forward, he couldn't see the can of petrol, and his foot caught against it, sending it clattering across the floor, its unsecured cap rolling under the pews. He hadn't stepped within St. Jude's for months and was unsure where the floor had caved in. Although confused, he was aware that if he fell into the crypt, it could be days before he was found and by then it would be too late. Survival would be unlikely; if the fall didn't kill him, the cold would.

He slid his hand onto the shelf between the books and two frayed hassocks waiting to be repaired. The box of candles was still there. He removed several, along with the matches. Lighting one of the candles, he made his way forward, carefully avoiding the slick where Clements' generator had stood. The smell of spilled petrol seemed stronger now.

Reaching the pulpit, he placed the candles about it and lit them, illuminating the area around the libation tube. He must not fail. Not this time.

Kneeling, he rolled back his shirtsleeve and ripped

the bandages from his arm. From his trouser pocket he produced a small knife, its blade shimmering in the flickering light. Very calmly and precisely, he sliced open his flesh and held the wound against the tube opening, rocking gently back and forth as his blood trickled down to the crypt beneath.

When the task was done, Pargeter rose unsteadily to his feet, blood still dripping from the wound. He felt light-headed and gloriously happy. The tree had been fed and things would once again be as they were before, he was sure of it. As he staggered back from the pulpit, his arm caught two of the candles, knocking them to the ground. He was surprised how far one of them rolled, its flame igniting the trail of freshly-spilled petrol. It seemed suddenly that the flames sought everything that was flammable and Pargeter reeled about, vainly trying to stop the spread.

By the time Laura reached the church, fire fighters were guiding the bewildered man out through the smoke-filled entrance. After tending to his wound, one of them wrapped a blanket around his thin shoulders and waited with him for an ambulance to arrive.

As Laura watched, serpentine flames reflected in the stained glass windows until they cracked and buckled from the heat. In a scene reminiscent of the London Blitz, the firefighters battled in vain against the inferno.

Laura crossed to where Pargeter was being helped into the ambulance.

"This wasn't meant to happen," he muttered. "I'd fed it. This wasn't meant to be."

It was clear he was suffering from severe shock and couldn't fully grasp what was happening. He'd received burns to his arms and legs but was lucky to be alive.

It seemed that most of the villagers had gathered to gape. Laura was soon joined by Larry and O'Shea. In silence, the three of them watched St. Jude's burn, and not one of them felt any remorse. They each had encountered evil within its stone walls, and each of them believed this was a fitting end for whatever lived there.

When the roof finally caved in amidst a fountain of sparks, the bystanders knew there was no hope of saving the church. Great billowing clouds of smoke coiled upwards from the blackened shell. They watched the small pinpricks of red against the night sky, before gradually making their way back to their homes.

"They say fire is cleansing," said Larry, the first to break the silence.

"Not if Hell is anything to go by," retorted O'Shea. Then, after a moment, he turned back to 'The Peal Of Bells', adding, "I need a drink."

Laura felt sick as she surveyed the burnt-out remains of the church. The charred wood of the rood screen still smouldered but little else remained. The stench of sodden debris churned her already delicate stomach. There was nothing left to save, but that, she thought, may be just as well. She'd had the chalice, crucifix and other valuables stored in the church hall for the services there, primarily to avoid repeated trips to the church. That would be one consolation for the diocese, albeit a small one.

A sound made her turn. Even now, with St. Jude's in ruins about her, it had the ability to make her nervous. She half-feared something would rise from its ashes like an unholy phoenix and then entwine itself about her with coils of darkness. O'Shea was standing a few feet from her, hands thrust deep into the pockets of his overcoat.

"A few hours ago it was a raging inferno, yet it still manages to chill the bones," he said. He crunched forward to where Laura was standing. "Did you get any sleep?"

"Not much," she confessed. 'Not any,' she thought.

"Come on, I'll buy you breakfast." He took her arm and led her through the wreckage.

"I don't think I can face food," she said, once they were free of the churchyard.

"The church may have gone but its legacy hasn't," replied O'Shea. "You should be eating for two, remember?" His words pulled Laura up short.

"What happens now?"

"It looks as if you'll be holding services in the church hall for a while longer," smiled O'Shea.

"To me, Dermot. What happens to *me*?"

"Well, that's something neither of us knows the answer to," he said gently, "but, whatever it is, I have a feeling you'll manage just fine."

Despite his words of comfort to Laura, O'Shea was worried. If he was to believe her, then whatever she was carrying was evil, at least in part. If anything, he was more mentally torn than she was. Dare he, in all conscience, allow her to give birth to what might possibly be the Antichrist? Would Laura even survive the birth of such a creature?

He had spent anxious hours going down every avenue of thought but he was still none the wiser. He'd even tried praying. All that achieved was a feeling of hypocrisy and deeper confusion.

He'd toyed with the idea of killing the child, but that would demand courage far greater than his. It was, after all, half Laura – or was she merely a host in which it grew? To prevent it from taking its first breath would mean killing Laura as well, which would be like killing his own niece. No, he couldn't go through that again. But to wait until it was born, would that be any easier? He doubted it, and it would no doubt mean he'd have to fight Laura as well as her demonic offspring. He felt as if he'd been catapulted into a horror film, with one half of his brain screaming in terror whilst the other half whispered, 'It's only a movie'. Reality was threatening his sanity, he thought, or was it the impossible threatening his reality. More cerebral circles into which his mind was inexorably drawn.

All he wanted to do was lose himself in a bottle of whiskey, but O'Shea knew he should stay strong for Laura's sake. He knew he was drinking too much. The new determination he'd found after Graham's death had been dashed by Laura's disclosure, and his greatest fear wasn't whatever it was that had defiled Laura, but his own lack of strength to oppose it.

Laura pulled up in front of the nursing home. It was a converted manor house, set in spacious grounds on the outskirts of Cambridge, and might have looked overly-imposing had it not been for a sunny aspect that softened its austerity. Early crocuses and snowdrops were peeping through the green lawns, and she tried to imagine how it would look in a couple of months when spring painted it with all its colours.

She knew that Social Services were working at

getting Leonard Pargeter to stay here indefinitely. He was deemed a danger to himself, and Laura, for one, would breathe a sigh of relief knowing he was properly cared for.

The matron, a pleasant woman in her fifties, led Laura along what seemed like endless corridors to Pargeter's room.

"He's shown no signs of violence," said the matron, "but we won't introduce him to the other residents just yet. He seems very confused. Is that normal?"

"Lately, yes, it would seem so." Laura felt the need to explain. "I've only become the Rector of St. Jude's recently and Mr Pargeter was no longer active with church duties."

"Ah, that would explain it."

"I'm sorry, explain what?" asked Laura.

"He keeps mumbling about not doing his duty one minute, then about doing it the next. It must be playing on his mind."

They'd reached Pargeter's door.

"He should be resting. He was put to bed an hour ago. I wouldn't normally disturb residents during their afternoon rest but…"

She had opened the door and stood back for Laura to enter. As the door swung wide, the scene that greeted them produced a choking scream from the matron. Laura had to grab the door for support.

Pargeter's room was bathed in blood. Sweeping red arcs decorated the walls, carpet, curtains and bed, and Pargeter's lifeless body lay crumpled on the floor.

Whilst the matron rang for help, Laura steadied herself and stepped forward to the body. Rigor was already setting in, confirming he'd been dead for some time, possibly shortly after he'd been left to sleep. Her first impression was that he'd been killed by whatever murdered the vagrant, but leaning towards him she saw that the wounds were self-inflicted. Whether he had meant to kill himself, no-one would know. It would seem he'd taken his own life whilst mentally unbalanced, but his death may well have been a final attempted act of appeasement. He had ripped his wrist open, apparently with a shard from his broken teacup.

Instead of returning straight away to Adderidge, Laura detoured into Cambridge. She knew she was pregnant and Doctor Reynalds had confirmed it, but she needed to see proof. She didn't like Cambridge but needed the anonymity of a city. There were plenty of chemists to choose from, and she wasn't sure if that was a sign of the populace's ill health or the reverse, merely an indication of society's paranoia.

Having picked a chemist at random, she hadn't expected the choice of pregnancy kits on offer. Although she suspected they were all equally reliable, she finally resorted to asking a female assistant and coming away with the most expensive.

Not wanting to wait until she returned to Adderidge, she headed for the nearest hotel. Availing herself of the Ladies Room, she followed the test instructions. Positive! Laura had the sudden urge to cry, although she couldn't tell if it was from relief or regret.

With her heart racing overtime, she sat in the lounge and ordered a pot of tea. When the girl carried the tray over, Laura slid her hands under her jacket to hide their trembling.

On the journey home, she tried to sift through her

feelings but disbelief and horror co-existed with awe and excitement. Having got to know Mrs Lyle's routine, Laura felt safe in taking a long luxurious soak without fear of being accused of hogging the bathroom. She needed to wash the day away. She wondered why everything seemed so normal when she knew that couldn't be further from the truth.

Later, sitting with O'Shea, she tried in vain to drive the sight of Pargeter's pallid features from her mind. The look on his face had been one of total adoration. Had he seen something in those last moments as the blood drained from his tortured body?

"I'm returning to Cambridge tomorrow," announced O'Shea, breaking into her reverie.

"What?" gasped Laura. "Dermot, you can't desert me now."

"I'm not deserting you, Laura. I need to catch up on a few things. The university has been very good about my extended vacation but I don't want them to get too used to doing without me." He gave a mirthless chuckle.

"Dermot, I need you here." Laura was devastated. She knew she was being unreasonable but it felt like a betrayal.

"I'll be back, I promise, before..." He stopped himself. "When are you telling Larry? Or aren't you going to?"

"Not yet. He'll have to know eventually, but I need to think of how to break it to him."

"He'll take it hard, you know," said O'Shea.

"I know."

It had been worrying Laura. At least O'Shea had heard her confession and knew what had taken place in St. Jude's. He had a better idea than Larry of what they were up against. No, there'd be time enough later.

As if heralded by the mention of his name, Larry appeared and joined them.

"Hey, I've been looking through some of that Cook guy's notes. Did you know there were stories of a dragon around here?"

"A dragon? No, I'd not heard that," said Laura.

"Well, they called it a 'wyrm' – W Y R M. It was supposed to live underground and needed regular supplies of virgins' blood." Seeing their astonished faces, he added, "Just kidding about the virgins, but it was given blood. We're talking late medieval times here. There's no mention of it since the fourteen hundreds."

"Maybe they found a more efficient way of feeding it," suggested O'Shea, not all together jokingly.

"Of course," continued Larry, "it may not be linked to St. Jude's – it just says Norfolk – but Cook thought there's enough to suggest the possibility and I agree with him. Apparently, it was the church's duty to keep the worm, sorry, wyrm, appeased," he said, pronouncing wyrm like wee-rum. "Sound familiar? And I'll tell you something else Cook found. It's from Indian Brahmin mythology, where a woman gives birth to a snake." He didn't notice the looks his friends exchanged as he fished a couple of folded sheets of paper from his pocket. "When it grew, the mother wanted to find it a wife, but the father said, 'I would have to go to the depths of Hell and beseech Pasuki, the King of Snakes, for who else, you fool, would give his daughter in marriage to a snake?'" Larry looked up. "You see, snake, Hell, the connection with evil is all over the world."

"Larry," cut in Laura, "Dermot is going back to Cambridge tomorrow."

"Just for a few days," added O'Shea. "Regrettable, but there's stuff I need to attend to. You'll keep on eye on things here, won't you?" Turning to Laura, he added, "I'm sure Larry isn't going anywhere. His journalistic nose is quivering like a bloodhound's."

"Sure, I'm hanging around," said Larry, looking from one to the other of his companions and trying to figure out what the fuss was about. "Although I'm not sure there's much more to find, especially now St. Jude's is burned out. Still, I'm finding weirdo Cook's file pretty addictive bedside reading."

"What else have you found?" asked Laura, relieved to bring his attention back to Cook's notes.

"This and that."

"Have you come across anything that might be of use?" asked O'Shea.

"It's all of use," said Larry, with a grin. "You just have to know how to use it."

"Whatever we're dealing with here, I can't fight this alone," said Laura.

"How does anyone fight it?" replied O'Shea. "How do you destroy a body like the church?"

It was Larry who broke the ensuing silence. "Like anything else, you go straight for the heart."

"It's not the church we need to fight, but a canker within it," said Laura, "one I doubt many people are even aware of."

FIFTEEN

A second body had been found in the vicinity of the docks. A security camera had caught a driverless forklift truck impaling one of the security guards and crushing him against a container. No-one had been able to work out how it happened. The bloodied container was now on its way to Vatican City and, according to the paperwork, contained an ancient religious artefact.

Benvenuti was thankful that the shipment wasn't further delayed. People were getting restless and he needed to get his charge safely to Rome before there were any more accidents. Up until now, he'd got away with waving his Vatican diplomatic passport to avoid close scrutiny of his cargo.

He breathed a sigh of relief as he watched Southampton grow smaller on the skyline. The swell of the English Channel was like the rise and fall of a woman's breasts and it comforted him. For a second, he thought of Laura and then, pushing her image aside, he concentrated on the task ahead and other pleasures closer to home.

With O'Shea back in Cambridge, Laura felt a loneliness envelope her, but it didn't last. She was aware of the child growing inside her, her child. Whatever the father might be, half of it was hers. There was one brief moment of desperation, when the only answer seemed to be to take her own life or that of the baby. However, she doubted the father would allow her that option; in fact, she felt sure of it.

Somehow that thought, however bizarre, comforted her. She wasn't alone. She doubted she'd ever be alone again.

She sat with Larry in 'The Peal Of Bells', which now felt very empty without O'Shea's blustering presence.

"Quiet, isn't it?" said Larry. "Without him here. Even when he wasn't speaking, he had the ability to make himself heard."

"Yes, he did," smiled Laura, already missing him.

They'd finished their drinks and, without O'Shea pushing for another, neither felt like making the evening last.

"I'll walk you back," said Larry.

"I'll be all right," said Laura automatically, then realised she'd be glad of his company, and was pleased when he replied that the fresh air would do him good.

It seemed odd, walking past the charred remains of St. Jude's. A full moon lit up the ruins like a Hammer film set, but they had lost their power to terrify. Even when clouds scudded across the moon, shifting and changing the shadows, it seemed to be nothing more than it was – an empty shell.

"It's gone!" said Laura.

"That's for certain," said Larry, believing she referred to the building.

Laura knew he hadn't caught her meaning but then, why should he? She didn't explain. Whatever had been beneath St. Jude's was no longer there, she was sure of it. She didn't know how she knew, but suspected it had something to do with the baby she was carrying. With its father no longer close, she felt hope soar briefly before she realised, with deadly certainty, that somewhere down the line it would return for its child.

Larry stood at the churchyard wall. He'd declined Laura's offer of coffee, but neither a nightcap nor retiring to bed appealed. He wasn't tired and felt caught in limbo. Half of him wanted to return to London and normality, but the other half didn't want to leave Laura here alone.

The pitiful remains before him should, he felt, give him some form of closure. He'd forcefully pushed the events in St. Jude's to the back of his mind, but they kept slithering forward again. When they did, his body remembered and responded, leaving him consumed by feelings of desire, guilt and regret. Try as he might to convince himself whatever he'd encountered was merely a product of his own twisted imagination, he never truly wavered from believing he'd encountered evil in its most primitive form.

A noise from the charred wood and stones startled him. Rooted to the spot, he strained his eyes as he tried to locate the direction of the sound, every muscle readied for flight.

Suddenly, there was movement and a scavenging fox appeared. He watched as it moved between the gravestones, pausing to dig in the thin grass before disappearing over the far wall.

Larry let out the breath he'd been involuntarily holding. Strangely, his relief failed to lift the feeling of misgiving that twisted in his stomach, and he hurried back to the pub. Maybe that nightcap was a good idea, after all.

O'Shea had needed breathing space. His thoughts were in turmoil and he didn't know what to do. It was an unusual state for him to be in and he wasn't enjoying the experience, but then, it was an unusual situation all round. To add insult to injury, he found the university had coped perfectly well in his absence. No-one seemed to even notice he'd returned.

He knew he couldn't leave Laura to face the future alone but, for now, she had Larry, that's if he stuck around once she told him about the baby. It was a lot to expect any young man to believe if he hadn't encountered the evil first hand.

O'Shea was forced to admit that he felt resentment for Laura's predicament and, having no source to vent his anger upon, he unfairly found himself blaming her. He knew this feeling would pass, but he'd needed to put distance between them for both their sakes.

Firmly placing his empty glass on the bar, O'Shea left the pub. His car was parked at the far side of the car park and now stood alone, most of the other vehicles having already left. He knew he shouldn't drive, but he'd done a lot of things lately that he shouldn't. Whilst he was fumbling in his overcoat pocket for his keys, for an instant he caught sight of movement in his car. He froze, but it was only the reflection of clouds being driven across the moon by a brisk north-easterly wind. No, he was alone. He'd always been alone. Funny, he didn't feel drunk. Mercifully, he didn't feel anything.

Turning on the ignition, he realised he didn't know where he was heading, but it seemed that had been the case all his life, or at least since leaving the seminary. He'd had no direction. Maybe that was how it was supposed to be and why he'd ended up here.

Reaching the T-junction, he turned left for no other reason than it was easiest. He didn't want to think. The headlights from what little oncoming traffic there was refracted off his windscreen as the wipers battled the rain. What had been little more than an inconvenience when he left the pub had turned into a heavy downpour. He automatically increased the wiper speed.

Stopping at traffic lights, he rubbed the steamed windows with his sleeve. There was something comforting about sitting in a warm car as the engine purred. Seemingly from nowhere, tears filled O'Shea's eyes and rolled down his cheeks. "Damn!" he said, and brushed them away. The roads were quiet at this hour and he watched the lights change from red to amber to green. He put his foot on the accelerator and pulled forward. He didn't even register what was happening as the speeding black car hit his right hand side with enough force to send him spinning across the empty highway.

The day hung like grey bunting from the rooftops, rain dripping into puddles, the wind whipping awnings like ships' sails, drenching passers-by in collected water.

Negotiating the miles of corridors and lifts within Addenbrooke's Hospital gave people time to adjust before and after visiting the patients. Laura's footsteps sounded brisk and confident as she hurried along their straight paths and read off the various wards within individual areas. Nothing could have been further from the way she felt.

O'Shea was in a small side ward and the bed next to him was empty. She was relieved that she'd be able to talk freely with him. A nurse intercepted her before she got to O'Shea's side.

"Excuse me, are you family?"

Laura had anticipated this. "Yes, I'm his niece.

When I rang the reception they said it would be all right for me to visit." How easily the well-rehearsed lie tripped off her tongue.

"That's fine, but please don't stay too long. He needs to rest." Those words must be indelibly imprinted on a nurse's soul, thought Laura, along with asking people to leave and 'I'm sorry'.

"Laura?" O'Shea heard Laura's voice and tried to turn. As she took his hand, he let out a low moan, relaxing back against his bolstered pillows. "How did you know...?"

"The police informed the university and they rang 'The Peal Of Bells', knowing you'd been staying there. They took a message and told Larry, who told me." She smiled, though it was an effort, faced with O'Shea's obvious pain. "God, you look a mess!"

"You look pretty good yourself," he retorted, "and it's not like you to take the Lord's name in vain." It was obvious it was an effort for him to talk. "I'm sorry I can't get up." There wasn't much of him that didn't seem bandaged, plastered or taped.

"You could have been killed, Dermot."

"Yes, but I wasn't. I think it just wanted me out of the way."

"It? You think this was deliberate?"

"Don't you?"

Laura had to admit she had immediately jumped to that conclusion, either that or...

"I wasn't drunk, if that's what you're wondering," continued O'Shea. "Yes, I'd had a few, but you know what I can down in an evening and I wasn't even close. The roads were practically empty and this car came from nowhere."

"And vanished into nowhere too, I'm told," said

Laura. "A hit and run."

She'd pulled up a chair and continued to hold his hand, surprised at how fond she'd grown of this gruff Irishman. She could feel the tears welling in her eyes, knowing how close she'd been to losing him.

O'Shea moved his head to look at her.

"Now, wipe your eyes, girl. It'll take a lot to knock me off my perch. But it does mean I'll be laid up for some time. I'd appreciate some good books if you can manage it. If I'm forced to read what the hospital library has to offer I really might give up the ghost."

Laura couldn't help but chuckle. O'Shea became serious again.

"Now, I have a favour to ask." He put his hand up to silence her response. "I have no intention of going anywhere but, just in case I'm not consulted on the matter, I want you to grant me the same service I granted you. It's been a long time, but I want you to hear my confession."

"But, Dermot…"

"No buts! Neither of us is averse to bending the rules and I might not ask again. You can't deny me the right to clear my conscience. There's no-one listening, except perhaps God, and I promise not to list every sin and keep you here for a week."

"Only a week?" said Laura, smiling.

By the time O'Shea had finally finished unburdening himself, his voice had sunk to little more than a whisper.

"Now, you must go and leave an old man to sleep. Besides, you have a job to do. You know your scriptures, Laura, better than I, I suspect. 'And the great dragon was cast out, that old serpent, called the Devil, and Satan, which deceiveth the whole world'."

175

"'He was cast out into the earth, and his angels were cast out with him.'" Laura finished the quote. "Can that really be what we're up against?" Even now, she found it hard to believe in a Devil.

"Whatever it is, Laura, it's evil and you may be the only person who can stop it. The Devil seems to be doing a damned good job convincing the world he doesn't exist."

"What makes you think a woman can defeat an evil that's lasted millennia?"

"Maybe because you *are* a woman or maybe because you carry that child within you. Remember Laura, there isn't a creature alive – and we are dealing with a creature of sorts, make no mistake about it – that isn't vulnerable when the life of its offspring is threatened. Think about it, Laura. I can't ask you to do anything more than that."

"Dermot, I have to go away for awhile." She spoke the words softly.

O'Shea took a shuddering breath. It was obvious even this caused him pain. He nodded, his eyes closed to hide his feelings.

"I understand. I wanted to be with you. When the time comes. I don't know if I'll be able to now."

Laura didn't confide her plans to him. He had to get well. That was all that mattered and worrying about her wouldn't help him heal.

"I know," she whispered.

It was obvious he needed to rest. Laura leant over him and gently kissed his forehead. Without opening his eyes, he smiled as she crept silently from his room.

"Do you think he'll pull through?" asked Larry, when he and Laura met for lunch.

"Physically? Yes. Addenbrooke's is a first class hospital. Spiritually, I'm not so sure."

"I don't follow."

"Something came close to ending his life, something stronger than him, and that might be something he has difficulty coming to terms with."

"The Catholic Church is a mighty powerful adversary. Many great men have tried in the past and failed."

"You forget, I'm a woman!" laughed Laura.

"Unfortunately, that's something I can't forget." Larry winked. "What has the Catholic Church got against women anyway?"

"It's not just the Catholic Church," said Laura. "Martin Luther said, and I quote, 'If women get tired and die of bearing children there is no harm in that; let them die as long as they bear, they were made for that'. And only a few hundred years ago, a C of E bishop said that women are intrinsically inferior in excellence, imbecile by sex and nature, weak in body, inconstant in mind and imperfect and infirm in character."

"Doesn't that make you want to give up?"

"Not at all. I simply intend to prove them wrong."

"Any more quotes like that up your sleeve?"

"More than I'd care to have, I'm afraid. Did you know that even today the Church of England cited menstrual impurities and women's inherent inferiority as valid reasons to exclude women from the priesthood? We made it, despite that." She fell silent as Larry strove to find words of comfort, and failed. Then she continued, "The Bible was a great piece of misogynist propaganda. Look at the Eden story. When the woman behaved in accordance with the desires she'd been given, God condemned her. And then, of course, you've got the misconceptions brought about by poor translation from the original Aramaic. The witch of Endor was originally 'woman'."

"How come you ever went into the Church?" asked Larry in amazement.

"For the teachings of the Christ," she replied. "They're still hidden in there somewhere. And he respected women. It's the church that's tried to grind us underfoot and I've had enough of eating dust. This woman is ready to fight back."

Larry grinned. "I was hoping you'd say that."

"The church isn't evil, Larry. Whatever denomination you follow, it stems from Jesus Christ, but something is using it, something ancient and evil, and it's time it was dragged into the light of day."

The shadow of a lone leaf fluttered over the sunlit ground like an early butterfly. A light wind was stripping away any remaining dead foliage from the bare branches and trees were showing signs of new growth. As Laura walked along the banks of the Cam, she placed her hand over her belly. No swelling there to notice, but she knew the baby was growing too. Soon, it would begin to show.

St. Jude's was nothing more than a quiet ruin. The sarcophagus and whatever it had housed was now safe in the confines of Vatican City, and Italian Catholic clergy were presumably feeding whatever had sought blood down through the centuries.

She'd thought hard and long of what to do. Today, as she'd sat with O'Shea, she'd finally realised that hiding away wasn't the answer. She could kiss her career goodbye, that was certain. She'd lost count of how many times she'd wondered what she would give birth to, whether she would survive or if she would become expendable once the child was born.

She needed answers if she was to protect herself and the baby she was carrying. She needed to go to Rome.

PART TWO

REVELATION

The children looked forward to the cooler autumn weather. Penance, by its very nature, was something to be endured, but the heat of the summer months made it so much harder to bear. Going without water on the hottest days had brought them near to fainting, and the tight cords they'd tied around their waists gouged painfully deep into their heat-swollen bodies, their skin already burning from nettle stings.

They crouched together, keeping an ever-watchful eye on the sheep, and waited.

Lucia reached out and took the hands of her cousins, Jacinta and Francisco. They had been told they were to be given something very important, a message, so they knew she would come.

As clouds began to gather over Cova da Iria, it looked as if it might rain. The sheep began to bleat and the children huddled closer. Then, as a shaft of sunlight burst through, they looked up.

It was Lucia who spoke.

"She's here!"

FATHER OF LIES

ROME

"For such men are false apostles, deceitful workmen, disguising themselves as apostles of Christ. And no wonder, for even Satan disguises himself as an angel of light. So it is not strange if his servants also disguise themselves as servants of righteousness. Their end will correspond to their deeds."
2 CORINTHIANS 11:13-15

"Hell is empty and all the devils are here."
WILLIAM SHAKESPEARE

SIXTEEN

It was blustery and cold when Laura stepped from the plane at Fiumicino Airport. She had never been abroad before and flying had left her a little disorientated. Sucking a sweet and sticking her fingers in her ears hadn't helped them to pop and she could barely hear a thing.

Following the other passengers, she made her way to the stream of taxis and masquerading private vehicles. Picking a yellow one with visible ID and a meter, she gave the driver the Trastevere address where she'd be staying. It was in an old quarter of the city, central but small, which suited both her pocket and inclination.

Larry had seen her off from Gatwick and she knew he didn't want her to go.

"This is downright insanity," he'd told her more

than once. "Why not just forget the whole thing?" He'd wanted first to stop her, then to accompany her, but Laura knew she needed to do this alone. She didn't know what she'd find, if anything, but the baby wasn't going to just go away and she needed answers.

The small family-run hotel was just to her liking, with hanging baskets of vivid purple flowers clashing with the green, white and red flag over the door. It seemed spring had arrived earlier here than in East Anglia.

Manuela Franci greeted her in the hall that served as reception and, after getting Laura to register, called her husband, Cesare, to carry the suitcase up to her room.

"We hope you will enjoy your stay in our beautiful city," said Cesare, in perfect English. "Just ask if you need anything."

Laura turned towards the open shuttered windows of her room. They looked out across the rooftops and down onto a flourishing roof garden below her, belonging to the house next door.

"I'm sure I shall be very comfortable. Thank you." She smiled.

The room was small and cheery, not too cluttered and, set at the back of the building, was relatively quiet.

Laura sat on the bed and rang Larry.

"Yes, safe and sound… No, I didn't take the train… Taxi straight to the door… Yes, I'll call you tomorrow… Who made you my keeper?"

Smiling, she finished the call. Larry had gone back to his bedsit. There had seemed little point in him remaining in Adderidge since, as he put it, 'all the action had moved on'. He'd made her promise to give him daily updates, though she wondered if there'd be anything to report.

Rome would have to wait. She'd hardly slept the previous night and was exhausted. After booking a light supper with Signora Franci, she lay down and was asleep before her head touched the pillow.

When she awoke a couple of hours later, she wondered where she was. The light was fading and her surroundings were strange. Gradually her memory returned and she wanted nothing more than to bury her head in the pillow and sleep on till daylight.

She checked her watch. Almost time for supper but just enough time to unpack. She took her clerical white collar from a pocket in the case and stared at it for a moment, before shutting it away in a drawer, along with the title of Reverend. For a while she needed to be simply Laura Coatman again. She wondered how safe it was to walk about the city at night. No, she must curb her impatience. Hunger pangs were making themselves felt. She thought of O'Shea telling her she needed to eat for two and hoped he was all right. Eating for two she might be, but she had a sneaky feeling a large dish of Signora Franci's spaghetti might just satisfy them both.

Larry was far from happy about Laura going to Rome but she'd been adamant and he had no way of preventing her. When he'd asked her to call him daily, she'd argued that it would be too costly and that he was being overprotective.

"If anything should happen to you, O'Shea would never forgive me," he'd said.

Laura had rather hoped it was because Larry would never forgive himself.

He still had the folder of Cook's notes, so decided it was time to knuckle down and finish reading them. The more he read, the more uneasy he felt. Not only had Cook researched the serpent in connection with St. Jude's, but he'd added accounts of serpents, both within the church and in other religions, with particular reference to the less obvious or rarely seen.

There was a photograph stapled to one sheet of notes, depicting the undulating snake on the side of the Chichen Itza pyramid in the Yucatan, Mexico. At the spring and autumn equinoxes, the sun would highlight this plumed serpent whereas, at other times, it seemed no more than the play of light and shadow on the stone steps. To the Mayans, it represented Kukulkan; to the bloodthirsty Aztecs it was Quetzalcoatl. Another illustration was of Quetzalcoatl from the Codex Telleriano-Remensis, depicting the snake devouring a man headfirst.

The Mayans, along with the Chinese and other races, used the representation of a snake biting its own tail for the Milky Way Galaxy. In fact snakes – or serpents – cropped up in most of the great religions of the world. Another picture, this time from Cambodia, showed the Great Sun Buddha seated in the coils of a snake.

What was it, Larry wondered, that made this such a worldwide symbol, often dating back long before there was communication between the continents. According to Cook, the first sighting of the Loch Ness Monster was right back in 565 AD. He flipped through page after page of photos and text, coming to an abrupt halt at a picture of a beautiful serpent door handle. What he found hard to believe was that it was located at St. Mary's Cathedral, San Francisco. Why, he wondered, was it in such prominence if it was linked to Satan? Seeing the snake as part of a representation of the Eden story was one thing, but this was on its own. Was this what Cook was referring to when he alluded to things getting interesting, he wondered.

He had no idea just how interesting. As he read on through the night, he grew more and more concerned. He feared Laura wasn't merely taking a close look at the Mother Church but was walking directly into the lethal jaws of a wily and age-old serpent.

Benvenuti had spies everywhere, or so it seemed to the other members of the Ordo Autem Serpens. They were quite sure that his sources relayed information through fear, not because they had any desire to help. It was therefore no surprise when he reported Laura Coatman's arrival in the Holy City.

"It is not totally unexpected," said Cardinal Scappucci when Benvenuti conveyed the news. "She seems to be an intelligent woman, so I'm not surprised she followed the coffin. She's curious."

"What do you want me to do?" asked Benvenuti, hoping that he would be given the task of showing Laura where curiosity led.

"Just keep an eye on her. Remake her acquaintance and show her our beautiful city. The chances are, with your guidance, she will find nothing, in which case she can return to England with our blessing."

"And if she does find out something?" prompted Benvenuti, hopefully.

"Ah, then it is you, Benvenuti, who will have our blessing to see to it that Laura Coatman learns the error of her ways, in whatever way you see most fit."

Benvenuti felt truly blessed. To do something one wanted was one thing, but to do it with the full permission of his superiors was almost enough for him to get down on his knees and offer thankful prayer.

Laura woke to brilliant sunshine and the sound of church bells. All the horrors associated with St. Jude's seemed so very far away. She would almost have said she felt reborn but a sideways glance in the mirror assured her that was far from the case.

She hadn't made any plans. This was unknown territory and she'd begin as any tourist would; she'd take in the sights of Rome, acquaint herself with the enemy's turf. She didn't fear the church, but there was an old evil hidden here amongst the grandeur and the ruins. Armed with a guidebook she'd bought at the airport, she stepped out into warm sunlight.

Laura soon discovered that the best way to see Rome was on foot. Leaving her clerical collar behind, she'd dressed in a light floral dress that made her look like any other tourist. She didn't want to draw attention to her presence here but to move incognito amongst the crowds. There was something of interest to see everywhere, carved keystones above every doorway, and church after church around every corner. Some streets were cobbled and her feet began to ache with all the unaccustomed walking. The buildings rose up around her, seemingly colour-washed in ochre, salmon and soft warm browns, their shuttered windows looking out onto narrow streets and open piazzas. Thanks to what seemed like endless steps, she also realised that she wasn't as fit as she'd previously imagined. Laura was lost in thought as she followed the routes taken by millions of tourists and pilgrims to the Holy City. No matter how often she relived the events that had brought her here, she still had no answers and couldn't think of any way of finding them.

When Benvenuti stepped from a doorway directly into her path, she almost fell over him. Her first instinct was to flee, survival at its most primal level, but instead she welcomed his arrival. His appearance seemed like the answer to her unuttered prayer. Nothing like facing a demon head on, she thought, and maybe this was the chance she had been waiting for. He certainly couldn't have arrived at a more opportune moment.

"Why, Reverend Coatman, this is extraordinary. What are you doing here?"

Laura couldn't believe it was a coincidence that the one person she knew in Rome should cross her path on her first full day in the city. She realised she was standing like an idiot with her mouth open.

"Monsignor Benvenuti! How amazing!" She couldn't think what else to say, then pulling herself together, she added, "I'm taking a short sabbatical. Did you hear about St. Jude's?"

"St. Jude's? Why, has something happened?" He was well versed in the art of lying but suspected Laura knew he was fully aware of St. Jude's fate. "Please, why not bring me up to date over a cup of coffee? Shall we?"

He led her across the square to a small coffee house with tables and chairs spilling onto the pavement. The aroma of fresh coffee billowed from the doorway as she sat at one of the mosaic-topped tables. Benvenuti caught the attention of an over-worked waiter and looked suitably thoughtful as Laura related the bare details of the fire. By the time she finished, she was almost convinced that the concern he showed was genuine. Almost.

"How long will you be in our beautiful city?," he asked.

"Two or three weeks," she replied. "Maybe a month. I needed a complete break before returning to my church duties."

"I understand. Perhaps you would do me the honour of letting me show you around? There is so much more to Rome than the usual tourist haunts. It would be a shame for you not to see everything."

Laura glanced up at him. Was his emphasis on the last word intentional, she wondered and, if so, what was the underlying meaning? Much as she disliked Benvenuti, this might be her one opportunity to see behind the façade of the Holy Roman Catholic Church, provided she was aware that he would only show her what he wanted her to see.

She smiled. "You're very kind," she said, wondering if anyone could truly refer to him that way.

Before separating, they arranged to meet the following day. He asked for her address so he might call for her but she picked a neutral café. She had no doubt he could find out where she was staying, if he hadn't already, but she didn't want to make life too easy for him.

As Laura walked back to the hotel, she made the decision not to tell Larry of her meeting. She knew how he'd worry and, if O'Shea heard of it, she was certain he would discharge himself from hospital and catch the next plane to Rome.

Besides, she told herself, as far as Benvenuti was concerned, she was no threat to anyone. She'd discovered he could be charming when he tried and, all in all, she couldn't have picked a better guide. If she appeared to be merely here to view the sights, he may let down his guard. As she passed some ancient ruins, wayside flowers exhaled their scented breath into the warm evening air. No, it was springtime in Rome and things had worked out very well indeed.

O'Shea cursed his body. The nursing staff were excellent and even the hospital food was tolerable, but he needed to get out of here. He'd had one relayed message from Laura, banally wishing he'd get well, and not one word from Larry. He felt he'd been sidelined and he didn't like it.

Admittedly, Laura had said she needed to get away but he wanted to give her his support. He wondered if she'd confided in Larry yet and if that was why he'd not heard from him. Too many unanswered questions, as usual, and it was not something he could get used to.

He had visitors, but they always came in his sleep. There was too much time to sleep in hospital. Graham, Dorcas, Clements. Sometimes they came separately, sometimes together and sometimes an amalgam of all three. O'Shea felt they were about to convey something of great import but he always woke at the crucial moment, frustrated and none the wiser. He knew it was no doubt the drugs he was being fed that brought the dead around his bed, but he wished they would go away.

"Either tell me something useful or bugger off," he grumbled to the empty room. Yes, he was definitely feeling more like his old self.

He was in no better humour when Larry arrived,

carrying a bunch of grapes.

"I'd have thought you could be more original than that," greeted O'Shea, nodding towards the fruit.

"I realise you'd have preferred them fermented and bottled but I doubt the staff here would approve." Larry grinned, pleased to see O'Shea back on form

"No, you can keep your wine," replied O'Shea. "The drink of sissies." Although he'd not say so, he was pleased Larry had made the journey from London to see him. "How's Laura?"

"Oh, she's fine," said Larry, making himself as comfortable as possible in a hospital chair. "She sends her love."

"What aren't you telling me, Larry?" said O'Shea. "Come on, it's written all over your face."

Larry didn't want to upset O'Shea but he couldn't keep his fears to himself any longer.

"She's in Rome," he blurted out.

"Rome? Good God! And you let her go?"

"Just how was I supposed to stop her? I don't think locking someone in a turret would go down very well in this century," he said rather peevishly.

"Then why, in God's name, didn't you go with her?"

"I tried, believe me. I'd have gone in a New York minute but she was having none of it. What would you have done? I'm not even supposed to tell you. There'll be all hell to pay when she finds out."

"Then you must follow her," O'Shea said firmly. "I'd do it myself if I wasn't laid up. You must go to Rome and keep an eye on her – from a distance."

Larry looked doubtful.

"I have the feeling you care about Laura too," continued O'Shea.

"Yeah, well, she's easy to care about."

"Then follow her," insisted O'Shea, pushing home the advantage. "I reckon she's going to need a friend watching her back. Oh, and Larry, before you see her, I think there's something you need to know."

Larry felt as if someone had hit him with an extra large brick. Had it not been for his own experience in St. Jude's, he would have thought O'Shea's revelation to be the result of the accident, a drug-induced fantasy, but hearing of Laura's ordeal brought home to him the horror he had felt and the self-repugnance that had followed.

He decided to relay his own encounter within the church to the astonished O'Shea. Although it had been a relief to unburden himself, he wished he'd kept silent. Watching the colour drain from his friend's face, he'd panicked and called for a nurse. As O'Shea grumbled at the fussing young girl, Larry felt he'd dealt the older man another blow. As he left the room and headed down the corridor, he heard O'Shea call out behind him.

"Please, Larry, go to Rome."

SEVENTEEN

Laura found herself looking forward to the day ahead. When she went down to breakfast, Signora Franci asked her if she'd mind being seated with a new guest, a Mother Dolores, who'd just arrived in Rome. Laura was delighted. Mother Dolores was charming. She chatted affably about her travels, her home town of Bristol, the convent in France where she used to teach and her excitement at finally being here in Rome. She was enthusiastically inquisitive about everything, including Laura, who thought she might suggest to Benvenuti that they invite the nun to join them on one of their sightseeing excursions. It would be doing the holy Mother a favour and reduce the time that Laura would spend alone with Benvenuti. It then occurred to her that, in doing so, she might be in a less opportune position to glean information from the reluctant Monsignor. She chose to say nothing.

She struggled through breakfast hoping she'd be able to keep it down. She wasn't sure when she'd get a chance to eat during the day ahead.

There were two walking sticks hanging on the back of Mother Dolores's chair and, when they rose to leave, Laura was shocked to see the nun needed both to walk. Although it hadn't been noticeable when they were seated, Mother Dolores was forced into a forty-five degree angle when she stood. A wave of pity washed over Laura. It must have shown in her face.

"Severe osteoporosis," said Mother Dolores. "I shouldn't complain. It may have stopped me teaching but I still get about with the help of these." She tapped one stick against the other. "Just don't point to anything in the sky," she added jokingly.

Laura had lingered over breakfast longer than she'd intended and was feeling flustered by the time she met up with Benvenuti.

"I'm so sorry," she blurted out. "Am I very late?"

Benvenuti noticed her flushed cheeks and approved. He just wished he'd been the direct cause.

"Buongiorno, Laura. Do not concern yourself. Are you ready to explore the New Babylon?"

"You mean Rome? Why do you call it that?"

"There is much in Rome, and indeed in the Roman Catholic Church itself, that comes directly from ancient Babylon, hence the name New Babylon. It's no secret." They had begun walking and Laura fell into step with her guide. "I thought we'd begin with the Pantheon, or as it is also called, the Church of Santa Maria ad Martyres"

"The Pantheon is a church?" asked Laura.

"It is now. It is our most complete ancient building."

"But I thought it was dedicated to 'all the gods'?" said Laura, struggling to remember her history.

He smiled. "It was, of course, re-dedicated when it became a church but yes, it was once a temple. You must be aware this was common practice even in your country, Laura, the church taking over pagan sites and shrines?"

"Of course," replied Laura. "I presume the temple statues were lost or destroyed?"

"Not at all. They were removed to the Vatican Museums, that is, apart from the large statue of Jupiter. It is said that is now seated on a throne in St. Peter's Basilica."

"I… I don't understand."

193

Benvenuti was enjoying Laura's confusion. "Oh, it would have been modified of course, but then presented as St. Peter." He smirked. "Pilgrims kiss the foot of Jupiter every day believing it is Peter, or so some people say. Whether it is true or not, I rather favour the idea. We will see it later."

Laura was horrified. "But that's so deceitful."

"Surely no more so than taking over religious festivals or changing pagan deities into saints? You see, we even recycle the gods."

Laura was forced to agree. She knew this had happened wherever Christianity had spread and absorbed other religions into itself. She was beginning to see it as having a life of its own as it expanded across the globe.

"I cannot verify it," added Benvenuti, "but I have read that during the Renaissance, the populace believed the dome was built by demons."

Benvenuti turned out to be an entertaining and informative companion, giving Laura his undivided attention, but failing to be drawn on his role within the Vatican. She couldn't fail to notice the admiring glances cast in his direction from those of her sex, and had to admit his dark good looks made him an impressive figure as he strode about the city. On occasion, when he held her gaze, it was all she could do to remember what she was saying. She'd wrench her eyes away and hope he hadn't noticed, but was left with the uncomfortable feeling he had. Recalling how she had once despised him, she could only put it down to misunderstandings and stress. She was still aware of an undercurrent of threat however, despite his charm, a threat she'd be foolish to ignore.

She noticed the number of ornate fountains and awe-inspiring statues in Rome. They adorned every open space but were spoilt by copious amounts of graffiti. Benvenuti followed her gaze as they encountered yet another semi-naked torso.

"You will have noticed, Laura, from ancient times through until now, the Romans have shared their love of flesh. So many naked or half-naked figures. Everywhere you look there is a surfeit of cold stone flesh. Look here, where the fingers press into the body. It appears so real." There was something distasteful about the way he admired the carved marble, although Laura felt aroused despite herself, more from Benvenuti's tone than the images of nudity.

She changed the subject.

"You seem to know a great deal about history."

"When one spends one's entire life here, one has much time to fill. The Vatican has a very fine library and I spend endless pleasurable hours there."

The rumour that the library in the Vatican City housed the largest collection of pornography in the world was, she knew, an urban myth, though she wondered what had given birth to the idea. What could not be so easily dismissed was its claim of owning the most comprehensive occult library.

There were long queues for many of the major sites, but Benvenuti used his influence to bypass the affronted tourists.

"Notice the sun wheel above his head? It looks like a halo. Also the pattern on the wall behind incorporating the symbol of Baal."

They stood looking up at the statue now posing as St. Peter. Laura was becoming irritated.

"Baal? What on earth do you mean?"

It was all Benvenuti could do not to laugh.

"It's the same symbol found on the front of the Pope's mitre, the symbol of sun worship. Once you look, you'll see it all over Rome."

By the time they came to part company, Laura's head was spinning. She was quite relieved there hadn't been time to include the Vatican Museums. Never had she imagined the church could have taken over other religions, monuments, statues and even symbols on such a grand scale. Benvenuti had been amused by her reactions and made no attempt to hide it. That aside, he had been attentive and the perfect gentleman. They had dined at a restaurant in the Appia Antica, close to where marks from Roman chariot wheels were still etched into the paving stones. So much history, thought Laura, and most of it violent. However, the pasta and wine banished all thoughts of warfare, bloodshed and the church.

Benvenuti had attempted to refill Laura's wine glass more than once but she was firm. She had the baby to think of now and, if that wasn't enough, she didn't want to let slip anything that might alert him to her real reason for being in Rome. It was easy enough to blame the effects of unaccustomed alcohol and fatigue for an early night and Benvenuti ordered her a taxi. He was happy to continue her charade and pretended not to hear her give the driver instructions. If it made her feel safe believing he was unaware of where she was staying, he'd play along. After all, wasn't he supposed to keep her happy – for now?

Back in her room Laura tried ringing Larry. There was no reply so she left a message. It was warm for the time of year and Laura leaned on her window ledge, breathing in the evening air. During the day the roof garden beneath was scorched by sunlight, and only plants from hotter climes struggled for moisture in their ornate pots. As darkness approached however, a dozen or so white orbs of solar lights glowed like mini galaxies in the dark garden of space. Laura leaned out, trying to catch a stray breeze. It felt as if she was looking out on a universe where good and evil were only words not yet spoken into being.

When she finally pulled back from the window, she felt calmer than she had in months. It had seemed a long while since she'd prayed, apart from when she'd been taking services, and then she'd just been mouthing the words she knew by heart, lip service and no more. Tonight, in a world she didn't understand, she linked her hands together and poured out her thoughts to Christ, the one person without whom there would be no church and the one person she felt would understand.

Maybe her prayers would have taken on an air of urgency had she stayed looking outside a little longer. She might have felt less at ease had she seen the shadow that encroached upon the moonlight. Obliterating the lights from the orbs, it slithered between the garden and her window, tenderly caressing the sill where Laura had been.

One missed call. Larry felt guilty not answering but an airport terminal speaker was the last background noise he wanted Laura to hear. At least he knew she was all right.

Fortunately he'd had the foresight to get the name of Laura's hotel; in fact he'd insisted on it, so was able to book into one close by. Thank goodness it wasn't the height of the summer season. He even bought himself a panama hat at the airport to hide his hair, which he'd pulled back into a short ponytail. Serious as his purpose might be, he looked forward to trailing Laura. How hard could it be, he thought. He'd had some experience at discreetly following newsworthy people and this should be no different.

It was too late to stake out Laura's hotel so Larry decided to take a walk before retiring. After seeking directions from his hotel porter, he made his way to the Tiber, known to the Italians, he discovered, as Tevere. In London, whenever he'd needed to think, he'd take a long stroll along the Thames Embankment. It felt only natural to seek out the river here.

The Tiber wasn't far from where he was staying. Once there, he turned left towards the Vatican City, wandering past a few straggling artists packing away their paints and canvases. Lights reflected down onto the water from streetlamps, bridges and buildings whilst strains of 'O Sole Mio' drifted on the breeze from unseen street musicians. It seemed like a clichéd living postcard.

On reaching the Castel Sant'Angelo, once Hadrian's mausoleum, he turned up the Via della Conciliazione towards the Vatican. There seemed almost as many people in the streets as during the day. A group of drunken revellers wove along a colonnade of Dickensian-style lamps sat upon modern stone pillars.

Approaching St. Peter's Square, quiet now despite a few remaining tourists, Larry found himself wondering about the pontiff, who was no doubt sleeping innocently just a short distance from where he stood.

Finally returning to his hotel and tired now from the walk, he quickly fell into deep sleep, dreaming of an ancient serpentine river flowing through the heart of holy Rome.

Mother Dolores was keen to hear of all Laura's exploits from the previous day. Laura felt guilty, knowing the nun must find it difficult getting about, especially on her own. Eventually she gave way to her conscience and invited the Mother Superior to join her when she met up with Benvenuti later.

"No, no, my dear, I wouldn't dream of it. I don't want to be a gooseberry." She winked, which made Laura smile. "Perhaps another time, when you're not meeting your friend?"

Laura had to admit she was relieved and wondered if it was solely because she wanted to tease information from Benvenuti or, more worryingly, whether she enjoyed his company too much to share. That was something she didn't want to admit, not even to herself.

She called Larry before leaving the hotel.

"Where were you? I left a message."

"Sorry," said Larry, half-smothering his phone to muffle nearby Italian-speaking voices. "I went up to Cambridge to see O'Shea. Must have forgotten to switch my phone back on when I left Addenbrooke's. I didn't pick up your message till late." He hated lying but he really had no choice.

"Dermot? How is he?" He could hear the anxiety in her voice.

"Doing well. Wanted to know how you are and what you're doing in Rome. I got the feeling he wasn't happy about you running off on your own any more than I am."

"Oh, Larry, I told you not to say anything."

"Sorry!" There was an uncomfortable pause. "Said to watch out for those Italians; they have a habit of pinching girls' bottoms, I gather."

Laura rather liked being referred to as a girl, but wouldn't want to be responsible for what Benvenuti might do to any young Lothario who tried it when he was with her. She laughed into her phone.

"I'll let you know. If they don't, do I take it my bottom isn't worth pinching?" It was safe to flirt from a distance but Larry, seated in a café a few doors away across the street, blushed, not sure what to say or what was expected.

Laura, realising she may have stepped out of line, hurriedly continued. "More sightseeing today. It's an incredibly beautiful city. You should make a point of seeing it sometime."

"I'm sure I shall," said Larry, feeling more uncomfortable by the minute. "Remember Laura, you're not on home turf now. Be careful and don't be seduced away from the reason you're there."

"Don't worry. I'll be fine. I'll call you tomorrow." Much as Laura cared for both O'Shea and Larry, she found she was enjoying her freedom. She felt far more light-hearted than she should be, and it was only when the occasional wave of nausea hit her that she remembered the baby inside her and why she was here. It was as if the city had lulled her with its beauty and, if anything, that should make her twice as wary.

She might have known Larry would tell O'Shea where she was, and could only hope it didn't cause him too much worry, though she guessed it was a futile wish.

Larry felt as if he'd taken a punch to the solar plexus.

FATHER OF LIES

That Laura should be meeting with Benvenuti was bad enough, that she had said nothing about doing so was perhaps understandable, but the look on her face when Benvenuti greeted her was almost more than Larry could stand. He stepped back and leant against the stone wall of a building, catching his breath before turning to take another look.

In that brief lapse, Benvenuti and Laura had disappeared in the crowd. Forgetting caution, Larry emerged from cover, only to dive into the closest doorway as the two of them passed within a few feet of him. Thank God Laura had been too intent on listening to her companion to notice him, but he must take more care in future. He didn't know what Benvenuti was up to but he didn't trust him, and whatever Laura's feelings might be, he knew she was dancing with the devil.

"You must promise me, Laura, that you will let me show you around during the evening. Many of Rome's sites take on a completely different atmosphere and beauty at night. The city becomes a giant stage where we mortals act out our parts."

They were standing in the shadow of the Colosseum, the greatest amphitheatre in the world, and Laura was in awe of its size and grandeur.

"Can we go in?" she asked, eyeing the daunting queue outside the high railing that surrounded the monument.

"I will arrange a private viewing when there are no crowds to trample us."

"You can do that?"

"It can be arranged. There are already moonlit tours but an individual viewing would be far preferable."

Two men approached dressed as gladiators. Laura had spotted some in a few of the tourist locations and had to admit they looked stunning, as if they had slipped through a time tunnel into present-day Rome. Benvenuti waved his hand dismissively at them and guided Laura away.

"Tourists enjoy having their photos taken with them," he said.

Laura imagined that standing with gladiators in front of the Colosseum must be the highlight of many a holidaymaker's visit. She had to remind herself that she wasn't here on vacation, and somehow she needed to get Benvenuti talking about things she was sure he'd prefer to ignore.

A moment later, he was talking rapidly in Italian into his cell phone. When he finished, he turned to Laura and smiled. "We will be given private access just before sundown," he said, gesturing back at the huge construction behind them.

"Sundown?" said Laura. "How will we see anything?"

"It will be well-lit inside, you will see. After all, we wish to show the world what a beautiful building it is."

"There aren't many to match its history of gory spectacle, that's for certain," said Laura, not sure she wanted to face the ghosts – humans and animals – slaughtered within those high arched walls.

What the hell was Laura doing with Benvenuti? Larry couldn't believe she would forget his unhelpful attitude in England. The thought crossed his mind that there was something going on between them, especially after seeing the way she looked at him, but he then dismissed it. After all, Benvenuti was a priest. Laura's words came back to him, 'I was a woman before I became a priest.' And Benvenuti was a man before he became a priest. Larry found no comfort in the thought.

EIGHTEEN

They had detoured down one of Rome's expensive shopping streets where prices reflected the wealthy tourist market. A light shower had thinned the crowds.

Quite suddenly Benvenuti spun about, grasping the arm of a middle-aged man in a vice-like grip. Laura couldn't understand what was being said, but it was obvious from Benvenuti's thunderous expression and raised voice that the man had committed some misdemeanour. The terrified man was talking quickly and shaking his head, all the while trying to break free. Finally, the pickpocket handed over Laura's purse and Benvenuti released his grasp, only to raise his hand and strike the man with unnecessary force, sending him sprawling into the wet road. Amidst the blaring of car horns and skidding bicycles, the man managed to haul himself out of the path of braking traffic.

Laura was horrified by Benvenuti's ferocity. Gathered onlookers averted their eyes, obviously sharing her discomfort.

"I cannot abide thieves," said Benvenuti calmly, as if nothing had happened. He handed Laura the purse and she mumbled her thanks, wanting nothing more than to put distance between her and the staring crowd. She was relieved to see the man being helped to his feet and out of harm's way. There was blood on his cheek where Benvenuti's ring had ripped the skin. Laura felt a sudden wave of nausea as the baby stirred within her, as if responding to spilled blood and fear. She fought the urge to be sick.

"Did you need to be so brutal?" she asked, when

they had turned off into a cobbled side street.

"Brutal? My dear Laura, these people need harsh treatment to keep them in line. Power is such a fragile thing, whether it be in the hands of governments, kings, the church or God. The Roman Emperors realised that. Brutality to the people for the people; let the disciplining of some feed the hunger in others. Now, shall we stop for some tea?"

Tea and cakes seemed less genteel now, despite the traditional surroundings of Babington's Tea Rooms. What should have been a pleasant reminder of home, instead highlighted for Laura that she was, after all, in another country. She couldn't rid her mind of the recent ugly scene and the ferocity on Benvenuti's face.

"Come, Laura, surely you're not still fretting over the pickpocket? He was out to rob you," he said, noticing how she toyed with the cream scone on her plate. When she didn't reply, he went on, "I believe it was an English judge who once said that justice must not only be done but must be seen to be done."

"There's a difference between justice and brutality," retorted Laura.

"Then I truly apologise if my behaviour caused offence. Now, do you think we can put the matter behind us?"

There seemed little point is creating an atmosphere between them so Laura nodded. She couldn't undo what her companion had done.

"Good," smiled Benvenuti. "I propose we visit the Spanish Steps next, if you feel up to the climb? I should warn you however, it is an area favoured by more of our light-fingered friends, so may I suggest you keep a tight hold of your purse.

The more Laura saw of Rome, the more she realised how far removed from the teachings of Christ the church had become. She felt it was a betrayal of their figurehead and that they had truly taken the name of her Lord in vain. She wondered when the rot had set in. Could any one person reverse the trend and prevent it all going to hell in a handcart?

Amidst stories of corruption, child abuse, cover-ups and Mafia connections, no-one seemed prepared to stand up for the teachings of Christ. Wherever she looked there was opulence and lavish splendour, but all the ostentatious trappings couldn't hide the decay beneath its glittering golden exterior. It brought it home to her that Christ hadn't been a Christian, any more than Buddha was a Buddhist or Mohammed was a Mohammedan.

But Benvenuti had been right about the Colosseum. When they arrived there, the last straggling visitors were being ushered towards the exit where attendants waited, ready to lock up. Benvenuti approached one of the men who nodded and showed the two of them through. It was still light but already long shadows were stretching out across the crumbling stadium.

Looking enormous from the outside, it seemed even larger from within. Laura tried to imagine what it must have been like when it was newly built, with fifty to eighty thousand Romans taking their seats for the spectacles. Benvenuti remained silent as Laura walked through the arches, admiring the architecture and grandeur of a bygone era.

She stood looking up at the vast circular walls, aware of Benvenuti standing at her side. He was close enough for her to feel the heat rising from his body. She turned and looked into his dark brown eyes. He reminded her of a musketeer, dark hair framing his aquiline face, his imperious gaze simultaneously arousing and angering her. She was at a loss to know which emotion was causing the rush of blood to her face. She gave herself over to her feelings and luxuriated in a femininity she seldom felt.

She managed to whisper, "It's magnificent."

The effect he was having on her didn't escape Benvenuti, but his boyhood idealism had long ago given way to darker passions. Still, it was a pleasant enough game to play for now.

Finally he spoke. "You approve then of our ancestors work, Laura? The gladiatorial games must have been a splendid sight, do you not agree?"

"Who wouldn't admire the builders of such an amazing arena," she said, "but not all the games played here were to be admired." She shuddered as she thought of the blood shed within these ancient walls. She'd read somewhere that it was estimated between five and seven hundred thousand people had lost their lives here.

"You are referring to the Christians burned alive? That was unfortunate, yes, but in those days it was as natural to watch as television is today. It was entertainment." He was goading Laura and she knew it. "Things have changed very little. We are not so far removed from those times. Violence lies just beneath the surface of our lives and it takes very little to release it."

Laura thought back to Benvenuti's outburst earlier in the day and knew this was true.

"We don't torture and kill people for mass pleasure any more."

"No, this is correct," acknowledged Benvenuti,

"but then we have the means now to simulate violence and death by way of films and computer games, something our ancestors were not privy to. It is still watching slaughter and destruction, but by proxy." To Laura's intense surprise, he produced a small packet of cat treats from his coat pocket and began sharing them out amongst a few stray cats that had followed them from the entrance. They seemed to know him and rubbed themselves affectionately against his legs.

"There are hundreds living here amongst the ruins," said Benvenuti, misreading the question in Laura's eyes.

As Laura stepped forward to look down on the exposed lower level, where animals and men had been kept in labyrinthine corridors and compartments, he came to stand beside her.

"It's like a village on its own," she said, marvelling at the work that its building must have entailed.

"Especially considering it was all built on marshy ground," said Benvenuti.

"Really?" Laura was even more impressed.

"There was once even an artificial lake here, in the grounds of Nero's palace. There were tunnels leading into the hypogeum, the lower area, from nearby stables and gladiatorial schools so that both men and animals could arrive here undetected. Come! I will take you down to that level."

"Are we allowed down there? I didn't think that area was open to the public."

"Normally, no, but we are not the public." He took a key from his pocket, opened one of the metal grid gates that sealed off numerous entrances within the Colosseum and led the way down steep steps.

It was dark out of the failing daylight but

Benvenuti had come armed with a torch. He shone the beam onto the steps for Laura, though he descended them as if he knew them well.

Emerging onto the lower level, they stepped once more into the open, but the walkways were in shadow from the high walls. The setting sun bathed the far side of the circular stadium in brilliant light, the stonework taking on a warm rosy hue, but down here, in the area that used to be underground, the temperature dipped away and Laura shivered.

"You are cold. How thoughtless of me." He began to remove his coat but Laura shook her head. "You can almost feel the fear down here, can't you?"

Laura didn't reply. The lights had come on, illuminating the huge building from the inside but, if anything, it threw the shadows into deeper darkness and she was no longer sure if the goose bumps on her arms were due to the chill or something else, memories etched into the stones two thousand years ago.

"Come, let me show you something." Pointing the torch at the pathway, Benvenuti led Laura back to the circumference wall and unlocked another gate. Steps led down again into a black void. Laura recoiled from the entrance but Benvenuti took her wrist and moved forward. "What you are about to see is something very few know of, outside the Vatican, that is." He pulled the gate to and took care to lock it again behind him.

Here the steps coiled round a central pillar. The walls were damp and smelled of mould. Laura didn't want to follow Benvenuti but neither did she want to be left alone in the dark. The descent was short and the torch beam revealed one central corridor under the stadium, with openings leading off on either side. A few of these were sealed with heavy doors.

"Where are we?" It was obvious they were still under the Colosseum but Laura had never been aware of this level before.

"Shhh," Benvenuti whispered, leaning forward and putting his fingers to her lips.

Laura could hear nothing except perhaps her own heart beating so loud she felt sure Benvenuti must hear it too. There wasn't a sound in the underground passage, not even the drip of condensation from the damp walls and ceiling. The stillness was almost tangible.

Benvenuti's face was only inches from hers. As he took away his hand, there was a moment when Laura was sure he was going to kiss her. Instead, he smiled beguilingly and stepped away. She could never be sure if he acted unconsciously or whether this was all an elaborate game for him, amusing himself at her expense. Whatever the answer, it didn't slow the beating of her heart.

"Please, let's go back," said Laura, trying to keep her voice steady.

"But Laura, don't you want to know our secret? I thought you'd be intrigued."

Laura had never felt the proximity of evil as much as she did now, not even within St. Jude's. She could feel the mud seeping into her shoes and felt unsteady. Pressure seemed to be building against her eardrums and her mouth was dry.

"Please," she whispered, angry at her own weakness. And then the light went out.

Laura couldn't remember when she had last been this afraid. She doubted she ever had. This far down beneath the Colosseum, there wasn't even the rumble of traffic. It was as silent as a tomb but for one faint sound, that of Benvenuti's steady breathing. Had Laura been able to read his thoughts, her fear may have plummeted to new depths but instead, quite suddenly, the torch went back on.

Laura hadn't realised she'd been holding her breath and it now came out in gasp.

"W-what happened?" She couldn't believe it had been deliberate. Surely no-one would play such an unkind trick.

"My dear Laura," said Benvenuti, noticing the sheen of perspiration on her pale face, "I am sorry if you were frightened. There must be a faulty connection in the torch."

"Let's get out of here before it does it again," said Laura, regaining a little of her composure.

It wasn't until they stood again in the open that Laura spoke. "What is that place and why is it so secret?"

"It has been convenient to keep it as a place of refuge or internment down through the centuries. The papacy has not always been held in high esteem. It stands to reason that outsiders should not be made aware of it."

"Then why tell me?"

"Perhaps because I trust you, perhaps…"

"Perhaps?"

"Perhaps because I think our secret will be in safe hands."

Laura had the feeling that wasn't what he'd been about to say but she just wanted to get out of here. She suppressed a shudder. Her emotions had taken a roller coaster ride and she longed to get back to her hotel room and sleep. She glanced back at the iconic landmark. Each stone archway glowed red, giving the impression the interior had been painted with ancient blood.

With Laura safely in a cab on her way back to her hotel, Benvenuti set out to walk to Vatican City. He had enjoyed his day and Laura's company, though he regretted not being able to subject her to the dark for longer. Still, he had the memory of her fear to take to his bed.

Perhaps he shouldn't have shown her the forbidden area, but the temptation had been too great and he always believed in giving way to it. Besides, the greater the likelihood of Laura being a problem, the greater his opportunity to feel her fear again.

Larry was tired, miserable and hungry, not necessarily in that order. He had been watching the Colosseum for what seemed like hours as daylight gave way to night. He had been consumed with jealousy, anger and concern, and they weren't necessarily in that order either.

"Son of..." he mumbled to himself, as he watched Benvenuti see Laura into a cab and turn and head off towards the Vatican. Larry couldn't follow Laura and guessed she'd be safe now, but he could follow Benvenuti. There probably wasn't much point in doing so, but then the evening was a washout anyway.

With hands thrust deep in his pockets, he trudged after his quarry.

It all seemed unreal to Laura as the cab crossed the bridge over the Tiber and she looked out at the lights of this captivating ancient city.

FATHER OF LIES

She was finding it hard to reconcile her feelings. It held such beauty and ugliness in its long history, light and shadow, good and evil, all lain out before her like an offering. Benvenuti, too, seemed a man of dual personalities, charming one minute, deadly the next. Rather like a snake, she thought. She smiled; he even liked cats. Had he deliberately caused her alarm in the subterranean chambers? Terror was more like it. She didn't want to believe he'd do that, though she knew he was more than capable, and that posed another question. Why didn't she want to consider it? She tried to shut down her mind so as not to pursue the answer.

When they finally pulled up outside her hotel, Laura stumbled from the taxi and up to her room. For a moment she thought of calling Larry but decided against it. Why couldn't she feel the same way with Larry as she did with Benvenuti? At least tomorrow she'd have time to get her thoughts in order. Benvenuti had duties to attend to and she hoped she'd see more clearly without his constant presence and maybe, if she was lucky, she'd work out a way to get some answers. Tonight she was too tired to even consider the questions.

Near the entrance to St. Peter's Square, a figure stepped from the shadows to intercept Benvenuti. Larry ducked back out of sight as he watched the hunched shape conferring with the Monsignor. When they had finished, the Monsignor strode out of Larry's line of vision but the other figure moved towards him.

He remained still, as a nun, bent double and using two walking sticks, hurried by. The speed at which she moved, considering her infirmity, was incredible in itself but, in her black habit, she resembled a giant spider scuttling along the web of streets. When Larry stepped cautiously from his hiding place, she had already disappeared from view.

"What have you got planned for today?" asked Larry from the safety of his hotel room. He tried to make his voice light and cheerful although he felt anything but.

"I'm not sure," said Laura truthfully. "I thought I might take a look at the Vatican."

"I would have thought that would have been your first stop," said Larry. "After all, this wasn't going to be a pleasure trip, was it?" He realised he might be sounding critical but he couldn't resist the dig.

Laura noticed the edge to his voice and felt a sudden pang of guilt. He was right; it must seem as if she'd been treating her visit as a holiday and seeing the sights. She could hardly tell Larry she hoped to lull Benvenuti into giving away useful information. The fact she'd been taken into the area beneath the Colosseum showed she was making progress, but time wasn't on her side, and he'd deftly fielded all questions, feeding her only the information he chose.

"How's O'Shea?" she asked, changing the subject.

"Probably worrying about you," said Larry, adding, "I haven't spoken to him for a couple of days."

The call was uncomfortable and strained and they ended it with Laura feeling aggrieved at Larry's attitude and him biting his tongue.

It had become routine for Laura and Mother Dolores to sit together for breakfast. Laura had warmed to the nun. Had she been Catholic, Laura could see herself becoming a Bride of Christ. The irony of her situation hit her. Far from being anybody's bride, here she was,

214

doubting her faith and pregnant. Thank Heaven Mother Dolores couldn't read minds.

"And where are you off to today?" asked the nun, as she reached for her third piece of cold toast. She had already downed a full English breakfast and Laura wondered where she put it all.

"I'm not sure," said Laura. "I was thinking of the Vatican City."

"Is your friend not with you today?" asked Mother Dolores.

"No, not today," said Laura and immediately realised her mistake.

"Maybe we could visit the Vatican together? That's if you can put up with an old slowcoach like me tagging along."

Laura could hardly refuse but made a mental note to think before speaking in future.

"Or the other place I really want to see is the Catacombs," continued the nun. "Maybe we could go there?"

Laura really didn't want to face them after last night's experience beneath the Colosseum. "Perhaps another time," she said. "Let's make it the Vatican today."

Mother Dolores never seemed to stop talking, yet, although Laura was careful not to divulge her position within the church, the nun still managed to draw her life history from her, or so it seemed. Thrusting first one stick forward then the other, her rolling gait caused many passers-by to turn and watch, but the holy Mother seemed oblivious.

The queues wound around the Vatican in anything but pious devotion. Mothers trying to quieten fractious children and small groups of chatting tourists outnumbered the occasional figure clutching a rosary and attempting to switch off the babble of voices. The Vatican Museums were far from glamorous on the outside, despite the heraldic crest above the door reading, 'Musei Vaticani'. Once they were finally inside, there was so much to see. Mother Dolores wanted to visit the Sistine Chapel next. They found they could hardly move for packed humanity, and any thought of quiet contemplation was quickly dismissed. It was exhausting.

As she had already visited the Basilica with Benvenuti, Laura chose to wait in the more airy plaza, whilst Mother Dolores went to touch the statue's foot. She hadn't the heart to tell her it may have been ecclesiastically recycled. She glanced up at the central loggia, the balcony on which the Pope made his appearances, half expecting to see him smiling down on the gullible pilgrims. Instead, 140 saints stared through sightless eyes from their statues around the square.

Since talking to Benvenuti, Laura found she was noticing more pagan architecture than she'd expected. Right in the centre of the plaza stood an Egyptian obelisk that Caligula had shipped from Heliopolis. Even Laura recognised it was a phallic symbol, and the rays emanating across the square from it formed the eight-rayed sun wheel of Ishtar. Would she have noticed, she wondered, if he hadn't planted these thoughts in her mind? To bring back trophies from different locations where Christianity had overlaid previous belief systems was one thing, but to proudly incorporate them into the fabric of the Mother Church was another. Now she thought about it, Laura remembered seeing other obelisks in Rome's squares. There'd been one, she was sure, in the Piazza Navona, surrounded by artists selling their work. She was trying to recall where else she'd seen them when Mother Dolores spoke.

"What are you staring at, Laura?"

Laura didn't want to offend the nun by revealing her thoughts. She doubted phallic symbols featured much within convent walls.

"I wasn't staring but thinking," said Laura. "I'm hungry. How about you?"

The two of them took their time as they made their way through squares full of artists, passed fountains and ventured down narrow side streets, glad to be on foot and not having to negotiate the traffic jams. Finally, they decided on a small restaurant and each of them ate enough for two.

It was an understatement to say Larry was concerned. One minute Laura was sightseeing with Benvenuti and the next she was in the company of a nun. The same nun he'd seen the previous night outside St. Peter's Square. Just what was going on? When Laura had emerged from her hotel this morning, he was astounded to see the nun in tow. It seemed too much of a coincidence for his liking that the nun just happened to be staying at the same hotel, given that she knew Benvenuti. Something was very wrong here and he couldn't make out what. His journalist antennae had never failed him before but, whatever it was picking up, it didn't make any sense. Not yet, anyway.

NINETEEN

There was a message from Benvenuti waiting for Laura at the hotel lobby. It seemed he was to be needed at the Vatican for the next two days, but he offered his apologies and regrets and suggested they meet for dinner. He had already given her a number where he could be reached so, unless he heard from her, he would call for her at seven thirty. She was rather taken aback as she hadn't realised he knew where she was staying, but reasoned that it really should come as no surprise.

Laura was forced to acknowledge a sinking feeling when she read the note. Despite herself, she was disappointed not to be spending another day in his company.

"What's wrong, dear?" asked Mother Dolores. "You look quite downcast. Bad news?"

"No, no, it's nothing." Laura smiled. Sweet as the nun was, two days in succession were more than Laura could cope with. She decided to skip breakfast in the morning to facilitate an easy getaway.

She tried calling Larry.

"Pick up, damn you," she muttered. She didn't leave a message. She'd only wanted to hear his voice. He seemed such a long way away and their recent conversations had been strained.

Crossing the room, she looked out over the rooftops. Although it was warm, she closed the window and pulled the curtains across. "Goodnight, Rome," she whispered, but it wasn't Rome that listened.

FATHER OF LIES

O'Shea had made life hell for the nurses. He wasn't exactly sweet-natured at the best of times and confinement wasn't doing him any favours. The staff at Addenbrookes were as keen for him to leave their ward as he was to go. Finally, with the help of Social Services, he was allowed to return to his flat, with care workers calling in twice a day to help him dress and undress.

He felt so helpless and, as a result, barked at everyone who came near. The few university visitors who called bearing gifts soon made excuses and left, and their visits became less frequent. He knew it was his own fault but couldn't change his nature.

Worry wasn't helping. Nor guilt. He felt as if he'd let Graham down even if he couldn't see what else he could have done. Had Graham felt as O'Shea did now, cut off from everyone he knew? He hadn't heard from Larry in days and, when he did, he felt he wasn't getting the whole story. As for Laura, he knew she wanted time alone, but running off to Rome? And now the silence? It wasn't surprising he was feeling helpless and afraid.

He couldn't go chasing after the pair of them and, although he was loathe to consider it, they may not want an interfering old man hanging round. He did the only thing he could; he called their cell phones and left the same message on both: 'Ring me!'

Benvenuti had a free day. Working on the age-old premise that absence makes the heart grow fonder, he thought a couple of days might heighten Laura's feelings, making it so much more pleasurable when the time came to dash her illusions and open her eyes to the dark. And come it would, he was determined on that score.

To his astonishment, he was enjoying the time spent with her. There was something about her innocence that made him long to corrupt her. If Laura was willing, she would make an excellent consort should he wish to take one, but he feared she had been brainwashed. Her nauseating devotion to sweetness and light was ingrained too deeply. No, he'd not convert her, but it would give him immeasurable delight to use and destroy her.

Today, she would be free to see the eternal city with, he was certain, Mother Dolores either accompanying or following her. He would put his mind instead to making certain Laura Coatman became troublesome enough to the Ordo Autem Serpens to ensure he was given a free hand with her, and to hasten the approach of that much anticipated day.

"Is your friend meeting you today?" asked Mother Dolores, catching Laura in the lobby.

Laura didn't want to lie but saw no other avenue of defence. "Yes, I'm meeting him later."

"Never mind," said Mother Dolores. "We can make the Catacombs another day."

When Laura left the hotel, she turned the opposite way from usual, so as not to be seen from the dining room. She felt guilty about leaving the clinging nun behind but couldn't face another day with her so soon after the last. Perhaps she'd have time to get her thoughts in order today.

It was pure good fortune for Larry that she didn't spot him standing in a doorway on the opposite side of the street. He'd been fooled by her change in routine.

FATHER OF LIES

Laura felt at a loss to know how to spend her day. She needed information but, without Benvenuti to question, she didn't know where to start. She decided she would explore some of the sites that so far she'd only seen in passing, the Roman Forum, the Imperial Forums and the Arch of Constantine. There was still so much to see, including a tour along the 800-metre passageway from the Vatican to the Castel Sant'Angelo. Finding that the Pope and those in high office had an escape route directly from the impenetrable Vatican to a fortress stronghold amazed Laura. However, the guide assured her it had been put to use more than once in the history of the Papacy, when Rome or the Vatican were under attack. There was even a torture chamber.

Although it was well-lit, the stone walls made Laura feel uncomfortable. It reminded her too much of the passageway beneath the Colosseum and the horror she had felt in the dark. There, Benvenuti's company had added to her misgivings, and a tremble went through her at the memory. She was aware it was purely physical and had never felt such an air of restrained excitement in someone's presence before, but there was a darkness inside him that frightened her. She wasn't so naïve that she didn't recognise it might well be that very darkness that made him so attractive.

She forced her thoughts back to her surroundings. It was cold out of the sunlight and she found herself thinking of its history.

Larry's words came back to her. 'Like anything else, you go straight for the heart'. Yes, she could see now that the only way to attack something like the church was from the inside.

Stepping once more into the open, it was apparent she hadn't counted on how much walking her sightseeing involved. The brilliant sunshine in a cloudless sky had sapped her energy. Far from clearing her head, she was still confused about everything and beginning to feel unwell. The only thing she could be certain of was that she was pregnant. Surely that wasn't a lie. As silly as it was, with that thought came the sudden need for further confirmation.

She left Rome's ancient glory to the tourists and headed back to the hotel. She needed to find a doctor and arrange for a scan.

Larry picked up O'Shea's message but didn't call back. He hadn't a clue what to tell him. 'No need to worry, but Laura's running round Rome with Benvenuti and a highly questionable nun.' No, he didn't think so.

After Laura had almost run into him first thing, he'd been about to follow her when he'd seen the nun leave the hotel and turn in the same direction Laura had taken. He'd hung back and watched. Sure enough, he wasn't the only one following Laura.

He wondered just what he had got himself into. What was a Blue Ridge Mountain boy doing skulking round Rome following two women, one a priest, the other a nun? Maybe he should just pack his bags and go home.

A car horn blared as he kept his eyes on the retreating figures and not on where he was walking.

"Son of a ..." He seldom did finish the expression.

It was obvious the nun wasn't trying to catch up with Laura but, like Larry, wanted to keep out of sight. Her rolling gait didn't slow her down at all and, once or twice when he got too close, he caught the sound of her sticks cracking against the paving stones.

If only he could think of how to alert Laura without giving himself away. He didn't like the way things were shaping up and besides, as confused as his feelings were in regard to her, there was a story in all this if he could just work out what it was.

It took a few calls before Laura was able to book an appointment at a private clinic with scanning facilities. She would have needed a scan sooner or later and she lied. "I've been experiencing sharp pains," she told the receptionist on the phone. "I really do need to see someone. I'm worried." It was going to cost her but she had to know just what she was carrying. Thank goodness she had some savings to fall back on, but she was only too aware her resources were limited. There would come a time when she would have to go home. Home! How odd that sounded. Norfolk, Adderidge, St. Jude's, even England, seemed like a memory that was already becoming hazy and distant.

She felt nervous as she walked to the clinic. Everywhere she looked there were couples, many hand in hand. Rome, like Paris, was a city for lovers and Laura felt very alone. She found herself wishing the impossible, that her child's father was flesh and blood, that she could share this precious time, hold hands, laugh and plan for the future. Before she knew it, she was standing outside the clinic, the piece of paper on which she'd scribbled the address crumpled in her hand.

The staff at the clinic were considerate and sympathised with her. Alone and away from home, it was only natural that she should be concerned. She gave her title as 'Mrs' although she wished she'd had the foresight to buy a ring. Still, even Rome must have its share of unmarried mothers.

Lying on her back, she turned her head to gaze at the screen. When she'd seen this done on television, the woman always looked huge and Laura was only too aware that she wasn't even obviously pregnant. The small bulge she had could easily be put down to a fondness for spaghetti or doughnuts.

The sonographer applied the electro-conductor gel and reached for the transducer. Laura was beginning to panic. What if the baby wasn't normal? What if it took after its father? She could feel sweat breaking out on her forehead. What would the nurse say if the foetus didn't show up on the ultrasound? Laura fought a dual battle, a desire to be sick and the inclination to run.

"Don't be afraid. Look, your baby is fine."

Laura stared at the screen but it just seemed an abstract picture in shades of black, white and grey. The sonographer smiled and began pointing out where the baby lay in the womb.

"Do you want to know its sex?" she asked.

Laura couldn't speak. For the first time she was aware of the baby as a living, breathing extension of herself. Her child! It was overwhelming and something she had never foreseen. Fighting the urge to cry, she answered, "Yes, please."

Outside the clinic, Laura paused to buy a postcard of Rome to send to O'Shea.

She made her way back to the hotel. There was just time for a shower and then she'd be meeting Benvenuti for dinner. She felt the now familiar rush of excitement at the prospect of his company and wondered if that was altogether appropriate for a pregnant woman, let alone a priest.

Benvenuti arrived at seven thirty precisely. He eyed Laura carefully as they sat opposite each other in the small, expensive restaurant.

"Are you well, Laura?" he asked, full of apparent concern. "You look a little pale tonight."

"I'm fine," she assured him.

"Maybe you have been overdoing things. Where did you go today?" Mother Dolores had faithfully detailed Laura's exploits to him but had been unable to enter the clinic without drawing attention to herself. Although it specialised in women's problems, its facilities were used for any number of complaints. He would like to know in advance if Laura suffered from any frailty that might impede his future pleasure.

"You're probably right. I do feel tired. There is so much walking to do in Rome and far too many steps." She laughed. "I can't remember when I last had so much exercise."

"Perhaps you should avail yourself of the Vatican's doctors, for a check-up you understand. I'm sure I could pull a few strings and get you a consultation if you wished."

"That's most kind but totally unnecessary," said Laura, smiling. "I forget though that the Vatican must have its own doctors on hand in case the Pope, or anyone for that matter, should become sick. So many of them are elderly."

"We have most anything within the Vatican City. We have our own army, our secret police, our own bank, radio, post office, even our own daily newspaper, L'Osservatore Romano."

"But you're not a self-sufficient country," said

Laura.

"True, but all countries trade, do they not? Rome has been a centre of commerce since ancient times. Come to think of it, we also have our own laws."

"Ah, yes," said Laura. "I read the age of consent is only twelve according to Vatican law." It was her turn to goad him and she couldn't resist.

"Actually, I believe you will find your information is out of date. We have increased the age in line with Italian law, but it is immaterial anyway. There are no children in the Vatican."

They continued to talk of Rome, the Vatican and their combined history throughout dinner, or at least Benvenuti did. For the most part, Laura simply listened and enjoyed the exquisite food. Once or twice she found she had stopped listening to his words, but was enjoying the sound of his voice and the passion behind the seductive Italian accent.

When they had finished, Benvenuti helped Laura with her jacket.

"I realise you are tired, Laura, but I wish to show you one of the beauties of Rome, the Fontana di Trevi, or Trevi Fountain as you would say. It is best seen at night."

Laura thought of their last sightseeing at night. At least there would be nothing underground this time.

"I'd love to see it," she replied, "but don't expect me to kick off my shoes and dance in it."

"Ah, 'La Dolce Vita' has much to answer for. It will please you to know it is actually forbidden." He lightly touched her arm and they made their way to the fountain.

"Aren't you meant to stand with your back to it and throw a coin in?" asked Laura, amazed by its grandeur and size. She was pleased Benvenuti had saved viewing this famous landmark till night. Well thought out light placements added magic to the smooth surfaces, the intricate carved figures and the constant rush of water. She felt she could stand here watching it forever.

"Don't waste your money. You should only follow that custom and throw a coin over your shoulder if you want to return to Rome; otherwise you are merely funding public upkeep.

"What makes you think I wouldn't want to return?" Laura was curious.

"I don't think there's anything here for you, Laura, do you?"

She felt instinctively there was a concealed threat within his innocuous words and couldn't help responding to it when she replied, "What makes you think I want to leave?"

It was only when Laura spoke the words that she realised, quite suddenly and unexpectedly, that she didn't want to go home. An overwhelming feeling of belonging spread through her, as if this was where she should be, was where she'd been heading all her life. She said nothing more to Benvenuti but kept these thoughts to herself. They were for her alone and, wherever they came from, she certainly wasn't meant to share them. If she could have physically clutched them to her, she would have. Instead, she made do with clasping her hands close to her body as if somehow the idea was within her grasp and nothing, or no-one, was going to pry it from her tightened fingers.

Benvenuti had been secretly pleased by Laura's

remark at the fountain. He was uncertain if she was under the spell all foreign locations cast on tourists who had left their troubles behind, or whether she really thought she could confront the Holy Roman Catholic Church in some way. He knew which interpretation he would relay back to Cardinal Scappucci. It was no coincidence that it would be the same interpretation that would best suit his own desires.

He stood naked before the full-length mirror and looked appreciatively at his finely-built physique, not a blemish to be seen. Turning first one way then the other, he smiled. A Roman work of art. He didn't need anyone else's admiration. He thought of Laura and turned off the light.

Laura had been about to sneak away again the following morning, but Mother Dolores had positioned herself by the hotel's entrance and there was no chance of escaping undetected.

"Laura, my dear, I missed you at breakfast. You're not trying to avoid me are you?" she said coyly.

"Oh no, of course not," replied Laura in mock horror, inwardly groaning at being caught. "What a dreadful thing to say."

"I'm teasing, of course. I know you'd never do such a thing. I was wondering if you would care to accompany me to the Catacombs today?"

It seemed that Laura wasn't going to be able to avoid another sightseeing excursion with the nun, but she sought frantically for an excuse.

"Perhaps later in the day?" It was only putting off the inevitable but she wanted to be alone to think.

"Shall we say I'll meet you here at one?" asked the

nun. She certainly wasn't going to give up.

"One thirty," said Laura. "I really must get on. I'll see you later. Arrivederci!"

She almost fled the hotel before she could be drawn into any more of Mother Dolores's plans, but she paused outside the door, unsure where to go that would be conducive to serious thought.

As her glance swept over the street and the buildings opposite, something familiar caught her attention and she looked again. Something – or someone – had registered in her line of sight. Like many in Rome, the café a few doors along had tables and white-painted chairs that had spread out onto the pavement, where one or two customers enjoyed a hurried coffee or more leisurely breakfast. A man sat facing her, reading a newspaper. Laura could only make out the top of his head, but knew her eyes hadn't deceived her.

"Larry!" she gasped in disbelief.

She strode over and stood a couple of feet from the table, waiting. After about thirty seconds, the paper was cautiously slid to one side, enough for Larry to peep around the edge. He visibly jumped at the sight of Laura standing before him, arms folded.

"Oh, fuck," he exclaimed softly.

"No wonder I haven't been able to get hold of you on your cell," began Laura. "Who's clever idea was this? No, don't tell me. Just what makes you two think I need a chaperone? And how long have you been following me? Is O'Shea here too? I don't believe this!"

TWENTY

Cardinal Scappucci listened intently as Benvenuti relayed the recent development with Laura.

"It would seem, Your Eminence, that the Reverend Coatman has plans that could prove – er – inconvenient to us should she remain at liberty."

"You have no proof of this, Benvenuti. She may have simply fallen in love with our beautiful city. Or," he added with an amused smile, "maybe she has misread your attentive overtures. Perhaps it's you she favours, not the city."

Benvenuti didn't share the joke. "Are we to wait until her prying causes us embarrassment? Or worse?" When the cardinal didn't answer, he went on, "Surely it's wiser to act now before the damage is done."

"Don't advise me how to act," snapped the cardinal. He took a deep breath. "Very well, do what you've had a mind to do all along, but Benvenuti…"

"Yes, Your Eminence?"

"Cover your tracks well. I know you're experienced in these things but we need no slip-ups. Do I make myself clear? Have your fun, but the Holy Roman Catholic Church must remain stain-free in this matter."

"Thank you, Your Eminence."

"And Benvenuti? You are very young to hold the position of monsignor. Young and ambitious. You have – er – certain talents which are undeniably useful to the Order, but don't let your personal desires reflect on the Holy See or you may well find you are not as indispensable as you think."

Benvenuti bowed and left the room.

FATHER OF LIES

Cardinal Scappucci crossed to the window and looked down on St. Peter's Square. He waited until he saw the pigeons scattering as Benvenuti strode between pilgrims and tourists already gathering below, then turned and made his way to his private rooms.

Larry sat on the edge of Laura's bed. It had taken a great deal of persuasion to convince her that he and O'Shea were not simply meddling, but acting out of concern for her. Deep down she knew this, but the shock of spotting Larry following her – spying on her was how she put it – had jarred her new-found confidence. It felt as if they were treating her like a child who couldn't be trusted to look after herself, never mind the fact she was soon to be a mother with a baby of her own to look after.

"Larry, there's something you need to know," said Laura, summoning up the courage to tell him about the child.

"I know."

"No, you don't know."

"I know," repeated Larry, taking Laura's hands in his.

"No, you can't. There's no way…" She stopped. "Unless… O'Shea?"

"He told me everything."

"He had no right." Laura pulled her hands away.

"Laura, he was worried about you. Is worried. Think about it for a second. He couldn't keep an eye on you so he entrusted me with the job. He had to put me in the picture. Don't hold it against him."

"And?"

"And what?"

"I don't expect you to believe me, about the baby.

Why should you? Did he tell you what that thing did to me in the church? Did O'Shea tell you that?"

" Yes, yes, he told me," Larry said, his voice low.

"It was as if it awakened some primitive response that I had no control over. Can you imagine how it made me feel, how unclean and, and…?"

Larry took one of Laura's hands again, struggling to subdue the memories that now threatened to engulf him.

"Actually, I know exactly how you felt."

She looked at him, startled, before the horror of his meaning sank in.

"How? I mean… oh God!"

"They say evil is seductive and I don't think that creature, that thing, whatever it was… is… cares too much about gender," said Larry.

Laura's response was instant. She wrapped her arms around Larry and they hung on to each other like two frightened children hugging in mutual pain.

"Did you tell O'Shea?" said Laura, finally sitting back.

Larry nodded and tenderly tucked a loose strand of her hair away, but it immediately fell back over her face. The sun had bleached her hair a shade lighter and it suited her, making her look prettier than he remembered.

"A few months ago I'd have put all this down to watching too many late-night movies." He smiled, locking his pain away for both their sakes.

"Larry, I'm so scared."

"Hey, you don't have to face this alone, kiddo."

Laura didn't return his smile. "I'm scared I'll die in childbirth," she blurted out. "It may look human but we both know it's not. How do I know it'll need me, that I'm not expendable?"

"You're forgetting one very important thing, Laura. This child doesn't just belong to its father. It's half yours and it'll need its mother, you'll see." Larry wished he was as confident as he sounded. In fact, he'd settle for half. "Let's grab some lunch," he said, lightening the tone. "Someone recommended a great little place in the Jewish sector."

"I don't have time. I promised Mother Dolores I'd accompany her to the Catacombs this afternoon. I'd never get back in time."

"Damn! I almost forgot. I've been keeping my eyes open and I'm sorry, but I really don't trust her. Can't you put her off?"

"I wish I could. She's harmless, Larry, just lonely."

"I wish I could agree. I saw her, you know, talking with your Benvenuti…"

"When?" Laura looked up sharply.

"The night… the second night I was here, near St. Peter's Square." He'd been about to say it was after he'd followed Benvenuti and Laura to the Colosseum but thought better of it.

"You must have been mistaken. Mother Dolores and I visited there together."

"Come on, Laura," said Larry. "Just how many nuns do you think run around Rome with two sticks and bent double?"

"Then maybe she was asking directions or something."

"I also saw her following you…"

"Stop it, Larry! You're seeing conspiracies everywhere." He opened his mouth to speak. "No, not another word. She's harmless, I promise." He didn't look convinced. "Come on, there's that café you were haunting over the road."

As they left the hotel, Larry said, "Well, maybe I'll just follow you and Scuttlenun this afternoon. From a discreet distance," he added as Laura turned on him.

"Scuttlenun?"

"My name for her. You're not going to change my mind, you know?"

"Nor mine," said Laura firmly. "Don't you dare try following us, understood?"

Larry had no choice but to capitulate. At least he knew where Laura and the nun would be. It was a popular tourist attraction so there was little likelihood of anything going wrong. He didn't like it. He was convinced the nun was up to something but he was being given no choice.

He found he wasn't hungry yet and decided he'd eat later. It would help fill in the hours whilst Laura was away. Besides, she was only too eager to finish his plateful as well as her own. Whilst Laura ate her lunch and Larry's, they talked of Rome's timeless beauty and its bloody past.

"What is it with the church and snakes, dragons, or whatever you want to call them? I thought they'd be against them. I read that one pope, Gregory something or other, even adopted the winged serpent as the device on his heraldic shield. Everywhere you go in this city you see serpents. They're legion," said Larry, as he drained his coffee cup and signalled the waiter for another.

"What did you say?" said Laura.

"I said, everywhere you go…"

"I know," interrupted Laura. "'And he asked him, What is thy name? And he answered, saying, My name is Legion: for we are many'." At Larry's enquiring look she added, "Mark 5:9."

"So what do we do? Wipe out every snake on earth?"

"It's been tried before. Look at St. Patrick, but all he managed to do was wipe out a populace of innocent creatures."

It was one fifteen when Laura got back to the hotel, just giving her time to freshen up before meeting Mother Dolores. She wondered if she should mention Benvenuti and watch the nun's reaction but dismissed the idea. If Larry really had seen them speaking, she was convinced it was pure coincidence and none of her business. Despite everything that had happened to her, her belief in honest clergy hadn't wavered, and she refused to give in to Larry's paranoia.

Laura found herself looking forward to the cool shade of the Catacombs. There were a number of popular ones and they mostly lay outside the city, dug out of the volcanic rock that Rome was built upon. It was ideal for tunnelling as it was softer when first exposed to the air, hardening as it dried.

The guide was enthusiastically relating how the early Christians dug out the rooms and corridors in the third and fourth centuries and used them initially as a depository for their dead, later adding chapels and even sleeping areas. In places, there were up to five different levels gouged out of the rock, the deepest as low as twenty metres beneath the surface.

"I was told of another entrance some distance from here. It's supposed to be more interesting and less commercialised," whispered Mother Dolores, pulling Laura to one side.

"We can't just wander off."

"Well I'm going to slip away," said the nun. "It's a lesser known part of the Catacombs and very informative, so I've been told. I know where I'm going." She hung back as the guide began leading the party round a bend in the passageway.

Laura was in a quandary. She didn't want to leave the main party but felt she couldn't let Mother Dolores go on her own. After all, Laura had only come to please her.

"We can maybe visit that one later or another time," Laura said, although she didn't really want another trip out here.

"It closes earlier than the rest. By the time we finish here it may be shut. I should have thought of it earlier." The nun looked contrite.

"Are you sure you know the way? I didn't see any signs apart from those at the recognised tombs."

"That's because they don't want all and sundry traipsing round there, but, I can assure you, you'll find it fascinating."

Perhaps if she gave way to the nun's request she might get away earlier, Laura thought optimistically. "All right, but let's hurry before we're missed," she said.

The nun led the way from the entrance. It was further than Laura expected and she soon regretted her decision. The different catacombs were spread out over a large area and Mother Dolores seemed to be leading them away from the main complex.

"I think we ought to go back," said Laura. They had completely lost sight of the main entrance and all signs of life.

"It's not far now," countered Mother Dolores, who seemed tireless despite the heat. "Here we are," she said finally, pointing to an open door in the rock face.

"There's no-one here," said Laura, annoyed they'd had a wasted walk. She was feeling the effects of the sun and longed for a cool drink.

"Wait till you see inside, my dear," said the nun, leading the way. At the door, she stepped aside, allowing Laura to go first.

"It's empty," began Laura, her foot on the threshold.

"Not for long, my dear, not for long."

The next instant Laura was shoved forcefully from behind and fell forward on the uneven ground. The door slammed behind her and she heard a key being turned in the lock.

"Wait," she cried, scrambling to her feet. She almost fell again as she threw herself back to the door and clutched the bars of a small grille set at about eye level. Her knees were bleeding and she winced as her grazed fingers gripped the iron bars.

Mother Dolores was already disappearing out of sight, her habit flying out around her in her haste.

He'd been watching her for some time. He'd watched as Mother Dolores led Laura away from the designated tourist route, the beleaguered guide and other tourists too wrapped up in their own lives to notice. He'd watched as they made their way to the remote hidden entrance and as the nun hurried away. Then he waited.

He had to be certain no-one else could hear Laura's calls for help, and she would call, he was sure of that. Benvenuti had pleasured himself before in the remote catacombs and no-one had ever found evidence of his handiwork, but it didn't pay to be careless. When they came, Laura's cries were music to his ears.

He let her call until her voice started to crack. A bead of sweat trickled down from his temple to under his chin, and then down and over the pulse in his neck. No-one had heard. No-one came running. Finally, and with some reluctance at concluding this part of the day's entertainment, he made his way down to the entrance, keeping to cover as much as he was able, and very quietly approached the door.

Laura called, then screamed, but no-one came. The guide had warned them not to wander off on their own but to stay in line together. There were about six hundred acres of rooms and winding passages in these vast catacombs, and he'd pointed out the very real danger of becoming lost in the maze of corridors. Exhausted, she turned from the door and leaned back against the solid wall by the opening, straining her eyes in the unaccustomed darkness. The light from the grille illuminated very little of the interior and although the floor sloped down as if to enter a tunnel, there wasn't an opening. It would seem this room had been dug out and left, perhaps with the intention of extending it at a future date, and it was never completed.

Her throat hurt and she could feel her eyes pricking with unshed tears. Her cell phone! She pulled it from her jacket pocket. Thank God it wasn't damaged. She punched in Larry's number but there was no signal, even by the door. Larry knew they were visiting the catacombs but he would have no way of knowing where to look. She must keep calling as long as her voice let her.

She turned back to the grille and visibly started.

Benvenuti was stood close to the bars watching her. A surge of relief was short-lived, replaced by dread, as she realised he had probably been there for some time and had made no move to free her.

Composing herself as quickly as she could, she tilted up her chin.

"Kindly open the door for me," she demanded, barely holding hysteria at bay.

He said nothing.

"I don't know what you hope to gain by this juvenile prank but I suggest you let me out of here if you know what's good for you." It was hard keeping her voice steady before his steely gaze. He still made no move to release her.

"Why are you doing this?" asked Laura, trying to remain calm.

"Because, my dear Laura, it amuses me and I can." He could smell her fear. It pulsed from her with her every breath and he, in turn, breathed it in. It was the most intoxicating perfume he knew. "You are not in rural England any more. This is my territory."

"And just what do you intend to do with me?" she asked. "Surely you realise you can't get away with this?"

"That is where you are very much mistaken, Laura. The Papacy is responsible for the maintenance of the Catacombs, those known to the tourists and those known only to the Vatican. No-one comes out here. It is well away from the guided tours and only Mother Dolores knows you are here, apart from me that is. She will say nothing."

"Mother Dolores! You must have some hold over her for her to do this."

"Mother Dolores? I have nothing over her, as you

239

so crudely put it. On the contrary, she is only too happy to do my bidding. She has needs, Laura, just like all of us, and I provide her with the means to satisfy her particular appetite. She will not help you; her hunger is too great."

Laura didn't want to know what those needs were and hoped fervently that Benvenuti didn't see any reason to tell her. She had trusted the nun, despite Larry's warning, and she smarted from the realisation he'd been right. What a fool she'd been and now she was at Benvenuti's mercy. Mercy! She doubted mercy and Benvenuti were acquainted. She fought back the tears, knowing he would derive satisfaction from the sight of her crying. She suspected weakness was an aphrodisiac to him and he was already enjoying her obvious vulnerability.

"I have been looking forward to this intimate time alone with you, Laura, although I feel obliged to tell you that the pleasure will be all mine. I have perfected the link between it and pain. The pain will be your part of the proceedings." He moved away from the grille and returned a few seconds later with the key that he'd retrieved from the crevice where Mother Dolores had dutifully left it.

As he inserted it in the lock, Laura backed away to the furthest wall, searching desperately with her hands in the near darkness for something with which to defend herself.

"There is nowhere to hide, Laura," mocked Benvenuti, pausing and glancing in through the bars. He imagined her soft flesh pressed firmly against hard stone and savoured the moment.

A second later he screamed and fell back, scrambling away from the door. Stumbling and falling, he tried to rid his mind of the image he'd just seen, the head of a monstrous snake inches from the grille, its yellow reptilian eyes fixed on him and filled with rage.

He remained sprawled in the dust for some minutes, his mind racing, trying to regain his composure. There was no mistaking what he'd seen. It was no ordinary snake. Even from the brief glimpse he'd had, he was aware he could see right through it, its shape held together more by a distortion in the line of vision than by an actual outline. It wanted Laura for itself, that much was obvious. Maybe he could salvage something from this after all.

Rising a little unsteadily to his feet, Benvenuti brushed himself down and warily approached the door.

TWENTYONE

Laura was confused. Everything happened so quickly. One minute she was trembling as she heard Benvenuti's approach, the next, something immense and powerful swirled up the dust in choking clouds and she heard Benvenuti scream. Something reared up between her and the door, something coiling in swift, fluid movements yet without substance. Something she'd encountered before.

She wasn't sure what frightened her most, being subjected to Benvenuti's sadistic pleasures or confronting the creature that had abused her within St. Jude's. Considering the creature – whatever it was – had not actually harmed her, she felt it was the lesser of two evils.

The dust was settling and there was no sign of movement. She strained her eyes in the poor light, aware she was still not alone.

Outside, she heard somebody approaching the door.

The spaghetti was to die for. Larry spent a pleasant few hours crossing the Tiber to visit the Jewish ghetto, and had indulged himself with local pasta and fried artichokes, washed down with half a bottle of Italian wine. Before coming to Rome, the closest he'd ever been to an Italian meal was a frozen value Bolognese from his local supermarket. Any resemblance was purely coincidental. Then, pushing his nagging concern for Laura to the back of his mind, something he hadn't been able to accomplish without the consumption of alcohol, he set off to explore further.

The afternoon was turning out to be far more

pleasant than he'd anticipated. He'd been too intent on cloak and dagger surveillance to appreciate Rome before, and it had impressed him as being just ruins, piazzas and fountains. Those and churches of course, and their seemingly endless bell ringing. Now that he had time to explore, unhurried and without any agenda, he felt himself drawn to the city. He found some Roman villas had been turned into museums and he ignored those, but their grounds had become parks and he could barely believe he was still within Rome's city limits.

Keeping as far as possible from the inevitable traffic jams, he sauntered wherever the whim took him. He glanced at his watch. Laura wouldn't be back yet awhile. He stopped by a stall selling gelato and took his time choosing his ice cream from the array of vivid colours and flavours, each adorned with the appropriate fruit and tasting so different from any he'd had before. Perhaps he was over-indulging himself, but he felt he deserved it after all the traumas in England and then the stress of following Laura. No, Larry was going to treat Larry, and to hell with the consequences.

He meandered in the general direction of the river, pausing on the Aventine Hill when he spotted a man peering through the keyhole of a weathered green door at the Cavalieri di Malta. Realising he was being watched, the man stepped to one side, grinning broadly and gestured for Larry to take a look. Feeling self conscious, Larry pressed his face to the hole and barely suppressed a gasp of appreciation. St. Peter's Basilica was perfectly framed, despite the garden on the opposite side of the door. A small spider had woven a web close to the keyhole and sat immobile, waiting for a fly. Larry adjusted his focus and the thought came to him that the Vatican sat like a fat spider with the web of Rome spun out about it. He suddenly saw himself trembling that web, alerting the spider, and he turned away and hurried back over the river to wait for Laura, his heart filled with dread.

Benvenuti cautiously leant towards the grille opening, prepared for a fast retreat if necessary. All seemed quiet but he was under no illusions; the Dark Lord wanted Laura and Benvenuti intended letting it know he would stifle his own desires and comply with his Lord's wishes. He spoke quietly, his voice gaining in strength when no further warnings came from within.

"Laura? I know you can hear me. It would seem there has been a change of plan. You must forgive me for not fulfilling my promise to you. When you achieve and have everything you've ever wanted, you begin wanting new things, different goals, different pleasures. Unfortunately, what I would like has to take second place to our Dark Lord. I had such plans, Laura, but even I have to defer to a greater power." He gave an exaggerated sigh, but one he nevertheless felt. He sensed her fear and longed to enjoy it further but all good things must end. He envied his Dark Lord and what it might do to her in the shadows of the tomb, but even he lacked the courage to stay and listen. His imagination would have to suffice and, after all, he'd had a lifetime of practice.

"Goodbye, Laura. I have to say I shall remember you with fondness. We would have had such fun together."

Laura sensed a stirring in the shadows as the sound of Benvenuti's footsteps receded. Had she been saved only to suffer a worse fate? She felt resigned, too drained to resist. It was as though all her fight had left with Benvenuti and she was too exhausted to even offer a prayer in her defence.

What Benvenuti had called his Dark Lord now slithered about her feet. She felt the cool air as it moved and a tingling, as though she was in close proximity to an electric current. The sensation slowly moved up her body and the outline of the creature wavered before her like a monstrous cobra, holding Laura in its thrall.

'It's studying me,' she thought, and suddenly it became clear why it had appeared and what it intended. She breathed out slowly, relaxing in the sure knowledge that the creature had, in fact, protected her. Protected her and her unborn child. 'It's aware of the baby,' she realised, '*its* baby.'

Something slid around her body and across her stomach, pausing there as if sensing the child in her womb and then withdrew. She became aware of other feelings, a brushing against her, slight touches that left her gasping, and then the gentlest of caresses on her face.

Quite abruptly, it released her. Laura heard the key turn in the lock and the heavy wooden door swung open. Briefly, dust swirled high in the airless room and the father of Laura's child was gone.

When Mother Dolores saw Laura walking into the hotel lobby, she felt as if her heart turned cold within her. She slunk back into a shadowed doorway until Laura had gone up to her room, then hurried from the building. She had no idea how Laura had escaped from the dungeon-like crypt but she could already feel

Benvenuti's wrath. She knew she had firmly locked the heavy door and left the key nearby as instructed. They had been alone, she had made certain of that. As far as she was concerned, she had played her part flawlessly but was equally sure Benvenuti wouldn't see it that way.

The thought of his anger and how it might manifest drove her scurrying towards the Vatican. If she broke the news to him herself, then it might stay his hand. She doubted it, but flight wasn't an option. There was nowhere to run to, and confronting him would be preferable to waiting in dread for his reaction. With her concentration now fully on how to break the news to a venomous Benvenuti, the nun pushed past a small group of students, scattering them as she expertly wielded her sticks for maximum speed.

Larry had been about to visit Laura when the nun made her hurried exit from the hotel. Sat outside the nearby café, sipping a hot black coffee and trying to stay calm, he saw Laura enter the hotel, followed by Mother Dolores's hasty departure. Had Laura deceived him? She had definitely said she was spending the afternoon with the nun but she'd arrived alone. He gulped down the remainder of his coffee, burning his mouth in the process, unsure whether to see Laura or follow the nun. Reasoning that Laura seemed perfectly all right, he decided to gratify his curiosity regarding Mother Dolores. Despite Laura's enduring faith in the nun, he didn't trust her and there was something furtive in her sudden ungainly sprint. Something had ruffled her black feathers and Larry was keen to know what.

In spite of her handicap, he had difficulty matching

her pace. She obviously had no idea she was being followed. When he caught the occasional glimpse of her face, her expression told of something being seriously wrong. Her sticks clattered on the cobbled streets whilst her wimple fanned out behind her. 'She's acting as if all the demons of hell are after her,' thought Larry. 'On the other hand, she could be running to meet them.'

Afterwards he remembered the next few seconds in slow motion. The driver of the car slammed on the brakes but it was too late to avoid hitting the nun full on with such force that she almost seemed to fly.

Larry was frozen to the spot, aware he was opening and closing his mouth like a fish in labour and unable to take in what he had just witnessed. For a moment he saw Mother Dolores's bloodied face, her dead eyes staring out unseeing, before a crowd gathered around the body and hid it from view.

Dazed and sick to his stomach, he retraced his steps to Laura's hotel. He wasn't sure how she would react to the news. She had defended Mother Dolores when he had voiced his reservations and he knew he must break the news of the nun's death as gently as possible. He was unprepared for what awaited him when he gently knocked on her door.

Larry sat in stunned disbelief. Any vindication he felt regarding his warnings about Mother Dolores was overshadowed by the horror of what might have befallen Laura. He blamed himself for not having done what he originally intended and followed them from a discreet distance.

"I'm sorry," she said. "I guess, despite everything, I'm having problems coming to terms with not being able to trust someone I should be able to."

"You've done nothing to be sorry for. We must notify the police," he said, rising to his feet.

"No," said Laura, firmly.

"No? He would have killed you, and that would have been the good part."

"What proof have we got?" asked Laura. "My word? My friend left me where, I might add, we had no right to be and I got shut in. No-one would have seen anything. There was nothing to see in fact. I got a nasty scare, end of story."

"Is that it? You're not going to do anything?" Larry was mortified.

"Oh yes, I'm going to do something, but I have to think this through. It's no use going to the authorities; at best I'd just be considered a delusional foreign tourist and don't forget, Vatican City is a law unto itself. The Italian police would have no jurisdiction there."

"So who *are* you going to?" snapped Larry, frustration getting the better of him.

"The Pope!"

Laura spent a good hour wording her letter, writing, rewriting, until she decided that, unless Benvenuti had been working purely for personal ends, the Vatican probably knew who she was, if not her purpose here in Rome. It was a chance she would have to take. She finally wrote a formal request for an audience with the Pope, giving no reason, but hoping it was forceful enough to let the reader know she wouldn't accept a refusal and meekly go away.

"Come on," she called to Larry, who had fallen asleep in a chair.

"Where are we going?"

"The Vatican."

"We can't just walk in there, you know? There's the Swiss Guard for one thing. It's protected like a prison."

"Have some faith, Larry. Come on."

"It seems to me it was faith that got us here in the first place," he mumbled, but was at her side before she was through the door.

The light was fading as they walked towards St. Peter's Square. Neither of them spoke. They'd both stepped out of their comfort zones over the last few days and were each finding it hard to adjust.

As they had anticipated, the Vatican guards blocked their way.

"This is of great importance," said Laura, handing over the envelope that was addressed to the Holy Father. "It is for his eyes only. I cannot stress how important it is that he receive it personally."

The guard was reluctant to take the envelope and called over to another.

"There are appropriate channels for communicating with His Holiness," said the second guard.

"Believe me," reassured Laura, "he will want to see this."

Finally, the guards accepted the letter.

Turning back towards Trastevere, Larry said, "You do realise that will go straight into the hands of a cardinal, probably the Pope's secretary?"

"I know," said Laura, "but we must hope it produces the desired result, whoever reads it first. If not, we try again."

"I think I'll need a stiff nightcap if I'm going to get any sleep tonight. How about you?"

Laura nodded. "The first bar we come to."

Benvenuti was not easily shaken, but the sight of Laura heading across St. Peter's Square turned his blood to ice.

That she was alive surprised him but, considering how he enjoyed taking his time in such matters, he could maybe understand that. Yet for her to march right up to the Vatican, apparently uninjured, was beyond his comprehension. He was still trying to come to terms with what he had seen earlier and the fact the dark energy was not, as he had believed, contained.

For a moment he swayed, unsure of his next move, then he raced along the corridor and descended the stairs three at a time. He paused before the Swiss Guard's booth, regaining control over his breathing before approaching them.

"The couple who were just here, what did they want?" he demanded. The guards glanced at each other. "I repeat, what did they want? Tell me."

Cardinal Scappucci slammed his fist down on the highly polished table.

"How could this have happened?" he shouted, staring Benvenuti in the face.

Benvenuti didn't flinch. After all, what was a mere man compared to what he had seen at the Catacombs?

"This letter!" The cardinal gestured towards Laura's request, open before him. "Have you read it?"

"No, Your Eminence. I brought it straight to you." Lying was so easy. Laura had mentioned nothing of what occurred at the Catacombs and, if it was discovered he'd intercepted a letter to the Holy Father, he would be in serious trouble. He'd carefully re-sealed the envelope and delivered it to the cardinal.

"She demands an audience. Why? To report your bungling?"

"That is a possibility, Your Eminence."

Cardinal Scappucci snorted. "I think it is time for you, Benvenuti, to enlighten the Reverend Coatman with regard to just whom you serve. The recent developments suggest she probably already has a good idea. The fact she has done nothing with the information means she probably wants something."

"Me! Your Eminence, is that wise?" Seeing the sudden flash of anger in the cardinal's eyes, he continued, "I'm not questioning your judgement, Your Eminence, but she will most certainly hold me in contempt."

"Are you afraid, Benvenuti?"

"I will never fear a woman, let alone a mere girl," said Benvenuti, straightening his back indignantly.

"Then perhaps you should," replied the cardinal. "This mere girl, as you call her, has somehow managed to outwit you and your permanent solution, something she would not have been able to accomplish without help. Considering the circumstances of her incarceration, one can only assume the help was not *human*. Do I make myself clear, Benvenuti? Not human."

Benvenuti stood silent, the full impact of the cardinal's words finally hitting him. He had hoped to keep the Dark Lord's intervention to himself for now, but Cardinal Scappucci was no fool.

The cardinal continued, "You will be humble when you speak to her, a new experience for you, I believe. You will explain the regret the Holy Roman Catholic

Church feels for her treatment and ask her what it is she expects of us. I suspect it will be answers, so give them to her. Are we clear on this?"

Benvenuti did what he always did when forced to smile – he faked it. "Perfectly, Your Eminence." It was certainly clear to him but he didn't have to like it. Humbling himself before Laura was almost more than he could swallow but, for now, he would play along. However, should the opportunity arise, and he was determined it should, he would make Laura Coatman regret the day she was born, and no intervention, human or otherwise, would be able to save her.

"And what of Larry Markham, Your Eminence?"

"He will leave Rome when she does. If not, we will be forced to deal with him. In the meantime, stay out of his way. And find out how this energy has avoided containment."

When he had left the room, the curtains opened and Cardinal Armatovani, secretary to the Pope, stepped into the light.

"Will he be a problem?" he asked.

"Probably! But if this Laura Coatman decides to denounce us, it is better if we distance ourselves as much as possible from a deluded monsignor with unbelievable fantasies. If he makes an attempt on her life, he will either succeed, thereby ridding us of an obstacle, or he'll be stopped and he in turn will no longer be a problem."

.

TWENTYTWO

When Laura came down the following morning, she was rendered speechless by the sight of Benvenuti waiting for her.

He greeted her as if nothing had happened. "Ah, Laura, I believe we need to talk." When she didn't respond, he went on, "Perhaps we can go somewhere private?"

Finding her voice at last, Laura tried to keep it steady. "We were somewhere private yesterday, or had you forgotten so soon? God only knows what you intended."

"I doubt it." Benvenuti paused, then, aware he was following instructions, he continued, "It would seem, Laura, that I am to – er – instruct you in just what does go on behind the closed doors of the Vatican. I personally see little point, but in this, at least, I have no choice. Now, if you refuse to be alone with me, which, I confess, is of no real surprise, let us pick a café in one of the busy piazzas in full view of the milling tourists. I doubt anyone will eavesdrop if we sit outside. Shall we?"

He turned towards the door, obviously expecting Laura to follow.

At last Laura was to get answers and, after all, wasn't that what had brought her to Rome in the first place? However, Benvenuti was the last person she wanted to be with.

"Wait! I need to make a call," she said.

"I would prefer it if this was just between the two of us, Laura. There is no need to call your lapdog. What I have to say is for your ears only. You will be quite safe, I give you my word."

"Is that supposed to reassure me?" said Laura, but she realised she'd learn nothing if she tried to bring Larry into this.

As they set off in search of a suitable café, Laura found herself wondering what she was about to hear. It would obviously be the result of her letter to the pontiff, though whether Benvenuti's instructions came directly from him she had no way of knowing. She found comfort in the knowledge that whatever had protected her at the Catacombs would see that she came to no harm with him now, or so she fervently hoped.

"Are you telling me there's no-one to hear our prayers," said Laura in disbelief. She was outraged.

They were sitting at a small table in one the square's many cafés. Those around them only had eyes for their surroundings or else were too busy with their food. Only one of the nearby tables was occupied and the young couple were far too interested in each other to listen, which was all to the good, considering Benvenuti's bombshell.

"Oh, how sweet you are," he replied. "No, your prayers are heard but they are simply not answered."

Laura was confused. "But you're telling me God doesn't exist…"

"Nothing of the kind. I am merely saying do not look for him within the church. The Order to which I belong consists of the majority of the highest-placed cardinals, those who make all decisions of consequence. *They* have the power, not the God-fearing clergy who follow orders. We all have a choice as to where our allegiance lies and that is usually based on what benefits us most. You believe, do you not," he continued, "that good can drive out evil, destroy whatever power it has? So why not accept that, similarly, evil can drive out good? That it can take away the power to answer mankind's futile little prayers? Besides, have you never considered that the devil could love you? What makes you think the devil isn't trying to save you from God?"

Laura was fully aware Benvenuti was teasing her or, at least, she hoped so. "If what you say is true, why isn't the world 'hell on earth'?"

"Some might say it is," rejoined Benvenuti.

"Most of us live in what we'd term an affluent society…"

"Affluence doesn't equate with good and never has, as I'm sure you know. Besides, *we* live here. Do you honestly think we would want to make all the world into a fiery pit?" He made a noise that was as close as he got to a chuckle.

"You said 'clergy'. What of the Pope himself? Is he a member of this Order?"

Benvenuti shook his head, dismissively. "No, he still innocently believes he is being guided in his God-given position by men as holy and dedicated as him. Deceit is easy in such a close-knit community, if those who pull the strings are joined in mutual interest. Popes are, as a rule, elderly and often in ill health. It is easy to put a puppet on what has been called the throne of Satan. Nothing reaches the pontiff except through the cardinals. What is referred to as the church is, in essence, the Ordo Autem Serpens, but then, it wouldn't be a secret order if the world aware of it, now would it?"

"I'm not sure where this is leading," said Laura. It

255

Serena Cairns

certainly wasn't what she'd expected, but then she wasn't even sure what that was. "So you're just a bunch of Satanists!"

"Nothing of the sort, Laura. Satanism is merely the reversal of Christianity. What the Ordo Autem Serpens acknowledges is older than Christianity, older than the Old Testament, older than any known civilization. It is primal power. It can be controlled to a point, but never destroyed. It is beyond that."

Benvenuti's passion for what he was describing was undeniable, but it was something far greater than Laura had imagined, even in her nightmares.

"If I accept what you're saying as true, how have I been drawn into it? What was it then, this *thing* that was unearthed under St. Jude's?"

"What you, I believe, Laura, would call Evil in its purest sense."

"Pure?" Laura spat the word.

"Laura, Laura, don't you see, good and evil are relative. You perceive that which pleases you as good, but there are many of us who have – er – shall we say, more refined tastes. Evil itself is both pleasing and stimulating to us. That which you would consider as good is quite nauseating to someone of our inclinations."

"But the church…"

"Oh come now, Laura. Where better to hide evil than behind the façade of holiness and piety?"

Laura felt as though Benvenuti was stripping her of everything she held dear, layer by layer, until there was nothing left.

"Let us walk," suggested Benvenuti, rising. At Laura's apprehensive glance he added, "We will keep to the thoroughfares."

FATHER OF LIES

It occurred to her that it would be all too easy for Benvenuti to topple her in front of the fast-moving traffic, if he had a mind to. It could easily be made to look like an accident, and she moved further from the curb.

As they crossed the Tiber, the ancient river that had witnessed so much of Man's aspirations and bloody failures, Benvenuti continued, "Many of our faults have been made public so, of necessity, we appear to change but we only concede on small issues. For example, the Catechism no longer forbids dialogue with the deceased, and we recently condoned the use of condoms, providing it is to prevent the spread of AIDS. In the great scheme of things, such concessions mean little, but give the appearance of moving with the times. You are right, of course, the average priest is full of good intentions and love for his fellow men, but he will always find himself in that niche, a servant, nothing more.

"However, there are those with ambition, those for whom hearing lurid confessions is not excitement enough, and they only need the right encouragement to forsake their holier-than-thou ideals. The more rotten the apple, the sweeter it becomes and corruption sets in before they realise it. A worm eating away at their convictions."

They paused and gazed out over the vast Tiber.

Laura was finding it difficult to hide her growing horror. She felt as if she were walking in a nightmare from which she was unable to wake. "So you exploit the baser instincts of certain individuals, giving them the opportunity to express their sadistic and sexual appetites, their greed, seemingly with the full backing of the church in the furtherance of its work? But what

257

about other branches of Christianity? This Order – you *are* talking purely within the Roman Catholic faith?" She deliberately omitted the word Holy.

Before Benvenuti could answer, a small child close by broke free of its parent's hand and staggered out in front of the oncoming traffic. Without hesitation, Benvenuti dived into the road and scooped the child up into his arms. As he leapt for the pavement there were screams from the parent and onlookers, and he fell forward on one knee, his free arm reaching out and breaking his fall. Catching his breath, he handed the child back to its distraught parent and acknowledged applause from the gathered crowd with a humble smile.

He turned to face Laura. "We have to live up to the public's perception of us," he said in answer to her unspoken question.

"You mean that was just an exercise in public relations?" she replied, wondering if she would ever get used to the contradictions in Benvenuti's character.

"Something like that." He took her elbow and guided her away from the excited chatter. "And to answer your question earlier, they are what you said, branches. That rotten apple does not fall far from the tree, Laura. Corruption is not the prerogative of the Church of Rome."

"So why isn't everyone aware of this. How can it be covered up?"

"Ah, Laura! It was Adolf Hitler – who, of course, had the Papal blessing – who said, I believe, 'Make the lie big, make it simple, keep saying it, and eventually they will believe it'. Once people believe a lie, they are willing to die in its defence, ignoring reason and factual proof to the contrary. It is a failing of humans.

FATHER OF LIES

Many have their suspicions, but who will listen when conspiracy theories are so prolific? Novels are taken as fact and facts are taken as fiction. Pseudo-science muddies the already murky waters. The majority think these stories are nonsense. They cannot believe so many people can be fooled for so long. Besides, in this day and age, very few people believe in the existence of a devil to whom they can attribute all the world's evil. Even where there is evidence of wrongdoing, such as child abuse within the priesthood, people prefer to think it is the fault of a minority. It offends their sensibilities. There are the rumours that the Vatican Bank is used to launder Mafia drug money and that the high positions within the Vatican are held by Italian Masons. Does anyone investigate? No, because few believe it and even fewer care. It was exposed recently that a member of the Mafioso had been interred within St. Peter's but the news quickly blew over. Historians are aware that the Borgia popes were involved in the black arts, and I believe The Grimoire of Pope Honorius is actually available on the Internet." He paused for a moment, savouring the look of desolation that had crept over Laura's features, before continuing. "Occasionally people ask questions, such as why name the near-infrared telescope in Arizona, 'LUCIFER'. It is laughable really."

"Lucifer?" Laura shook her head.

"The Vatican and the Jesuit Order united with the University of Arizona to build a huge stellar observatory. 'LUCIFER' allows astronomers to observe star-forming regions in young and distant galaxies in unprecedented detail, despite their dust clouds. Questions were asked why it was built on

Indian holy land, why the Vatican should be interested and why it was named 'LUCIFER', but even I do not know the reasons. However, I do know the questions were ignored and soon the questions ceased. Everything is in the open but the people choose not to see. A pope is named Vicarius Filii Dei, Vicar of the Son of God, but the numerical value of the Latin letters comes to 666. Names, numbers, all in the open. Even the name 'Vatican' comes from 'vatis', meaning prophet, and 'can' meaning serpent. No-one outside of our Order suspects, because it all seems too improbable. If there are rumours, it is put down to the imaginings of deluded conspiracy theorists."

"And what of Jesus?" she ventured. She leaned against an old stone wall for an instant, needing the touch of something solid and reassuring in her swiftly-changing world view.

"Do not worry, your precious Jesus had nothing to do with us. The dark energies have always been instrumental in religious belief systems throughout the world, ancient Egypt, Judea, Babylon, Sumer, India, to name a few. The birth of Jesus Christ gave the Order the perfect vehicle to spread out from one central source. They became less fragmented, more organised, and consequently more deadly. You will find, if you do your homework, that the saviour gods, Christ, Bel, Osiris, Prometheus, Mithra, Krishna," he paused and waved his hand as if summoning them from the air, "they all shared much the same story. There was no need for the church to be inventive. We, or perhaps I should say, the dark energies, didn't infiltrate the Christian religion until 325 AD when they began making changes with the First Council of Nicaea. It was then the Order was formed and put your Jesus back on the cross."

Letting his last comment go unchallenged, Laura pushed again for an answer. "You still haven't explained just what lay beneath St. Jude's." Laura wondered if Benvenuti was avoiding her question.

"Ah, yes, St. Jude's." It crossed Benvenuti's mind that perhaps he was telling Laura more than was intended but he was, after all, following orders. "There is a balance in all things, I am sure you will agree. The Kabbalistic Tree of Life highlights the balance of good and evil perfectly. It is one of those universal laws that even you must have battled to come to terms with. Good needs its evil counterpart and vice versa."

Laura still wasn't sure where Benvenuti was going with this and was feeling decidedly uncomfortable.

Benvenuti smiled. "You must have asked yourself why, if God created all things, he created evil as well, our salvation and damnation, if you will. Leaving God – any god – out of this, it really does come back to that balance. As the world was formed, so also were good and evil or at least the essence of good and evil. Man's perception plays its part here, though both of these energies were always present long before man emerged on the scene, for that is what good and evil are, energies. Rather like matter and anti-matter, except that, unlike them, they don't cancel each other out but co-exist."

"I don't see…" Laura broke in.

"Bear with me!"

Laura narrowed her eyes but kept silent. Her gut instinct told her he was at least telling her the truth, and it was a truth she had perhaps always been aware of. Not for the first time, her cell phone gurgled out its tune from her pocket. She checked the caller and ignored it.

"When man appeared," Benvenuti went on, "he unwittingly gave form to those energies. At its base level, anything that didn't threaten his existence was good and that which did, was evil. There have always been those who swam against the tide but, for the most part, the so-called good things became linked with passive images, whether animal, vegetable or mineral."

He was enjoying himself. Rarely did he have the opportunity to instruct, and destroying Laura's faith had a sweetness to it that he could almost taste.

"What man referred to as evil took on the shapes and forms of those things he found threatening, the serpent for example. Once man gave form to the energies, the energies in turn took on those forms. To get back to your question then, the creature that lay beneath St. Jude's was one of the original serpent energies that came face to face with a zealot called Jude. Jude was able to subdue the creature but could not, of course, kill it."

"Why was that?" interjected Laura in the vain hope he would give away a vital clue.

"One cannot kill energy, Laura. It can change its shape, but the primordial energies we are talking about here are what they are, and nothing and no-one can kill them. You will no doubt take some consolation in the fact that good cannot be killed either." He smiled. "Jude was merely able to contain the energy and was, no doubt, buried with it. It would have needed feeding. To keep it imprisoned, one of the reliquaries in the tomb will have contained a potent holy relict, such as the blood of the Virgin Mary. Now do you understand what you are dealing with, what was sleeping in the crypt at St. Jude's?"

"If it was such powerful energy, how come it lay dormant for so long?" Again she pried for information that might help; again none was forthcoming.

"It was suppressed, true, but as mankind's faith in reliquaries and their contents diminished, they began losing their power to contain the energy. It is perception that shapes reality. It would have burst forth before now had not its hunger been appeased down through the centuries."

"By the feeding of blood? This was what Pargeter was doing."

"Well done, Laura. I do believe you are beginning to comprehend at last. Yes, Pargeter was the last in a long line of feeders. With him becoming negligent in his duties, it was only a matter of time before the energy broke free. The accident at the church merely brought that time forward. If, that is, it *was* an accident."

"I don't understand," said Laura. "No-one could have shifted that beam."

"Exactly, Laura, no man could. Kinetic energy on the other hand…"

Laura's head was reeling. She was desperately trying to absorb all that Benvenuti was saying.

"You said 'one of the serpent energies' earlier. Do you mean there are more of these things?"

"Ah, yes, many more. There are similar places to St. Jude's around the world, where evil sleeps, waiting – entities born of mankind's imagination since he first formed thoughts of deities, gods and demons. We have located and released some of them but there will still be many more that we need to find. It is a case of watching carefully for the signs. That is why evil constantly seems to be on the increase. Each time a new, shall we say 'serpent' for want of a better word, raises itself from slumber, a new war breaks out, a killer epidemic spreads across a country, a famine, an earthquake… well, you get the picture."

"If what was beneath St. Jude's is pure energy, why did you have to ship the sarcophagus to Rome?" asked Laura.

"We were not forced to, but it was much easier to transport it in what it has come to know as its lair. It was more containable and easier than trying to ride the whirlwind. Jude's remains were of no interest to us."

They had walked past many of Rome's famous sites, though Laura had barely noticed them. Now, as they passed the Colosseum, she paused.

Benvenuti glanced from Laura to its high walls. "What better place for the serpent energies to lie than beneath an ancient arena dedicated to death and base pleasure?" he said, almost reverently.

"You mean, this is where…?"

"I told you, did I not, that there was more than one of these energy manifestations, not just the one buried beneath St. Jude's? The subterranean passages beneath the arena are ideal for sleeping dragons." He smirked. "Not all areas are seen or opened to the public. You have been in one of the lower regions. There are others in a lower level still that are dark enough even for the blackest of thought-forms." They walked on a few paces, before he continued. "Roma is littered with pagan temples and imagery, so is the perfect place for us to contain the serpent energies. We erected churches over the temple ruins, our altars above earlier blood-drenched ones and preserved the scenes of execution, torture, death and debauchery in the name of religion and archaeology. The city has a wonderful old drainage system, one part dating back as far as the 6th century B.C., and this, along with underground caverns and tombs, has proved invaluable for concealing various deeds from the public eye. Although many of our museums contain priceless works of art, for those who wish to see them there are relics of a more macabre nature. I particularly like the Museo della Camera Storica myself. You should take a look if you have time. There is much to be learned there of papal justice."

The warning didn't go unnoticed by Laura.

"And what of the energies we would term good? Where are they?" she asked.

"They turn up too, in a different guise of course," replied Benvenuti. "They appear in more benevolent forms, such as visions of angels, gods and goddesses. Throughout the world there are holy wells and places of healing, such as Fatima and Lourdes, for instance. There were healing wells all over the Celtic world, the Roman too. India has its fair share of holy shrines and religious sightings. Seek and you will find, Laura. Remember what I told you, always a balance, but there is no reason to assume a bright light is a holy vision. Who knows what beast may be hidden in its brilliance."

Although Benvenuti wanted to see Laura back to her hotel, she needed time to absorb all he'd told her. Already questions were bubbling up in her mind. She also had to think up what to tell Larry. Would he believe she'd wanted time to herself? She was sure he would be waiting anxiously at the hotel, and she wouldn't want to be held responsible for the outcome if he ran into Benvenuti.

She couldn't tell Larry what she'd found out, of that she was certain. No, it would have to be a lie. Sudden stomach pains and a further scan seemed the best she could come up with, and he wasn't likely to check. Why would he? He trusted her. And tomorrow? It had been left that she should ring Benvenuti when she'd had time to assimilate all he'd told her. Would there ever be time enough for that, she wondered.

So immersed in her thoughts was she that she almost fell over a small child playing behind its parent's back. Staggering, she swerved to avoid knocking it over. The mother turned and glared at Laura as if it was deliberate and Laura noticed the child had both legs in metal braces.

"I know what you're thinking," said a man who had been standing near, as Laura mumbled her apologies. He was a tourist by the look of him.

"What do you mean?" said Laura, startled.

"How can the innocent be allowed to suffer so? It is a question we all ask."

"I think I know the answer to that one," Laura replied, more to herself than her surprised companion.

As she'd expected, Laura found a disgruntled Larry waiting at the hotel. He accepted her explanation but pointed out huffily that she could have rung him, especially after all that had happened.

"I'm sorry, truly I am," she said. "I was panicking and hadn't realised my cell was switched off."

"Anything could have happened to you. You could have been abducted; how was I to know? A little longer and I'd have been battering down the Vatican's doors."

Larry being so upset compounded Laura's feelings of guilt. She really wished he'd stayed in England but, even as she thought it, she realised how glad she was that he was here, despite it making everything so difficult. She didn't need a testosterone-fuelled champion impeding what she had to do though. What was it Benvenuti had called him? Her lapdog.

Much as she would have preferred to be alone, Larry had no intention of letting her out of his sight. It made for an uncomfortable few hours. He was still grumpy, whilst she felt as if she'd just had everything she held sacred turned inside out and shredded.

"I wonder how long we'll – you'll – have to wait for a reply to your letter," Larry mused over dinner at the café opposite.

Laura shrugged. She could hardly say it had already produced results. She wasn't hungry and idly twirled the spaghetti about her fork, but there was too much Bolognese and not enough pasta. The strands reminded her of a mass of pale worm-like serpents writhing in a thick primordial sea, and she pushed the plate away in disgust.

"Look, Larry, it's been a stressful day all told. I know I got the 'all clear' but I'm tired. Do you mind if I turn in?"

"O.K., but I'll be round first thing. No running off again without me."

That night she couldn't sleep, but lay on top of her bed turning first one way, then the other. It was oppressively warm and the room seemed stuffy despite the open window. Finally sleep overtook her and she dreamed of a giant snake uncoiling from the shadows of her room. Its head rose up above her, and it held her with its deep brown eyes until they were all she could see. They were somehow familiar. She tried to focus on the head and, as she did so, it changed and became that of Benvenuti. The eyes remained the same but the mouth twisted into an ugly smile and she woke with a gasp, looking about wildly, convinced he was in the room with her. She allowed herself the comfort of a silent prayer. All was quiet. The curtains swayed gently as if moved by a soft night breeze and the moon reflected on the sill, but there was no breath of air from the window to cool the moisture on her skin and Laura lay exhausted, sticky and uncomfortable until sleep again claimed her.

TWENTYTHREE

It was late when Benvenuti was summoned into Cardinal Scappucci's private chambers.

"This woman, Reverend Coatman, is she still a problem?" The cardinal scrutinized the arrogantly confident man before him.

"She is dangerous, Your Eminence."

"I believe that's obvious, but it would also seem, from what I've been told, it's now too late to do anything about it. Have you told her about us?"

"Yes, Your Eminence, today."

"And?"

"And I believe she understands."

"Of course she understands," snapped Scappucci. "She's encountered the serpent energy and survived. What I want to know is what you think her next move might be."

"It's hard to tell, Your Eminence."

Benvenuti knew he must tread carefully. To condemn Laura as a threat to the Order might have repercussions he wouldn't want to face. If it was considered that she had to be disposed of, he was the obvious choice to deal with it, yet he had no desire to confront the Dark Lord again. However, if he played down the threat she posed, he would be answerable to the Order with all its awesome power. Considering the last conversation he'd had within these walls concerning Laura, he found it odd to now be in the role of defending her.

"It's clear the energies want her alive," ventured Benvenuti, "but to what end is anyone's guess."

"I don't want guesses. Stick with her and watch her every move."

"She's an intelligent woman, Your Eminence. I suspect she'll have more questions. Do I have a free hand in answering them?"

"At this stage I see no alternative, but, if you feel at any time she's a threat to the Holy See or the Ordo Autem Serpens, then…..," Cardinal Scappucci paused.

"Yes, Your Eminence?" Benvenuti was rigid with apprehension.

"Then we will arrange an audience and I shall meet with this Laura Coatman in my chambers. Whether she leaves the walls of Vatican City will be another matter."

Benvenuti bowed his head, exhaling quietly.

"It has not gone unnoticed, Benvenuti, that you have a tendency to think you know better than the rest of us, and that you sometimes act without thought. Remember, we have more experience than you in dealing with meddling intruders, and the Order also knows how to deal with those who reach beyond their station. It's a long time since we had a burning in the Campo de' Fiori."

"Your Eminence," acknowledged Benvenuti.

Taking his leave of Scappucci, he waited until he was in the corridor before snorting with displeasure. That he should be admonished like a schoolboy was bad enough, but Laura being the cause yet again of his embarrassment cut him to the bone. He vowed, somehow, someday, he would make her pay.

Laura felt bereft of all that made life worth living. She picked at her breakfast, wondering how she could get away from Larry. She had things she needed to ask Benvenuti and there'd be no chance with Larry shadowing her every move. She doubted Benvenuti would discuss anything except in person.

"Right," she said under her breath, "here goes."

It was easier than she thought. Playing upon the supposed scare the previous day, she merely said she was going to rest.

"I'll meet you tonight for dinner if you like," she added, trying to soften the blow.

"Perhaps you should see a doctor again," suggested Larry, unable to disguise his concern.

"Nonsense! I'm just tired," she reassured him. "It's hardly surprising considering all the stress I've been under, and worrying about the baby too. No, I just want to stay quietly in my room and relax." The lies dripped off her tongue so glibly but, surprisingly, she felt no remorse. She began to wonder what she was turning into. The old Laura would never have sunk to lying.

"You'll call me if there's anything wrong, won't you?" asked Larry. "Anything!"

"Promise. Why don't you make the most of the day? I believe you can get an excursion out to Naples and Pompeii."

"And if you *should* ring?"

"I won't! Please! I hate to think of you sat in that café all day on my account, twiddling your thumbs. You can tell me all about it over dinner. And take lots of photos!" she added.

"I would if I still had a half-decent camera," he grumbled. He didn't want to leave Laura alone, but she was adamant and he'd learned that arguing with her was useless.

Laura hoped she hadn't sounded too keen for him to disappear, even if it was true.

Next, she rang Benvenuti and arranged to meet him

at the same café they had stopped at yesterday. Again, she preferred to risk being overheard than place herself in a vulnerable situation.

On leaving the hotel, she was so intent on watching out for a distrustful Larry, possibly sat in the nearby café, that she nearly knocked Cesare off his ladder. He was busy watering the flowering baskets and showering the narrow pavement beneath.

"Ah, Signorina Laura, good morning," he laughed.

"Good morning, Cesare," she called back.

She had only taken a few steps when it suddenly occurred to her that, if Larry should call by the hotel or even ring the reception, to hear that she'd gone out only minutes after speaking with him would not go down well.

"Cesare," she called back, "would you do me a huge favour?"

"Si, signorina." He paused from watering, can held high.

"If anybody should come looking for me or ring for me, can you say you haven't seen me today? I don't like lying, but there's something I need to see to alone and I don't want to hurt anyone's feelings."

"Si, signorina. Do not worry about a thing. I will keep your secret. Ciao." He waved the watering can dangerously.

"Grazie!" She didn't like doing this at all but it seemed what people said was true, that lying became easier the more you practised it. She was afraid she would soon become accomplished in the art.

"I'm rather puzzled," said Laura over coffee, "about your mention of relics. Surely if the energies you speak of can be so easily subdued, they can't be that strong. On top of which, the majority at least of what were termed holy relics were in fact fake. How does that work?"

"Do holy relics have power? Of course, but it is the power human beings give to them."

"You mentioned the blood of the Virgin Mary."

"I was being facetious, using that as a silly example, Laura, but certainly a saint's blood was considered a reliquary. In fact, when Saint Vibiana, who became the patron saint of Los Angeles, was excavated from the catacombs of San Sisto, here in Rome, her tomb housed not only her body, but also a vessel containing her blood. Both were shipped to America." Benvenuti didn't seem to notice Laura's reaction at the mention of the catacombs. "A chip of the crucifixion cross, bones of just about anyone, holy or otherwise, I understand even Rasputin's dried penis, were all considered holy relics. And of course, these things *did* have power if people believed it of them. The power attributed to even the basest article imbues it with that power, its potency if you like. Look at the Communion wine and wafer."

Laura was appalled.

"You yourself know the power of prayer," continued Benvenuti, "not just to your god but to any deity, even a lump of rock for that matter. Every thought is a powerful thing and has the power to create. If the horned devil, God or feathered angels didn't exist to begin with, then they, or something very similar, surely do now in some form. And that's due simply to the amount of thought that has been invested in them. Pour energy into these thought forms and you give them life. If enough people believe they can subdue evil with good, then the chances are they can.

And it goes without saying, the reverse is also true. Even today, the Vatican trades in relics. Of course, if you require a splinter from the Holy Cross, you need an application from a bishop."

Benvenuti's dark eyes sparkled like morning frost on black marble. Laura looked away; they made her think of tombstones.

"I also find it hard to believe the Order has managed to keep its existence a secret for two thousand years," she said.

"Not quite two thousand. It was not until three hundred and twenty five AD that the Order formalised its structure and intent. Before that, the energies were totally unchecked. It was then that we, and I use the term broadly, linked our own desires to those of the energies. Naturally, there have been individuals – even popes who were not elected from the Order – who have stumbled on the truth, but they were seldom believed and, if they did become a problem, it was easy enough for them to disappear."

Laura felt a sudden chill. "As I would have done?" she asked.

"Indeed!" Benvenuti seemed totally unabashed.

"You choose to worship that which is evil rather than that which is good. Why? I don't understand."

"No, Laura, your use of the word 'worship' is incorrect. We, how shall I put it, we *align* ourselves to that which is most profitable to us as individuals, as it ultimately makes no difference to which we give our allegiance. Neither can be destroyed. We merely use what best suits our purposes."

"And to hell with the rest of the world?"

"Ha, I think we have already established there is no Hell, but, to answer your question, it is so important to enjoy what you do. Don't you feel that, Laura? I enjoy my work. I can only surmise, but I suspect the early church elders were no different from us, and that some preferred the idea of hedonistic pleasure to sackcloth and ashes. Excess is so much more rewarding than self-denial." He waved to a young waitress and ordered more coffee and pastries.

"But to seem so pious in church rulings..." Laura was still struggling with the fact that millions of devoted followers accepted laws they believed came from God's representative on earth.

"As I have already stated, it is very easy to deceive, Laura."

She glanced up, wondering briefly if he had been reading her thoughts.

"For instance, the church is against birth control. It states that all human life is sacred and the unborn baby has the right to life. To destroy it is murder, but that very ruling causes untold suffering, especially in third world countries where there is famine and drought. You see how simple it is? Think the policies through and you will see the suffering they cause." He bit down on a pastry and added, "You really should try one of these."

Beneath the veil of brightly striped tablecloth, Laura placed her hand on her belly. Soon the baby would be noticeable. She could already see the gentle swell in her curves when she stood naked before her mirror. Did this child too have that same right to life that the church purported to advocate? She looked up at Benvenuti.

"And what of love? Does that not touch your world at all?" she asked, feeling a lump in her throat as she spoke.

"Love?" He gave a shallow laugh. "Of course! I *love* what I do. I *love* life. *My* life! Why do people always think love is something they have to share?"

Laura fought back unexpected tears.

"Are you going to eat that?" Benvenuti added, motioning towards her pastry.

Laura shook her head. Despite everything that had happened, she couldn't help but wish the man opposite her had chosen a different path, and she wondered what black events in his past had moulded him into the monster he'd become. Could he have been different once, she wondered, or had he always harboured this darkness in his soul? She pulled herself together. Wishing achieved nothing and Benvenuti wasn't about to change.

If he noticed Laura's silence he didn't show it. "Sometimes the church does what is says on the packaging. After all, wouldn't you say it has always been expected to support the underdog? Surely what has been described as the devil fits this bill? Even your Rolling Stones recorded a song called, 'Sympathy for the Devil'." This obviously amused him and he smothered a smile with the last of the coffee.

Laura was becoming aware of zigzag lines blurring her vision. Considering how stressful the last few days had been, it was not surprising she should feel the onset of an optical migraine. Fortunately they were pain free, but trying to focus became nigh impossible. She needed to lie down.

"So what happens now?" she said, trying to keep Bevenuti's face in the outer periphery of her sight.

"What do *you* want to happen, Laura?"

She was taken aback, expecting him to suggest options, if indeed there were any. She'd wanted and received answers but hadn't divulged her pregnancy. She wondered again what Benvenuti's reaction would be. No, this was something for the ears of the Holy Father himself. She needed reassurance that both she and the baby would be safe, and she needed that from the man at the top.

"I want what I requested in my letter – an audience with the Pope."

Larry took Laura's advice and checked out the tours. Not only were they pretty costly but he didn't like the idea of relying on excursion companies' timetables. He wanted to be able to get back to Rome quickly if Laura needed him. Finally, thankful that he'd thought to bring his UK driving licence with him, he decided on hiring a car. This gave him the freedom he needed.

Once he'd left the chaos of the city's congestion behind, he felt himself unwind. Every bend in the road brought breathtaking views. He found himself wishing he were just another holidaymaker soaking up the Italian sun. Maybe, when all this business was over, he and Laura could come back here on holiday. The thought brought him up short. It would *never* be over. And where did he fit in if she was going to give birth to god knows what? What made him think he had any role in her future?

He stopped at a picturesque trattoria for lunch: cold cuts of meat, truffles, local cheeses and bread, all with the pungent aroma of garlic, and washed down with a glass of white wine from a nearby vineyard. Any other time, he would have felt mellow and satisfied, but his concern for Laura hung about him like a cloud, until he finally gave in and turned the car back to Rome.

As Larry entered the small but mercifully cool

foyer of his hotel, the porter at the desk signalled that he had a visitor in the lounge. A wave of relief washed over him; Laura must be feeling better after her rest.

In a chair by the window, one leg resting on a stool, sat O'Shea.

"Where the hell have you been and where the devil is Laura?"

"L-Laura wasn't feeling too good. She's taking it easy today. This may sound a silly question but what are you doing here?"

"Well, as neither of you thought to keep me abreast of what's happening, I decided I'd better come and see for myself."

"You could have phoned!" said Larry, taken aback.

"Lost your number," huffed O'Shea.

"But not the address," said Larry with sarcasm.

"Confound it, I wanted to be here. All right?"

"There, that wasn't so hard, was it?" Larry smirked as he straddled a chair facing O'Shea.

"How is she? Laura? You said, 'resting'? I went to her hotel. Some woman, Manola or someone, …"

"Manuela!" Larry interjected.

"Yes, well, she said Laura was out. She went up and knocked on her door but there was no reply, so I came on here."

Larry was already ringing Laura's cell, visions of her laying unconscious playing in his head. "Pick up, pick up," he kept repeating.

When she finally did, she sounded far from pleased.

"Are you all right?"

"Of course I'm all right except you just woke me up. I told you I'd meet you for dinner." Her voice sounded croaky. She peered groggily at her bedside

278

clock. At least the numbers weren't jumping around any more.

"I'm sorry! It was just that …" Larry began.

"Seven thirty!" said Laura and hung up.

"It looks as if she'll have the delightful surprise of dining with us both," said O'Shea, the thought of food obviously improving his mood. "In the meantime, I suggest we find the bar and you bring me up to date with everything you've not been wanting to tell me."

Laura struggled to hide her displeasure as O'Shea loudly hailed her over to the table where he sat with a sheepish-looking Larry. It was bad enough trying to shake off one lapdog but now there were two of them. Double the deceit, double the lies and double the chance of being found out. There had been a message from Benvenuti waiting at reception when she'd left, saying an audience had been arranged for the following afternoon. At least she wouldn't have to lie about her whereabouts on this occasion.

"What a wonderful surprise!" she said. "It's so good to see you. When did you arrive?"

"Before lunch," said O'Shea, as Laura wrapped her arms around his neck. He tried to stand, slightly overwhelmed by her greeting, but gave up. I came by your hotel but that woman, Mag…, Mon…"

"Manuela." Larry came to the rescue again.

"Yes, she knocked on your door but there was no reply."

Laura didn't stall for an instant. "I got something from the local chemist to help me sleep. It seems it actually worked," she joked.

Despite the problems it would cause her, she was pleased to see O'Shea looking so well. "As good as new?" she asked.

"It's too late for me to ever be that, but better than I have been. Larry's been bringing me up to speed. I see now why I hadn't heard from either of you. It would have scared me half to death. I understand you're trying to get an audience with the big man himself?"

"Yes, I've just heard in fact that I have an audience booked for tomorrow afternoon." She hadn't been surprised by the speed with which it had been arranged. Obviously the Vatican wanted this English upstart of a girl dealt with as quickly as possible. "Maybe you can let Larry show you the sights of Rome tomorrow," she suggested. "I'll need the morning to prepare myself."

Neither Larry nor O'Shea were keen on the idea, but Laura was adamant that she needed some time alone to think through all she had to say and ask. She already had most of the answers but they weren't ones she could share. Not yet, anyway. She could see herself spending most of the morning working on a story that would satisfy them both.

"Where are you staying?" she asked O'Shea.

"As luck would have it, I managed to get a room here, two doors down from Larry. Had to say I was his uncle, heaven forbid." They laughed but Laura picked up a tension beneath their idle chatter.

"You're looking well, blooming in fact," said O'Shea, still skirting around something.

Laura realised then why the conversation had felt strange. Neither of the men had wanted to touch on the subject of the baby.

"I've never felt better," said Laura truthfully, "but mother and baby need their sleep. I'll ring you when I get back to my hotel tomorrow." At last she was able to escape, but she wasn't sure how long she could play this game. She hoped fervently that tomorrow might provide the answer.

After Laura had left, O'Shea leaned across the table.

"On your life, Larry, you must promise me you'll protect Laura."

That night, as Laura lay in bed, she thought back to Benvenuti's words, that all life was sacred. It hit her as strange that not once had she seriously considered aborting the child she was carrying. She doubted she'd ever had that option though. If this energy, for she accepted that's what it was, had wanted a safe vessel for its seed, then it could not have found a better one than a woman of the cloth. Perhaps she'd been chosen not by chance, as she had once thought, but because, as a priest, abortion was something she would never contemplate.

As though the baby read her mind, she felt it stir within her. She laid her hand above it, then pulled back in horror. Her skin rippled beneath the touch as though the child was rubbing itself against her fingers.

She pulled back the quilt and swung her feet onto the floor. She sat on the edge of the bed, uncertain if her legs would support her. She'd broken out in a sweat. Finally the full horror of what she was carrying hit her. It was like waking from a dream only to enter a nightmare. "The scan looked normal," she repeated over and over, trying to convince herself that the baby would be too. 'What was I thinking? How could I have been so stupid?' Even as the full awareness of her situation hit her, she knew there was nothing she'd be allowed to do to alter it. She'd suffered these bouts of panic less since coming to Rome, and always they'd been replaced by a comforting blanket of reassurance, but, this time, none came. The undulating movement in her womb had ceased and now, feeling cold, she crept beneath the cover, like a child trying to lock out the dread with tightly squeezed lids.

TWENTYFOUR

The following morning, Laura was surprised she felt so calm, despite thinking she was, in the words of a Bob Dylan song, 'going ninety miles an hour down a dead end street'. An audience with the Pope was something most Catholics could only dream about, but then they didn't know what she knew. She felt exhilarated, but was aware she had to appear cool and in control. It helped that she felt sure in herself that she was on the brink of something momentous.

She viewed herself in the mirror. She'd heard how women who were pregnant seemed to glow but had never thought to see herself this way. There was a radiance about her that even she recognised. For one rare instance she found herself admiring her reflection. The girl looking back at her from the glass had come a long way, but only now was she fully aware of each step that had brought her to this place, this point in time, and for what? Maybe today she'd finally understand.

Her audience wasn't booked until late afternoon. With Larry showing O'Shea some of Rome's sites, she had a few hours to herself. Neither of the men had felt it appropriate to go sightseeing. but they finally gave in as they could do little else but wait. O'Shea had fought long and hard against Larry pushing him around in a wheelchair, so they had finally settled upon taxis to various landmarks with Larry providing a supportive arm whilst there. She didn't envy him the job.

Still smiling at the thought, she decided to stroll to the Campo de' Fiori, where the open market sold flowers of every description. Basking in the array of colours and perfumes would maybe take her mind off the impending meeting, the dread of the night before now forgotten.

Around the edge of the piazza, a number of gypsies approached the tourists, offering them lucky heather and palm readings. It all added to the holiday atmosphere.

"Signorina, you buy?" The woman looked elderly but maybe it was her brown weathered skin that made her appear older than her years.

"No, no thank you," replied Laura, turning to move away, but the woman grasped Laura's wrist, halting her.

"I read signorina's palm? Tell of tall dark man," she insisted.

Laura was in no mood to argue and she resignedly let the gypsy take her hand, thinking that one tall dark man was enough to contend with.

With a sudden cry, the woman released her grip. "La Papesse," she hissed, then again, louder, "La Papesse."

Despite the heat of the day, Laura felt a coldness envelope her. She'd heard that name before but couldn't recall where. The woman had turned, about to scurry away.

"Wait," called Laura. "Please, I must know what you mean."

The woman scrutinized her. "La Papesse," she said again, this time in no more than a whisper.

"What do you mean?" Heat flushed Laura's cheeks and made her unsteady, replacing her initial chill.

The woman tentatively took Laura's arm, leading her away from the milling tourists and curious onlookers. "You do not need a man, my lady," she said in an accent more cosmopolitan than the one she'd used previously, her voice low, almost reverent, as if fearing to be overheard, "but you must beware of one." She pointed now at Laura. "La Papesse!"

She reached out and took Laura's hand and raising it up, brushed it with her lips. Uttering "My lady" once more, she turned and vanished into the crowd.

Laura stood transfixed, trying to extract meaning from the gypsy's words. Not for the first time she wished she'd brought her laptop to Rome with her. There must be an Internet café somewhere but she hadn't much time. She knew she needed to find out what the woman had been referring to, and she needed to know before her audience with the Holy Father.

It took three attempts before Laura was able to get directions but fortunately, once there, the staff spoke English and showed her how to log on. She typed 'La Papesse' into the search engine, guessing on the spelling, and was quickly able to find a wide variety of links. The second card of the Tarot's Major Arcana, La Papesse was, in older versions of the pack, what later became known as The High Priestess. It was thought by some to refer to her beloved Pope Joan. Of course, that was where she'd heard that name before, in Larry's flat in what seemed like a lifetime ago. It had meant nothing to her then but now, as she read on, she smiled. When she'd finished, she headed for the Vatican. The clock was ticking and she had an appointment to keep.

Benvenuti was waiting to greet her. 'Step into my parlour...' thought Laura.

"Good afternoon, Laura. I hope you slept well last

night and are feeling recovered."

"I'm sure it will come as no surprise to you to learn I had a dreadful night."

"As always, you are correct," said Benvenuti, touching Laura lightly on her arm to guide her. Although she managed not to flinch at his touch, it amused him to watch her reaction. "I assume you lay in bed or maybe paced your room, trying to rationalise everything I told you. I should be interested to hear your conclusions."

The palatial opulence of the Vatican rooms was beyond Laura's most wild imaginings. They'd entered through St. Anne's Gate, the main entrance, and passing through high arches, came into a square. The building rose up on all sides, looking austere and unfriendly, reminding Laura of her university, but it belied its interior. Stepping into the elaborate hall of the apostolic palace, she gasped. Everywhere she looked there were works of art and excessive use of gold leaf. In a world where there were still starving millions, she found the grandeur obscene. It had the air of something that should have died but had somehow overcome death and gilded over its corruption and decay. She could feel the weight of the shadows like a living presence. She was not going to this meeting as a supplicant but as an equal and she felt she was not there alone.

"In bocca al lupo!" murmured Bevenuti, as they reached Cardinal Scappucci's apartment.

The cardinal reached out to her. As she bent forward to kiss the proffered ring, repugnance crawled like worms beneath her skin and she recoiled from him.

"Come now, Laura – I may call you Laura, may I

not? – am I really so bad?" he asked, scrutinizing the woman before him. He was curious. According to Benvenuti she had almost cost him his life.

"That can't be a serious question," said Laura. "And I was led to believe my audience was with Pope Gregory."

"Surely you did not think we would allow you to go telling tales to our beloved pontiff. He is old and in ill health, and such stories would upset him, do you not agree?"

"But I thought..." Laura spluttered.

"That he belonged to our Order, perhaps that he was the head of it? No, not this pope, though many in the past have had that privilege. The Order of the Serpent is not for everyone. Monsignor Benvenuti has enlightened you regarding our true nature, I understand. You see, we do not worship a god of whom we have no proof. We prefer to deal with energies of which we are very much aware, and to which you too can testify. It must seem a little strange to you, but I feel sure you will grow to appreciate what they... we can do for you."

"And this in return for what, my silence?"

"Of course. I am sure you will concede that we are not forced to bargain as a rule."

"If folk tales are anything to go by, bargaining with the devil never ends well. You're trying to whitewash something that's too dark to be covered."

"We have succeeded for two millennia, Laura, and done it very well, don't you agree? The people were only too ready to hang their Christ upon a golden cross, condemning him to an eternity of suffering in their sight. It will take more than you to prise loose those nails."

287

"You use these... these things, these energies, to cause suffering whilst you profit."

"Not just me personally. We placate the Dark Lords, this is true, in return for... favours. They would cause suffering just as much without our help. If you were the Devil, where better to hide than within the organisation duty-bound to destroy you?" He smiled sweetly. "But then I am not the Devil. I find that to become head of our Order within that organisation, a position so powerful that no-one can touch you, is all the reward I need. As for all the sins you no doubt lay at our door, you can't alter history, young woman."

"No, Your Eminence, but I can help even the score."

"And what do you intend to do, expose us? Think about it. You would be responsible for the destruction of millions of people's lives. Destroy their beliefs and they would be left with nothing. Would you really want that on your conscience, even if we were prepared to allow it?"

"I am fully aware, Your Eminence, that I wouldn't be believed even if I tried," said Laura.

"Ah, a little wisdom at last," sneered Scappucci. "So what is it that you do want?" He was at a loss to see what the dark energies would want with this slip of a girl and it made him uneasy.

"I want to be Pope."

Scappucci blanched. Only he and one other trusted cardinal would understand the danger Laura posed.

Laura had expected her words to enrage the pompous and highly unpleasant cardinal, but, instead of derisive laughter, she had struck a nerve, yet wasn't sure why or how to press home her advantage.

"You are a little too ambitious, I feel," said

Scappucci, recovering quickly. "Do you really think that office is an enviable position? It is the loneliest on earth."

"There is always a price for power."

There was a pause. "So tell me, Laura, do you believe in God?"

"I don't have to believe in God to believe in the teachings of Christ."

"This is true. He was not the only man – or woman for that matter – to preach that particular code of living, but you mustn't mind my observation when I ask, isn't the idea of a priest who doesn't believe in God an unusual concept?"

"Unusual maybe," conceded Laura, "to an outsider but, looking back over the history of the papacy, I doubt many of the popes believed in God, any god, or else they would have expected eternal damnation for their unholy behaviour. I certainly don't see God's hand in the running of the church."

"Harsh words! I note that you no longer wear your priest's collar. Is there a reason for that?"

Laura was not about to admit that she hadn't wanted to draw attention to herself. "It seemed rather hypocritical for me to do so whilst having a crisis in faith."

"And have you resolved that crisis?"

"Yes, Your Eminence, I believe I have."

The cardinal was silent for a moment.

"I don't believe you wanted to see me merely as a job-hunting exercise. Let us cut to the chase, as the saying goes. Apparently one of the Dark Lords wants you alive and unharmed, so I am obliged to ask what you want, apart from the highest position in the Vatican, in exchange for your silence?"

"I can only answer for how I feel at this moment," said Laura.

"That is all any of us can do." He loathed having to negotiate with this base female who, but for Benvenuti's bungling, would already be food for worms.

"I want both protection and upkeep for myself and my child." There, it was said. She waited for the cardinal's reaction.

The meaning of Laura's request took a moment to register. When it did, a surge of anger rose in its wake.

"Child?" He spat the word.

"That is what I said, Your Eminence," Laura calmly replied.

"You think the church will take responsibility for you and Benvenuti's bastard? If we paid out for every child springing from the loins of our clergy the church would indeed be poor." He laughed, a coarse sound with no humour in it. "After all I'd heard about you, *Miss* Laura Coatman, I'd thought there was more to you than just being a whore. You can tell your lover that your scam has failed. You have nothing. You *are* nothing. Crawl back to your gutter and take Benvenuti with you." His laughter was tinged with hysteria born of relief. This girl was no threat at all.

"The child is not Benvenuti's," said Laura, after waiting for the laughter to subside.

Scappucci waved his arms dismissively. "Then go back to your loser journalist or could it have been that drunken Irish schoolmaster? Is that it? You and the failed priest? Or do you not know which? I would ask you to come back later so I can have my turn with you, but you are really not my type."

"The baby was conceived within St. Jude's by one

of your Dark Lords, as you call them. That is why it protects me and why *you* should bow your knee to *me*." She spoke with a confidence and authority that surprised the cardinal. He stopped laughing. "I'll leave you to consider my terms shall I? Your lackeys know where to find me."

With that, Laura turned and marched out of Scappucci's apartment. She was trembling and, although she tried to hide it, she knew Benvenuti would notice. He was stood a short distance from the doors, waiting to escort her back to the world outside.

Laura felt as if she didn't breath again until she was in the square amongst amorous cooing pigeons and gawping tourists. Benvenuti touched her arm again and she hoped Larry and O'Shea weren't among the crowds nearby.

"Laura, I obviously do not expect you to tell me what went on with Cardinal Scappucci, but you seem very shaken. Perhaps you will allow me to buy you a coffee?"

Laura turned to look at him. Could it be he was actually concerned for her or was it a ruse to get her to talk? She decided she could do with a coffee, strong and black, and let Benvenuti guide her out of the square and towards the Tevere. She'd just faced down one of the most important and influential men in the church and her nerves were raw.

Laura was tempted to tell Benvenuti about the baby but held back. She wanted to wait until she heard from Cardinal Scappucci. She was certain she wouldn't have long to wait. They'd crossed the river and were now seated outside one of the cafés in the Piazza Navona, where buskers provided the background music to street artists' negotiations with enamoured tourists. Benvenuti had, perhaps a little too obviously, steered her away from the vicinity of the Vatican.

"If you must know, His Eminence was trying to buy my silence. I'm sure you've already worked that out," said Laura over the coffee, feeling a little more like her old self.

"And did he?" he asked. He seemed almost disinterested but the small tension lines about his eyes told another story.

"Let's say negotiations are in progress."

"I see!" Benvenuti paused as if considering his next words carefully. "I would urge you to take great care, Laura. You believe me to be dangerous, but I am as nothing compared to him and he has resources beyond even my knowledge."

Laura looked at him in astonishment.

"Who are you and what have you done with the real Monsignor Benvenuti?" It was a limp attempt at humour that failed to raise a smile.

Abruptly, Benvenuti rose. "I am glad to see you are recovered. You will excuse me; I have things I must attend to." With that he was gone, leaving Laura feeling as if she'd been slapped in the face. She slowly finished her coffee. 'La Papesse' may be the High Priestess card but right now she felt as if all she'd managed to conjure was a deeper pit to fall into.

"Well?" Larry and O'Shea almost spoke in unison.

"Let me at least sit down and order," grinned Laura, when they met for dinner. Whatever she may be feeling inside, she mustn't let them know she was concerned. Worrying about them worrying about her was the last thing she needed.

Over seafood pasta and salad, she explained that it had been Cardinal Scappucci whom she'd seen.

"Pope Gregory seems to be a pope in name only; it's Cardinal Scappucci and the Ordo Autem Serpens that pull the strings of their puppet pope. He is frail, from what I can gather, and is probably relieved to have decisions made for him."

She filtered the information Benvenuti had given her, inferring it was Cardinal Scapucci who'd explained it all. The answers she'd been unable to give them previously now stunned them into silence. The explanation of the entity in St. Jude's was difficult to digest and needed to be washed down with copious glasses of red wine.

By the time she'd finished talking, the two men were mesmerised.

"There's one thing I don't understand," said O'Shea. "If these energies are contained in some way, how has this particular one been able to appear when you're in danger?"

Laura paused before answering. "I wondered that too, and can only assume it can link with the child. I am carrying a part of its energy, and it draws on that to manifest. I can see no other explanation."

"And the great unholy holinesses expects you to keep quiet about all this?" It was Larry who spoke.

"Don't be a fool," she said, more sharply than she'd intended. "Even with your connections, Larry, no-one would believe it. It's National Enquirer material and I, for one, don't want to spend the rest of my days in an asylum, thank you very much."

"She's right," O'Shea reluctantly agreed. "There are some truths that will never be believed."

"So what do we do? Just stand back and let it go

on?" The wine was taking effect and it was no good trying to reason with him.

"There's not much else we *can* do, not for now at least," said O'Shea.

"Not for now? What does that mean, for Christ's sake?"

"You're forgetting the baby," said O'Shea, looking regretfully at Laura.

"Baby? What…?" Larry looked confused.

"He means," said Laura, "that we don't know what I'm going to deliver to the unsuspecting world, or the Vatican for that matter. Scappucci thinks one of you is the father."

"Would that was the case," groaned Larry, sinking deeper into despair.

"I think," said O'Shea, "that what you've learned is only the tip of the iceberg, a mere fraction of the whole, so take great care. Keep your wits about you."

Laura nodded. She was eager to change the subject. "Do you remember, Larry, back in your flat that time, a tarot card fell from the pack I was looking at?"

"Tarot cards!" exclaimed O'Shea. "And there I was thinking you were only shagging!" The wine was, it seemed, also affecting him.

Laura tried not to smile. "Not really," said Larry.

"You said it was the High Priestess and commented on it being strange, what with me being a priest."

"Oh yeah, vaguely."

Laura went on to tell the two men about her meeting with the gypsy.

"So this means what, exactly?" asked Larry.

"Hold on, I looked it up on the net," said Laura. "I wrote down its meaning." She fumbled in her bag. "Here we are."

O'Shea sighed.

"Amongst other things," she continued, "it means secrets, spiritual forces and matters not yet revealed. It can also mean esoteric knowledge, occult wisdom and hidden influences. Don't you find *that* strange, considering all that's been going on?"

Perhaps it was the alcohol but neither seemed as excited as Laura had hoped. Still, at least it had drawn Larry away from his previous thoughts, so she thanked 'La Papesse' for that.

Later, alone in her room, Laura considered the evening had gone well. The two men had expected answers and she'd managed to satisfy them. She couldn't tell them what would happen next because she didn't know.

Before climbing into bed, she took from her bag the piece of paper on which she'd written the tarot definitions, smoothed it out and placed it between the pages of her Bible. For some unfathomable reason it comforted her, and she needed all the comfort she could get.

TWENTYFIVE

Benvenuti had been standing by his window since dawn. He'd watched the sky grow pale and the sun touch the rooftops of Rome, but none of its beauty registered. Throughout his long association with the Ordo Autem Serpens, he had often been asked to perform unpleasant tasks. Usually he was able to extract some pleasure from them and the rights and wrongs held little meaning for him. He was allowed, even given the opportunity occasionally, to pursue his own pleasures, but it was always understood that his desires came second to those of the Order.

Until recently, it was Cardinal Vanni who'd instructed him in his duties, or at least he had until now. This time he had been called into the Cardinal Scappucci's presence in the early hours.

"It's essential that you finish the task you were appointed earlier, Benvenuti, and that you waste no time. Laura Coatman has to disappear, quickly, quietly and above all, permanently. Am I fully understood?" The cardinal fixed him with a steady gaze but, before Benvenuti could answer, he continued, "How you accomplish this is up to you, but failure isn't an option this time. I suggest you put your own pleasure on hold and get the job done. There are plenty of tarts in Rome to take your mind off this one."

"But the Dark Lord, Your Eminence..." he began.

"There can be no excuses. Furthermore, you will say nothing of this to anyone, you hear me? Not Vanni, not anyone."

Benvenuti nodded. None of this was to his liking and if things went wrong, as his every instinct shouted they would, he'd be made the scapegoat. That's if he managed to kill Laura and live. This was what he'd been dreading.

Taking leave of the cardinal, he spent the next few hours in thought. Finally, as soon as etiquette would allow, he silently made his way to Cardinal Vanni's apartment.

Laura had not yet dressed the following morning when there was a knock at her door and she heard Manuela's voice.

"Signorina Laura, you have a visitor. A holy man of the cloth."

Pulling on a dressing gown, Laura went down to the reception area. Perhaps it was already a messenger from Cardinal Scappucci. Benvenuti was standing imperiously near the desk. As he turned to greet her, there was no sign of a smile.

"Are you insane coming here?" spat Laura. "If Larry should see you or even O'Shea for that matter…"

"I need to speak with you on a matter of great importance," he replied.

"Could you not have just rung me?" said Laura, not only annoyed at Benvenuti's uncharacteristic lack of guile but also him catching her in a state of disarray.

"It cannot wait."

"Not here then. I'll join you at the usual café in about twenty minutes. Now please go before you're spotted." Laura could hardly be seen pushing a Vatican representative from the building but she came close, glancing anxiously up and down the street. "Twenty minutes," she repeated, before darting back to her room. She wondered what could be so important that it warranted this early morning visit.

Once in the café, Laura ordered a coffee and croissant. It seemed highly likely she would now miss her usual breakfast.

"All right, what's so urgent?" she asked.

"There are certain cardinals at the Vatican who would like to speak with you."

"Why should I want to speak to them? I'm waiting to hear from Cardinal Scappucci."

"May I suggest," said Benvenuti, "that you reconsider? Earlier this morning he gave me direct instructions to take your life. If you want to go on living, I recommend you take the other cardinals up on their invitation."

Laura struggled not to choke on croissant crumbs. She looked at Benvenuti in disbelief.

"Whatever was said in your audience with Cardinal Scappucci has convinced him you are a threat of some kind, or at least an inconvenience he would rather be without. What you might call a loose end that needs to be tied."

"And you were given the task of tying it," she stated, numbly.

"So it would seem, yes."

"Why should I believe you?" Even as she asked the question she knew Benvenuti wasn't lying. She had seriously misjudged Scappucci and it could have cost her dearly. Although reluctant to admit it, she realised she owed Benvenuti her life.

"Because, if you think about it, I have never lied to you, Laura. Besides, there is one thing I will not do and that is accept a suicide mission. You will need someone to, how do you say it, watch your back."

Laura thought him stabbing her in the back might be closer to the truth. What he was suggesting was like giving the position of chef to Hannibal Lecter, but he was probably being honest, and she was willing to listen to what he proposed.

"I don't need anyone's help but, if I did, it would need to be someone I could trust," she said.

"Come now, Laura, surely someone familiar with the manoeuvrings of those in a position of power might be more useful to you right now. After all, trust can be broken, especially at a price. Do you really expect your two lame terriers to do more than bark when your life is threatened?"

"Your Dark Lord stopped you. It'll shield me again if need be."

"Nevertheless, the cardinals appear eager to meet your demands, provided they are not excessive."

"When do they want to meet with me?" said Laura.

"Now!"

'Carpe Diem,' thought Laura, 'as if I have a choice.'

As they headed towards the Vatican, Laura said, "It has occurred to me that I may be walking into a trap. You could be working for Cardinal Scappucci, after all."

"Be assured, Laura, the head of Ordo Autem Serpens does not stain his own hands or put himself at risk. If I wished you harm, I would hardly be leading you to the Vatican when there are far more appropriate places to take a life."

"If that's supposed to give me comfort, it doesn't. Your own guard wouldn't breathe a word against you."

"True, but it would be too obvious. I prefer to maintain a little discretion. Besides, where would the fun be in that?"

They had arrived at St. Peter's Square where they

passed the crowds gathering about the Basilica.

"It is no coincidence that St. Peter's church, the largest Christian church in the world, by the way, was built on the site of Nero's ancient circus grounds where he had hundreds of Christians executed." He smirked. "It adds a certain ambiance to the place, don't you think?"

He left Laura standing alone as he spoke to the Swiss Guards on duty. They nodded their red-plumed helmets and stood to attention like fairytale soldiers in their armour and yellow, blue and red uniform. Then he raised an arm in her direction. She was ushered through and taken quickly up a back stairway. They hurried across marble floors and through more immense arched doorways to a room where the assembled cardinals waited.

Before opening the door, Benvenuti paused. "You will not be aware of it, but I believe you ought to know that the members of the Order, although assisting Cardinal Scappucci in managing the Order's affairs, do not follow his wishes as a matter of course." He stepped to one side to allow Laura through.

"Miss Coatman, please come in." One of the cardinals stepped forward to greet her. "Cardinal Vanni," he said, guiding her into the room. "Monsignor Benvenuti, you will stay. We may have need of you."

Benvenuti flinched. To be put in his place quite so obviously jarred his ego. He stood watching as Vanni introduced Laura to each of the cardinals present.

"It has been brought to our attention, Miss Coatman, that not only has your life been threatened but, if Monsignor Benvenuti is to be believed, one of the Dark Lords has other plans for you. Here in the Vatican, we have learned never to accept anyone's word, but the monsignor is not known for admitting defeat. I personally agreed with Cardinal Scappucci's decision to ask him to explain the situation here to you, and it was after his doing so that you requested an audience with the Holy Father. I can only assume you either threatened our Order in some way or your demands were deemed too excessive.

"Within the church, the Holy Father is considered infallible, but I feel we both know otherwise. No one man has the right to be all-powerful but it is good policy to let it appear that way, and our Order has managed papal affairs for centuries. Occasionally, in extreme circumstances, we need to intercede in a more forthright way. If it is true the Dark Lord saved you, then we have no desire to anger it. Even we know our place."

Laura remained silent, wondering where this was heading.

"Perhaps you would kindly let us know why Cardinal Scappucci is willing to bring the wrath of the Dark Lords upon us and why they are intent on protecting you."

Laura glanced at Benvenuti, who was looking decidedly uncomfortable.

'Here we go', she thought. 'Showtime.'

"I agreed," she began, "to keep my silence in return for the upkeep and protection of both myself and my child."

Benvenuti's head shot round as a murmur rippled through the room.

"I was unaware we needed to congratulate you, but I don't see…"

"It was fathered by one of your Dark Lords."

There was silence as the cardinals absorbed what Laura had said.

Vanni stepped forward and laid his hand on Laura's shoulder.

"My child, that would make you the second Immaculate Conception, something we never dreamed we would see. Of course, you will have everything you need, the best doctors..." He seemed overwhelmed but then added, "But we will, of course, wish to confirm your condition."

"I welcome it," said Laura.

"Very well," said Vanni, "I believe we should leave it there and arrange for a consultation with one of our physicians at the earliest possible opportunity. Monsignor Benvenuti will see you out."

Once Benevenuti had escorted Laura from the chamber, one of the cardinals approached Vanni.

"Are we to believe her? How are we to know who the father of her child might be?"

Vanni smiled. "Don't fear, my friends. We'll put Laura Coatman to the test, but all in good time. We'll see for ourselves in what regard the Dark Lords hold her, but we must use caution. We don't want to bring their wrath down upon us all. If there are any reprisals we must be sure they fall on Monsignor Benvenuti. As I said, all in good time."

Laura was surprised she was being allowed to leave, but then there really was nowhere for her to go.

Once clear of the Vatican, Benvenuti turned to her.

"You should have warned me," he spat, trying to regain control over a situation he hadn't foreseen.

"And why would that be? I told you I could look

after myself," Laura replied.

"Until the child is born maybe, but I will be surprised if you are allowed to live once the Dark Lord and the Order have no further use for you."

"Do you really think a bunch of cardinals know anything about bringing up a child? Tell me, what do you know of 'La Papesse'?"

Benvenuti looked at her strangely. "The female pope, Pope Joan? There is no proof that she even existed."

"There is no proof she didn't. Even some Vatican officials have thought it possible. In a time when few outside the clergy could read or write, there were more books written about her than about Christ. She's always been a heroine of mine."

They had stopped walking and now Benvenuti looked directly into Laura's eyes.

"I see you are ambitious, Laura. Excellent," he said, with what passed for a smile, "and how far do *you* expect to rise within the church, you who are not even Catholic?"

"There isn't a vacancy at the top," she replied.

Benvenuti lowered his lids. In little more than a whisper, he said, "That can be arranged."

It was almost lunchtime and Laura knew Larry and O'Shea would be waiting for her. She could tell more evasive lies or risk telling them the truth. Lies made things so much more complicated. She decided there was nothing to be gained from keeping the meeting with the cardinals secret, but she'd skip telling them she was on Scappucci's hit list. She'd forgotten that Manuela would have told them of her morning visitor.

The two men were seated outside the nearby café

and Larry rose to greet her as she approached her hotel. She braced herself and crossed over to their table.

"What was that bastard, Benvenuti, doing at your hotel and where have you been all this time?"

"Good morning to you too, Larry."

Larry looked the worse for last night's over-consumption of alcohol.

"O'Shea!" She nodded over to him and he nodded back, staying remarkably quiet for once. "You look dreadful, Larry."

"Fuck it!"

Laura sat down, ordered a salad and coffee and began to explain.

"Yes, Larry, it was Benvenuti who called by this morning, 'though I'm sure Rome is full of clerics who fit his description. He was summoning me to meet with some cardinals."

"And you just went wandering off with the psycho?"

"When are you going to learn, Larry, that I don't need or have to ask your permission to do anything? Is this getting through to you?"

"And?" said O'Shea, at last breaking his silence.

"And?" repeated Laura.

"The cardinals," O'Shea prompted.

"Ah, yes, they are being supportive of my requests concerning the child. They want me to see one of their physicians, but that was to be expected really."

Larry had sunk into an even fouler mood, if that was possible. "Then you don't need us any more, is that what you're telling us?"

"No, of course not, but I need space to sort this out for myself. Surely you can see that?" When Larry didn't answer, she looked at O'Shea. "Dermot?"

"We're only concerned for you, Laura, you know that. Would you rather we went home?"

Home! It seemed so strange a concept now. She hadn't given a thought to her life in England.

"No, no, of course not." She reached out, laying a hand on the arm of each man. "I treasure your support but please, do just that, support me."

"Humph," said O'Shea, patting the hand on his arm.

"Sorry!" Larry added, though somewhat reluctantly.

"Good," said Laura. "Now, as there's nothing we can do until I hear from the Vatican, I suggest we grab some picnic fare and head off to one of the wonderful parks around here, the Villa Borghese maybe. And talk of babies, Benvenuti and the church is strictly taboo. What say you two?"

"Here, here," said O'Shea, and was echoed with less enthusiasm by Larry.

Laura didn't have to wait long for a summons to see a Vatican doctor. She doubted he had ever been called upon for his gynaecological expertise before. Though somewhat bemused, he quickly confirmed what Laura already knew, and she was once again ushered before the cardinals. Glancing around, she couldn't see Benvenuti and found this disquieting. She had become used to his presence whenever she was inside the Vatican walls.

"We are satisfied that you are indeed with child," said Cardinal Vanni, "and the fact the Dark Lord has protected you seems to confirm it may well be the father. However, as a token of – er – shall we say, commitment, we wish you to prove yourself."

Laura couldn't look away from his face. It was totally immobile. Just his jaw moved, and this seemed to only rise and fall, giving the impression he was a ventriloquist's dummy. She wondered how he enunciated each word without moving his lips.

Slowly she registered what he'd said. "Prove myself? How?"

"You will have no doubt discussed your condition with your friends. No-one is going to listen to the ravings of an ex-priest, especially one who holds a grudge against God. In any case, he can be dealt with later, if need be, but Larry Markham is a loose cannon and could become a nuisance to us. It's simple. Kill him."

Laura's mouth fell open and a choking noise came out. She looked from one cardinal to the next in disbelief. They remained stoic.

"And just how do you propose I go about that?" asked Laura, incredulous now that she should even be having this conversation.

"We suggest poison." It was a cardinal who until now had remained silent.

"Ah, yes, a favourite I believe with many of the early popes." She looked about. "And what makes you think I would agree to this?"

"You really have little choice. You cannot afford to be squeamish now, considering what you are carrying."

Laura had to play for time. "Very well, but in my own time and in my own way," she said.

The cardinals nodded their assent.

When she left the Vatican, Laura felt numb. Killing Larry wouldn't prove her child's parentage, something the cardinals seemed to accept far too readily. She suspected this was just her first ordeal and wondered what else they had in store for her. She only just managed to get to the nearest public toilet before throwing up.

TWENTYSIX

Dermot O'Shea felt old. He felt it in his bones. He'd seen too much and been through too much and was tired of it all. He was alone when Laura found him sat at the hotel bar. She looked around but there was no sign of Larry.

"Dermot, we need to talk." She looked dreadful and her voice was shaky.

"Good God, Laura, what is it?" O'Shea was about to order her a brandy, remembered the baby and changed it to a pot of strong tea. Drink in one hand and guiding Laura with the other, he hobbled over to some chairs by the window.

"Dermot, I don't know what to do. I…"

O'Shea motioned her to silence as the waiter arrived with the tray of tea.

"I'll be mother, shall I?" he said, pouring Laura a cup but leaving his empty, the irony of his comment failing to register. "Now tell me, what's going on?"

Laura told him what the cardinals had asked of her.

"What am I to do, Dermot?" She was once more the vulnerable young woman he remembered.

"If you want security for yourself and your baby, you have to appear to agree to their demands," said O'Shea. "Larry must be made to leave Rome. I doubt they'd harm him once he's out of the picture and they could hardly expect you to chase after him."

Laura wasn't sure O'Shea was right. As Benvenuti had pointed out, like the Mafia, they liked tying up loose ends, but voicing her fears would do little good.

"And you?" said Laura. "They seemed to know all about you. What if they want rid of you, too?"

"It's not surprising they've checked up on Larry and me, but I doubt they'll consider me any sort of threat. I'm not as volatile as Larry. Nevertheless, I'll return with him, if it makes you feel any better. At least that way I can keep an eye on him."

Larry arrived in the doorway. Laura noticed with regret that his features now supported a permanent frown. Maybe his leaving was best all round. She could hardly believe it had come to this.

"Hello, what are you two cooking up?" said Larry, sounding cheery but devoid of humour.

Before Laura could speak, O'Shea answered. "We were saying that it's probably time you and I returned to England."

"And leave Laura here alone with that Benvenuti hanging around? No way!"

"Have you thought, Larry, that us being here might actually compromise Laura's safety?" O'Shea knew that Larry wouldn't leave on his own account but might be persuaded for Laura's.

"You've been building up to this, haven't you?" Larry looked resentful.

"Don't be foolish," said Laura.

"Foolish?" he began. "Look, if you want to get rid of me, at least have the decency to say so outright." Laura flinched at his words. "I gave O'Shea my word I'd protect you."

"If my protection is the only thing that's keeping you here, then there's no need to stay. I'm protected enough."

"And just what is *that* supposed to mean?"

"It means the devil protects his own." She looked away, not wanting to see the impact of her words on Larry's face.

"So that's it? You've become one of them?"

"Larry," interjected O'Shea.

"Where I'm going, you can't come with me," said Laura. "Neither of you can. You two are the closest I have to a family but it's time to let go."

"Right, I'll leave you to your precious Benvenuti and the church." Larry raised his hands in a gesture of defeat. "I guess I lost that battle before it began."

"Larry!" Laura protested, but O'Shea put a restraining hand on her as Larry pushed his chair back from the table.

"Let him go," he said. "He'll cool down and when he does, I'll talk to him."

"But not before you're safely away from Rome," said Laura, tears brimming in her eyes.

"No, not until then," he agreed.

Benvenuti had spent the last few hours trying to come to terms with what he was proposing. It was not that he had any problem with taking a life, but he had to be sure there'd be no repercussions. He was a great believer in careful planning.

He had no fondness for the pope in office and a radical change might be beneficial in many ways, particularly if he became indispensable to the new pontiff. To have a woman in that role could offer unforeseen opportunities in both career and personal areas. He was definitely warming to the idea.

He'd been summoned to Pope Gregory's chambers more than once, so there was no reason for anyone to be suspicious. However, a straightforward act of violence would be too easily traced back to him. Anyone wishing to see the Pope had first to talk to the Prefect of the Pontifical Household and then take a lift, whereas the Pope's secretary and bodyguard were responsible for who was allowed to use the back staircase. The Secretary of State used both freely.

No, it would need to be less obvious. He cursed the fact he'd lost Mother Dolores as an ally. She'd had years of experience in the use of drugs, especially as suppressants, and would have known the variations in dosage between subduing, immobilising and producing a fatal overdose.

Immersed in thoughts of Borgia popes and Catherine de Medici, he was jolted back to the present by the ringing of alarm bells. The sound of running and doors slamming brought him to his feet.

As he rushed out into the passageway, he heard raised voices and began hurrying towards the papal apartments. The guards were struggling to open the doors that were apparently locked from within. Perhaps Benvenuti, alone of all those gathered, guessed the reason for the screams issuing from the Pope's throat.

More hurried footsteps and a cardinal appeared with keys, but the key on the inside prevented their use. The now guttural sounds died away leaving an ominous silence. Frightened glances were exchanged and even the guards seemed too afraid to move. In the seconds that followed, the sound of a key turning in the lock from the inside held them all immobile.

Benvenuti felt the hairs on his arms stand on end, and he hung back as the others leaned forward to watch a lone guard reach out and turn the handle.

Pope Gregory's eyes seem to stare out at them from his livid purple face, whilst the rest of his body was draped across the bed, blood trickling from every orifice. His torso appeared strangely misshapen, twisted and crushed as if by the coils of a gigantic snake. Most disturbing of all, he was alone.

As the murmurings rose to confused and frightened shouts, Benvenuti stepped back, distancing himself from the turmoil. It would seem he'd been saved the task of killing his Pope after all. Once away from curious glances, he hurried along the corridor and slipped out into the lengthening shadows of St. Peter's Square. It would soon be dark and the timeworn city waited. He needed to make a grateful offering to his Lord.

Cardinal Zafrani donned his cloak and hurried through the empty streets. It was barely four a.m. and the stones underfoot were wet from a light rain. He'd already risked much by seeking out Benvenuti and demanding Laura's address. There was urgency in what needed to be done. He kept glancing behind, wondering if Benvenuti would dare to follow him, but there was no-one in sight.

Dealing with Cesare was another matter. It took Zafrani valuable minutes to calm him down and persuade him to rouse Laura. Had it not been for Zafrani's position in the church, he was sure Cesare would have physically thrown him into the gutter.

When Laura almost stumbled down the stairs to reception, the cardinal ushered her out of Cesare's earshot.

"Pope Gregory has met with a dreadful accident."

"What?" gasped Laura. "What happened? Is he badly hurt?"

"He is dead. The cardinals will not release the information till later this morning. There is some confusion as to the cause."

Benvenuti's words came back to Laura, 'It can be arranged'. Had she inadvertently signed the Pope's death warrant, she wondered. She swayed, suddenly feeling nauseous.

"There is something you must see," Cardinal Zafrani began in a hurried whisper. "If what you told the cardinals yesterday was true, there is something you should know, *must* know. Please, get your coat."

As they hurried back in the direction of Vatican City, Laura questioned the cardinal.

"You said 'if' what I said was true. I thought the cardinals believed me."

"Delaying tactics for the most part, I'm afraid, until they work out what to do with you. Tonight's events will only remove an obstacle, not provide proof of your story."

"Why are you telling me this?" said Laura, struggling to keep up with him.

"Because I *do* believe you. I am privy to knowledge the others do not have. There were only two other people who knew of what I am about to show you, and now one is dead."

They had reached Viale Vaticano and Zafrani produced a key to the Vatican museums. Once inside, he retrieved a torch from under his cloak and led the way down through the lower level and into the vaults.

Laura guessed this was how Howard Carter must have felt when he first glimpsed the interior of Tutankhamun's lavish tomb. Everywhere she looked there were historical relics not on display to the public, a treasure trove of value far beyond its mineral wealth.

"I was given instructions yesterday by Cardinal Scappucci to destroy what you are about to see," said

313

Zafrani, his voice hushed despite no-one being about to hear. "It is the only time I have disobeyed or lied to His Eminence."

Laura was too in awe to answer.

Cardinal Zafrani continued, "There have been many prophecies regarding the papacy and its end, Saint Malachy, the Monk of Padua, Nostradamus, and they were all wrong. It has mostly been linked to some calendar event such as the Millennium, the end of the world, of the papacy, or even the birth of the Anti-Christ, certainly the world as we know it anyway. People do love to dwell on Doomsday. However, what I am about to show you came directly from the Virgin Mary herself."

Laura was startled. She found it hard to believe that a man so corrupted by the order could still believe in anything beyond his own personal needs.

The cardinal had come to the oldest area beneath the Basilica, The City of the Dead, grottos where hundreds of human remains were discovered. It was presumed these were early Christians but now Laura wasn't so sure.

"There were only ever two people with knowledge of what I am about to show you. One was, of course, His Holiness, and at present the weight also rests on my shoulders. But not solely," he added as an afterthought. "There has to be two, you see. Should anything happen to the Pope, it is my duty to show this to the next elected pontiff, and if anything should befall me first, the Pope will choose my replacement. I should never have told Cardinal Scappucci about the item's existence, but the Order can be very persuasive."

The cardinal counted along the ancient brickwork

and then began to carefully remove one of the narrow stones. Wrapped in plastic and looking incongruous in this setting was a small envelope, barely visible in the freshly opened recess.

"My personal protection policy," he declared, removing the envelope almost reverently.

Laura might have guessed he wasn't helping her out of kindness. He was assuring he'd be on the right side of the fence when things got rough. Still, if what he'd kept hidden was to help her own plans, she wasn't going to question his motives. If she was to live in the world in which she now found herself, then she would have to learn to live by its rules or change them.

The cardinal placed the envelope onto a low wall and carefully opened the seal. A small sheet of yellowed paper was pressed between two pieces of board. The dry air down here had ensured it hadn't suffered from damp but, even so, the writing was faint.

"I don't have to tell you what this is, do I?" asked the cardinal, his eyes unusually bright with excitement.

Laura finished reading. She felt breathless. "No, you don't, Your Eminence. You most certainly do not."

Laura's head spun as she walked back to her hotel, in awe of the possibilities now laid before her. She'd just been handed her salvation and a way to protect her friends, and had been given the gift of infallibility in the eyes of the people. She watched the city coming to life, the early traders laden with flowers, paintings, food, the cafés and pizzerias opening up and tables and chairs being arranged under awnings, early-rising tourists hoping to get the first places in queues.

The Papesse card had meant the unlocking of mysteries and access to hidden knowledge, knowledge that needed to see the light of day. Rome was fresh after the night's gentle rain and the sun was shining. What better day to reveal a secret already kept too long?

Benvenuti was startled to receive Laura's call.

"I realise the cardinals will no doubt be in turmoil following Pope Gregory's death, but I need you to call another meeting," she instructed.

"How did you know…?" Benvenuti stopped himself. Zafrani! He wondered what possible reason the cardinal would have for betraying the Vatican's self-imposed silence.

"It doesn't matter. Tell them I demand to be seen, that Cardinal Scappucci should be present and…" she paused, "and tell them this time *I'm* chairing the meeting."

She then rang O'Shea.

"Laura! You've only just caught me. We are due to leave for the airport."

"Don't go! I can't explain now but there's been a development. Larry will be safe; you both will."

"But, Laura…"

"I'll explain everything tonight," she said. "Trust me, I'm a priest."

"Laura… Laura?" O'Shea was left talking to air and wondering how he was going to explain this to Larry. "Damn!"

Benvenuti turned up in person to escort Laura to her meeting with the cardinals.

"I hope whatever you have to say is enough to warrant this unheard of breach of etiquette," he said. "The cardinals did not take kindly to being summoned, especially during a crisis. Nor did they appreciate having to explain their meeting with you to Cardinal Scappucci. Tread carefully, Laura. I fear you may have placed yourself in jeopardy as a result."

"I can assure you they will want, no, 'want' isn't perhaps the right word, they *need* to hear what I have to say, and there is no better time than now. When are they releasing news of Pope Gregory's death?"

"After the meeting, no doubt. I gather you learned of the circumstances surrounding his death from Cardinal Zafrani, so will understand when I say that a believable account has to fabricated and as swiftly as possible. Would I be right in assuming you initially thought I might be to blame?"

"It crossed my mind," said Laura. "Perhaps I owe you an apology."

"There is no need. The Dark Lord merely beat me to it." Benvenuti showed no remorse at being thought the murderer.

The cardinals were waiting when they arrived at the Vatican. Cardinal Scappucci stepped forward as Laura entered the room.

"What gives you the right to demand we see you? You are overstepping your mark, young woman. It is only in deference to your condition and the possible parentage of your unborn child that we have agreed to see you. It will not happen again." There was no mistaking the hostility in his tone. It was clear he was in command again, despite the mutinous attempt by the other cardinals.

"I think it might, Your Eminence," replied Laura.

"May I suggest that perhaps you listen to what I have to say before you make any rash statements?"

Scappucci was taken off-guard by the authority in her manner. He had expected a timid apology but was faced with open defiance.

"Monsignor Benvenuti," said Laura, turning to include him before he left, "I should like you to hear what I have to say to the others."

It was obvious this also met with displeasure from Scappucci but, when Benvenuti caught his eye, he nodded. Benvenuti closed the heavy doors and waited. He had never heard anyone speak with such disrespect to one cardinal let alone a company of them, and was secretly afraid Laura had signed her own death warrant. What worried him even more was who would be asked to carry it out.

"Perhaps you would care to be seated," suggested Laura. "I shan't keep you overlong. I know it's customary to make speedy arrangements for a pope's funeral; six days, isn't it?"

"We care to stand," said Scappucci stonily.

"Firstly, I think you should know that I am fully aware of the circumstances surrounding Pope Gregory's death." A gasp went up from the cardinals. Before they could ask questions, Laura continued. "What did you expect your Dark Lord to do when you were secretly plotting the downfall of the mother of its child? The church has always instructed its followers to have faith, but where is yours when confronted with the birth of a dark saviour, for surely that is how you must see my child."

"I don't know where you got the idea..." began Scappucci.

"Please don't insult my intelligence, Your

318

Eminence. Haven't you yet learned to appreciate the powers that you're dealing with? I find that surprising." The other cardinals murmured their discomfort. "I was still in England when I began uncovering disturbing evidence pointing towards the dark side of the church and, although I had no idea then of the existence of your order, it's all written down and out of your reach."

Scappucci smirked. "Do you honestly think there is anything you could find out that is capable of turning the people against us? It is you who would be considered a charlatan or, at the very least, mad."

"I'm not about to put it to the test," said Laura. "It's sufficient that I know what's going on and I've shared that knowledge with others."

Scappucci now laughed. "You mean that jumped up journalist and the washed out drunkard? You must know you cannot protect them."

"That's where you're wrong, Your Eminence. I can. I've also placed the information where even you will never find it, including an exposé on your Ordo Autem Serpens." The last part was a lie but she had got proficient at telling them of late.

"As you have not as yet made this public, I presume you have a price. Otherwise you wouldn't be here."

If the ace Laura was holding had been anything less, she knew she would never be allowed to leave the building alive. To bluff would have been useless. If she was to play this card to win, she must not weaken now. She felt the baby kick in her belly. Perhaps it too could sense its father in the airless corridors and chambers.

Laura's head swam as she fought against an

unexpected desire to surrender, to sacrifice herself as so many had before her, unquestioningly offering their souls on the altar of deception.

Another kick jolted her back into her surroundings. Perhaps the baby was on her side after all, or did it now fear for its own existence at the hands of the disciples that evil had spawned?

The cardinal was speaking again in soft hypnotic tones. "Surely you aren't going to ask us to change? After all," he chuckled, "you, more than most, must understand how reluctant we are to do that?"

"But changes are inevitable, Your Eminence, and I'm not asking for anything to change, not yet, not at once, not so soon. We mustn't destroy the people's belief for, without belief to feed upon, the church would become hollow like the shell of St. Jude's."

"So what *is* it you propose?"

Laura took a deep breath. Even the devil admired courage.

"See to it that I am elected Pope."

TWENTYSEVEN

Laura could feel the shadows gathering as if they too were listening, waiting for the answer to her demands.

"What you propose is preposterous and totally out of the question," shouted a burly cardinal, holding his pendulous belly as if he were about to give birth. "You are a woman and not even Catholic."

"Thank you for stating the obvious. I realise there's nothing we can do about my sex, but surely it's within the church's capabilities to baptise me here and now and raise me up to the position of cardinal. They're *your* rules, so break them."

There was an audible gasp from cardinals.

"I have been doing some research," she continued. "Are you aware that in 767AD, a layman was ordained as a cleric, subdeacon, deacon and priest, then consecrated as a bishop and Pope, all on the same day? At least I have a head start, being a priest already, albeit in the Church of England. Furthermore, in 1501, the illegitimate daughter of Pope Alexander VI, none other than Lucrezia Borgia, took the Pope's place in his absence and dealt with all business affairs."

"What you're suggesting wouldn't just split the church, it would destroy it," snarled Cardinal Scappucci.

"There would undoubtedly be ripples."

"Ripples? Tsunamis!"

"They would level out eventually. You're all-powerful and you've had millions of followers accepting every ruling you've passed, no matter how unpopular they may be. And why? Because they believe that the Pope is the representative of God and infallible. You have only to make a statement saying Pope Gregory had a premonition he was about to die, and this was a revelation given to him before his untimely death, an inspiration from God, if you like. If they truly believe in the Pope's infallibility and that it's God's will, they'll believe it's the divine word speaking directly through him. I'm not denying there'll be a storm, but we can ride it out. If things should turn ugly, we can do what the papacy has always done, retreat, barricade ourselves in and wait out the furore."

The cardinals began talking rapidly amongst themselves. Laura didn't need to understand Italian; their body language showed their agitation.

"There's one more thing you might want to consider," she continued. "Electing a female to the position of Pope might have the reverse effect. It could, in fact, bring more people to the church. After all, in the past, women have had a pretty rough deal under your patriarchal system. Maybe they'd welcome a change."

There was uproar in the room.

"This is madness, sheer madness," snapped Cardinal Scappucci. "What makes you think we would agree to such a demand based only on a few scurrilous accusations, and an unproven claim to be carrying what? The Anti-Christ? And what of the child? How would you explain that?"

"I'm sure your public relations department will think up a suitable explanation." She paused. "There's also something you aren't aware of and I think this might be the right time to bring it into the open. I believe, when this is publicly made known, you'll find acceptance follows."

FATHER OF LIES

Laura reached into her pocket for a photocopied sheet of paper and handed it to the cardinal.

Turning to the others, she continued, "Let me tell you all a story. It began on the thirteenth of May, 1917, and involves three children who were tending sheep near their village. The village was in central Portugal and was called Fatima."

A gasp went up from the cardinals. Laura waited for quiet before resuming. She glanced at Scappucci, who had turned deathly white.

"These three children saw something that day, a vision of a lady who asked them to recite their rosary. She appeared on six occasions. On the final visitation, on the thirteenth of October that same year, she revealed she was the 'Lady of the Rosary'. The vision was adjudged by the Bishop of Leiria in 1930 to be a genuine appearance of the Virgin Mary."

One or two of the older cardinals were now fingering their rosaries nervously.

"I see I have your attention," said Laura. "As I'm sure you are all aware, the lady also gave the children a message with instructions it should not be made known until the 1950s. The message was then written down, put in an envelope and sealed. By 1960 it should have been made public, but an official press release from the Vatican stated that it was, and I quote, 'most probable the secret would remain, forever, under absolute seal'."

A few of the cardinals were shifting uncomfortably whilst Scappucci, now slumped in a chair, supported his head with one hand. In the other was the crumpled sheet Laura had handed him.

"In June, 2000, a four-page document was released, supposedly being the message that had been kept

323

secret for so long, but there were many who suspected the original was still locked away, and how right they were."

Laura walked over to Scappucci and retrieved the sheet of paper. "Only two amongst you knew of this besides the Holy Father. Yes, you've all been kept in the dark until now."

Her taunt brought Scappucci to his feet.

"This is a forgery," he shouted, snatching the sheet back, "obviously some sick joke. Who gave you this?"

Ignoring the question, Laura said, "No, Your Eminence, we both know it isn't fake, although of course what you have in your hand is only a copy. But then you know that, don't you? The original is again well out of your reach. The person who safeguarded this note also had the presence of mind to keep internal memos regarding it. It is *not* a forgery. You'll see that, alongside the original, there is a translation into both Italian and English."

"The cardinal responsible will pay for this."

"No, he is under my protection."

"*Your* protection?" Cardinal Scappucci sneered.

"If anything should befall either of us, or my friends for that matter, then the contents of my files will be made public knowledge. As long as they are beyond your reach, your only concern must be to keep me alive." Her mouth twisted into a smile worthy of Benvenuti. "With all your resources, that shouldn't be too difficult."

"No-one will believe you," said the cardinal.

"Your faith in people is touching," said Laura, sounding far more confident than she felt, "but your timing is out. Women are taking positions of power now and you've lost favour with your 'pro-life' war against contraception and abortion. We're no longer easily deceived. The people that matter will listen."

Cardinal Vanni stepped forward.

"I should like to see what is written," he said, holding his hand out to Scappucci, who reluctantly handed over the paper. Vanni read it in silence.

"I had heard rumours, unofficial of course, that the Holy Father who first read this fainted. I can now understand why."

Turning, he handed it to the other cardinals to read. Finally, Benvenuti was handed the paper.

"'When a Holy Mother forms the rock, two in one will govern Rome.' Is that all there is?" Cardinal Vanni looked at Laura.

"What more is needed, Your Eminence?" she replied. "'Thou art Peter and...'"

"You don't have to instruct me on the Bible, young woman. It would seem indeed that your arrival was prophesised and I for one will not fight you. However, there will be many from all echelons of the church that will refuse to accept you. If you rock the ecclesiastical boat, it is inevitable some of its crew will drown. Are you prepared for this?"

"There are always casualties with change. No doubt, you'll see that those who count are given lifebelts."

The cardinal smiled. "Perhaps you have the diplomacy to make this work after all."

At this last remark, Cardinal Scappucci rounded on the others.

"Can't you see what's going on here? This is a confidence trick almost worthy of us, but still a trick, no doubt concocted by this woman and her lover." He swung round pointing his finger accusingly at

Benvenuti.

"Cardinal Scappucci, I protest," said a shocked Benvenuti.

"So do I," said Vanni.

"Why?" responded Scappucci, his voice growing louder in an effort to be heard above the other cardinals. "Are you blind? We are all aware of Benvenuti's ambitious ways. If he couldn't gain power himself, what better way than be the power behind the throne?" Spittle was now accumulating at the corners of his mouth.

Laura had remained silent as the cardinals argued, amused to begin with but now growing increasingly angry.

"What manner of devotees are you," she finally called out above the noise, "that you don't even show your Dark Lord respect?"

"How dare you..." began Scappucci.

"No, how dare *you*!"

A current of air caught the paper in Vanni's hand and he turned to find the source. Even as he did so, the gust increased till it reached a spiralling vortex of energy that whipped the cardinals' garments about them, pinning back those near to the walls and buffeting those closest to Laura, sending the most elderly and unsteady to their knees.

Laura remained an oasis of calm in the eye of the storm, as the spiralling force took on a dark hue, like black clouds billowing around a tornado. It swirled about her feet and then rose up behind her, now a shadowy outline around clear shimmering energy.

The battered cardinals threw up their hands in a useless gesture of protection as the head of a gigantic cobra hovered above Laura, turning slowly as it eyed the terrified clergy cowering before it.

Vanni was the first to react. He threw himself forward on his knees, his head touching the floor. For a moment, it looked as if it might be a suicidal gesture as the snake's head inclined towards him, but it jerked back up to look at the others, who all followed Vanni's example. Benvenuti was the last to bend his knee and lower his head. As he did so, he saw Laura raise one hand above her and watched as the monstrous serpent swayed into her caress.

"Thank you for staying another day," said Laura later, when she was seated with Larry and O'Shea in their hotel. "I needed to let you know that you're now both safe from any action by the Order. You can return to Rome in perfect safety whenever you choose."

"How come?" It was Larry who spoke. "You seemed only too eager for us to leave yesterday."

Laura told them of the day's events as gently as possible. She realised it must sound like an Ali Baba fable to the two men, but they had both seen and experienced enough to accept all she told them. When she got to her demands of the Order, O'Shea produced a handkerchief and wiped his face.

"Do you really feel you're up to this, Laura?" he asked. "Be certain now, for it's a heavy load you're planning on carrying."

She laughed. "You ask as if I have a choice," she said.

"I must say, it will make a change having someone young in the position of Pope, still with their wits about them, but there's one thing that bothers me," said O'Shea, frowning.

"Only one?" interjected Larry.

O'Shea ignored him. "Why would this, this serpent energy, want you to be Pope?"

"I've thought about that," said Laura. "Maybe that was always the plan."

"But why? Or are we assuming it's doing it out of fatherly love for its child?"

"Benvenuti told me there are good energies too. If a female pope was predicted by one of them, perhaps the dark couldn't prevent it. What better way to control the outcome than by impregnating me and seeing that I come to Rome? It would seem to have turned things around through my – our – offspring."

"There was no way it could know you'd come to Rome," said O'Shea.

"I had no choice if I was to learn about my child's father. It occurred to me," continued Laura, "that if Larry and I *had* made love, I would have assumed the child was his and stayed in England. The fact that Larry wasn't able," she looked apologetically across at him as he rolled his eyes, "sorry, but maybe it managed to influence how that turned out."

"Thanks a bundle," snorted Larry.

O'Shea sighed. "No wonder I'm going grey," he groaned.

"I'll be fine, I promise you. Besides, I know where my true friends are if I need you."

"If you think we'll just run off and leave you to…" said Larry.

"That's exactly what I want you to do."

Larry shook his head, trying not to let his tears show.

"You once told me that the way to bring something down was from the inside. Well, I've also come to learn that it's from the inside that changes can be made."

"So you think you can single-handedly turn everything around?"

"I don't know, Larry, but I'm going to try. The girl you first met was a Reverend trying to spread the word of Jesus in her own simple way. That girl is still there, inside me, only now I have the chance to do so much more."

"That's not all that's inside you or have you forgotten?"

"I know! Do you think I haven't given this hours of thought?"

"Hours!" Larry mocked.

"Whatever it is I'm carrying, it doesn't just belong to that … thing. It's half *me*. You said so yourself. It may have whatever passes for DNA from its father, but it's being nourished on *my* blood and will be suckled on *my* milk. Don't you think I'll have some say in what it believes, what it thinks, how it feels? According to the scans, the baby appears normal. As I'm not being forced to give birth to a physical monster, don't you think I'll do my utmost to ensure love and compassion subdue any traits it might inherit from its father?"

O'Shea had remained silent until now. "She's right, Larry," he cut in. "It's an infernal nuisance but…"

"I know," said Larry, "but we don't have to like it." He grimaced, knowing he'd lost the battle. "And 'infernal' sums it up, doesn't it? Why couldn't you have taken up something simple, like crochet or quilt-making?" Glancing about, he said, "I hate saying goodbye to a place even if I've only known it a short while. I'm always aware I may never return."

"That's not the way to look at things," Laura

replied.

"You're right, but it doesn't make it any easier."

"Then I'll make it easier for you. I'll ensure you return, both of you." She took their hands. "I'll send you an invitation every year until you accept."

"Bloody hell!" O'Shea brusquely hid his emotion. "On headed papal notepaper, I hope."

"You must choose a name," said one of the cardinals. "Pope Laura doesn't sound quite right, now does it? It is customary for a new pope to take on a name befitting his – her status." He sounded almost patronising, as though he was talking to an infant. "Have you given thought to what name you will adopt?"

Laura didn't mind the cardinals talking down to her. They would find out soon enough that she was no child to be manipulated and moulded into the token head of their church. She didn't hesitate.

"Joan!" she said. "I will be Pope Joan."

"It has become usual to take the name of an apostle."

"But I'm nothing if not unusual."

"An excellent choice," said Cardinal Scappucci, in an attempt to redeem himself with both Laura and the Dark Lord. "St. Joan of Arc was canonised in 1920, and you honouring her in this way will please many Catholics."

"Joan it is then." She nearly added 'the second' but held her tongue. She had sat up late the previous night, studying the numerous female saints and martyrs. Joan of Arc seemed by far the best choice, as it was advised to pray to her in times of opposition by church authorities to hopes and dreams. There would certainly be plenty of opposition as she brought hers to fruition. That the saint shared the name of Laura's own personal heroine merely doubled its suitability. "But I'll not be the first to be called that."

"Even Pope Joan – *if* she existed – called herself John."

"Only because she was passing herself off as a man. Perhaps there'll come a time when popes can use the name with which they were christened." She smiled and couldn't resist adding, "We may even end up with a Pope Elvis!"

Scappucci snorted. "Must you make a mockery of everything?"

"I have no need, Your Eminence, it's already been done."

The great wheels of papal propaganda had begun to turn. Laura looked at the world's newspapers spread out before her. "Well, we've made the headlines at least," she light-heartedly remarked to Cardinal Vanni.

"'The 1.2 billion Catholics of the world, who are mourning the loss of their pope, are now being forced to come to terms with more disruption within their church'," she read aloud.

Cardinal Vanni nodded. "Rumours have been leaked via the Vatican Radio of a great revelation about to be released to the public, one that will change the way the Holy Roman Catholic Church is perceived in the eyes of the world. We also have various Catholic magazines poised to print whatever we tell them."

"Very clever," said Laura. "As I pointed out previously, the people, primed and expectant, will accept anything if it's presented as the will of God."

"That remains to be seen," said Vanni, crossing the room to see for himself the papers spread across Laura's desk. "'Whilst the church is in turmoil following the announcement of Pope Gregory XVII's death, news of a woman being ordained and raised to the position of cardinal has sent shock waves throughout the world.'"

"I think you'll find," said Laura, "the news will receive mixed criticism. The world may be shocked, but I doubt it will question the papacy and the all-powerful Holy See. Besides, the church has always been referred to as 'she' and 'Mother Church'."

Vanni shook his head. Laura had noticed him doing that a lot during the last week, and she felt she might warm to this man. Only time would tell.

Leaving Vanni to continue fretting alone, she made her way down to the Sistine Chapel, where the Conclave would gather to choose the new head of their church. The fire and rescue service was on the roof, attaching the six-foot-long copper chimney that would keep the outside world informed. Within the chapel, two stoves were set up, one for the ballots and one for the chemicals that would turn the smoke either white or black. They both fed into a common pipe leading into the chimney. Ritual had to be followed, even when the results were already known.

As Laura gazed up at Michelangelo's famous ceiling, her attention was drawn to a painting that she'd failed to notice before. One of the triangular corner pieces, 'The Brazen Serpent', showed the all too familiar coiling reptiles. She shuddered and, despite it's air of expectant preparation, the chapel suddenly felt chill.

Later, with the outside world still reeling from the recent disclosures, and believing the cardinals were shut away in the conclave deliberating on Pope Gregory's successor, she went through the Department of Propaganda's statement one more time. Tomorrow would be the final test of the people's belief in infallibility.

Alone now in her apartment within the Vatican, Laura was aware that this short time before the announcement was probably the last she could call her own. In a matter of hours she would be a figurehead, the public property of the all-seeing world. 'Not quite all-seeing,' she thought. Soon she would be surrounded by the dark-clothed security force, the Vatican Secret Service, and seated on a red and gold throne, wearing white and gold vestments, a silk mitre on her head. She would hold the golden crosier, the shepherd's crook, in her left hand as she blessed the crowd in St. Peter's Square – and her life would never be hers again.

There was a knock at her door.

"Monsignor Benvenuti," announced the guard.

She would have to get used to the security her new position afforded. She motioned Benvenuti to take a seat but he remained standing.

"To what do I owe this visit?" she asked.

"You have done well, Laura, far beyond my imaginings, but now is the time for you to consider your unborn child."

"Don't you think that's what I've been doing, securing its future?" replied Laura, somewhat surprised.

"Security is one thing but a mother's love is another. How much time do you think your new-found high position will allow you to spend with the baby?" He moved closer till Laura could almost feel his warmth against her, and she felt his hand slither across her shoulder. "Whereas," he continued, with a voice like black velvet, "if you were to take a consort, someone capable of the everyday mundane papal chores…"

"You have ideas above your station," cut in Laura.

"You can say that to me after all you have achieved?" Benvenuti was taken aback. "The situation may have changed but do not expect me to pay homage…"

"Homage? I want that from no man."

Benvenuti softened his tone. "A woman like you needs a strong man by her side."

Laura couldn't believe her ears. He must think she was a complete fool. Now she was in a position of power, he was running scared. Could he really believe her attraction to him would somehow override the fact he'd left her to the mercy of the one being he feared?

"Such a man as you?" she replied.

"You know we would be good together."

It would have been so easy for Laura to give way to his touch but she recognised that, although he excited her, it was the danger that added to the pleasure, a pleasure in which she could not afford to indulge.

"Do you think I fought for all this," she gestured about her, "only to share it? You have your answer. No."

She had never seen him looking so handsome – or so deadly.

It was not what Benvenuti wanted to hear. "Bitch!" he roared.

There was a time when Laura would have cowered before such an onslaught. That time seemed so very far off now. She didn't flinch and her silence angered Benvenuti even more. For a fleeting second, she thought back to the gypsy's warning. Was she only turning him down because of a warning from a street vendor? She was aware that part of her still wanted him, but she couldn't afford to risk everything on this man.

"You're nothing," he shouted, "nothing but a vessel, like all women. That's all you're good for, a fleshly plaything for our lust. Even the Great Serpent used you. If you think that *thing* you're carrying will save you, you're wrong. It's a while since I've taken a woman with child."

He lunged towards Laura, roughly grasping her shoulders. One arm circled her waist and he smothered her mouth with his as she remained motionless in his embrace.

"Fight, damn you," he roared. "Fight!"

As he lifted his bejewelled hand to strike her, her indifference to him showed in her eyes, staying his blow. For a second, his cruel mouth curved into a smile before he brought the back of his hand slicing towards her.

It never made contact.

Dust motes swirled as a force as old as time and stronger than life sent Benvenuti crashing against a stone pillar. He looked about in desperation to find something, anything, with which to defend himself, but again he was seized and felt something circle his throat and tighten. He was lifted up and thrust against the wall, where he hung like a flayed Christ upon the cross.

"No," shouted Laura, above the sound of his choking, "I don't want him dead."

The pressure round Benvenuti's throat eased instantly and he fell to the ground, where he lay crumpled, slipping into unconsciousness. Again the motes spiralled as something shifted across the room to the sound of rustling satin and coiled itself about Laura.

She felt no sympathy at the sight of Benvenuti. Such emotions were becoming alien to her. She'd no room for feelings that might cloud her resolve and threaten both her and her child. Coldly, she turned and walked away.

ASCENSION

"…and the dragon gave him his power, and his seat,
and great authority."
REVELATION 13:2

Benvenuti stirred and reached out to the wall for
support. Every part of him hurt and his throat felt
constricted. He turned his head, trying to make out a
familiar shape in the dark. He must have been
unconscious for hours. No light shone through the
windows. Perhaps the shutters were closed because,
whichever way he turned, there was nothing but
blackness. He struggled to his feet, finding it hard to
maintain his balance.

Hearing footsteps in the corridor and keeping close
to the wall, he made his way to where the door should
be. He stumbled once against a stool, falling heavily
and cursing the lack of light. Finally he reached the
door and pulled it open.

Everything remained dark.

In the hotel, O'Shea turned away from the window as
a deafening cheer went up in the piazza, accompanied
by the ringing of the enormous campanile bell in St.
Peter's Basilica. "White smoke! We have a new pope,"
he said flatly.

"That's not her, not Laura," said Larry. "It's
whatever she's carrying."

"No," answered O'Shea. "It's Laura. We just didn't
recognise it in her before. I believe she's the same
young woman, but now coping with what's been thrust
upon her."

Larry was less forgiving. "And when she's a mother? What then? What of her child? Do you honestly think she'll be able to teach him about beauty, compassion and love?"

"I believe she'll try and, after all, that's all any of us can do. Oh, and by the way, it's 'her', not 'him'."

"Son of a …"

"I think the cardinals will be more surprised than you," said O'Shea, with what almost passed for a smile.

"She's relying on the fear they have of the child's father to keep them both safe. Will that be enough?"

"We must wait and see, Larry. Only God knows that. Come on," he added, "we've a plane to catch."

Laura peered into the shadows.

"Are you there?" she whispered, but there was no sound from the darkness, no mirage movement at the edge of sight. She was standing in 'The Room of Tears' where she'd changed into her papal robes. Everything was still and as it should be. To the cardinals' dismay, she'd refused to spend three days cooped up within these walls, as was custom. After all, who outside those in the Order would know?

She pulled the white skullcap down firmly onto her head and slipped into the red leather shoes. She'd thought to tease the cardinals and ask that the shoes have high heels or be covered in sequins like Dorothy's in 'The Wizard of Oz', but had taken pity on them and remained silent. As it was, she'd grumbled about the vestments made by the papal tailors, Gammarelli. They were too cumbersome for a female but, unless she wore the smallest of the three sizes usually made to fit whoever was voted in as Pope, it would alert outsiders that the choice had already been made.

A gentle knock sounded at her door.

"It is time, Holy Mother."

Laura smoothed her hands down over her vestments and opened the door. A gathering of red-robed cardinals, and bishops in purple, waited patiently, as she was handed the crosier and the ribbons of her mitre were adjusted. She couldn't miss what seemed an excessive number of the Vatican's Secret Police and security guards hovering behind the clergy. She was well aware of their fears for her life, but Laura was confident she wouldn't be allowed to come to harm.

Through the windows, she could see the piazza brimming with expectant faces, the devout, the curious and maybe the hostile.

"Right, let's do this," she said, stepping forward.

Much later, with the day drawing to a close, Laura looked back over the most momentous few hours of her life. There was so much to take in: the white smoke from the Sistine Chapel's chimney, her ordination in the Basilica, the angelic voices of the Pontifical Choirboys, all recorded by the Pope's photographer and all co-ordinated by the Master of Liturgical Ceremonies. The crowds had spilled out of the square into the Via della Conciliazione, every pair of eyes trained on their new pope.

A tapping sound came from the corridor. She glanced out of the door to see Benvenuti making his way towards her. In dark glasses and rapping the wall with a white stick, he was a pitiable sight, unsteady, like a child learning to walk. There was a time when

Laura would have felt the compassion she now denied him but, instead, she watched as he suffered the fate he had forced onto others. She didn't want him dead, but had discovered an appetite for revenge that surprised her. Alone in the dark, but for the images crawling from the lurid recesses of his own mind, he was dependent now upon her and maybe he too would have his uses. She was a woman after all, as well as being the Pope.

She fought the urge to go to him. He would have to come to her, but when he did, it must be on her terms. She stepped back quietly into her chamber and, though he paused and tilted his head to listen, he had no idea he was being watched and moved on. She wondered if she was becoming as corrupt as the ecclesiastical brethren of the Ordo Autem Serpens, to whom she had now become the Most Holy Mother. No, not as corrupt as them, but wasn't there a danger in lying down with the Devil? She could no longer afford to be sweet, naïve and innocent and, if she had to impose changes, then she saw no reason why she shouldn't enjoy the methods.

Popes, after all, were not known for being angels. They were *not* infallible. They were human, with frailties, both physical and spiritual, and a morality not always fitting their high office. She expected she would be no different but, hopefully, the legacy she would leave would be more worthy than those of many of her predecessors. She thought back to the Tarot card that had highlighted her path, La Papesse. Amongst its meanings were 'female pope' and 'life without men'. She didn't want a life of celibacy but this was not the time to think of that. There was precedence aplenty of popes taking lovers but, for now, her world had turned upside down and it would take all her concentration to maintain a steady footing on the storm-tossed 'barque of Peter'.

She went to the window and looked out. The light was fading but the rooftops were still golden in the last rays of sunlight. Rome lay out before her and, despite all its history and its hidden secrets, it was still the most beautiful sight she'd ever seen.

Rome, her city. Hers and her daughter's.

FINIS

COMING SOON:

SET IN TIME

EGYPT, 1823 BC: MIDDLE KINGDOM

Holding the burning torch at arm's length, Neferwer ran his fingers along the wall. The stone in the passage was roughly hewn, unlike the smooth, painted surfaces in the chamber they had just left. The uneven floor led sharply down, making it difficult to maintain a balance and the sound of Heqaib and Ankhef behind, stumbling in his shadow, added to the tension. Only the promise of riches drove them on.

Keki and Henenu had fled with what they could carry rather than descend beneath the burial chamber, but there was no sign of what had spooked them. They were men used to stealing from the dead and weren't prone to fanciful fears, but, when they had stumbled on this passageway, something had sent them scurrying away with only what they'd already ripped from the folds of cloth wrapping the mummy. Disappointingly, there had been little else worth stealing, and what there was had been piled in a heap as though it had been dumped and left. The prospect of further riches was too much for Neferwer and his friends. Ankhef's story had sparked their desire for gold.

The tunnel finally opened up into a vast chamber. Neferwer stopped abruptly, his two comrades crashing into him. Their curses died away as they moved to stand at his side.

The light from the torch failed to reach into the shadows, but all three men were aware of movement in the darkness. The torch flames wavered for a moment as if something had passed close by, yet they appeared to be alone. Neferwer raised the torch higher, lighting the recesses in the wall. Nothing.

They were nervous. The old man, Ankhef, had never said why he hadn't taken the riches for himself. They presumed that he'd intended to return later to plunder the tomb. They'd never thought to ask why he'd failed to do so. An oversight they now regretted. He'd died penniless, but not before they'd wrung the directions to the tomb from him and left his emaciated body lying in the alley.

Again, there was movement, sudden and swift, as a shape, barely visible in the flickering light, circled them, disturbing the accumulated dust of centuries.

"Aieee!" Ankhef screamed, his voice high-pitched with terror. His companions whirled about. Ankhef, struggling in the grip of something they couldn't see, was suspended high above the floor of the chamber, his eyes popping whilst he fought to cry out, as his assailant slowly crushed his writhing form.

A moment later, his distorted body dropped to the ground and continued to twitch as blood poured from his mouth.

As one, the two remaining thieves made for the tunnel entrance, Neferwer scrambling through ahead of his companion. The steep incline made speed almost impossible as they strained for purchase, kicking back debris and sand, blind panic driving them upwards. Neferwer could make out dim light from the burial chamber above, where a reed torch had been left burning. He increased his efforts.

A scream from behind made him turn. Heqaib was reaching towards him, arms flailing.

"Help me."

There was nothing Neferwer could do but watch as Heqaib was dragged back down the tunnel and out of sight, his screams raking the silence.

Finally exiting from the tomb's opening, Neferwer's feet churned up clouds of dust as he half-ran, half-slithered down the slope, loose rubble avalanching before him. He reached out his arms to steady himself, shredding the skin from his fingers as they grazed the rock face on one side. He didn't even feel it. All he knew was he had to escape, put as much distance between himself and the tomb as possible and do it fast. The screams of Ankhef and Heqaib were still ringing in his ears.

Something caught at him, sending him sprawling. He looked back in blind terror, but it was Keki's scarf that had wrapped itself about his ankle, gold rings and trinkets knotted into its folds. There was no sign of Keki. Or Henenu.

He staggered to his feet and looked back up towards the tomb entrance and, as he did so, the moon came out from behind a bank of clouds, illuminating the craggy hillside. Nothing moved. Neferwer turned to the shale and rocks ahead. In the distance, the Nile glittered like a giant snake, winding its way to the Middle Sea.

He tried to control his breathing; now was not the time to panic. He needed to negotiate the path downhill. If he lost his footing again it could be fatal. He'd had a bad feeling about this tomb all along. Why was it on the left bank of the river? All the other tombs were built on the west bank, the land of death. Whose rock-hewn tomb had he just entered, that defied death itself?

He thought he heard movement. It could have been a settling pebble from his own headlong race down the hill. His eyes scoured the incline behind him. He turned again to the west and screamed. Something rose up before him, shimmering in the half-light, indistinct and monstrous, swaying menacingly. Neferwer realised he could still see the glistening Nile through its body.

He took a step back and almost fell, before scrambling sideways, trying to get hand and footholds on the rugged slope.

In one fluid movement the creature scooped him up, tightening its coils about him, holding him high in the air. The clouds once more obscured the moon, as Neferwer's gurgling screams choked to silence. The grip loosened and his lifeless form was dashed to the rocks, where blood pooled black in the dark Egyptian night.

Serena Cairns says she finds the writing process akin to magic and attempts the art of literary alchemy, turning mere words into evocative stories. She won a short story writing course with The London School of Journalism, and went on to have stories, articles and poetry published in a number of magazines, ranging from Australian Cosmopolitan to The Criminologist. Serena now lives in Devonshire, England.

Her web site is at www.serenacairns.co.uk

Lightning Source UK Ltd.
Milton Keynes UK
UKOW06f0055120515

251317UK00010B/77/P

9 780993 160080